Don't Believe the Hype

Natalie Lewis is an expert with over thirty years' experience working in fashion PR with the biggest names in the business including Net-a-Porter, Jimmy Choo, Matches, Diane von Furstenburg and Anya Hindmarch. After selling her agency in 2007, Natalie consulted on a freelance basis with a range of high-profile clients including Bella Freud, Robbie Williams, Victoria Beckham and Claudia Schiffer. In June 2020, Natalie took a sabbatical from the fashion world to write *Don't Believe the Hype*.

NATALIE LEWIS

Don't Believe the Hype

HODDER

First published in Great Britain in 2023 by Hodder & Stoughton
An Hachette UK company

1

Copyright © Natalie Lewis 2023

A CIP catalogue record for this title is available from the British Library

Paperback ISBN 978 1 399 70578 3
eBook ISBN 978 1 399 70577 6

Typeset in Plantin Light by Hewer Text UK Ltd, Edinburgh
Printed and bound in Great Britain by Clays Ltd, Elcograf S.p.A.

Hodder & Stoughton policy is to use papers that are natural, renewable
and recyclable products and made from wood grown in sustainable
forests. The logging and manufacturing processes are expected to
conform to the environmental regulations of the country of origin.

Hodder & Stoughton Ltd
Carmelite House
50 Victoria Embankment
London EC4Y 0DZ

www.hodder.co.uk

For Catherine, Emma & Goo. Wish you were still here. You may have found it slightly funny.

Author's Note

While I have indeed worked as a PR in the fashion industry for many (many) years, the story and characters in this book are entirely fictional and are all figments of my imagination.

PUBLIC RELATIONS (PR) – the practice of managing and disseminating information from an individual or an organisation to the public in order to affect public perception.

More commonly known as engaging in the practice of smoke and mirrors.

Prologue

'You remember that pair of boots last winter that you absolutely had to have? You saw them in every magazine you flicked through: at the hairdresser, in the doctor's waiting room, in the checkout line. You noted every celebrity wearing them proudly and looking effortlessly amazing. You heard there was a waiting list, that they were a limited edition. You were desperate for those boots. How did those celebrities get them? Could you get them? Would your friends get their hands on a pair before you did? They were the ultimate statement in fashion that season. If you had those boots, well, you'd look amazing too.

Let me tell you what really happened.

A pair of boots was created six months earlier. They were given by the designer to the fashion PR. The PR gave them a name. The "Cassandra". They had those boots photographed, artfully. They then called up their favoured publication and told them they had an exciting exclusive for them. The boot of their dreams. They could write a story about them using images of all the VIPs wearing them in the pictures everyone was going to see. The PR wouldn't let anyone else write about the boots until their story had come out. The magazine eagerly agreed.

That same fashion PR then told the designer to make twenty pairs of those boots to give to their chosen celebrities, who were never going to buy them themselves. They sent them out with a personal note from the designer, as a gift.

The PR had written the note. The grateful celebrities wore those boots when they knew they were going to be photographed. They posted a picture of them on their social media when they were told they could – by the PR.

You wanted those boots so badly. You still believed there was only one pair left in your size, on a resale site based in Sweden.

In a fashion PR agency showroom somewhere in London, those boots had sat on display in five different colourways for months. They had been sent with couriers to photographic shoots on a daily basis, shoved in paper bags. The factory was poised to make thousands of them, once thousands of you believed there were none left.

That boot became the "it" boot. For one month. You bought those boots using your "buy now, pay later" app, to try to convince yourself they weren't the price of a small car. You wore those boots twice. You swooned when your pair arrived, but they didn't look quite the same on you as they had in the pictures. And by the time you had tried them on in your bedroom, a new summer sandal, the "Frida", had arrived in another PR showroom and was about to go through exactly the same process. You would feel as passionate about Frida as you had about Cassandra in approximately six months' time.

And that, in a nutshell, is fashion PR. Any questions?'

'But what do you actually *do*?'

Oh, for fuck's sake. Really? Even after all these years, it's constant. Today I'm back at my old university's careers forum to address it. Again. *Fashion PR? Q&A with Frankie Marks.* I stand at the lectern, look out at the sea of students and try to focus on the task at hand, rather than the packet of crisps stuffed into my handbag and the fact that I am absolutely starving. But let's be honest, if only they had seen me at the beginning. I was just as confused as they are . . .

PRESS NOTE

It was a momentous day in the world of fashion PR as Frankie Marks made her first appearance inside the doors of leading agency Georgina Galvin Communications. Frankie was at once inspiring, enigmatic, modest and exceptionally well prepared.

'Frankie who?' commented the members of the GGC team as they sipped their skinny lattes.

ENDS

The wooden floor of our bedroom was covered with a piled tangle of clothes and shoes and tights. There wasn't really that much room for such a big pile. But there it was. And so many tights. Ribbed. Opaque. Plain. Patterned. Woollen. Silk. The shutters were half open, the bed wasn't made, and I was struggling to decide what to wear. The options were all impossibly unsuitable for where I was heading. I had veered all the way from jeans and plain black polo neck, through to an A-line skirt with striped shirt, via a dubious dungaree dress and flared burgundy cords. I opted for my original choice. Jeans, polo neck and the one blazer I owned. Casual but formal. Confident but low-key. No tights required. *Jesus, I couldn't go through this every bloody morning*, I thought, as I yanked my head though the polo neck for the tenth time. I also knew James couldn't go through this for five more minutes.

'Just wear the jeans, for God's sake. You're interviewing to be the intern. No one will be looking at you.' He laughed at me from the tiny adjoining bathroom before switching on his electric toothbrush.

I poked one denim-bedecked leg through the bathroom door into his line of sight and wiggled it dramatically for confirmation.

My boyfriend of four years came into the bedroom, all tousle-haired and minty. 'You'll be fine. They'd be lucky to have you. Frankie Marks, the most unlikely candidate for fashion PR. Oh, this could be funny.'

I looked up at James and stuck out my tongue as I continued my deep dive into the sock drawer. He bent down to kiss the top of my head and gave my hair an affectionate ruffle.

'My hair!' I screeched, frantically patting the tonging down. 'You're such a fucking pain. Now look at me.' I scowled.

'Now now, Frankie, you're going to have to remember to keep your thoughts to yourself. From what I understand, PRs have to smile. And be nice to people. Even when they hate them. Just try to remember that.'

He had a point. I wasn't entirely renowned for my people skills. Generally, if anyone tried to embark on polite chit-chat and ask how I was, I liked to reply 'terrible' to end any potential ensuing conversation. Same went for the interminable question, 'What have you been up to?' My standard reply – 'nothing' – normally did the trick. I also had an extensive list of behaviour I found unacceptable in others – chiefly, I absolutely could not bear to hear anyone chew or swallow loudly. *Ever*.

But, as the dozens of letters I had written to art galleries and auction houses since leaving university the previous summer, extolling the virtues of my degree in art history and my unparalleled willingness to intern for nothing but my bus fare, had resulted in no joy, I was determined that this would finally be my employment break. Of sorts. I hadn't been fussy. I'd thrown the net wider. Publishing, PR, marketing, production – you name it, I had sent them my sparse CV. I was desperate. I urgently needed to get on to the career ladder, and my mountain of rejection letters and emails was depressingly high. But a friend-of-a-friend had known some-one's sister's boyfriend who had once met Georgina Galvin and had sent her an email on my behalf, which she had promptly forwarded on to her PA, who had called me out of the blue. Fashion wasn't exactly my forte – my wholly unsuit-able pile of clothing options was testament to that – but I believed there was room to manoeuvre.

'If Sotheby's don't appreciate what I have to offer in rela-tion to my thoughts on seventeenth-century Flemish art, then surely I can apply myself to growing an interest in hem lengths for a finite period of time?' I said to James, with abso-lute false confidence.

'I'm sure you can find as much value in velvet as you would have done in Vermeer.' James laughed. Again.

The call had come in unexpectedly the day before, just as I was debating whether it was too greedy to have sour cream AND cheese on my daily baked-potato lunch for one. *If I have both today, I can have just tuna tomorrow?*

'Frankie? This is Debbie. From GGC.'

'Hello, hi, GG who?' I had frowned, scrambling to remem-ber what GGC was.

Noticing my hesitation, she went on, 'Georgina Galvin Communications. We've had your CV in and would really like it if you could pop into the offices tomorrow. We've had an unexpected vacancy come up – an intern who didn't quite . . . well, anyway, are you free to come in for an interview?'

'Oh my God. Yes, of course. That would be wonderful. Thank you.'

'Ask for me. Let's say ten a.m. See you then.'

I hadn't heard of Georgina Galvin before. I came to understand she was legendary in the fashion world – the woman everyone knew of, feeling they knew her intimately while not actually knowing anything about her at all. She had moved through the industry seamlessly, having first come to its forefront as the right-hand woman to one of the most significant designers in Milan. How she had got there, nobody knew. Her age, a mystery. But when, after a number of years, she announced she was moving back to London to set up her eponymous agency, every designer and brand clamoured to be a part of it and be represented by her. Now she was something of an enigma. Floating in and out of the public eye. Appearing when necessary. Disappearing whenever she felt like it. But the mention of her name in fashion circles garnered attention and admiration in equal measure. She was the epicentre of numerous urban myths. And I was about to be placed in front of her – totally and utterly unprepared.

Debbie, who, as it turned out, was a perky, freckled brunette, met me in the hallway when I arrived at the imposing Georgian townhouse in Marylebone that was home to GGC. She efficiently placed me in a light-filled meeting room with a quick and terrifying pep talk.

'Don't be nervous. Georgina likes confidence. But don't be too confident. Be friendly. But don't be overfamiliar. And ask questions. There's nothing she likes more than giving advice. But don't ask too many questions. She'll wonder why you don't know anything.'

I sat down, sweltering in my coat and scarf until it occurred to me that I could perhaps disrobe. I placed them on the chair next to me. I sat at one end of an incredibly long glass table, the walls around me covered in framed magazine covers and pictures of a woman I assumed must be Georgina, with clients all over the world. None of it really meant anything to me, but there was the iconic eyewear shoot with the dripping lipstick that even I was aware of because we had talked about it in one of our Dali seminars in my first year. My interest was piqued. Here was the designer duo Dante, renowned for their A-list celebrity following, hugging Georgina backstage after what I would later learn was their infamous show on the tube tracks at Old Street station. Clearly Georgina knew them well, because scrawled at the bottom of the white surround was a message: *We'll always have Old Street! Love, your Dante boys.* Further along the wall I spotted an image of a Hollywood A-list actress – whose name I couldn't quite remember – leaning over a tray of diamonds, with Georgina just out of focus in the background. I sweated and fidgeted, waiting for what felt like an interminably long time. Just as I was about to grab a mint from my bag to combat my increasingly dry mouth, the door flung open. I stood up.

'Hello, I'm Georgina, sit, sit, please.' The woman standing at the door gestured. She was beautiful in a masculine kind of way. Brown hair, slightly messy topknot. Make-up minimal. Age undefinable. Anywhere from a mature forty to a brilliantly surgically refined sixty. Jewellery delicate but deliberately styled. She didn't pause for niceties. I would find out she never paused for niceties – and that she was never really around.

'I'm running late, and I've only got five minutes, I'm afraid. Debbie went through your CV and she's shared it with the team, and quite honestly this is just for us to meet so I can put a face to a name. We need someone with energy, enthusiasm and a can-do attitude. This job involves a lot of running around, anticipating everyone's needs and thinking on the go. Our last intern didn't quite cut it,' she said, glancing down briefly at my CV, 'but I'm sure you're more than capable. This is most definitely *not* a nine-to-five job, so the most important question is, can you be flexible with your working hours?'

Despite the inflection, this was most definitely NOT a question.

Georgina's phone rang then, and she put it on silent and turned it face down.

'Oh yes, absolutely. No problem.' I nodded fervently.

'Great. Let's make this quick, then. We'll start you on a three-month trial. From Monday. Debbie will explain how to claim expenses, and if you do well, we can look at a permanent position depending on how you manage. A lot of the team started as interns. Do you have any questions?'

Of course I froze, my mind a perfect blank.

'Umm. Not that I can think of right now. But I just want to say, thank you so much for the opportunity. I'm so excited to learn. You're such an inspiration.'

'Oh really? Why?'

Shit.

'You know . . . just so inspiring?' Oh, the shame of it. Good grief. *Think before you speak, Frankie.*

Georgina left an agonising silence as I floundered and tried to look meaningfully into the distance.

'I mean . . . Dante . . . so great . . .' I whispered, pointing at the photo on the wall.

And with that, she raised an eyebrow, pushed her chair back, pulled down the cuffs of her immaculate white men's tailored shirt and left the room as I sat, my toes curling in painful silence. Later on, I would often replay this moment in my head and the memory of it would make my eyes water.

'You're such an inspiration.' For fuck's sake. Had I really said that? I wanted the floor to swallow me up. And *no* questions? I had a hundred questions. Mainly, 'How did I end up here?', 'How old actually are you?' and 'Did you tie your hair up with pins or a band?'

I picked my bag up off the floor and shuffled from foot to foot. Was I supposed to follow her or wait to be fetched from the room? As I considered the merits of either approach, the door opened.

'Come on, then, don't just stand there!' Georgina said sharply from the other side. I grabbed my things, left my CV on the table and followed her out to where Debbie was waiting in the hallway, holding her laptop and staring at a diary screen. The two of them walked and talked as they went down the stairs. I followed gingerly behind.

'So, you have a ten thirty a.m. with the guys from *The Forward* to talk about their special sustainability issue; they're coming here. Then at midday, you need to sit down with the team to go over the dinner tomorrow night; they urgently need you to give final approval on seating plans. Then you're done for the day here. Lunch is at Zaffano's with Amanda at one thirty. You have a facial at three thirty and drinks tonight to discuss Dante's show music with Marcel.'

Georgina nodded while checking her phone. 'We need to change Zaffano's. Amanda is on some new keto diet – she can't eat Italian. She can do sashimi. Can you change it? To that Japanese I like in Mayfair. But get a table by the window. On the ground floor. Not the basement. Too stuffy down there. Get Andrew to package up that Dixie scarf for me to take for her as a gift. I know she liked it. Let's have some gluten-free breakfast in for *The Forward* guys – one of them is coeliac. Ask Nicky to email me that plan so I can look at it in the car on my way in first. Can Marcel come to my house? I don't want to have to go out and put make-up on after I've had my face done. Oh, and did you tell them I want the oxygen facial this afternoon? And not with that new therapist. She gave me a rash.'

I needed a lie-down just from listening to Georgina's list of demands. She took a sharp left into another room, and Debbie told me she would take me on a quick tour of the building.

'This is the office and where we all sit – Georgina likes to be able to see us all when she's in.'

Debbie gestured towards a separate glass office with one desk at the far end of the room, where I spied Georgina already talking on the phone, simultaneously applying hand lotion and sipping a coffee.

'We all work incredibly hard but it's fun and she's a great boss. I mean, she has high expectations, but she's the best. Just ignore everything you've heard.'

I nodded. *Yup – I'll ignore everything I've never heard.*

I looked around a double-height room filled with desks in arrangements of two, three and four. A gentle vanilla scent wafted from numerous large candles strategically placed between phones, laptops, whirring printers and a crowd of perfect, shiny people.

'Guys, this is Frankie, our new intern,' Debbie said.

'Hi, Frankie,' the perfect people mumbled, barely looking up. I smiled and gave a sort of half wave with my free hand to anyone who was looking. Which they weren't. In the other hand I was heaving my coat and scarf and bag.

'That's Andrew, he's one of our account directors, and next to him normally is Jemima, but she's dropping something off somewhere at the moment, I think – clients are always scrimping on courier bills.'

Debbie pointed at one of the groups of glass desks covered in laptops and a printer, magazines, chargers, notebooks and litre bottles of sparkling water. Andrew was immaculate – alabaster-skinned with symmetrical features and perfectly coiffed hair – and I watched as he flicked through a magazine, inserting coloured Post-its while dialling someone frenetically on his landline. I glanced down quickly at my own jeans and platform loafers with a significant tassel detail and saw, with a sinking heart, the glittery Elsa embroidery snaking up my navy socks that I hadn't noticed in my bedroom. An emergency Disney store purchase at the airport last year when I had aptly frozen ankles preflight. *I want to die. Right now.* I was definitely going to be uncovered as a fashion imposter by Day Two. But I needed this job. And in the meantime, I'd carry on writing to every single gallery in London just in case something more suitable came up.

'Over in this corner is Nicky's team. She's the Senior Account Director but she's on holiday this week. She doesn't really *do* winter in England. Her Account Director is Zoe but she's not here either. She has boyfriend troubles. I saw her scrolling through Tinder and crying so I sent her home.' Debbie corrected her overshare and got back to the task at hand. 'You'll be sitting at that desk with them.' She pointed to an empty desk. 'I'll get IT to set you up with a laptop and email address on Monday. Always keep it password-protected, and if you leave it here overnight, remember to lock it up in the drawer next to your desk. Don't eat hot food in the office, Georgina hates it. And never, ever wear open-toed shoes unless you've had a pedicure. She has a thing about it.'

I made a mental note to ask my best friend Charlotte where on earth to go for a pedicure should we encounter a sudden heatwave in January.

We wandered out to the hallway and Debbie directed me back down the stairs, passing a small room on the half landing.

'This is what we call the sample room, but really it's a cupboard where all the samples go in and out of every day. It's where Eloise, the Showroom Manager, sits. No idea where she is, though,' she said with a shrug as we moved past.

I managed a fleeting glimpse into a dim box room, crammed with a desk and paper bags filled to the brim with clothes and shoes. There was a rail haphazardly stuffed with an array of hanging clothes in a cacophony of colours and materials. Post-it notes covered the walls with scrawls, dates and a lot of question marks. *A lot.*

'And this is the main showroom.'

We were back on the ground floor. I peered inside a large, white-walled space. Rail after rail of clothes. Shoes in rows all along the perimeter. Plinths holding expensive-looking hand-bags. Glass boxes full of jewellery of all shapes and sizes. Sunglasses in rows on display stands. I'd never seen anything like it.

'There's a second adjoining room for the other clients, but that can wait till next week,' Debbie said, waving her hand. 'So that's pretty much it for now. You need to provide all travel expenses to claim back at the end of each week and I'll see you nine a.m. on Monday.' She was ushering me back to the front door and checking her phone. Clearly my time was up, and clearly no one at GGC did only one thing at a time.

Stuttering my thanks into thin air, I emerged on to the pavement, reeling. I felt like I'd been whacked around the head by ten metaphorical patent shoes. I had questions. So many. Primarily, how on earth had I just got this job? I turned back expectantly to Debbie, who promptly smiled and closed the door behind her. Who were these people? What did they actually do? How could I ever survive in that environment? Did they really all look like that, every single day? *Shit*. But regardless, and most importantly, I realised I had an internship. Georgina had seen some sort of value in me and I would make it work for as long as it took to get a glowing reference and something else. I wrapped my scarf around me and texted James.

> **Frankie**
> I really am going to work in fashion PR. Who knew?

Next, Charlotte.

> **Frankie**
> I have a job. Sort of!

Then I called my father. He didn't do texts.

'Fashion PR? What on earth is that? And what do you mean, for free?' He sighed down the phone.

'They'll pay for my travel.' The panic about how much longer I could get by without an income was real, and I could hear myself whining slightly, my pitch going up a notch and betraying my anxiety. I always regressed when I wanted my father's approval, and I hated myself for it. His mantra to me had always been to look after myself. The day I lost my pocket money, age ten, on the way to buy a KitKat, and sobbed inconsolably when he refused to advance me the following week's fifty pence, was my first harsh lesson about taking responsibility for my own actions. Plus, my father had memorably added, 'Who wastes their money on chocolate when they could have bought a newspaper instead?'

'You need a salary . . . you need to start paying James a fair share of the rent. There's no such thing as a free lunch. All those university loans for *this*?'

'I know. I really know. But Georgina said it's likely, well, it's *very* possible I'll get a paid job there. It could be a good opportunity, and let's be honest, it's my *only* opportunity at the moment. It's not like I haven't tried. I'm sure I'll find something better soon. It's just a stepping-stone – it'll look good on my CV and get me a professional reference for a start. I'm sure James will understand.'

'It's a ridiculous world, full of ghastly people, and a total waste of your education. Try Christie's again. Use your degree, for crying out loud.' Apparently, as far as my father was concerned, I was the only art history graduate on the job hunt. 'Find yourself a real job, don't get stuck there for too long.'

'Oh God, I won't be there long,' I said quickly. 'No way. What do *I* care about fashion anyway?'

PRESS NOTE

GGC is delighted to announce the appointment of Frankie Marks to the highly sought-after role of intern. CEO Georgina Galvin said, 'With her exceptional passion for the industry, Frankie will be a wonderful addition to the GGC team and we look forward to welcoming her next week.'

Frankie Marks commented, 'I am thrilled to be joining GGC and to gain further insight into how appalling my wardrobe is. Opportunities likes this come around once in a lifetime.'

ENDS

'But they're all so well dressed, like they haven't tried at all,' I wailed to Charlotte on the phone, while crunching on a poppadum, the Sunday night before I was due to start at GGC.

'Which means they've probably all tried incredibly hard to look like they haven't tried at all,' she retorted.

That was easy for her say. She hadn't seen the team at GGC in all their full designer glory. My notoriously lacking sense of style extended beyond the aforementioned Disney socks to a terrible mistake with pleather jeggings purchased for Charlotte's eighteenth birthday party – which was followed by six months of begging her to delete all photographic evidence of the catastrophe that was my thighs. High fashion was way out of my depth, but I was determined to be the best badly dressed intern they had ever had. Now I just needed to make sure the curry I had devoured last night hadn't been too garlicky. Should have thought of that. I took a discreet breath test against my wrist and checked I'd remembered my mints.

Okay, so: there was Andrew, someone missing called Jemima, Zoe, and another one who was on holiday. And a girl in the sample room. I couldn't for the life of me remember her name. I reached into the recesses of my brain. Nope. Nothing.

I sat on the jammed top deck of a bus on my way from Ladbroke Grove to Marylebone for the first morning commute of my working life, to a place I would never have imagined myself working in, with the kind of people I would never have imagined working with. I fiddled with the top of my polo neck as I stared out the window, watching a freezing London morning pass me by. I stared furiously at anyone who tried to sit next to me until they moved past. James wasn't wrong. I wasn't good with strangers.

James and I had been together since my first year at the University of Manchester, having collided drunkenly into each other by the warm vodka station at some godforsaken house party. We had been a couple ever since. I was up from London, studying History of Art. James was a third year with a no-nonsense attitude to . . . well, to everything, including me, apparently. He had studied something to do with economics and was now working in something financial that I didn't understand, but he was assuredly on the first rung of his solid and well-paid five-year plan. He had always known what he wanted to do. We couldn't be more different, but quite frankly we couldn't imagine not being together – as much as we sometimes annoyed the hell out of each other. I adored him. He was laconic and dry-witted. He loved a balance sheet. I didn't understand what that was. I was prone to outbursts, didn't suffer fools gladly and never quite knew when to bite my tongue. But James grounded me, and as much as I detested the thought of it, he looked after me. And let's face it, he put up with me and happily acted as my social wingman when appropriate interactions failed me.

'A PR intern. Being polite *all* the time. Thank you, Lord, for this gift that will just keep on giving,' he had said that morning as I was leaving the flat. My new job was going to present him with hours of anecdotes and one-liners, I just knew it. And it was going to be really irritating.

We lived in his minuscule one-bedroom flat off the less salubrious end of Ladbroke Grove, where he subsidised me – and I, in return, perfected the art of the takeaway order and attempted something vaguely akin to keeping things ticking over while he was at work.

'Subsidised *until* you get yourself a job,' James had jokingly specified on numerous occasions. A joke which I suspected had a time limit, and a job which I had so far spectacularly failed to deliver. *Until possibly now*, I thought, as the bus veered left after Marble Arch.

I decided to get off a stop early to gather my thoughts and give myself a little pep talk from under the woolly hat that was pulled down to the top of my eyebrows.

'You can do this. You *can* smile at everyone. You will *not* speak out of turn. You *will* learn to love lurex. The girl on holiday was Nicky! Yes!' I remembered. Now God help me retrieve the sample room girl's name. I took a deep breath and rang the buzzer of the glossy black front door. No answer. I rang again. 9.04 a.m. Was I the first person in?

At 9.06, Debbie hurtled around the corner, clutching a coffee.

'Oh God, sorry! Isn't Eloise here to let you in? She's always bloody late. Hold on, let me find my keys, hold this. Don't spill it. It's for Georgina. She's coming in today.' Debbie thrust an oversized takeaway coffee cup into my gloved hand

and rooted around in her significantly large bucket bag. 'Here, found them.' She waved the huge bunch of keys triumphantly before she unlocked the door, quickly punching in a code on the alarm inside the dark lobby.

She flicked the switches and the lights came on one by one. She unlocked the doors to the showroom on the left and carried on up the stairs. She unlocked the sample cupboard on the half landing and took a look inside.

'Shit, she really left it a mess on Friday, fucking Eloise,' Debbie muttered, her perkiness drooping for a second. She carried on up another flight to unlock the doors to the main offices, switching on more lights as she went, while I mentally unpicked the chaos behind that sample cupboard door.

I followed in her wake, still clasping the huge coffee and praying it wouldn't slip through my gloves and stain the immaculate grey carpet, as the building snapped to life around us. I could hear the front door beginning to open and close two flights down, and the sounds of chatter echoing up the stairwell.

'God, how is it already Monday again?' Andrew walked in with a messenger bag, a croissant, and sporting an interesting take on a deerstalker hat with fur inlay that I was pretty sure Harry Styles had worn in his latest music video.

'I really am over him now, I promise you.' A girl was talking intently down her phone as she walked into the room. So, that must be Zoe with the boyfriend trouble. She was beautiful. A cropped pageboy cut, cartoon-sized, almond-shaped hazel eyes and a heaven-sent set of full lips. Did she look in the mirror every morning and say, *Thank you, God*?

'Hi, everyone! Good weekend?' A tall, striking black girl with a broad smile shook off a camel coat at the other empty desk Debbie had pointed out to me last week. Jemima, I guessed.

'I cannot believe my holiday's already over,' groaned someone glossy with a mahogany tan who must be Nicky, relieving herself of a quite excellent cross body bag which she flung on to her desk. She threw herself into her chair with a flourish and a sigh. 'This weather doesn't suit me. At all.'

'Okay, everyone, Georgina's on her way,' Debbie announced, looking up from her phone. 'Let's get into the meeting room with the papers. Frankie, can you stay down here and answer the phones till Eloise appears? Just press whichever line is ringing. Don't forget to take a message and always take their numbers to call them back. Even if they say we have it.' She pushed a pack of Post-it notes and a biro in my direction and swiped the coffee from my hands.

'Where the hell is Eloise, anyway?' I heard Nicky asking as they all trooped up the stairs holding their newspapers.

'Oh, and Nicky, this is Frankie. She's our new intern; she wears glittery Elsa socks,' Andrew added with a wicked grin as he left the room.

'Hi, Frankie. Ignore him. Welcome. And I know . . . my tan is fabulous.' Nicky smiled as she sashayed out.

Note to self: do intensive shiny-sock clear-out tonight. Urgent.

The room was silent. I stared around me, shell-shocked. I didn't have a computer yet. I didn't have anything. In fact, I didn't have a clue. *Holy fuck, I'm fucked.*

The door opened and shut again, throwing in a quick icy blast from the street.

'I'm heeeere.' I recognised Georgina's voice as it carried up the stairs and heard Debbie run down to greet her.

'Morning. How was your weekend? Let me take your coat. Did they send the right driver? We're all ready for you . . . your coffee's up there. Eloise still hasn't shown up but Frankie's manning the phones.'

'Who's Frankie?' I heard Georgina ask indifferently.

'The new intern? You met her last week,' Debbie replied.

'Oh, right, right. Of course. Yes. Okay.'

As James had reminded me, no one was looking at me. My new boss couldn't even remember hiring me.

I sat in the silence contemplating what I was doing there, why I hadn't eaten breakfast, what time I would have lunch, and how I could ask Nicky where her bag was from (so I could look for a high-street equivalent. I found myself quite liking the idea of a crossbody bag).

Suddenly the phone rang, interrupting my reverie. Line one flashed. I picked up the receiver.

'Good morning, GGC,' I said in what I hoped was my best proper-job voice.

'Can I speak to Andrew, please,' replied a weary female voice.

'Oh, I'm sorry, he's just in a meeting. May I take a message?'

'Urgh. Yes. Okay. It's Natasha from *My Style.*'

'Can I have a number for him to call you back?'

'He has my number.'

The line went dead before I could reply. More ringing as line two flashed.

'Good morning, GGC.'

'Nicky, please. It's Amanda Starling.'

'I'm sorry, Nicky is currently in a meeting. Can I let her know you called? Is that starling as in the little bird?'

'Seriously? Just get her to call me back asap.'

And once again, I was left speaking into the ether as the line clicked dead.

I googled Amanda Starling. Editor-in-chief of *Avalon* magazine. Shit. I really needed to do some homework. No wonder her keto diet had been high stakes for that lunch I'd heard Debbie and Georgina discussing on the day of my interview.

An hour passed in much the same vein, a rinse and repeat of 'Good Morning, GGC' followed by a flurry of names I'd never heard of and numbers I somehow never managed to get. By 10.30 my head ached from the effort of so much enforced politeness, and my stomach had passed the growling stage and was positively baying for food. The elusive Eloise still hadn't shown up by the time the team drifted back into the office.

'God, that was awful.'

'We've never had such a bad weekend haul of editorial.'

'Georgina was in foul mood.'

I scurried from desk to desk, sticking my scribbled Post-its in front of each of my new colleagues and wondering if Georgina was watching my efficiency from her glass box.

'I'm really sorry, most people wouldn't wait long enough to give me their numbers for you,' I apologised repeatedly.

'Don't worry about it.' Nicky waved her hand. 'Can you go see if Eloise has arrived yet and ask her to come up? Meanwhile, do we all feel like a cup of tea?'

'That's the royal "we", Frankie,' said Andrew. 'What Nicky means is *she* would like a cup of tea. But actually, while you're down there, I wouldn't mind one too. Builder's. No sugar.'

'See, I knew I wouldn't be the only one who wanted a cup. Same for me, please, Frankie. No sugar. But strong. Not too much milk. And I only like the mug with the blue and white stripes.'

I headed down to the kitchen on the ground floor. It was tiny. I had a poke around the fridge. Two dairy-free yoghurts. One half-eaten punnet of grapes. Half a pint of skimmed milk and someone's leftover salad that had seen better days. I opened up the cupboard, took out the mugs and after a quick rummage, located the teabags. I had a sinking feeling I would be spending a lot of time in this room.

As I was squeezing the life out of Nicky's teabag, I heard the door open and close quietly. I stuck my head around the door and saw an average-build brunette who looked to be pretty much my age and in startlingly bright purple tights, phone clamped between her ear and shoulder, whispering urgently.

'Yes, yes, I know. Look, I'm late again, but I'll have a look at everything later and let you know. Got to go.'

I put the spoon down with enough of a clang to cause the brunette to look up and in through the kitchen door. When she did, I waved the spoon aloft in a vague gesture of hello. She looked at me suspiciously.

'You must be the new girl. I'm late,' she said as she ran up the stairs. That must be Eloise.

'Nicky asked if you could go up to the office. If you're Eloise? I'm Frankie, by the way, nice to meet you.'

'Fucking Nicky,' she said distractedly, climbing the stairs and disappearing round the corner, hurriedly stuffing her phone in her bag.

'Nice to meet you too, Eloise,' I muttered to myself and the teabag as I heard the sample cupboard door slam shut.

Eloise had clearly been at the back of the charm queue with me. This could be interesting. She was either going to be my new best friend or my new worst enemy.

PRESS NOTE

Frankie Marks is delighted to announce that her first month at GGC learning how to take lunch orders and pick up dry cleaning was heralded an enormous success and she looks forward to discovering even more about tuna baguettes in the coming days.

Nicky Harris, Senior Account Director, commented, 'We are so impressed with how Frankie navigated the deli counter. We can't wait to see what further skills she brings to the team in the future.'

ENDS

'Oh hi. Remember me? James? I think we met once by the fridge. Or was it next to the recycling bins?' James called me as I was rearranging hangers in the showroom, a few weeks after my first day at GGC.

'I'm not really sure. I think those bins were part of the set for an *Avalon* shoot last week. Were you there?'

He said he was pleased for me, despite my sudden interest in duchesse satin. I wasn't entirely convinced, but I didn't have time to worry about it as I spent that first month absorbing, listening, eavesdropping and nodding a lot, in between getting lunches, picking up coffees, running errands and hanging clothes. GGC was a machine. The door buzzer went continuously. Couriers came in and out of the building constantly. Dropping back samples from publications, picking up samples going to publications. Stylists came in for appointments, selecting clothes, shoes and jewellery for their shoots. Everyone was working a full season ahead. The summer collections in the showrooms in January would be replaced by the winter collections, after all the shows in February and the selling campaigns in March were finished. Then there were the collections called pre-collections. They were created in between seasons, and were also in the showroom. 'They're more commercial, Frankie – by which I mean people actually want to buy them because they haven't been designed for the catwalk,' Zoe had explained. I didn't understand. Why design anything in the first place that wasn't going to be sold?

'The catwalk collections create a halo effect. They're then adapted to fit someone who isn't seven feet tall, for a start,' she added. *Ridiculous.* I struggled to get my head around it. And curiosity was already getting the better of me. I wanted to see one of these shows. I just needed to last long enough to be there for London Fashion Week in a month's time, to see the catwalk clothes created for seven-foot models that no one would buy.

'It's like they're all on a hamster wheel, with no breathing space to get off and rest their legs, let alone hand-hold the intern. And that's just in the office. There's a whole life out of hours that they have to fully embrace ... drinks, dinners, cocktail parties, openings, galleries ...' I breathlessly relayed my observations to Charlotte in between mouthfuls of crisps one day, as I marched back to the office with a matcha tea for Zoe. My new colleagues' lives were relentless, but also kind of exhilarating, and as I watched each of them spinning twenty plates in the air every day, my fascination with the team and the agency grew. As someone who found very few people tolerable or remotely interesting, their allure was not only perturbing to me, but increasingly compelling.

Georgina was hardly ever in the office, but I observed everyone else with fierce concentration and started to engage with them a bit more day by day.

Zoe loved to overshare. She was beautiful, with an ability to carry off that pageboy cut hairstyle with a high-waisted jean that bewitched men and women alike. For some reason she couldn't hold down a relationship, but careered endlessly from man to man. I spent a lot of my day staring at her and considering her love life. She just couldn't work out what she wanted. But while she figured it out, she was an infamous beauty on the fashion circuit.

Nicky – well, Nicky was a law unto herself. Permanently tanned and always in the most beautiful and extortionately priced clothes, with perfect hair thanks to her brunette bob being blow-dried twice a week. I was shocked by the extravagance, but she entertained press constantly – breakfast, brunch, lunch, afternoon tea, cocktails, dinners – although she was always on a diet. And she was funny. She had a husband Mark who no one ever saw, but who definitely had a job in the City and definitely adored her, but hated her job. She didn't want children yet but planned to start trying soon – after the next Fashion Week, but before her next holiday. I kind of really wanted to be Nicky.

Then there was Andrew, who was just brilliant. Full of gossip and breathless stories, potty-mouthed, and always exhausted from unspecified late-night shenanigans. He was also very kind, and the others all adored him.

I tried to not dislike Eloise following our first encounter. I really did. But she had no interest in pretending she didn't dislike me, squinting and sighing loudly whenever I asked a question, so I gave up. I mean, I wasn't quite sure why she had taken such an aversion to me so quickly. I had truly been on my best behaviour and had even once asked her where she procured her neon Post-it notes from. She was always dressed in her own weirdly self-conscious interpretation of the latest trends, which always included terrible purple or pink tights and huge platform lace-up boots. She was stand-offish, constantly seemed to be on the phone, had frayed nerves and kept a lot of apples on her desk. Which she crunched on really loudly. Therein sealing her fate as someone I could never be friends with anyway.

And then there was Jemima. She had come to GGC straight out of college and was a Londoner born and bred, like me. She had also started as an intern, one who they all realised they couldn't live without. Tall and languid, she had the sweetest temperament and was consistently good-natured. Nothing was ever a problem. On my second day, it was Jemima who had taken me to the deli around the corner to talk me through what everyone did and didn't eat.

'When Nicky says she wants a chicken salad, she wants the chicken on the side. She doesn't want the dressing. She keeps a bottle of balsamic in the kitchen. Zoe doesn't eat tomatoes or garlic. And when she says she wants a ham baguette, she means she wants a wholemeal baguette with ham *and* cheese. And when she says she needs the low-fat mayonnaise, you'll tell her it is the low-fat – they don't have low-fat, but she won't notice, and as she'll never step foot in here, she'll never know. She also likes it cut into four pieces. Andrew always thinks he'll have a soup and then remembers he's not allowed to have soup if it's a day Georgina is in. He'll still ask you every day to call him to tell him what the soup of the day is, and will take ages deliberating. But he'll always end up having a tuna sweetcorn sandwich. And you'll never have to get Georgina anything. Unless Debbie isn't in. Although Georgina's rarely here, and when she is here, Debbie wouldn't dare not be here, and on the very off-chance it does happen, you'll be getting her sushi. And it won't be local. But even if she's on her death-bed, Debbie will talk you through that potential minefield.'

If my father could see me now, I thought to myself, as I carefully placed everyone's lunches in front of them. He'd be mortified.

Oh, it's great, I had emailed him that first month. *I'm learning so much. It's really exciting. I'm getting involved in everything. It's really going to help me when I reapply to the auction houses.*

The team had all seen my CV, so they knew my background – they weren't astounded by my average intellect. As it turned out, Andrew had a First in English from Edinburgh, Jemima a 2:1 in Psychology from Sussex, Nicky a 2:1 in History from Bristol, and Zoe had a 2:2 from Durham in Anthropology. Which would have been a 2:1, she assured everyone, if she hadn't split up from her boyfriend just before her finals. They were all really, really clever. They had all fallen into the industry by chance, mistake or good fortune. I put the information in my back pocket for when I needed to rebut my father's next onslaught. I had always been creative when trying to bring him around. Like the time I proudly told him what a great essay I had written about the scrotum – the holiest place in the Roman Forum – for my year seven history test. And when he exclaimed it was the *sacrum*, not the scrotum, and told me what a scrotum actually was, I insisted it must just mean I had an excellent grasp on biology. I wasn't certain he bought it – and at some point in the conversation he definitely lost the will to argue the logic – but I focused my efforts on getting top marks in my next biology test to prove my theory and appease him. I would now need to apply the same logic – work hard, excel, and invent a new mathematical theorem for the exacting job of spacing the hangers in the showroom.

In the first week of my second month at the agency, I marched down Oxford Street, clasping a bikini in the branded GGC paper bag that Eloise had pushed into my hand with an address label on it and no further direction or word of thanks. I deeply regretted wearing stiff leather boots. They were rubbing against my heels and I could feel all the hallmarks of blisters starting to take shape. My Google Maps kept flipping the wrong-side up as I navigated the side streets of Soho searching for the address. When I finally arrived at an annoyingly inconspicuous entrance with a door buzzer marked 'My Style', I was flushed and ever so slightly sweating, despite the winter chill.

'Bikini from GGC,' I said to the girl at the nearest desk to the door and handed it to her without further introduction or niceties. She reciprocated in kind, stretching out her hand and grunting a barely audible 'Thank you' under her breath.

Back on Oxford Street, across and down from Selfridges, through garden squares, criss-crossing my way on to the high street, I checked my pocket for Nicky's ticket for the dry cleaning she had asked me to collect. Shit. I checked my other pocket. My back pockets. I must have left it behind. My panic escalated as I pushed open the door to the steaming hot dry cleaners.

'Look, I've left her ticket, but I have to pick up a dress for Nicky. You know Nicky?' I implored. 'I'm in a bit of a hurry.'

'Nicky?' said the man behind the counter, who was wearing little round-framed glasses and a tape measure around his neck.

'Yes, we know Nicky. She wants the silk dress? Hold on. But I need the ticket. And she also left two jumpers and a suit,' said an older lady, rummaging through a sea of hanging plastic bags, pulling down four and placing them on the counter in front of me. Nicky had insisted she needed her dress by five p.m. for some drinks do. I couldn't fail.

'I don't have either ticket. I really, really need the clothes. Please, I can't leave without them. It's an emergency,' I begged.

'Well, I don't know . . .' The woman looked at the man. He looked back at her. This gaze between two dry cleaners became the singularly most important moment in my new professional life.

'It's my first month at work. I can't go back without them. I just can't.' I tried to muster a tear. I bit my bottom lip.

'She's another new one from that office.' The woman tipped her head knowingly to her partner in crime. He in turn shook his head in pity.

'Remind Nicky we do delivery,' the woman said as she pushed the bags in my direction and I gratefully swooped them up, swallowing down my irritation that Nicky could actually have had these things delivered.

I clutched the plastic bags over my forearm, which was now raised to stop the dress hem from sweeping the streets. The plastic stuck to my cheek. The top of the wire coat hangers banged not so gently into my right thigh with every step. My arm started aching. My blisters were burning. I carried on marching. Wearing my arctic parka with intense insulation didn't seem such a smart idea anymore, as I felt a trickle of sweat pool down my back with another stop to make. I still needed to get Andrew's coffee.

'An extra shot, caffeinated, low-fat cappuccino, please,' I said briskly at the coffee counter. It was 4.44 p.m. I now had sixteen minutes to make Nicky's deadline. Ninja-like, I pushed the door open with my elbow, caught the bottom of it with my foot, and edged myself through the narrow space back on to the street. Burning coffee on one side. Dead arm on the other. Blisters. I was nuclear red, and a bead of sweat neatly ran from my hairline down the side of my cheek.

Oh God, did I put enough deodorant on this morning?

I rang the GGC doorbell with my non-dead elbow. No answer. Through gritted teeth I buzzed again, and as the door opened I could hear Zoe cursing Eloise from inside the showroom.

I felt like I'd just completed some kind of bizarre obstacle course as I walked up the stairs into the office, but remembered to switch on a magnificent smile as I came through the door.

'Thank you! And my Saint Laurent suit and my jumpers! I totally forgot they were all still there.' Nicky extricated the pile of bags from my hands and threw it down. 'Drinks aren't happening now. Apparently, I got the wrong day. But I never do that. And it was in the diary.' She was frowning at the shared office calendar on her computer. 'Anyway, it's great to have everything back.'

Not. Even. Going. For fuck's sake. I had practically been on my knees negotiating the release of those clothes. I slumped into the chair at my desk, yanked off my boots and lowered my socks. Peeling raw skin and burst blisters. Great.

Andrew absent-mindedly put his coffee to his lips as he scanned his emails, and just as quickly banged it back down.

'NO!' he screamed. 'I don't fucking believe it.'

'Is it the wrong coffee?' I sat bolt upright.

'We're losing Cooper & Co.' He began reading. '"Such a great job. Been a wonderful two years. Time for a change." Blah, blah.' He took a gulp of coffee. '"Termination in two months, as per contract. At that time, please send all samples over to ... FUCKING FIVE STAR." Okay, so they didn't call them "fucking" Five Star. That's my artistic licence. Shit. *Shit.*'

'Sunglasses client,' Jemima explained to me.

'That fucking Dominic Carter. Georgina's going to kill us. And then him,' Zoe chimed in.

'Who's Dominic Carter?' I asked, understanding immediately that this was information I needed to know.

'Literally our arch-rival. He runs Five Star PR. He's always on our tails,' Jemima said. 'So losing a client to him is painful, Frankie.'

'And channel that pain into hating him. It's an important part of the job,' Zoe half laughed with a grimace.

'Let's not tell Georgina till she's back from New York.' Andrew gestured Debbie over. 'When's she back? And for how long?'

'In the office on Monday week, for the day. That's as far as we've got with the diary,' Debbie said as she walked over studying her laptop. 'You can tell her then.'

'Well, I'm one hundred per cent taking the cat's-eye pair in black before they go,' Nicky said. 'They'll go really nicely with my new bikini.'

PRESS NOTE

Navigating showroom appointments is a sought-after skill set. We are delighted to confirm that Frankie Marks' inaugural press appointment in the GGC showroom was a huge success. It was a testament to her people skills and in-depth understanding of our valued clients.

'It was humbling to watch our new intern handle herself so well in such a high-pressure environment. We continue to watch and learn,' said GGC's Account Director, Andrew Davies, as he scrolled through Instagram.

ENDS

'And so, to make money, you either need high-street or big-brand clients. But to get those clients, you need to have one of the cutting-edge designers everyone is talking about. To *get* those designers, though, you need to *already* have a great designer on your books. But you can't afford to take on those great designers till you have the high-street fees.'

'Right. Okay . . .'

'Exactly. And then apparently, you have to have some accessories clients because you need the showroom to be a one-stop shop for stylists.'

'Uh huh.'

'Right, so that's it. That's sort of how Georgina made

GGC so successful. I think? And then you also need to understand the metaverse. Now designers are creating virtual clothes, which I still don't really understand. I mean, someone was talking about how to buy something on a blockchain and I suggested calling a plumber.'

'Of course you did. Who wouldn't?'

'Exactly. So, I think that's how it works. Charlotte, are you still there?'

'Still here, but got to go. Let's talk virtual reality later. Or not . . .'

'Urgh, don't tease me, Charlotte. I feel like I'm literally on a speed-dating course with the world of fashion,' I wailed.

'Fine, but let's talk about it just a little more speedily, shall we?' my best friend replied with a sigh.

Over the years, Georgina had made GGC the prime example of how to make a fashion PR agency work in London, and while she may not have been around much – 'much' being a loose term for 'really hardly ever' – when she was, she was not one to hold back.

'Remember when Georgina noticed I'd left a third-row seat empty at Dixie's last Spring/Summer show?' Zoe said. 'My God, she made me watch the show video on a loop for about two hours to remind me how sloppy it looked on film.'

'What about when Amanda Starling told her the Dante dress I'd sent for her to borrow for the BAFTAs had arrived with a sweat stain under the armpit? I mean, you'd have assumed the last shoot team would have had it dry-cleaned before they returned it to us, or that Eloise would at least have checked it before sending. I was demoted to the sample cupboard for weeks to steam and clean and suffer Eloise's interminable silences,' Jemima said, picking at her sandwich. It must have been bad. Jemima never complained.

'Don't worry, Frankie, it's all part and parcel of the job. It's why Georgina's so successful – and also why she can be such a bitch. I think that's probably why we all secretly worship her,' Zoe said reassuringly, when she noticed my eyes widening as I chewed.

But I wasn't worried. No. It wasn't that at all. I was just concentrating on all this new information and trying to make sense of everything. I was considering the frankly astonishing fact that I found it all interesting. And that earlier that day, I had learned a non-fungible token wasn't a mushroom. I was also wondering where everyone else on my degree course had ended up working. Were they fetching lunch orders, and happily listening to stories about steaming and armpit stains? Or had they got the jobs of their dreams and were spending their days walking around silent white galleries nodding in front of abstract art? *And wasn't that my dream, too? Or had I somehow crash-landed in an alternate universe that I was always meant to be in?* But also, and perhaps most importantly, I was regretting not having bought myself a packet of crisps. The buzzer interrupted my thoughts.

'BUZZER. ANSWER THE DOOR,' Georgina shouted out from her desk suddenly. I hadn't noticed she had come in. But there she was, picking at some sushi behind her laptop. Had she heard the team discussing her? Could she even hear the office chatter through the glass?

'Where's Eloise?' Nicky threw her arms in the air. 'For God's sake.'

I ran to the intercom. 'Hello?'

'Hi. It's Laura, here for an appointment with Andrew.'

I pressed the button and released the door.

'Andrew, someone called Laura for you?'

'Oh shit, I totally forgot,' he said, taking an enormous bite out of his tuna sweetcorn sandwich. 'Frankie, it's just a showroom appointment. She's from *Madame* magazine. Calling in clothes for some awful "How to Wear" shoot. Do me a favour – can you go and see her into the showroom and tell her I'm on a call and will be down soon?'

He took another bite and sat back in his chair, scrolling through Instagram.

Me? An appointment? Shit. I ran down the stairs to be greeted in the hallway by a petite brunette in a black jumpsuit and, quite frankly, ridiculously high stack-heeled boots.

'Hi, Laura. Andrew's just on a call. He's coming down shortly but has asked me to start the appointment,' I said, trying not to reveal the fact I had absolutely no idea what I was supposed to do. This was the first time I had been face to face with a real-life member of the press. Turned out they were only human – and this one was wearing a terrible musk perfume.

'Oh, okay. No problem. I know what I want to look at,' Laura replied, pushing open the door to the first showroom and heading straight to the Dante rail.

Within minutes, she had picked out a selection of tops and dresses and handed them to me in silence before moving on to the Giovanni Castani shoes. I was back at my teenage Saturday shop-assistant job.

'Can I have those and those, please. Oh, I like that shoe,' she said, pointing at a pair of patent stilettos with an ankle-strap detail and pulling them out of their neat line before moving swiftly on to cast her eagle eye around the showroom once more. *That shoe? It's a pair. Plural.* I had started to notice every item of clothing was talked about in the singular by everyone in the fashion industry. That *trouser*. The *culotte* hanging over there. That *jean*. I made a mental note to follow suit. Even though it was absurd.

Andrew came charging in.

'Soorrrry, Laura!' he gushed, emitting a faint waft of tuna.

'No problem.' She leaned in to kiss him on both cheeks.

'Oh. Tuna. How are you? Someone's already helping me.' She vaguely gestured in my direction as I stood there, still holding the Dante clothes and hanging on to the shoes in the crook of my little finger.

Andrew turned to me and I registered him quickly scanning the clothes in my arms.

'Oh, I'm so sorry, Laura, those pieces are already going somewhere this afternoon. In fact, the entire Dante rail has been booked out,' he asserted as he carefully lifted the pieces out of my hands and walked over to the rail to rehang them. 'What about some Dixie? Or the new collection from Darcy Girl? You know Darcy Girl, don't you? Everyone in the know loves them.' He was directing her firmly to the rail of our biggest high-street client.

'But I don't want Dixie and I don't want high street, Andrew. And if you don't want to lend me what I wanted, why didn't you just cancel the appointment?' Laura almost stamped her tiny feet.

'It's not that I don't *want* to, Laura, it's just that the Dante collection is already committed, and I didn't know until just this second. That's why I was still upstairs. On the phone.'

I observed the exchange, back and forth. Laura knew that Andrew knew that Laura knew that Andrew was lying. I would be excellent at this game. I had joined the chess club at university for a laugh. It turned out I was an unbeatable and manipulative strategic thinker. And this wasn't just about clothes. This *was* chess. PRs were the bishops, manoeuvring, thinking ahead, opening up the game and taking pawns – or in this case, velour suits.

'You know how big our circulation is, Andrew, and this inverted snobbery is very old-fashioned.' She sighed and walked over to Darcy Girl, gave it the once-over and picked out one daisy-print balloon-sleeve shirt. 'I'll have this. And the Castani shoe. I can't take it with me now. I'm going to other appointments. Please can they be sent to me this afternoon?'

And with that, she turned on her gigantic heels and exited the showroom and the building in a puff of musk.

Andrew fixed the rails and grabbed the shoes and shirt.

'Give these to Eloise and tell her to book them out to Laura today. We don't lend Dante to *Madame*. Not high end enough. I should have warned you. My bad.'

The team was used to being screamed at regularly by outraged press. Dante clothes were a valuable commodity.

'You asshole,' someone had yelled down the phone to Andrew the day before when he explained that there was no more suiting to send. He had put them on loudspeaker mid-rant for all our enjoyment.

'Our whole story is based around those leggings,' another pleaded.

'It could make the cover,' the next one bribed.

'The *Gloucestershire Daily* is exactly the right market, we really need those silk shirts,' a frantic voice had beseeched.

The hierarchy of publications, the status of stylists, the jostling for cover credits. The relevance of social media, influencers, online stories, number of views, celebrity dressing. This was what counted. This was life or death in the world of fashion PR. This was what I would need to get my head around – and fast. As it turned out, I was a quick learner. I could be the king of this particular chessboard.

PRESS NOTE

We are pleased to announce Frankie's resolve today was matched only by her tea-making skills and her decision to wear all black.

'I personally was thrilled to see Frankie embrace a new dress code while ensuring the office was fully hydrated at all times and adhering to our bathroom rules. It was an exciting day,' commented Nicky Harris, Senior Account Director, GGC.

ENDS

I wasn't to go to the London Fashion Week shows in February, I was told. It was only my second month at the agency. I was surprised to find myself more than slightly disappointed, but was pragmatic about it. The shows were clearly the pinnacle of what the team all worked towards. Like an artist doing a painting and then seeing it in an exhibition. What I hadn't anticipated was the workload in the weeks before. We stayed in the office until after midnight every night. As stress levels rose, so did office consumption.

'We all smoke, eat pizza and drink coffee all day and night,' I said to James as I drank yet another double espresso at home before I left one morning.

'But what do you actually *do?* In between smoking, eating and drinking?' he asked.

I was stumped. How could I explain the intense discussions about the average width of a bottom (sixteen inches) for the seating plans, without sounding ridiculous?

'Think of the front row as your bottom line – pun intended – when you're talking about your money stuff. If that's wrong, the whole thing doesn't work.' I tried to validate the absurdity.

He raised an eyebrow. I couldn't blame him. I could barely contain my eyebrow raises when he banged on about currencies at work – but I always made an effort. Same with Charlotte, who struggled to hold any interest when I messaged her details.

> **Frankie**
> Anyone from a Danish publication has to sit fourth row!

> **Frankie**
> No one is allowed to speak to Amanda Starling unless spoken to!

> **Frankie**
> Shows only last 8 minutes!

> **Charlotte**
> Did you read that article I sent you on the crisis in Yemen?

But I didn't have time to worry about life outside the office. I was fully invested in making myself an indispensable part of the team and securing my reputation as a brilliant Deliveroo specialist.

'Two Margheritas with extra cheese. One Four Seasons. Dough balls. One mixed salad.'

'Two packs of Marlboro Lights, two lighters.'

'A six-pack of Peronis. Four Diet Cokes. Pellegrino. Not Perrier. Too many bubbles.'

'Snickers. Maltesers. Oh, and let's get some Jammy Dodgers.'

The Dante show was the most sought-after ticket in London. They held the prime Fashion Week schedule slot on the Sunday night. 'They' were Jonathan and Lloyd, the co-designers who headed up the brand – and this season they were going for something different. Smaller, more intimate, and it was causing Nicky a multitude of problems. She spent the week before the show between their studio and GGC, troubleshooting as she went. Problems with production, models, music, venue, after-party, collection.

'It's a fucking nightmare. Let's look at this front row one last time. The boys have told Amanda she can bring her daughter, she's eleven – so that's eight inches. Which bench can we squeeze up?' I momentarily wondered what I had done with my mother aged eleven on a Sunday night. I thought most likely I was watching *Hannah Montana* while eating fish fingers as a special treat.

I heard similar conversations about the Dixie Triton show. She had been in the business for decades, designing clothes for women who knew what they wanted and didn't want to be slaves to trends. Which meant she wasn't a hot ticket. More of a respected ticket. I kept my head down, digesting every detail. Occasionally I would be sent out with invitations to hand-deliver. To hotels for foreign press and buyers who had flown in. To private homes for the journalists not going back into their offices before the gruelling fashion month they had ahead of them. I dropped off outfits for VIPs and influencers to wear to the shows, and be photographed in. I booked cars and couriers. I confirmed hair and make-up teams to attend to any VIPs coming on the promise of a blow-dry and makeover.

'Seven a.m. tomorrow to start final prep for Dixie's show, Frankie,' Nicky said as I was leaving past midnight on the Saturday night. 'And I'd also like you to come help at the Dante show. All hands on deck. It's going to be chaos.'

I went home feeling a mixture of emotions. I was exhausted, and I wasn't going to get more than four hours' sleep. I was going to be working at least a sixteen-hour day tomorrow. I hadn't seen James properly all week – but on the other hand, I was actually going to experience a show.

'How was it?' a voice came from under the covers as I tiptoed into the bedroom.

'I smoked twenty cigarettes and ate ten Jaffa Cakes. That's the bad news.'

'Excellent. And the good news?'

'They asked me to help at the Dante show tomorrow night. That's the biggest show of Fashion Week. It's going to be amazing,' I said as I peeled off my jeans and sat on the loo. 'And I think I'm going to see all the really big editors in person, and . . .'

'Oh, your mum called earlier, I think. Didn't leave a message but it must have been her because it was the landline and no one else even knows what that is.'

'The thing is, I just really hope they let me watch the show and don't just leave me outside or something . . .'

'Are you even listening to me? I called BT about the inter-net being down last week and they're sending someone, hopefully on Monday.'

'. . . And Lord knows what I'm going to wear. I really don't want to stick out like a sore thumb . . . did you say someone was landing . . . ?'

'Nope, not listening to me. Should have told you – we've run out of toilet paper. There's a couple of squares of kitchen roll by the kettle. Hear that?'

The alarm woke me up rudely the next morning. I slammed it off so as not to wake James up, while secretly hoping I had slammed it hard enough to accidentally wake him up. Today was my first full and proper day as a fashion PR. Today was the day that I went to work on a Sunday on minimal sleep and would see a show. I may even get to wear a headset. Or carry a clipboard. But before my moment of high-octane glamour, I had at least ten hours of making tea, running around London, stuffing envelopes, buying out the local newsagent's entire supply of Haribo and Marlboro Lights and saying 'yes' to any request. I picked out an efficient outfit: black straight-leg trousers, white shirt and a black cashmere crew neck I had been saving for a special occasion. Well, to be honest – the only outfit I owned for special occasions.

They were all already there when I arrived at the office, sitting on the floor surrounded by colour-coded name cards and a seating plan.

'Better to see it laid out visually like this than on a computer screen,' Nicky said, by way of explanation. She was inexcusably immaculate for so early in the morning. Swinging bob, cream silk shirt, tan trousers and a flat-woven loafer. *Look at me, Nicky! I wore smart black trousers. Please want to be my friend. What has become of me? Since when did I care what other people think?*

I went into the kitchen and put the kettle on, determined to be proactive. They all looked shattered. After I had handed out mugs of coffee, I hovered at the periphery watching them assemble their seating puzzle. They had to accommodate buyers, press, friends, sponsors, potential sponsors, high-net-worth customers.

'There was just no budget left to pay anyone to come for the front row,' Nicky said as she swapped over some name cards. 'And Dixie just doesn't have the pull anymore, she's been around too long – we're going to have to really juggle these seats.'

'You *pay* people?' I might have shouted this. But this was the first time I had heard that some celebrities weren't just at fashion events for the love of the designer, they were *paid*!

'You have much to learn, Frankie. Much to learn,' Nicky muttered as she continued shuffling names around.

I fleetingly imagined that one day perhaps it would be me integral in making the decisions, having arguments, throwing names in the corner and relegating Danes to the fourth row. The quicker I understood, the sooner I would be involved. It was slowly dawning on me – I was getting sucked into this weird world.

'This bench definitely has a better view.' Nicky was pointing to the map on the floor. 'Amanda needs to be bang in the middle of it.'

I finished my coffee, and as the caffeine took effect, I realised I needed to go to the loo. Now. And not just for a wee. Holy-mother-of-fucking-God. It was that takeaway Lebanese we had all ordered in the office last night. I one hundred per cent overdid it on the jalapeños in my kebab. Disaster. I could barely do a poo when James was in the flat – and had been careful to ensure my routine avoided the necessity at work – but I'd not had time to have my morning coffee at home today, and anyway, James had swiped the last of the kitchen roll. What was the etiquette here? Did anyone in fashion actually have bodily functions? What did I do? Were they all going to be sitting up here for a while? Would they notice if I slipped off? I ambled over to my desk, trying to look purposeful, and picked up my mug as if headed to the kitchen. That would do. The bathrooms were on the half landing a floor up, near the meeting room. I ran two steps at a time, bolted myself in one of the two cubicles, balanced the mug on the sink, ran the tap, sat down and prayed. *Hurry up, poo.*

'Frankie's smart, I think.' The door was opening. Oh, good Lord, I couldn't take it, now I just couldn't do it. Not now. *Oh yes, we had a good intern, sadly she stank the loos out in her second month, so we had to let her go.*

'Yes, I like her too.'

It was Nicky on the phone. Why now? Seriously?

'Yup. Okay. See you there later. You need anything? No, okay. Yup. Just usual seating crap. Same shit, different day, basically.'

Oh the irony!

The other cubicle door closed; I clenched and flushed. The agony of my bloated stomach was only relieved by the knowledge she had been talking about me. I was in! I practically sailed down the stairs.

'Any takers for some Snickers mini bites?' I beamed.

'JUST HOLD ON,' Nicky shouted at the crowd waving their tickets in the air and jostling at the entrance to the basement show venue.

'Frankie, stand here. With security. We're not ready for anyone to come in. Unless you see Amanda. And don't forget: do not speak to her unless she addresses you directly. You do know what she looks like, don't you?'

I smiled and nodded. I absolutely did not. Holy fuck. I pulled out my phone the minute Nicky disappeared down the stairs and did a frantic Google image search.

As I looked out at a sea of belligerent faces, I felt a drop of rain plop on to my head, and with that, the assembled crowd let rip.

'It's raining out here, you know.'

'Jesus, this jacket is going to be destroyed.'

'When will the doors open?'

'I have a ticket. I lost it. Can you just check my name is on the list?'

'For fuck's sake, it's freezing.'

They were coming at me from all sides. Any previous vestiges of courtesy dropped. I looked up at the security. They were expressionless. Seen it all before.

'Here.' Jemima appeared at my side holding a clipboard, and thrust a headset into my hand. 'Channel one.'

A headset. The holy grail. I had arrived. My cashmere was taking a real hit in the rain, which was now coming down heavily. I didn't care.

'Nicky. Come in, Nicky. Can we open doors?'

Crackle.

'Yes. Ready.'

Jemima looked at me. 'Brace yourself,' she whispered as she opened up the rope.

'One by one, people,' shouted security.

And absolutely not one by one, pushing and shoving, they threw their invitations into our faces while Jemima either scanned the list – holding a hand up in a gesture to *just wait there* – or gushed a greeting to someone she recognised while pushing them quickly through.

I spotted Amanda Starling in a beautifully tailored navy trench coat coming through the crowds and felt a sudden rush of adrenaline.

'Amanda!' I shouted and waved. She gave me a withering look as Jemima looked at me in horror. I had already forgotten the cardinal Amanda Starling rule. *Do not speak unless spoken to.* Much less scream out her name as if we had just bumped into each other at a club next to the speakers, and I was waving a pint of warm beer in a plastic cup at her.

'Amanda on her way in,' I said authoritatively into my headset as the Editor-in-Chief of *Avalon* pointedly ignored me, and I reached out to shove someone in a red leather jumpsuit to the side to make room.

'Right. That's everyone,' Jemima assured me after a fraught half hour and as the last ticketless stragglers dissipated. She then repeated the same into her mouthpiece. She exuded an essence of calm. *How does she do that?*

'Come. Let's go.' She pulled me by my hand, and we descended the stairs.

Inside the basement, it was exhilarating. The room was so dark it was almost black. Background music playing, chatter, bustle, flashbulbs popping, people taking their seats, photographers taking their marks at the end of the catwalk, which still had a polythene cover on it to protect it from wet shoes and spiked heels. The heat was overwhelming from the sheer numbers packed into such a small space. I knew the designers had wanted intimate. This was positively tiny. Despite the freezing rain outside, people were fanning themselves with the press releases they had found on their seats. I could almost feel the steam rising from my soggy cashmere. Girls in full Dante looks were having their photos taken before sitting down. Amanda Starling was expressionless. Then a team of men started peeling back the cover on the catwalk as I listened to the instructions being relayed through my headset.

'Front row full.'

'Girls in line-up.'

'Music on my cue.'

When the lights went up and the music crescendoed and the first girl stomped down the tiny catwalk, I was enthralled. So, this was what it was all about. I tapped my feet and started happily singing along to the lyrics of the pseudo-ironic Bradley Cooper/Lady Gaga duet that interspersed the heavy techno-beat mix.

'May want to turn off your headset, Frankie.' Jemima nudged me as I wailed *sha-ha-sha-ha-sha-ha-low* for all the GGC team's listening pleasure.

PRESS NOTE

A successful PR prides themselves on their innate understanding of when to leave work at the office. The way Frankie has juggled her personal and professional life has been a masterclass in balance.

Frankie Marks commented, 'I am delighted to have learned so quickly that the industry is just a part of my life. Not its entirety. Learning how to implement that delicate balancing act has been incredibly rewarding. The fact that both my best friend and my boyfriend think I'm a fashion bore is puzzling.'

ENDS

Fashion Week had left me feeling almost euphoric. It puzzled me. I tried to engage with James the first night I was able to get home at a normal time once all the shows were done. I couldn't wait to fill him in on all the gory details of my Fashion Week debut. We went for tapas and a glass of wine so I could tell him all about my near-death Amanda Starling moment, re-enact my *Star is Born* debacle, fill him in on what channel my head-set was on and how incredible Nicky was at managing everything and still making time for a blow-dry. I thought he'd find it all highly entertaining, but it turned out not so much.

'I sort of can't understand what it is you actually like about it all,' he said over the patatas bravas. I stabbed a meatball as he took my other hand, giving my knuckles a little rub.

'I can't really understand it myself. But I feel a part of something. A team. And given that I hate most people, the fact that I want to be in their gang must mean something. Plus, I'm working really hard. Really fucking hard, James.'

'Sorry, sorry . . . I'm happy if you're happy . . . but it's all just so . . . I dunno . . . bizarre? I'm just worried you're going to lose sight of what you really want to do. Did you get anything back from any of the galleries yet?'

My mailboxes, both physical and virtual, were empty. I shook my head woefully and tried out my best doe-eyed look as I attempted to chew on a piece of calamari seductively.

'I can't believe you're not finding any of it funny,' I went on between mouthfuls. 'I'm funny. I'm a funny person in a ridiculous environment. And in that ridiculous environment I may have found my people. Against all the odds . . .'

'You need to relay this all to Charlotte. You always do that . . . err . . . *great* "Shallow" rendition together . . . she'll appreciate that story more than me,' he said. I nodded, pacified. I *did* do a superb Bradley Cooper. James' reaction to my new job was surely temporary. He'd come around to GGC. Like he did the time I impulsively got a feathered haircut he hated, but he waited patiently until it grew out and managed to only make Bon Jovi references for the first month. I just had to wait for things to settle. When we got home, I called Charlotte. I was sorry I hadn't been around. I was dying to see her. We made a plan to meet up.

Charlotte had been my best friend since we clashed metal train-track braces at senior school. Aged fifteen, she had understood my aversion to the gangs of girls avidly debating `fringe or no fringe', and – with as much intensity as if it were a GCSE subject – how to smoke menthol cigarettes without violently coughing and risking their crop tops falling down on a Saturday night (I mean, it did fall under the laws of gravity in Physics, but they weren't to know that). Charlotte had always been my barometer of good and bad. My sense check on the world. She knew I was unswervingly loyal, prone to tiny temper tantrums, unable to ever remember anyone's birthday. Ever. But she always reminded me that I was the best friend anyone could have. And she made me funny. She brought out the best in me, and I wanted to share everything with her. When I left for Manchester, Charlotte had chosen not to go to university. She wanted to get straight into what she called 'the university of life' while I spent three years ruminating on portraiture. A job rising through the ranks at Amnesty fighting for human rights gave her a gravitas and integrity I often felt acutely lacking in.

'Tell me everything, then,' she said as she stuck her fork into her beetroot and goat's cheese salad. We were in our favourite local restaurant, tucked away in a corner table by the window.

'Well, it's kind of surreal. People are so rude . . . all the time. I've learned that a mule's not just a donkey but a backless shoe. Who knew!' I laughed at my own joke. 'I mean, you literally couldn't imagine me anywhere more unsuitable. But the irony is that I'm beginning to love it.'

'There are people ruder than you? I don't believe it,' she said, smiling at me with what I wanted to believe was endearment. 'On a scale of one to ten, are they ruder than you when you asked to move tables that time because the man next to us was eating too loudly with his mouth open?' I gave the question serious consideration.

'I give them a strong nine . . . And I'll never understand how you couldn't hear him? He was chewing that chicken like it was still alive and about to escape. And I had a full visual of his fillings.'

'I just felt sorry for him . . . you weren't subtle. So, what are these people in the office like?'

'Well, there's Zoe, who's beautiful. I mean, just breathtaking. She has a pageboy haircut. Who can carry off a pageboy haircut? She bloody can. And she's nice. Properly nice. And a laugh.'

I ate a mouthful of my shepherd's pie. I had accepted many years ago that I was never going to be thin like Charlotte. I enjoyed food too much. Though I had already gathered that this much red meat and carbs was simply not tolerated in the fashion arena. They were a guilty pleasure to be enjoyed in secret.

'Then Andrew's just your archetypal gorgeous gay guy. Handsome. Immaculate. Spiky. We'd want to have him join us for every girls' night out. Jemima, she's just the calmest, nicest person ever. Tall, I come up to her belly button. She told me everything I needed to know when I started. Then there's Nicky. We want to be Nicky. I've honestly never seen her without a blow-dry and a suntan. She's magnificent. And hilarious. Not quite as hilarious as you. Or me. Obviously.'

'Anyone who isn't nicer, prettier, funnier or more tanned than me?' Charlotte enquired, with a rather tighter smile.

'That'll be Eloise, who basically lives in the sample cupboard. That's the room where samples move in and out all day long to the publications. She was an intern at one point. But had to intern for a year and is still only in that cupboard. Haven't quite figured it out, but basically we don't like her. She crunches apples loudly and she's a bit useless at her job. Oh, and then there's this PR guy called Dominic Carter. They hate him. I'm learning to hate him too – I think it's a prerequisite of having a job there.'

'That's right up your street. And what about Georgina?'

'You know, I've barely met her – well, not properly at least. I see her once a week when she comes in for the Monday morning meeting with them all, and then she mostly just disappears. I guess you can do that when you're her . . . She can make stuff happen over one lunch, one coffee. It's what she does outside of the office that's so impressive. Her reputation precedes her. And they all always tell me, as tough as she can be, she's genuinely nice. She may not show it very often, but they know she cares. In her own way. But she's like a rocket when she's actually at the office.'

I thought back to overhearing her and Debbie going through her diary on the day of my interview and the volcanic speed of the instructions, and gave Charlotte a precis.

When I finished relaying the potted version of the exchange, her eyes widened. 'Crikey.'

'I know, right?'

'And I'm fine, by the way, thanks, Frankie,' Charlotte said, shaking her head. 'You know, you haven't asked me one single thing about how I'm doing or how the Venezuelan intervention is going. I mean, I know I asked you, but you've just talked about yourself without coming up for air for, oh, let me see' – she made an exaggerated gesture of looking at her watch – 'yup, twenty-seven minutes. You must really love it . . .'

I was feeling too high on life and light-headed to really feel bad. And I was sure she was teasing like she always did. *Wasn't she?*

'I know. But I'm finally working. I really did get a job. Okay, an internship that may turn into a job. But you're right. I'm sorry. How are you? What's happening with Venezuela?'

There was a prolonged silence as Charlotte dug her fork back into her salad and went to put it in her mouth before waving it dramatically in the air.

'Well, since you finally asked . . . I'm good, but I'm not sure we're going to have any movement on that case.' She paused. 'I am slightly concerned you're going to turn into a PR monster.'

I sobered up immediately.

'Oh, no chance. I mean, it *is* highly unusual that I like them all – well, most of them. And I admit I have got a bit of a girl crush on Georgina. And you spend so much time together and everything's so intense that I guess I've just got a bit too wrapped up in it all. But you know, there's a business being run alongside dissecting the width of shoulder pads . . . Oh fuck. I won't turn into a fashion bore, promise.'

'You can be a bore if you get us free clothes.' She laughed. 'So, what's the plan?'

'Well, now I've mastered the lunch orders, am friends with the local dry cleaner, can keep hangers straight and make a perfect cup of tea – I'm hoping Georgina will invite me to their Monday morning meetings soon, and that's going to be my first step towards getting involved in the nitty-gritty. Look, it's not where I thought I'd end up. But turns out I'm really not that bad at it, and that fashion people aren't as shallow as I'd always thought they'd be – and it's all a tiny bit fascinating. I'm actually praying they take me on full-time.'

'I'm really glad you're enjoying yourself.' Charlotte raised an eyebrow as she swirled the dregs of her wine around in her glass. 'But . . . I mean, you're clever, Frankie. I just hope you really do get to use your brain.'

'But that's the thing, they've all got amazing degrees, you know. They all fell into it. And they're all super smart. And by the way, let's not forget, no miraculous job offer from Christie's arrived by courier pigeon the last time I looked.'

I had also realised from watching the team at work that this job, if I progressed, was going to exercise all of my analytical and strategic skills. It may be about mohair and not Matisse, but it was gripping.

'And look! I ditched the tasselled loafers.' I waggled my foot in the air.

'Thank God for small mercies,' she whooped at my square-toed pumps.

The waiter brought us another carafe of house red.

'Shall we go "out out"?' I said, getting more excited the more I drank.

'We will not go "out out",' Charlotte replied. 'You've got work tomorrow and I've got to prepare for a conference call.'

'We're old,' I lamented while I surreptitiously looked at my mobile to see if Zoe or Jemima had messaged me from the office drinks. They had said they would. No text just yet. I was sure it would be incoming.

'We're just responsible twenty-somethings. With jobs. As you keep reminding me,' she replied. 'Stop checking your phone. I haven't seen you for ages. How's James?'

How was James? That was a valid and excellent question. He was currently on the five-a-side pitch in terrible green and yellow striped socks.

'He's good. Yeah. He's great. Work's going well.'

Charlotte looked at me in the way only Charlotte could. I felt myself welling up. She had that effect on me. Only her, the doctor and my father. The minute anyone in authority asked me how I was, even if I was completely fine, I would burst into tears and need to be handed a box of tissues as they nodded soothingly.

'You don't look or sound like it's "great" though.'

'No, no . . . we're fine. It's just a bit tricky at the moment. I don't think he loves that I don't howl with laughter about the job being so ridiculous. I think he thinks *I've* become faintly ridiculous – like you. I guess you both think I'm mildly idiotic. I find it a bit irritating when he's dismissive but I'm sure it'll all settle down. Oh God, we *are* fine, aren't we? That's just me and James, isn't it? Although he didn't laugh when I told him about singing "Shallow". And that was highly disappointing.'

'Definitely not ridiculous, potential to become mildly idiotic, I fear . . . but I'm happy for you. Look, it's getting late and I don't want to miss the last tube. Let's finish our drinks and get the bill.'

Maybe I already *was* a crushing bore, I contemplated. Surely not? Anyway, now at least I could go and meet the team for the tail end of their drinks. Zoe had just messaged me where they were. I was sure something had happened at Andrew's lunch with the *Avalon* team today. Or that Nicky had a good tale to tell about her appointment with that Korean stylist this afternoon.

As Charlotte and I gave each other a hug on the pavement outside, I wondered if she was disappointed in me as she went to save the world and I went to gossip about gaberdine. But as I jumped in an Uber to meet the others, I felt invigorated. I was embarking on a new journey and I was going to make something of it, and even more of myself. I had found myself somewhere unexpected, and I was going to be the best bloody PR in London. *Well, if Georgina offers me a job, that is.* Just a small technicality.

I texted Zoe.

Frankie
Wait for me – on my way!

PRESS NOTE

GGC are delighted to announce that as of today Frankie Marks has been invited to their Monday morning meetings. Her perceptive analysis of the weekend tabloids spoke volumes to the hard work she has so far invested in her role.

'Who knew the News on Sunday *would prove to be such a riveting read. I learned so much about breakfast TV presenters that I am excited to share with everyone,' Frankie commented. Miss Marks is certainly a name to watch.*

ENDS

Show season was officially over. Reviews for Dante had been glowing. Dixie's had been reverentially polite. For us, it was back to the daily grind. Monday mornings were when the team newspaper meeting happened. At 9.15 a.m. sharp, everyone gathered around the glass meeting table with the weekend papers and supplements they had each been assigned to pore over spread out in front of them, small Post-it notes affixed to pages. Month three at the agency and I had finally been invited to join, much to Eloise's thinly veiled fury.

'I've never wanted to go to those meetings. Listening to everyone whittle on about how well they've done for their clients,' she had sneered when I mentioned it to her the preceding Friday.

Everyone shuffled their publications and waited for Georgina to arrive.

'Anything interesting happen this weekend, Andrew?' asked Jemima, sitting to his left.

'What *didn't* happen this weekend, more like,' he replied with a wicked smile.

'What have I told you about being more discerning?' Zoe smacked the back of his hand. 'Who'd you end up with this time?'

'It's complicated. But it started at Rotundo in Brewer Street, took me to Maze under the arches at King's Cross, over to Shoreditch for a dawn chorus breakfast. Back to a studio flat in . . . actually I'm not sure where that was, and I'm not actually sure exactly who I was with. Apart from one really hot guy I met by the DJ stand at Maze who I think works for the Marriot Hotel group.' Andrew was just about to launch into the juicy details when the door swung open and Georgina entered the room.

'More details later, please,' whispered Zoe, and then quickly and even more quietly mumbled to me out the corner of her mouth, 'He has a habit of having affairs with entirely inappropriate fashion friends, clients and enemies. And that club closed in 2015, so he's hiding something . . .'

'Morning, everyone. Good weekend?'

Georgina wore a black and white pinstripe trouser suit, white tee and plimsolls. She looked both immaculate and casual. I had serious outfit envy as I looked down at the boho floral skirt I'd picked out so carefully that morning, which now felt just casual. Without the immaculate.

'Well, Andrew most definitely had a good weekend.' Zoe smirked.

'Zoe!' Andrew smiled coyly, fiddling with his string bracelet.

'I don't think I want the details on that before I've eaten,'

Georgina said. 'Right, who wants to start? Oh, I like your hair wavy like that, Frankie.'

Much to my dismay, I felt myself go red. It was too much to be so delighted that I had been singled out for my excellently tonged hair – which had just so happened to go better that morning than usual. I needed to pull myself together in front of them all. I wanted to be one of them. *Oh yes, Frankie. She's hilarious. We can't remember life without her, honestly – she's the glue that holds us all together.*

The newspaper allocation was in accordance with office hierarchy. Newest team members got the tabloids. As you rose through the ranks, you reached the higher echelons of the broadsheets. The hallowed *Herald* and so forth.

'You'll know you're in for a promotion when you get moved on to a broadsheet,' Zoe had told me on the Friday afternoon. 'This weekend you'll have the *News*, *News on Sunday* and *Brilliant!* magazine.'

I had spent Saturday and Sunday mornings lying in bed and going through them; James laughed at me as I studiously inserted my Post-it notes and explained the importance of mass media, as he made a big show of turning the pages of his broadsheets.

'Can I remind you you're not middle-aged and on Wall Street?' I had poked him.

'And can I remind you that I love you but don't love the fact that you're literally examining what someone wore on *Britain's Got Talent*?' he'd replied. I had laughed over my quiver of fury at being patronised, but his words had annoyingly stayed with me on my journey into the office that morning.

'I'll start. The *Herald* story on Dante came out and it's great.' Nicky opened up the paper to show everyone the double-page spread. She had allowed a journalist to join them in the run-up to the show. 'They used all the right images from the show, and there's just one misquote, which isn't bad going. I mean, Harrods will be furious that Selfridges was listed as the main stockist, but I really needed to share those credits out. Selfridges went mad last month when Harrods got the *Daily* credit, so they can sort of shove it.' Everyone murmured in agreement. I murmured too. Authoritatively, I thought.

'In other news, Celia Johns got the front cover of *My Style*, which is absolutely infuriating.'

The whole table groaned. Again, I groaned with them assuredly. Celia Johns was a luxury womenswear client of agency rival Dominic Carter. Annoying. Nicky pushed the papers into the middle.

'Here's your latte, Georgina. Sorry it's late. There was a queue.' Debbie had slipped into the room, placing the cup in front of her. Georgina nodded indiscernibly as she focused on us all.

'Morning, Debbie,' the table chorused as she exited as quietly as she had entered.

It was my turn. I coughed nervously and pulled down my shirt.

'I did the *News* etcetera this weekend. It was all pretty banal stuff. But a great picture of Stacey Powers from *Breakfast Banters* wearing a Dante top in her interview shot—'

'WHO LENT HER THAT?' Georgina slammed her hands down on the table, causing everyone to jump.

'Nope, not us. Definitely not us,' said Andrew. 'I'd know if they'd called it in and would never have let Eloise send it. Never.'

'Find out how the hell that happened,' shouted Georgina, 'and if any of the stockists' press offices sent it, you tell them from me that NOTHING by Dante gets sent anywhere without OUR APPROVAL.'

I pretended I understood how this would be so important

to anyone. In the meantime, I nodded vigorously in support of the collective uproar.

'I mean, there's always a chance she already owned it and brought it down to the shoot,' Zoe ventured, 'but I'll get on to it straight away. Stacey Powers cannot be wearing Dante publicly. It's a total disaster. Andrew, let's make some calls after the meeting.'

'Well, at least it wasn't on that ghastly Melissa Bailey,' Nicky said, holding up a picture from one of the supplements of a former *Carlyle Bay* soap star turned A-list celebrity with the universally derided worst fashion sense known to mankind. We all sniggered.

'How she snagged that total Hollywood hottie Gabriel Bannon is a total mystery. That red hair. The *clothes*. She wasn't a good actress. I didn't even cry when her dog got run over in season four.' Andrew was in his element. This was deadly serious.

'We're just lucky she didn't request for the Dante show. Can you imagine?' Nicky added.

'Well, if she'd brought the husband, I'd have made room and had the argument with the boys,' Andrew said.

'Moving swiftly on,' Georgina snapped, sipping her latte. I could feel everyone's tensions rise. 'Jemima, what have you got for us? Did you do the *Daily*?' Georgina turned to her left.

'Ahem, yup. I mean, yes. I did. We had main fashion for Jessy in their swimwear resort special here' – she pushed the page across the table for everyone to see – 'but the annoying thing was that Dixie should have been in this "Working Women's Wardrobe" feature, but she isn't. And they asked for look thirty-four from the show, which Eloise told me she'd sent them.'

'Add that to our list this morning, people,' said Zoe, running her fingers through her extremely short hair.

After a few more round-ups, some more shaking of heads

and confusion over things that shouldn't have gone wrong, Georgina made a move to leave. 'I think that's it. I don't like these misses. You let me know any good news later. I want to know any monthly cover credits or misses. Full lists, please, and all online and digital stories. By end of the week.' She had the attention span of a gnat and she was bored already. And clearly irritated. 'By the way,' she added as she stood to leave, 'has anyone seen Eloise? I've heard her timekeeping's getting questionable.'

As we all came down the stairs, Eloise was hurriedly taking off her coat.

'Morning, Georgina, sorry I'm late, trains were dreadful this morning.'

'Seem to be dreadful every morning, from what I'm hearing,' Georgina said. 'Get it together, Eloise.'

'Yes, sorry. Sure. I will.' She turned back to her Post-it notes.

'She's getting worse by the day,' Jemima said as we walked to our desks. 'Need to keep an eye on her.'

I was delighted to be conspiratorial with one of my more senior colleagues.

'Oh yes,' I whispered back. 'I'll do some expert hovering and report back. And what's with the tights?'

Jemima ignored my last comment. *Too much too soon.* I needed to learn to hold back a bit. *Remember to keep your thoughts to yourself.* James was right. Shit. He was always right. As annoying as I sometimes found his unsolicited advice, no one knew me better.

PRESS NOTE

After a sparkling first few months, Frankie Marks has proved she is an expert at negotiating industry events. The Society.com spring party was a hugely dull success. Minuscule canapés and not-quite-cold-enough champagne were served to the great and bored in the private surroundings of a suddenly fashionable gallery in East London, where the exclusive crowd mingled, trying to one-up each other.

'I was blown away by the attention to detail tonight. There can be nothing better than an evening spent with fine wine, food and friends,' gushed a sockless Dominic Carter.

ENDS

After spring was over, my internship was extended, and I started getting paid. Minimal pay. But pay nevertheless. The team began taking me to their external breakfasts. I took more appointments. I was brought into client catch-up meetings at the office to be introduced and exalted as a 'new and invaluable member of the team'. I soon understood this was also their way of gradually handing over any conversations they didn't want to have – a prolonged initiation ceremony of sorts, more commonly known as passing the buck. 'You can handle it, Frankie. It's good for you to deliver news like this. You can only learn on the job.' I listened intently as Jessy raged that she hadn't been included in a cut-out, high-leg swimwear story in *The Forward* summer special; I heard how Darcy Girl were 'really disappointed' (translate to furious) not to have secured editorial the week before; I tried to explain frantically what had happened with the Dixie sweaters that had been FedExed to a shoot in Barcelona but were lost in transit. I found that I loved every single second of the pace, the aggravation, the highs and the lows. I prayed to the employment gods every night that Georgina would realise she couldn't live without me and make me an actual job offer soon. And it wasn't just the work that had me hooked. It was the people. I liked them. I was happy to see them every day. This was the real revelation.

Time flew, and in between the daily mechanics and methods of PR – and the rising panic I wouldn't be offered an official full-time job while managing my eye-watering overdraft under James' raised eyebrow and my father's continued latent disapproval – I began to appreciate the power of fashion in a more cerebral sense. I started to train my eye. I became fascinated by the industry and how we messaged it. I stopped writing any application letters to galleries and auction houses. I panicked about how to tell my father I was planning on staying put. I stopped questioning where and when Georgina would appear. She was like the Wizard of Oz and I grew accustomed to her prolonged absences. I revelled in my new-found status within the team. *We can't remember life without her. She's the most naturally gifted paid intern we've ever seen. Just watch her in action with high-waisted bikinis and FedEx!*

'For fuck's sake. Five Star won that enormous Australian UV-friendly swimwear account I pitched for. My pitch was excellent. I even photoshopped pictures of myself in all their swim trunks for the presentation. I was wondering why I hadn't heard back from them; I gave myself such a great six-pack.'

Andrew was scrolling through a PR directory one lunchtime a few weeks after my internship had been made semi-permanent. 'And Dominic Carter went to Bondi for the launch. I want a client to send *me* to Bondi. I hate looking at his fucking Instagram. It enrages me.' Andrew waved around the post with an offensive image of our number one enemy flashing very white teeth under mirrored sunglasses against a background of sea and sand. We all listened to the rain hitting the windows. It was a poignant moment.

'He lost that big hosiery account though. Bet he didn't announce *that* on social media,' Zoe said, breaking the wistful silence.

'No, too busy wearing Cooper & Co sunglasses on Bondi to announce any losses. Oh, and hold on . . . with the hashtag *clientsynergy*. Oh, he can just fuck off.' Andrew threw down his phone in disgust.

The hostility between GGC and Five Star couldn't be more serious. Georgina loathed Dominic. With a passion. It was the only time I ever witnessed emotion from her that wasn't about a piece of editorial. She viewed her rival with utter derision. It was like he was a buzzing pest in her ear that she was constantly having to bat away. But the threat was real. Contract renewals came with anticipation. We were neck and neck in the client stakes, and one of us was always ready to poach from the other. The gloves were well and truly off.

'I look forward to meeting and hating him in person,' I said. I was inhaling the low-fat chicken salad that I'd copied from Nicky (while silently bemoaning how it would never fill me up), as I looked at an irritatingly smug image of Dominic Carter beaming in the party pages on *Avalon* online. 'But God, I actually already hate him. I really do. He looks so bloody arrogant.'

'He's everything I aspire not to be in this industry,' added Andrew. 'He's manipulative, he treats his staff terribly, he'd step over his dying grandmother to get a new client. Georgina may be tricky and unpredictable, but she has integrity. And by the way, may I add he's also *deeply* unattractive. Just putting it out there. There is nothing and no one as repellent as Dominic Carter. Even *I* wouldn't sleep with him. And as we know, that's saying something.'

'You're coming to the Society.com summer solstice drinks with me tonight, Frankie,' Zoe announced. 'Jemima can't come – and I can't face going on my own. Borrow a dress from the showroom, we'll leave from here.'

'Sure,' I said, as I texted James to tell him I wouldn't be home to murder the two chicken breasts I had been planning to try to cook for him for supper.

Two chicken breasts saved from certain death I guess, he texted back.

We clocked Dominic the minute we walked into the venue. Swept-back hair, Bondi tan, impeccably tailored suit, bare ankles and a signet ring on his pinkie finger. I recognised him instantly from the numerous photos and posts I had taken to stalking on social media. He clocked us. He clocked my Dixie dress, which was two sizes too small for me, with buttons pulling at the seams over a really bad minimiser bra that wasn't minimising anything. He approached us. We air-kissed. Game time.

'Ah, the infamous Frankie,' he said, as he looked me up and down.

He had seemingly made it his business to know who I was before he ever met me. I was secretly overjoyed before I remembered he was our nemesis. But that surely meant someone, somewhere, on the fashion circuit had discussed me? I was going to enjoy this evening. Here I was among the great and the good, a legitimate PR who would learn to socialise without telling someone they really shouldn't have eaten the mackerel canapé before speaking to me. I wouldn't worry about exactly what 'infamous' meant. I'd take it. I had arrived.

'God, I can't believe we're out again? I mean, who does this – has a party on a bloody Wednesday?' I blurted, trying to sound like the seasoned PR partygoer I had now decided I was. We were at a gallery that, once upon a time, I'd have given my right arm to work in. It was a classic fashion industry drinks party – that is, thrown for no particular reason, except a constant competition of discreetly looking over shoulders for someone more important to network with.

'I know,' he replied smoothly, 'it must be exhausting for you. You're still so new.'

I wanted to thump him. He was as ghastly in person as he was in photos. Fortunately, he spotted someone more important to him than me across the room. The sunglasses client he had stolen from us.

'Oh look. Sorry, I see Clive from Cooper & Co. Better go say hello. Lovely to meet you in person, Frankie.' He gave the top of my arm a patronising squeeze. 'By the way, your dress is stuck in your knickers,' he whispered.

Yeah. And? It's a LOOK, said my game face. *Shoot. Me. Now,* said my internal weeping. If I hadn't been infamous before, I was going to be now.

As I frantically unpicked my dress, I also pleasantly recalled I was wearing my haven't-had-time-to-do-a-wash-this-week, last-chance-saloon, back-of-the-drawer, should-really-throw-these-away, greying-white period-emergency knickers. I somehow shook off my deep humiliation at the fashion fail as Dominic and I edged into opposing corners of the room and spent the rest of the evening in silent but deadly social one-upmanship. What was I trying to prove? I found small talk excruciating. I hung on to Zoe, smiling, air-kissing, nodding effusively, checking my bottom every five seconds.

'When can we leave?' I turned to her. 'It's going to take hours to get home and I really just want to put on my slippers and burn my pants.'

'One more round of the room,' she insisted, poking her finger in my back and pushing me to complete a final circum-navigation of the terrace. 'Your knickers are concealed, and don't forget to smile.'

Once we were finally able to slip away, we stood on the pavement ordering our respective Ubers and sharing a Marlboro Light.

'Do you think Dominic really wants to steal all our clients?' I asked.

'Yup. Well, definitely Dante. He'll also go for Dixie just to twist the knife.'

'How can he be bothered? He's got enough business; he's been doing this for years.'

'When Georgina started the agency, he asked to join her. Apparently, she said no and he's never got over it. At least, that's the story I've always heard. It's like he's playing the lead in his own drama. He wants revenge. He wants to prove to her she made a mistake, plus schadenfreude and all that. The problem is, she's refused to ever show she cares. Which isn't entirely true. We know she can't bear him. But as far as *he's* concerned, she couldn't give two hoots. And that's just poking the bear. I think he secretly worships her.'

Well, this was new and fascinating news about the rivalry. I wanted to dissect this information with Zoe, piece by piece.

'Oh look, Karim's coming down the road in a black Prius.' Zoe stood in the middle of the street to make herself known.

'Damn Karim the efficient Uber driver. I've got so many questions. Tony in a white Honda Civic is three minutes away.'

'Mind if I don't wait? We can discuss Dominic in detail tomorrow.'

'Definitely don't mind. See you in the morning.' I grabbed Zoe's cigarette off her and waved goodbye, tracking Tony on my phone.

Suddenly, Dominic Carter appeared next to me. Smarmy smile, blazer sleeves pulled up, glitteringly white teeth, sock-less ankles.

'Funny bumping into you here,' he quipped.

Hilarious. His presence was making me distinctly irritable and I was tired. My jaw ached from all the fake smiling and I had a crick from rubbernecking. The social side of the job definitely wasn't going to be my strong point. I was ready to be at home.

'Ha. I'm just waiting for my car. That was fine but point-less, no?' *Urghh. Don't always give yourself away, Frankie.*

'I never consider these things pointless. It's always good to go out and see everyone outside of the office. I had a great chat with your client Dixie just now. She's wonderful, isn't she?'

And there it was. He had spun a bit of post-party chit-chat into what I recognised as a veiled threat.

'Oh yes. We love Dixie. She is wonderful, you're right.' I kept my tone light.

'Love that, by the way.' He was pointing at my Samira K clutch bag. 'Didn't she walk in Dixie's last show?'

Had he just assigned my bag a gender? And given it limbs? God give me strength.

'Oh, here's Tony. Bye, Dominic,' I called out as I opened the car door.

'See you around. And by the way, Vanish will really bring out the white in your whites.'

I felt like shit the next day. I hadn't drunk so I had to assume I was ill. I decided to blame Dominic Carter's hairy ankles and my exposed knickers for making me feel sick. I had learned that being ill at GGC was never really an option. They just all popped an ibuprofen, drank a vitamin infusion and went to work. They named every ailment a 'low-grade infection'. They didn't give any bandwidth to actually feeling properly unwell.

I messaged Zoe horizontal from bed half an hour after I should have been in. *Going to be late. So sorry. Think am sick.*

She wasn't having any of it. *Take Nurofen. A being strange. N furious with E. I need you in office.*

I need you. Greatest text message of my life thus far.

I dutifully popped two pills, ate a KitKat, gulped a coffee and shuffled myself into the shower before deciding what to wear, which was becoming distinctly easier.

With the new discount codes Debbie had handed me for every brand represented by GGC, I had managed to find some surprisingly excellent Darcy Girl pieces. It was amazing what the high street could do if you did a careful select and you were paying wholesale. Plus, I had lost a *little* bit of weight, invested in a top-of-the-range hairdryer with incorporated straightener, and had a revolutionary miracle serum that gave my skin a dewy shine, however jaded I actually was. And by God, today my face needed it. Insider knowledge was one of the perks of the job. I had got one of my new professional friends – the assistant to the Beauty Editor of *Avalon* – to procure some for me.

I was morphing into someone new and I knew it. More than that, I was delighted.

'Here. I'm here.' I sat at my desk and popped two more Nurofen. My 'low-grade infection' was going to give me ulcers but at least my skin was looking refreshed.

'Oh good,' said Zoe. 'Thanks for coming in. Andrew's being odd. Nicky's screamed at Eloise about the wrong dress going to *My Style*. Crikey, you look like shit.'

'I'll go and talk to Eloise in a minute, but can we discuss Dominic last night? He hit me with a snide Dixie comment. He wasn't wearing socks. He saw my grey knickers.'

I rested my chin on my hands and leaned forward over the desk. I could feel my headache beginning to numb as the Nurofen kicked in, although I still felt as though I was dragging my body through treacle.

'The whole evening was a bore. Your knickers fiasco was a highlight. Meantime, what do you think of him?' She held up her phone with an image of Jake, twenty-five years old, shirtless, with his hands up above his head holding a bottle of beer.

My extension rang. Saved by the bell from giving an answer. Zoe swiped right.

'Hi, GGC, Frankie speaking.'

It was just a call in from the *Saturday Daily Magazine*. The story was black and white. They wanted something from every client. I took notes. They needed it by end of day. I went down to Eloise.

'Morning. All good?' I placed the request in front of her as she continued eating an apple and didn't make eye contact. 'This is for today. I'll go down to the showroom and pick some pieces out. Want me to bring them straight up? Have you got room in here?' Eloise glanced at the call-in note as I looked around the rails. I carried on talking, eager for anyone to know that I had been at an event – and having exhausted the conversation with Zoe, anyone with a pulse and a working ear would do. 'Oh God, I saw that awful Dominic Carter last night. He was all over Dixie, he knew who I was. Couldn't believe it!'

'Maybe your reputation is already preceding you.' Eloise crossed her pink legs, still seemingly emotionally invested in her apple. Was she being even more sarcastic than usual? Why was she wearing pink tights?

* * *

Turned out, the black and white pieces I gave Eloise didn't all arrive at the *Saturday Daily*. As summer rolled on, we all worked so hard, but things still weren't going exactly to plan. Jemima got an earful from our bag client Samira K when her most expensive clutch ended up in a tabloid still-life feature alongside a high-street equivalent – not a brand adjacency she could countenance. The Dixie dress Amanda Starling had called in to wear to a style awards dinner apparently never reached her, so she wore an outfit from Celia Johns, one of Dominic Carter's top clients, instead. These kinds of mistakes could be catastrophic when it came to contract renewals. All the other agencies were always circling. And of course, any of these slips would be glorious for Dominic Carter. The errors incited Georgina's wrath when she heard about them. We witnessed Eloise getting the kind of dressing-down from behind Georgina's glass windows that made us all retreat to the loos for a quiet moment, but Eloise simply didn't seem to care. It was baffling. And when we all individually queried the slip-ups with her, she shrugged and told us there was a lot going on, a lot of samples coming in and out. She said she just didn't know and were we *sure*. We were sure. And when we saw her receiving yet another warning, I asked Debbie for some insight. Or more to the point, and urged on by the others, I asked why Eloise was still there at the agency.

'Go on, Frankie, you ask. Not thinking before you speak will work in your favour on this one,' Zoe said, throwing me in front of Debbie and her laptop. Debbie reluctantly explained that Eloise had begged for another chance after the latest mistake, said that the job was everything to her, she was still paying back her student loan, she'd try harder. Georgina had taken pity. She'd even given her a small pay rise last season to motivate her.

'She does have a heart – and Eloise is the daughter of an

old school friend of Georgina's back up in Norwich,' Debbie had clarified as she started typing, to signal the conversation was over.

'Wait, whaaat? Georgina is from NORWICH?' I couldn't help myself. In my mind, she was born in the GGC central London office. In a Celine trouser suit. Probably paired with a white cotton men's shirt.

We were gobsmacked. Eloise, like Georgina, never gave anything away about her personal circumstances. I had tried to get something out of her, and Zoe had told me she had always been so guarded with them all it had got to the stage where they just gave up. They had no idea what her motivations or ambitions were, but tried to keep it light and genial for the sake of office atmosphere. Now at least we knew why Georgina kept her on, albeit still stuck with the samples. I was baffled. Here I was, fully immersed in learning every nuance and method of the business, and Eloise seemed to have given up at the first cotton-mix jumpsuit hurdle. How could she be throwing away such a golden opportunity?

'How could none of you have found out this vital piece of information before?' I asked.

But we had no time to dwell on Eloise. I mean, there literally was just no time.

PRESS NOTE

Frankie Marks' meteoric rise in the industry has taken everyone by surprise. Rarely does someone come in and take the PR world by storm while wearing floral midi skirts and eating quite so many crisps.

'We have high hopes for her. Once she has grasped that the virtual world of the metaverse isn't about poetry, we are confident Frankie will continue to excel,' Nicky Harris commented via voice notes as she scrolled through a travel brochure.

'It's just a phase. I hope,' added Frankie's loyal boyfriend, James.

ENDS

A new intern had started, giving me the exalted role of *Senior Paid Intern*. Admittedly, a title I assigned myself. I took her under my wing and gave her the same attention Jemima had given me when I'd arrived. I told her about Nicky's balsamic vinegar. I warned her about keeping her toes hidden. I introduced her to Claudia at the deli, who she needed to be best friends with to avoid the lunchtime queues. The intern was clearly overjoyed to be there and was efficient and bubbly. Plus, she always asked me if I wanted a packet of crisps with my salad each day. I liked this new intern. She knew I secretly loved carbs. I also liked her because her arrival coincided with Eloise being off work with the flu for a couple of days, throwing the intern into the sample cupboard to cover her absence. It was a glorious 48 hours when every sample went to the right place on time. Eloise really was the broken link in a very well-oiled machine, and she made it clear that she simply didn't care if tartan or tweed were the next big thing. She absolutely couldn't give a damn about ankle straps on shoes. And she wasn't interested in who was on the cover of the next issue of *Avalon* magazine, but she still resented us all. No wonder she had been left languishing in the sample cupboard.

I, in the meantime, was falling in love with my job. As I continued to hone my professional skills, I felt a quiet joy at seeing someone on the bus wearing the Darcy Girl culotte she didn't know I had been instrumental in persuading her to buy – via our showroom, my press appointment, and sending the one sample we had left to the shoot three months ago, landing it on the pages of *Madame* magazine's 'How to Wear Them' story. When I wasn't howling with laughter at some of the industry's inanity, the cultural commentary fashion could play a part in was actually fascinating to me.

'Doesn't everyone get a slight spring in their step and fifteen minutes of feeling fabulous when they buy something new to wear?' I explained to James and Charlotte, earnestly banging my fists on our kitchen table one warm night a month or so later when we all had a chance to be together in one place and pretend I hadn't overcooked some pasta.

'Not me,' said James. 'Unless a football shirt counts?'

'I really don't like culottes,' Charlotte said.

But for me, the thrill of the journey of that culotte was addictive. And I wanted more and more.

One sunny Friday morning I settled down at my desk, waiting for the usual flurry of instructions. There was surely a call-in to sort out in the showroom, a rail to be tidied, an appointment no one else wanted to take, a cup of tea to be made, a reservation for lunch to organise, a new post from Dominic to bitch about. I was humming to myself when my internal extension rang. From Georgina's phone. My stomach dropped to my knees.

'Hi, Georgina.'

'Can you pop into my office, please.' I could see her gesturing to me from her glass box.

Oh God, what had I done? I didn't want to be let go. I'd been working so hard, learning on the job. It was so different from anything I had ever anticipated doing, but I now definitively knew I wanted to stay. I understood that fashion PR was a skill, it was strategic, and it wasn't only about the clothes. I took a deep breath and entered Georgina's office.

'So, how do you think it's going, Frankie?' Georgina looked up.

'Yes, I mean, good. I think. I'm loving it. I'm learning a lot. It's been great. Thanks so much for having me these past months.'

She left an agonising silence. My stomach dropped from my knees to my newly pedicured big toe. I was just doing a quick mental inventory of how quickly and calmly I could clear my things at the end of the day while saying a graceful goodbye to everyone, when she looked directly at me.

'You've been here for . . . what is it . . . over six months now? And we're impressed. We'd like you to stay. Full-time. How do you feel about that?'

Disney fireworks exploded above my head.

'That would be wonderful. Really?'

'Yes, really.' She actually smiled. 'A few hiccups here and there. Pants, singing . . . but we think you're going to make a good PR. Sometimes coming into this industry without any desperate desire for fashion is what makes the best account directors. Having said that, what I'll now do is authorise

Debbie to ask the clients for bigger clothing discounts for you. This' – she made a vague gesture, looking me up and down – 'needs some work.'

I looked down at my midi-length skirt paired with open-toed flats and a pedicure. I had been certain I had nailed a laid-back summer boho look that morning. Apparently not.

'Thank you so much, Georgina. I won't let you down. Can I ask what the salary will be?'

'Debbie has the details. Thanks, Frankie.' And with that, I realised I was dismissed.

I walked back to my desk grinning like the Cheshire cat. I had a full-time job – finally – and I knew I was going to accept whatever salary they offered. James would understand. He could make me a profit and loss document. I would manage somehow.

'You're stuck with me!' I announced gleefully to them all as I walked back into our office.

'Yes!' Zoe exclaimed.

'I knew it.' Jemima beamed.

'You'd better warn your boyfriend.' Nicky winked.

'Yup. He needs to know you'll be spending even more time with us than with him,' Andrew added.

My stomach sank as fast as my heart had leaped. *How will he react?* I thought as I stroked the desk that was now mine. James had been just about tolerating this temporary new version of me, and I now had to tell him it was here to stay. There were only so many jokes we could entertain about how only meeting by our toothbrushes each night counted as a hot date before one of us really lost our shit. I went down to the sample cupboard to let Eloise know, my good news buoying my goodwill. In my new capacity as an official PR, I would attempt to use my PR skills on her. It would *definitely* make my life easier. When I reached the room, I stood leaning against the door frame.

'Hey, just wanted to let you know I'm staying on. Let me know how I can help. I know you've got a load of things you can teach me.'

'That's nice. Another intern who's been promoted above me. Great. I'm actually just packing up a massive call-in from *Avalon*.' And she turned away.

I couldn't work her out. I thought it may be a punch in the stomach for her, but I was valiantly attempting pleasantries, and she showed no inclination to move up or out, even as she watched upstarts like me come in and leapfrog her. She still didn't engage with any of us, except to discuss how a bra top or pink leather shoe had been called in simultaneously for two shoots and which publication's request was more important. And even then, it was like pulling teeth.

'They took me on full-time!' I performed the first moves of my electric slide as I threw my denim jacket on to the kitchen counter that evening.

James had tried to warm to GGC over the past few months. I'd remembered to send his mum a birthday card, made a concerted effort to understand why I had no money; I had empathised over the end of the premiership season but shown great joy at the friendly summer international fixtures that filled some gaps, and promised not to mention again the French lace story in *Avalon* that I had sent in a Dixie top for and got my first full-page credit confirmed. I would have to wait three months for the magazine to come out, but it was worth the wait. It would be particularly special now that I knew I would be looking at it from my desk at work and not from the sofa with my baked potatoes. Now that I. Had. A. Job.

James high-fived me. 'Salary? How long d'you think you'll stick it out?'

'Starter salary. But that's okay with me, if it's okay with you. I think it's just about enough for now. And I'll definitely stick it out. I like it there . . . I really do. I don't think it's just a phase. I like fashion. There, I said it.'

'You should call your parents and let them know. But don't forget, if you change your mind, I *am* earning enough to get us through a few months while you look for something better.'

It was a passive-aggressive comment but I chose to let it go over my head because I was dreading telling my parents more than I was irritated by him. I wasn't entirely sure how excited my father would be about the fact that I now recognised *Avalon*'s Editor-in-Chief Amanda Starling and knew that the average model's shoe size was a thirty-nine. I needed to work out what information to disseminate to him in order to mini-mise his disappointment. His affirmation that I was doing the right thing was everything to me. But at least I was now in a position to contribute to the rent.

'Let's get a pizza. A celebratory one. You're paying, now you're earning.'

'Oh, err . . . can we not? Can we get sushi instead?'

'Okay, listen. It's strange enough you're working in fash-ion. Funnier that it's as a PR. And disastrous that I now appear to know the difference between French and Chantilly lace. But where I draw the line is if you start eating like them. I've had months and months of hearing about how tired you are, and what someone called Nicky was wearing. I want to eat pizza with my girlfriend. The one who always gets extra toppings. Who loves me so much but still won't share the extra pepperoni? Remember her?'

'Sure,' I said brightly. I put on my best PR voice. 'Pepperoni. With extra mushrooms. And onions. Extra thin, crispy base.'

I could try a liquid diet for the rest of the week?

PRESS NOTE

Frankie's time in the fashion industry so far has taught her invaluable lessons in shopping and style over the past months. Her ability to mix and match cottons and cashmere has moved on exponentially. If not yet flawlessly.

'I am encouraged by Frankie's progress in the wardrobe department. She will soon learn that a too tight white jean isn't perhaps the best choice with a navy poplin shirt. But I have every confidence her taste levels can only improve,' commented Georgina Galvin via her assistant Debbie.

ENDS

A month or so sped past as we geared up for the new season.

'I'm heeeere . . . Who's been eating eggs? What have I said about hot food? I can't STAND the smell,' Georgina yelled up the staircase.

Andrew raced from his desk to the kitchen with the offending McMuffin under his top, just as Georgina turned the corner on the landing. I sat smugly with my low-fat yoghurt and granola pot.

'And I'm wearing my new heather-grey Celine cashmere,' she announced. 'If that smell lingers on me, I'll be furious.'

She glared at Andrew running back to his desk, but I definitely noted a hint of a smile. This was how Georgina always operated so successfully. Instilling fear and terror that we would fall short of her gimlet eye for professionalism, with sudden flashes of friendly warmth keeping us all on our toes and confusingly wanting more of her impromptu office visits. For my birthday a month earlier, she had given me a dressing-down for missing a swimwear story along with a beautifully wrapped home pedicure kit. I had thanked her profusely for both.

'Your jumper *is* sensational though,' Andrew said as he shook the crumbs out from under his shirt.

'I know – it is, isn't it?' Georgina's tone warmed immediately.

'Georgina, I've got Lloyd on the line. He said it's urgent.' Debbie nodded towards her glass box. 'I'll bring you in your coffee, he's on line two.'

'I'll take it in here, I want to catch up with everyone anyway,' she said, nodding to an empty chair. Our collective astonishment was tangible as we watched her sit at the desk next to me. I stopped eating, overcome by the fear of chewing or swallowing too loudly. Debbie transferred the call, and to even more of our astonishment, Georgina clicked him on to loudspeaker as her latte with almond milk and sugar-free vanilla was placed in front of her.

Lloyd Danes, the designer and co-founder of Dante – revered and adored by A-list celebrities and fashion editors alike. I had witnessed it at their shows. I had seen it in the metaphorical fist fights over their samples. And the fact that their basement show had been the first I'd ever experienced gave them a special place in my fashion heart. Together with his boyfriend, Jonathan, Lloyd had started the label straight out of college and the pair were famous for their refined tailoring. They were a PR dream – good-looking and articulate as well as creative and conceptual.

'Lloyd, hi, how are you? I loved the images from the new lookbook shoot, I saw them yesterday,' Georgina said soothingly down the phone, as she applied lip balm. 'They're strong, the model's great – so pleased you used her, every-one's talking about her at the moment.'

'Those assholes at Society.com just posted a negative review on the pre-collection. How did the images get leaked a day early? How did no one know? Have you seen it? And worst of all, they didn't like the velour. How could they not understand it's ironic? That it's a commentary on the leisurewear of the nineties and conspicuous consumption? What don't these people understand?'

Lloyd was breathless down the phone. We could hear him inhale deeply on a cigarette. Georgina knew everything about Dante, having mentored the boys out of Central Saint Martins, after she saw their graduate collection and immedi-ately offered to represent them for free. That was three years ago. They had brought her client after client on the back of their success. They were her special project.

'It's really not a problem.' She was lying. The fact that those images had been leaked was an almighty problem. 'We would have sent them out today anyway.' She kept her tone even. 'But we'll call them . . . and I'll be finding out how they got them. Don't panic. It's not a disaster,' Georgina cooed as she admired her immaculate nude nail colour. 'How was your meeting with Lucy?'

Lucy Collins was one of the most elite stylists in the world. She had been enlisted by Georgina to guide the boys since their very first show as she herself was rising through the ranks. That was one of Georgina's greatest gifts. The innate ability to recognise emerging talent ahead of the pack and reel it in before it became shark bait for the competition.

'Yeah. It was good. She wants to change hair and make-up teams for the next show. She wants to show in a white box somewhere and she wants the models to be holograms.'

'Uh huh. Good, okay. I'm going to get off the phone, I want to give Society.com a call right now. And you know you can call me ANY time. Except not tomorrow. I'm on a spa day tomorrow.'

'It's a total disaster!' she screamed at all of us as the phone went down. 'How the hell did they get those images a day early?'

Although Georgina tried to be in the office for a portion of every day when she was in London, she was always perfectly happy to let us all get on with it, knowing that we knew what she expected of us. After so many years in the business, she wasn't interested in the daily minutiae anymore, but she was still the figurehead and was omnipresent. She always knew exactly what was going on even if she wasn't actually doing it herself. Her delegation skills were legendary. But this was unfathomable. She would one hundred per cent get Nicky to make that call for her.

'NICKY,' she yelled, although Nicky was only a few feet away.

'I have no idea. I have those images here.' Nicky pointed at her laptop and a pile of photos on her desk. 'I haven't sent them anywhere yet, obviously. How the hell did they get them? But to be honest, the velour is tricky. We can only work with what we're given. I've talked to Lucy about it as well.' She gestured in exasperation as she crossed her skin-tight black-jeaned legs, which rose to reveal the delicate star tattoo on her ankle that I envied approximately eight times a day.

Georgina eyed her.

'Take the boys out drinking. Get a bigger story up on *My Style* to make up for it. Andrew, go for drinks too. Make them feel loved.'

Andrew mumbled something about having a really full schedule.

'I don't care if you've got tea with the King. Make time,' Georgina snapped. 'They're our most important client – and since when have you turned down a night out on company expenses?'

Andrew mumbled something else indiscernible but nodded meekly. Zoe raised her hands to him in a what-the-fuck gesture.

'Frankie, what news do you have?' Georgina turned to me.

This was another one of her gifts. The ability to switch focus at the drop of a hat and put any one of us under the spotlight of her attention. I pushed my yoghurt to the side. *Don't go red, be cool, be Nicky for one second.*

'I'm working on a Darcy Girl story with *Madame*. Laura decided she liked it after they shot that balloon-sleeve daisy shirt and she's now gone fully into wanting to do a two-page feature on their new poppy-print collection. Using celebrities. They won't pay anyone, so we've put asks into a couple of the *Breakfast Banters* weather girls, that woman who just came out of the jungle, and one of the baking finalists. Darcy Girl are thrilled. I'm just waiting to see who we can secure. Then I'll work on getting the samples over.'

My nonchalant yet efficient telling of this story belied my joy at having Georgina's undivided attention to tell it to. For me to get our high-street, highest-retainer-paying client a double-page spread in the biggest middle-market monthly was – well, honestly, it was amazing. It was a shot of adrenaline. These were the moments I was learning I thrived on. It wasn't about the poppies placed on shirting. It was the strategic thinking, the negotiating, the execution of a plan. Even if it was with reality TV stars, a weather girl, and a lot of polyester.

'Nicely done. Keep me posted.'

I smiled so widely my jaw started to ache.

'And where's your shirt from?' She pointed at my newly purchased and much-prized navy cotton poplin wide-collared shirt. I had copied it from the Fashion Editor of *The*

Forward who had been wearing it to a press appointment a couple of weeks ago. 'It's good.'

I fingered the collar, blushing.

'But not with those.' She pointed at my slightly too tight white jeans. 'That doesn't work.'

And with that, she picked her coffee up, swept into her office and shut the door.

'It's half a compliment.' Andrew slapped his thigh laughing as my blush mottled down my neck. 'Just take it and run with it.'

I looked down at my legs. I thought I'd got it so right. And now I'd have to spend the rest of the day in my outfit of shame. Oh well, at least that made it an entirely appropriate outfit for dinner at my parents' that night. I hadn't seen them for months. I was dreading it.

'How's it going at your new job, then?' my mother asked me.

'Yes, good. I'm doing okay. I mean, I've been there the best part of a year, Mum. So it's not really *that* new.' I laughed nervously.

'Goodness, is it that long already? Anyway, I like your outfit, sweetheart. Very smart,' she said kindly.

I shuffled in my chair and spread my napkin over the white jeans that had caused Georgina such offence earlier.

Dinner with my parents took place in the familiar cosy dining room of the family home that I had been raised in. The same faded maroon curtains with the swirl embroidery I had stared at, mesmerised, as a child, were still there. The same plaster was falling off the cornice as it had done for twenty years. My mother handed me a bowl of steaming roast potatoes. My favourite.

I always had mixed emotions going home. A sense of security enveloped me whenever I walked through the familiar space, quickly followed by a sense of acute irritation at being treated like a child, which then led me to behave like a child. And so, the cycle prevailed.

'Thanks, Mum. I just bought it last week.'

Oh, I'd mentioned spending superfluous money I didn't have to spend. Amateur mistake. There was an uncomfortable silence as eating resumed. I looked back at the curtains. My younger sister Tilda was away at university. Two years behind me. I really needed backup, but there was none to be found. I pushed a potato around my plate as I waited for the inevitable inquisition.

'Have you had a pay rise yet?' my father asked me.

'Umm, minimal. But I get a clothing allowance.'

I was talking quickly. I had made another mistake I knew immediately he would have picked up on. I got a clothing allowance but was still buying extra clothes.

He shook his head silently. My father was an academic. Locked in books and papers as long as memory served me. Highly intelligent, hugely well read, and clearly unimpressed by me.

My mother had been a secretary. Fastest typist in the West, according to her. She gave up work to raise my sister and me, and truth be told, all my parents wanted was for us to utilise the education and opportunities that they had worked so hard to provide. That meant us going into the arts, or law, finance, architecture – anything where we could 'use our brains'. Fashion was not part of the equation. That, with my degree, I had somehow been unable to secure myself a job that my father considered worthwhile was still a lingering disappointment. That I now felt fashion was my chosen career – and had stopped searching for any other type of job – hadn't gone down well. My mother was much more forgiving and was forever trying to keep the peace. She was now operating all her diplomatic know-how to smooth the rift between my father and me over my chosen employment.

We ate the remainder of dinner listening to my mother chatting about Tilda and their upcoming all-inclusive touring holiday of the historical sites of northern France with their best friends, the Freedmans. I managed some 'lovely's' and 'lucky you's' while I picked at my food, as my father ate in silence and my mother chatted on encouragingly and then tried to engage him back into a conversation about my dreaded job.

'Well, I think if you really believe you're where you want to be, then that's a good thing. I'm proud of you. Martin, aren't we proud of her?'

My father pushed his chair back and stood up while I froze in silent anticipation of his next move. He said nothing but simply walked out of the room and into his study. This was not the ideal scenario.

My mother sighed. 'I tried, dear . . . He just assumed you'd end up using your degree.'

'Yes. I know,' I said as I too pushed my chair back. I left her sitting there as I went into the kitchen across the hallway.

I would take my father in a coffee and his favourite short-bread biscuit as a peace offering. I stood staring at the garden out of the window above the sink, waiting for the water to boil while my eyes welled up and I felt my throat contract. I was a daddy's girl at heart, and all I wanted was his approval, no matter my protestations to the contrary. When I had got my 2:1 degree, he was my first call. When he said 'well done' and didn't ask why it wasn't a first, I did a cartwheel (metaphorically, obviously – I could barely do a somersault).

I walked across the small hallway and tentatively entered his study, placing the tray down on the desk in front of him and clearing some papers.

'Please don't be irritated. I really just want to get as far as I can. I'll prove it to you. It's more than just fashion.'

He took the coffee and biscuit and furrowed his magnificent eyebrows. 'Francesca, it's a waste of your extremely capable brain, not to mention education. I've said it already: ghastly people, and a shallow world that I would rather you had no part in. I still don't understand what it is you even do.' He took a sip of coffee and bit off a chunk of shortbread.

He had called me Francesca. I knew it was time to back off. He picked up his book. The conversation was over.

I shut the door quietly behind me and went to find my mother, who was nibbling a digestive as she sipped her own coffee, ensconced in the hideous but unbelievably comfortable seventies beige leather sofa in the sitting room.

'On second thoughts, I'm not so keen on those trousers, dear,' she said as I sank down beside her.

'What on earth are you wearing?' James exclaimed. A couple of months had passed since my disastrous visit home, but my outfits were clearly still a cause for concern.

'A tulip-festooned all-in-one. Obviously.'

'You're changing before we go out. Yes?' He was laughing rather too joyfully.

I had spent my day at the Darcy Girl childrenswear launch, Darcy's Little Darlings, the brainchild of their super keen CEO, Malcolm. To my utter horror I had worn the same tulip jumpsuit as one of the not-so-darling guests, the five-year-old daughter of an X Factor 2018 runner-up. I took a look at myself in the full-length mirror in the bedroom. I had honestly thought I'd pulled it off. No. I had not. My sports bra had caused an unsightly ridge mid-ribcage, the plastic buttons were shiny, and the multi-coloured tulips shaped over my bottom did me no favours. I looked like a clown. Fashion fail number 3,001. I undid the buttons as quickly as I could and scrunched the jumpsuit into the back of my cupboard, throwing on my trusty boyfriend jeans and favourite faded sweatshirt and an enormous puffa jacket to fend off the biting cold.

James and I walked down Ladbroke Grove, holding hands in amiable silence. We seemed to have reached a balance: I was learning to not be a work bore and discuss everything that had happened in my day. He had learned to not call me a work bore and still ask what had happened while praying I didn't answer. Happy days.

The tiny Thai restaurant was crowded but we spotted them at a table tucked away in the corner by the bar.

'Hello, stranger!' Charlotte held out her arms and I leaned down to give her an exaggerated hug. She had lost more weight since I last saw her a few months earlier. The new Cambodia case was taking it out of her.

'Well, hello to you too!' I extracted myself and parked my bottom on the seat next to her. I held my hand up in greeting to the others, including one olive-skinned newcomer. Felipe. Charlotte's new boyfriend. Or 31D, as I liked to call him, indicating the seat he was sitting in when they met on the plane to Cambodia.

'I have to have pad thai AND green curry AND prawn crackers and then I don't care what else we get,' I said.

'More importantly, I want a beer,' James said, 'and then I want you to tell Charlotte about wearing a romper suit with tulips. Because even I could tell it was a fashion disaster.'

Oh, how they all fell about laughing. I tried to maintain my dignity. But now I thought about it, there was indeed a comedic element.

'I had to. I had to wear the client. For God's sake. I know. I know. I even outfit-matched a five-year-old, for fuck's sake. Pass me the wine, I need a drink, I've been with screaming kids on sugar highs all afternoon, and some agonising D-list celebrities. It's not all glamour, you know . . .'

My emphatic noodle consumption was interrupted by my phone ringing. Zoe. I answered, ignoring the looks being exchanged around the table.

'Houston, we have a problem.'

'I can't really talk, Zoe. I'm at dinner.'

'It's quick. The model for the Giovanni Castani lookbook shoot tomorrow just cancelled. Nicky needs you to be the foot model. The shoot's at Camber Sands. Car is collecting you at five a.m. I just redirected it. Make sure you've waxed your legs.'

'Don't be ridiculous. Why can't you do it?'

'My feet are too flat. Nicky's are too small. You, little bear, are just right.'

'For fuck's sake.'

'For the sake of the client, actually. Get an early night.' Zoe laughed and hung up.

I shoved my phone in my bag as some spicy crackers were placed in the middle of the table. I dipped one in the sweet chilli sauce and crammed the whole thing in my mouth.

'And when I said it's not all glamour, let me tell you, I'm bloody serious,' I announced with my mouth full, while simultaneously reaching down to have a quick feel of the hair situation around my lower calves. I picked up my bag and said a hasty farewell while they all groaned, and James' face froze in a disappointed grimace.

PRESS NOTE

The Giovanni Castani lookbook shoot was a magnificent success. Frankie Marks stepped into the model's shoes, both figuratively and literally, to great acclaim.

'It was a pleasure to watch Frankie give it her all in the triple, strap Gladiator sandal. Her commitment to running in sand dunes was unquestionable. Her slightly swollen ankles are nothing we can't fix in retouch,' commented the incredibly good-looking and renowned photographer Greg White.

ENDS

I didn't have any home wax in the bathroom. I had to shave, ruining my monthly waxing cycle. I was almost more furious about that than I was about my 4.15 a.m. wake-up and the fact that when I left dinner early, Charlotte had sent me a spiky message: *Not okay by the way. You barely met Felipe.* When James had come home, he got into bed and rolled over to his side, dramatically huffing and puffing.

The photographer at the shoot was Greg White. He specialised in on-location shoots and was known to be the best of the best. I moisturised my legs and feet and toes in the back of the cab. The driver didn't seem delighted by the aloe with lavender aroma, which I thought rather churlish given it was distinctly preferable to the stale

Christmas tree air freshener hanging off his rear-view mirror, and the lingering waft of greasy kebab that had greeted me when I opened the passenger door. The journey time was going to be just under two and a half hours, he told me. I was desperate for a power nap after only four hours' sleep – and was maybe a teeny bit hungover. I may have left dinner early but apparently had managed to wash down copious glasses of wine in record time. What I needed was a mug of builder's tea and a vast bacon sandwich. But sleep proved impossible as the driver listened to Soft Rock FM and proceeded to tap the steering wheel and hum along in between cracking his knuckles for the duration of the journey.

I scrolled through the online images from Darcy's Little Darlings instead. We had done well. Top of the *Daily Post* bar of shame, with a succession of images of each of the dubiously recognisable attendees. Darcy Girl would be delighted. I sent them an email with Georgina and the team in copy, subject heading 'Images!!'.

> Hi guys. Yesterday was a great success. Please find attached this morning's online coverage. Bear in mind it's only 5.30 a.m. so plenty more to come!

Yup. *Your faithful PR was up and working before dawn had broken,* was my subtext. And I was going to get that email in before anyone else did. They may be my friends, but Nicky and Zoe had stitched me up and were still snoring, so I would take credit where credit was due.

I watched the signs for Gatwick Airport fly by me as we sped down the M25. My eyelids started getting heavy. I remembered hearing the driver hum along to 'We Built this City' before I eventually succumbed to my sleep deprivation. I must have slept the rest of the journey, because the next thing I knew the motion of the car had stopped, and I was aware of my open mouth and a small trickle of drool on my chin. Most attractive. Thank God they were only going to be looking at my feet and ankles.

I looked around to see I was in a car park, right on the edge of what looked like a sandstorm on the beach. A white over-sized location van was parked on the other side, housing all the shoes and catering. I clambered out of the car, straightened my crumpled sweatshirt and jeans from the night before – no need to dress up, and they were the quickest things to hand – summoned all my courage, and edged my way in.

I immediately spotted a God-like creature that must be Greg inside, chatting animatedly to the designer, Giovanni, and his assistants as he held up an orange patent three-inch stiletto, marvelling at it. I, in the meantime, marvelled at Greg. Salt-and-pepper hair, cheekbones I could cut into a baked potato with, and two snaggle teeth that were so sexy it wasn't normal. I mean, I had heard about his infamous sex appeal – and the stories about what he could do with those teeth and how many supermodels he'd done it to – but I was still taken aback.

'Yes, yes, the light will really hit the heel perfectly at this angle,' Greg was saying.

'Morning, morning. Your model has arrived. Not perhaps the one you were hoping for. But I've moisturised my ankles for you,' I said in a bleary attempt at breezy early morning humour.

'Darling!' Giovanni clasped me in a bear hug. '*Grazie* to you.'

'Hi. Greg,' said Greg, who as it turned out was even more sensationally good-looking close up. Zoe was going to really regret her flat foot claim. He glanced down at my feet. 'Can you take your socks off; they're going to have left marks.'

'Yes, of course,' I said, less breezily, as I sat down on the beige leather seat edging the van and feeling, well, completely stupid.

'Can you do anything with that swelling?' Greg beckoned the body make-up artist over while pointing accusingly at the double ridge marks above my ankles and my swollen flesh above them. The humiliation was real.

Barbara the make-up lady grimaced.

'Will do my best. Maybe stick your feet up on two cushions in the meantime, to try to take the puffiness down?'

My late night, lack of sleep, and lack of the carbs I needed to soak up my hangover were making me dangerously tetchy. But still I smiled and obediently positioned myself lengthways on the narrow banquette, stuck my legs up in the air and planted my feet against the side wall of the toilet at the end of it. I lay there, apparently invisible, for a good half an hour while Greg and Giovanni discussed heel and toe details in depth – *kitten, block, pointed, round, natural light, overhead, side, flash, no flash* – until Barbara finally popped back to check on the progression of my puffiness.

'Not sure they're going to go down much more, Greg,' she sighed. 'I'll stick some tinted moisturiser on them and you'll have to do the rest in post. Let's get an express pedicure done quickly.'

I turned and smiled wanly at Greg, being careful to clench my jawline to minimise my double chin.

'Sorry about that. It was an early start. I didn't think.' *Plus, I'm doing you all a favour, I'm not being paid to step in, it's fucking freezing, and I'm hungry and hungover.* Feeling my bare, sockless toes turn numb from cold, I also wondered aggrievedly why I hadn't brought a coat, and why had no one offered me a bacon sandwich yet?

'Barbara, can I get up now and have a quick cigarette?' I couldn't believe I was actually asking for her permission as she shoved my just-painted nude toes into a pair of polystyrene flip-flops. This was not a career high.

'Go, go,' Greg interjected, 'then let's get started. The light's really good right now.'

'So just walk up the dunes and I'll be catching your feet in motion,' Greg yelled at me as the wind started whipping the sand up around us.

I was wearing a pair of green stilettos with an open heel and a strap across my ankles. They were half a size too big so the toes were stuffed with tissue. My jeans were pulled up to above my knees to be out of shot. I tried my hardest to walk gracefully as I sank into the dune.

'Longer strides, Frankie!' Greg yelled, even louder. 'Towards me now. Lovely. Oh great. Yes! Look at the light on this shot, Giovanni.' He held his camera up for Giovanni to look at the images on the digital screen.

'*Bellissima!*' beamed Giovanni.

'We got it. Let's move on to the pink kitten heel,' Greg instructed one of his two assistants.

My feet were already in agony. My calves were aching. I gave an emphatic thumbs-up as I took the green shoes off and shuffled over to the assistant who was cheerfully waving the next instruments of torture at me.

'This time let's do it seated, cross your feet over each other. No, this way. Angle to me. No, that way. Up. Down. Perfect. Love this. Cross them the other way.'

If Greg wasn't so exceptionally good-looking, I'd have told him to shove it. As it was, I was smiling serenely. *Whatever you need, Greg, with your salt-and-pepper slightly floppy hair and oh-so-green eyes.*

My pink stilettoed feet went up, down, sideways, in circles. I marched across the sand in lemon-yellow leather slides. White flats had me running. Strappy high purples saw me kick my feet up with joy. Gladiator sandals were shot in motion – there would be a lot of retouch required around my not-stick-thin calves. But by shot number seven, I was almost enjoying myself as I imagined Greg's adulation at what an exceptional shoe model I was.

We broke for lunch just after midday. Which was just as well, as I might have fainted from starvation otherwise. We crowded into the location van to eat hummus wraps and couscous salad. Hardly the bacon sandwich I craved, but at least I would no longer be in danger of passing out on set.

'So, we just have another eight shots to go,' Greg said, looking through his shot list. 'We're going to have to move fast before the light goes. Frankie, let's get going as soon as you're ready.'

I settled into my prawn mayonnaise on brown, bestowing Greg with my most beatific beam, and crunched my poor toes open and shut to get some circulation going again. I thought I would have time for a little rest and was just contemplating my next witticism when Barbara appeared at my feet, brandishing more tint. The ridge from my socks hadn't fully dissipated but the swelling had almost gone, she told the table. *Cheers, Babs.*

Lunch over, the wind had started to pick up. So had the pace.

'Great. Hold it there. No. Hold it. Stay still. Can you lift both feet high, almost vertical? Run, Frankie. Jump, Frankie. Jump again. Leap. Forward. Point them both in front. Wider! Bring them together! I said wider! Jump! Lift. Higher!'

I had sand between my toes. In my hair. Up my knickers. By the time I heard the blessed 'It's a wrap' and a bit of clapping and Giovanni enthusing, I was crunching sand in my teeth.

'Got any plasters, Barbara?' I muttered as I limped back to the van. My feet were ravaged. It was five p.m. The light was already going. I would be home by eight, I reckoned, if traffic was okay, and I certainly wasn't sticking around to look at any of the shots Greg was currently downloading on to his laptop for everyone to see. Thankfully my car was already there to collect me, as promised by Zoe. I just needed to do a humiliating wee in the internal toilet with everyone in the van listening, and escape.

'Thanks for stepping in.' Greg smiled. Those teeth. I felt my legs slightly buckle.

'Oh, no problem. It was really good fun.' I smiled bashfully in return as I felt the raw skin on my big toe rub against my trainers and crunched another bit of sand in my mouth.

I turned and hugged Giovanni and pegged it to my car, throwing myself into the back seat and undoing the laces on my shoes to release the tension against my – possibly permanently crippled – feet. Not that I was ever one to overexaggerate.

You owe me. Big time, I messaged Nicky.

Big mistake. Greg White is sensational-looking, I texted Zoe.

Do you think if I only drink green juice for a week my ankles will get thinner? I asked Charlotte.

The next three hours were spent crawling back to London on the M25 in rush-hour traffic, during which I idly fantasised about my imaginary shoot with Greg White, the one where the wind was blowing my hair in the right direction as I gaily laughed and skipped along the seashore, Greg's oh-so green eyes shining with admiration as he called out to me, 'Divine, Frankie. Absolutely bloody divine.'

Was this what being a PR was all about?

My phone pinged.

Hi. It's Greg. Got your number from Giovanni. Fancy meeting up some time to discuss the images?

The photographer was such a bore, I quickly WhatsApped James, as my heart thumped.

PRESS NOTE

The great joy of fashion PR is the opportunity to create the next big thing out of nothing. Frankie Marks' ability to embrace new challenges is what stands to mark her out as an industry 'one to watch'.

'As soon as I met Melissa Bailey, I knew I'd possibly stumbled across the greatest PR opportunity of all time. Never have I seen anything so awful that made me itch to make good. Sadly, I didn't understand that this would mean never again would I not work on a weekend,' commented Frankie, working from her bed on a Saturday morning.

ENDS

Time seemed to speed up as the team completed two more show seasons. My feet were featured in every new magazine shoe story, I perfected the art of the press release and was promoted to Account Director. My mousey brown hair now had some soft lowlights, and I was able to contribute towards mine and James' holiday in Spain and a new winter duvet.

The team had just got back from a lunch with the *Herald*'s fashion department, fully fashioned in our clients' new Autumn/Winter collections. Zoe needed to get a story on the Jessy Galway expansion into beach jewellery. Nicky wanted to push Giovanni Castani's new range of ankle boots. I just really liked the chicken paillard at the restaurant they had chosen, so offered to go along and sell in the new jersey range Dixie was launching next month. We pitched what we needed to, found out that Five Star were having problems with their big menswear client Hunter & Fitch, and were indulging in some self-congratulation when Debbie walked in.

'There's someone from Melissa Bailey's office on the phone. They've asked for Georgina, but she doesn't want to take the call – which of you wants to deal with it? I've put them on hold.'

Me. Me! I'll take it. Give me that ex soap star with the famous Hollywood husband.

'Not me, not a chance. She's absurd.' Nicky looked up from her desk. 'I heard on the grapevine she wants to do her own collection. Acting roles must have dried up. Not touching her with a bargepole.'

'Don't look at me. I spend my life refusing to send her any samples for events,' Zoe said.

I spoke up, trying to sound vaguely disinterested but instead achieving utterly desperate. I wanted my own client. Maybe this was the one? 'I'm happy to take it, Debbie.' She forwarded on the call.

'Good afternoon, GGC, Frankie speaking.'

'Oh hi, Frankie. This is Martha. From Melissa Bailey's office. She's looking for fashion representation and has asked if I could put in a meeting with someone from GGC. Not entirely sure who the right person to speak to is. Can you help?'

Melissa Bailey. Representation? I looked over at Nicky and Zoe, pointing to the phone at my ear.

'What?' they said in unison. I grabbed a piece of paper and scrawled a barely legible note which I held up.

Wants PR.

'Nooooooo, we can't,' they both whispered.

'Sure, Martha. Why don't you shoot me over some dates that work for you and I can talk to Georgina this end?'

I put the phone down with my mouth still open like a goldfish.

'What do we think, people?'

'Gripping,' Zoe said. 'Absolutely gripping. In the worst way possible. I've known Martha, her PA, for years,' she added. 'Was that her on the phone? You would LOVE her. Martha, that is. As for Melissa Bailey, well, she isn't famed for her fashion sense. More for her fashion faux pas ... That would be one hard sell.'

Jemima looked over and momentarily stopped typing.

'Tragic.'

Andrew walked into the room with a cup of tea in his hand, having been out all morning.

'Who you talking about?'

'Melissa Bailey,' Nicky said wearily.

'Shut. The. Front. Door.' Andrew put his tea down and his hand to his chest. 'Be still, my beating heart. It's too much. Too much. You know how I feel about the husband. OMG. Why did I have to be out?!'

'Apologies. I feel your pain. But I have to say, I'd absolutely love to meet her,' I said. 'I'm fascinated. Plus, you know, if you stopped disappearing all the time you could have swiped that call.' Andrew had developed a new habit of going off-grid in the last few months. He would leave for a press appointment and vanish for hours on end, with long-fangled stories about why his phone had no service. He took a sip of his tea and offered no explanation. Meanwhile, I saw that Martha's email had already popped into my inbox.

Melissa Bailey had been a soap star, the main female character in *Carlyle Bay*, the UK's equivalent to *Knots Landing* combined with *Neighbours*. We had all watched it religiously, following her preposterous on-screen trials and tribulations. She had been adored by the UK press. Her every step was trailed by them for years and years, and enthusiastically pored over by us in the trashy weeklies. Then she had left for what she believed would be greener pastures, but she quickly became old news and had taken herself off to find better fame and fortune in the States. It hadn't quite taken off professionally, but after a year or so there, she had met world-wide sex icon and Hollywood A-lister Gabriel Bannon when they had been seated adjacent to each other front row at a Lakers game. He had been charmed by her English accent and self-deprecating humour. They dated – every move, dinner, kiss, and trip to the shops tracked by the press. They quickly went global as the biggest celebrity power couple in the media and she became a bona fide A-lister herself. But she still couldn't quite shake off the remnants of the soap actress reputation that dogged her new-found status.

Her manager was legendary. Cole Fisher. Creator of concepts. Maker of stars. He criss-crossed continents forging relationships, creating brands, saving faces. He had looked after Melissa when she was just starting out. He had stuck with her through the bad times. He had spotted the relationship with Gabriel as her golden ticket and had carefully navigated its progression through perfectly timed photo opportunities and paparazzi tip-offs. They were, it seemed, genuinely in love; she got pregnant; they had a lovely wedding in Malibu with three tabloid helicopters circling above them. Cole probably hadn't needed to stage-manage the whole thing at all.

Now he had the full package. Melissa was beloved in the USA. She got pregnant again. They now had two impossibly perfect girls, Dandelion and Delilah, who cemented their almost cult status.

But Gabriel was away a lot on set, on promotional tours. Melissa got bored. She had been used to working the gruelling hours demanded of soap stars. And it was then that Cole got to work on her second career. He secured her deals with flip-flop brands. She promoted toothpaste in Korea – where *Carlyle Bay* had belatedly become a craze – and attended garden parties in LA. Still unsatisfied with her 'personal brand', Melissa needed a new outlet. Thinking fashion was the obvious choice, she honed her focus. Did some terrible collaborations. Wore some terrible clothes.

She wanted more. I wanted more. I had been involved with so many clients and campaigns by now, but I hadn't yet had a project to really call my own. Melissa Bailey could be a godsend for me and I couldn't wait to meet her, out of sheer curiosity if nothing else. And I was more than mildly surprised that I was the only one who could see the potential in taking on a project like this.

'She's a laughing stock in the industry. Everyone knows that,' Georgina said, scanning the new influx of monthly magazines that afternoon.

'I know, but that's exactly why she could be our biggest challenge, the biggest surprise success story. I'd really like to go for it. I think I'll die if I don't get my hands on her.' I could see Georgina's interest already beginning to wane. 'Imagine if she went to Five Star? If we said no?' I had thrown down my ace card.

Georgina looked up. 'I think you'll regret it. But you can go for it. I don't want anything to do with it. Really. You can tell her I felt you would be best placed to do the meeting. But she has to pay the maximum monthly retainer' – she looked at me sternly – 'and if you do like her and want to take her on, it mustn't be at the expense of any other clients.'

I was elated.

'Working with Melissa Bailey? Surely not, Frankie. Isn't that a step too far?' Charlotte said. 'Although obviously I'll want all details,' she added thoughtfully as we discussed it a week into my binge-watching reruns of *Carlyle Bay* in case Melissa asked me anything about it. Charlotte, like all people, was secretly fascinated.

I had told James as we were sitting on the sofa in our pyjamas. A rare evening in, just the two of us, pasta on our laps and my giant sheepskin slippers on the ottoman slash table, so they kept blocking his view of the TV. These winter evenings when we could argue about what to watch, and why I couldn't buy smaller slippers, were still heavenly. I ruined it by talking about work.

'I thought you loved the job because of the fashion and the journey of culottes . . .' James said witheringly. 'How does that involve working with an ex soap star?'

And that comment sealed the deal for me. I would meld the two. I banged my slippers together twice high in the air so James couldn't see the TV at all.

And two weeks later, the pitch meeting arrived. I had woken up early, full of anxiety. I wasn't sure I was ready for this solo, with no wingman or woman to bounce off, but Martha had said Melissa preferred a one-on-one initially. I had spent a week with Zoe finalising the pitch document, samples of editorial, ideas and strategies. I practised my authoritative yet nonchalant oh-are-you-globally-famous-I-hadn't-noticed voice on James, who cocked his head to one side, trying to pretend he was a) listening, and b) interested.

I went into the office that day in a black cab. I needed to be pristine and was mindful of preserving the precise middle seam of the navy gaberdine Dante trousers off the showroom rail that I had somehow managed to squeeze myself into. The cut was perfect; I almost looked thin. I had paired them with a slogan-emblazoned heather-grey cashmere jumper from an upcoming streetwear label and a Castani heel. A mix of hi-lo. A wardrobe signalling that I was confident, fashion-forward, not that bothered.

'Don't fuck it up!' Andrew said, grinning as I gathered all the documents up and left to take a taxi to the offices of Melissa's management company in Notting Hill. I texted Charlotte. She was in Guatemala working on a prisoner release, but I knew I could interrupt for breaking news.

> **Frankie**
> Guess where I'm going now.

Charlotte
Where?

> **Frankie**
> Into the meeting with Melissa Bailey.

Charlotte
Nooooo. It's today??

> **Frankie**
> Yesssss.

Charlotte
Report back.

I called Zoe.

'Remind me just one last time what she's like?'

'Well, her assistant Martha says she's a laugh. But can be a total pain in the neck. Desperate to prove herself, hard to engage with on any meaningful level, taste level of zero. I reckon you blind her with fashion science. Show her all the Dante editorial from the beginning as your opening gambit.'

'Okay. This'll be interesting. Wish me luck. Will report back as soon as I'm done. Oh, I'm here already.'

I pulled up outside a purposefully modest white stucco building squeezed into a terrace up a side street. I examined the buzzers. 'Magnificent Management' – I pressed it and a voice came through the intercom.

'Hello?'

'Hi, it's Frankie from GGC. Here to see Melissa Bailey.'

'Second floor, I'll buzz you in.'

The door was released, and I walked into an unassuming front entrance with one lift. I decided to take the stairs instead of waiting, and climbed them with purpose. I reached the door with a large 'Magnificent' logo. It was off the latch and I walked directly into a room with a reception desk.

'Hi, Frankie to see Melissa.'

'Take a seat. I'll let her know you're here,' said the entirely disinterested girl behind the desk. 'Would you like something to drink while you wait?' she added with what sounded like a sigh.

I did her a favour. 'No, I'm fine, thanks.'

As I sat down in a large cream leather armchair, I sank so deeply that I knew immediately it was going to be impossible to achieve a graceful rise back to my feet. On the coffee table were piles of magazines, cover stories of other Magnificent Management clients, gossip weeklies featuring babies and houses and weddings and divorces.

'Come with me,' said the girl from behind the desk.

I clumsily heaved myself out of the sunken depths of the chair, put my crossbody bag back on, and clutching the pitch documents carefully, followed her down a narrow, quiet corridor into an equally quiet and surprisingly small meeting room with terrible overhead office strip lighting. My stomach was churning.

Melissa Bailey was sitting at the head of a small white Formica meeting table, with an enormous black telephone in the middle, a bottle of alkaline water, two glasses, a container of paper straws and a flickering fig-scented candle.

'Hi.' She extended her hand, smiling. 'Thanks for coming to see me.'

'No problem, really glad to be here.'

I could feel the treacherous onset of a blaze in my cheeks as I carefully took off my bag, lowered myself into the seat and positioned the pitch documents on the table in front of me, trying to stop the slight tremor in my hands. And then I finally got a good look at the infamous Melissa Bailey. My God, she was tiny. Much smaller than she looked in the pictures. Scarlet red bob. Wonderful boobs, or a great push-up bra. Huge diamond ring. Fat watch. And terrible, no, not just terrible – utterly unspeakable clothes. One-shoulder black top with a diamanté situation across the chest line and, from what I could make out from my vantage point, shiny black satin hot pants and platform-heel shoes.

'So, the thing is, I'm sure you know I did a great collaboration last year with Satsumi Satins.' She stroked her abominable shorts. 'It did really well. But now I'm ready to do my own thing. I've got great ideas and Cole – my manager – has found backing for me to get this off the ground pretty quickly.' Melissa started talking at pace, sipping her water through a straw in between breaths, at which point the door swung open and a quite peculiar-looking man entered the room. He had what I could only describe later as helmet hair, swept back and so wet with gel he looked like he'd just been caught in a monsoon. He wore a pale pink shirt with a frightening sheen which was, wholly inappropriately, open two buttons too many.

'Hi. Sorry to interrupt. Cole Fisher. I just wanted to come in and say hi and thanks so much for coming in.' He didn't extend a hand but instead came around to my chair and squeezed my shoulder. *Strange.* 'I believe in Melissa and her vision. I really feel if we think outside of the box and commit ourselves to getting her out there, it can become a reality. We need expertise and we believe we need you and GGC. But I've got to run. I'm due at the recording of my new show, *Animals at Altitude.* So great to meet you. Melissa, this is all *magnificent*, I love you and I'll call you later. Leave you two ladies to it.'

And with that, he spun on what I highly suspected were stack heels and left the room. I was so taken aback I had to remember to start breathing again.

'Maybe I can run you through how it works, and you can tell me where you are with everything?' My voice was ever so slightly shaking but at least my cheeks were back to normal thanks to Cole's interlude. 'So, GGC is actually fairly small. Everyone thinks there's loads of us because we get such good results. But in reality, there are two core teams. Georgina isn't someone you would see very often but she's ALWAYS there to give an opinion and an overview of any strategy. What you would get is me, my Senior Account Director, our other Account Director, our Account Manager, and a great position in our showroom, which press are in and out of all day long.'

Suddenly Melissa interrupted and beamed. 'Cole is SO supportive. Isn't he great?'

'Oh yes, yes, he seems great. Really enthusiastic.' I fixed a smile.

'So.' Melissa banged her manicured hands on the table. 'What do you think?'

'Do you want me to finish telling you more about GGC?' I queried. 'Or maybe you can tell me about what the vision is for your collections? Or here, this is the press book for Dante. They've been a huge success story.'

Melissa waved the book away as her mobile phone started ringing.

'No, no need. I'm a very spiritual person. My instinct tells me we'll get along just great. I always go with my astrological readings. Do you go with yours? What's your star sign? Can you go away and have a think about what you can do for me and let's meet again next week? You can talk about fees with Cole's team. I really have to take this call.' I could see the name 'Martha' flashing up.

'Hi. Hold on,' she spoke into the phone and whispered across to me, 'Can you see yourself out? Would you mind? Great to meet you.' And with that she turned away, speaking rapid fire into the line.

'Look, I really need a facial today. Can you see if she can do it at five thirty p.m.? Then Brian could come to the house to do my hair. I know I said tomorrow morning, but now I'm going out for dinner. No, I don't need make-up, I can do it myself, but can you call the house and ask Loretta to get out the black satin suit hanging in the furthest cupboard on the left and steam it for me? And you know what, I won't like the food tonight. Can Chef please prepare some papaya for me? One sliced. One cubed. One scooped into little balls. Thanks.'

I tuned into the conversation as I picked up my things and exited the room. As I walked back past the girl on reception and out the door, I started to gather my thoughts. A lightbulb went on in my head. *Melissa Bailey was magnificent*. That is, she was a magnificent gift for me. I wanted this. *Who wouldn't?* She was the greatest PR experiment of all time. She was globally famous, slightly ridiculous and she wanted a foothold in fashion. I quickly texted Charlotte again. Always my first port of call for significant news and gossip.

> **Frankie**
> Fascinating.

> **Charlotte**
> Like what?

> **Frankie**
> Tiny. Preposterous. Badly dressed. But nothing that can't be fixed. I will learn to love her.

> **Charlotte**
> Shame you can't fix the childrens' names.

> **Frankie**
> I will learn to love those names too.

> **Frankie**
> By the way, what's my star sign?

I pressed last number dialled, skipping past a series of 'good luck' and then 'how did it go' messages from James. I'd talk to him later.

'Well?' Zoe asked as she picked up the phone.

'She's sort of absurd. Literally has no idea what she's walking into. But intriguing too. And I reckon she's clever. This could be huge. I was strangely mesmerised by her. Will you call Martha and get any feedback? Although I do know she's in the middle of organising a facial, some papaya, a blow-dry and an outfit change for Melissa. I'm coming back to the office now. We need to talk to everyone about it. But I think we should do it if she wants us. And we should do it together. She's going to need everything we've got.'

'Oh God, Frankie. Okay, I'm in.'

We had absolutely no idea what we were getting ourselves into.

PRESS NOTE

Today the greatest PR lunch of Frankie Marks' career thus far took place at the highly lauded Cinquecento in Mayfair. She stunned both her client and the invited editor with her electric company and sparkling wit. It was truly a lunch to remember.

'I was fascinated to note how Frankie managed to eat a full-fat pasta dish with no hint of shame. It was a remarkable achievement, and something I will take away with me – and that will sit on her thighs – for some time to come,' gushed Amanda Starling, Editor-in-Chief of Avalon *magazine.*

ENDS

It didn't take long to negotiate with Cole Fisher. Melissa wanted GGC. She decided she wanted me specifically, for reasons that were still not entirely clear.

'It's all about star signs,' I insisted to anyone who asked.

I got to work on her very fast. There was a lot of ground to cover and not a lot of time if Melissa really wanted to do a proper collection for next season. The head designer at Celia Johns was summarily poached for a hefty can't-say-no salary increase and a backhander pay-off to release her from any gardening leave. The floor below the Magnificent offices was secured and remodelled as studios and more office space at record speed. I spent the first month explaining why we had taken her on as a client to aghast key members of the press.

'She has a vision. Yes, a good vision.'

'You'll be so surprised. Of *course* pleasantly.'

'She's not how you imagine. No, not like that at all. She's a Scorpio. With Aries rising.'

'She wants to do this properly. We're excited! Yes, really.'

'We can do this,' I had announced to Melissa one night – eight vodkas later and horizontal on one of the enormous satin pouffes in her magnificent drawing room, wearing a pair of her giant sunglasses. It was just one of the many planning nights we had spent together that always seemed to end up like this. I discovered she was complex – funny, annoying, clever, stupid and generous. She found out I loved to eat, had a short fuse and did a brilliant Bradley Cooper impression. Turned out we liked each other. A lot.

'I can do this,' I had whispered to James one night as I started to panic, lying in the dark.

'C'mon, Frankie, are we really talking about that woman again?' he said.

I wondered what Greg White would have said. I hadn't heard from him since the shoot, apart from one winking emoji text with a screenshot of my heavily retouched ankles, to which I replied with a gif of a supermodel with hair blowing in the wind. He sent me back a laughing emoji. I couldn't decide what hilarity to reply with but as I was fiddling around, I sent back a heart. By mistake. He didn't reply. I was simultaneously humiliated and furious he hadn't fallen madly in love with me and begged me to go on a date with him, while grateful that he hadn't given me the option to. Charlotte questioned my moral compass as I talked about his teeth on a more than regular basis. But the fact was that I had a fully blown, needed a poster on my wall, was-thinking-about-someone-else-during-sex crush. It didn't help that I felt

James slightly withdrawing too. He had given up making bad jokes about my work ever since I signed Melissa. Instead, he pointedly tried not to talk about it at all. I couldn't work out whether to be relieved or even more offended.

Luckily Melissa Bailey was an excellent distraction. I spent a lot of time thinking about her, and wondering what I could do to set the ball rolling in our favour. I needed to establish her in the fashion firmament. I had to change her public image. All preconceptions required turning on their heads. I asked my mother what she thought of her: 'Oh, I did love *Carlyle Bay*, but I don't like her hair.' Claudia from the deli: 'Literally obsessed with how absurd she is.' The dry cleaner: 'I liked that last film her husband was in.'

I realised I needed her endorsed by just one major player in the fashion industry. *The* major player. And fast.

My fingers hovered over the keyboard. Yes, I was going to do it. I was going to email Amanda Starling – who I knew had scathingly and publicly belittled Melissa's fashion sense at *Avalon* magazine, along with the rest of the industry, over the years. I was going to show all the detractors that I had made the right decision taking her on to our books.

I started to type.

Hi Amanda,
Hope you're really well.
I had a thought – I hope you don't mind me asking – but would you be interested in lunch with Melissa Bailey? I'm sure you know we've just taken her on as a client and I wanted you to be the first editor to meet her.
Not a problem if you're not interested. Just thought it was worth putting in the ask.
Have a great weekend.
Thanks,
Frankie (GGC)

My hands shook, poised over the send button. After conducting my rudimentary market research and taking into account the press and retailers' reactions, I had come up with a plan which had been discussed endlessly with everyone in the office, who agreed. I shook as I contemplated the send button. I took a deep breath. I pressed.

This excellently developed strategy was totally reliant on three things: that the *Avalon* team returned every awful rhinestone-embellished top from Melissa's diabolical collaboration with Satsumi Satins from their fashion cupboard, to erase them from memory; my new and enhanced belief in horoscopes; and my hope that Amanda Starling wouldn't be able to resist a meeting with the infamous Melissa Bailey. And if I prepped Melissa properly, and if we played it right, then I could begin to implement the plan I had been hatching.

Dear Frankie,
Yes, why not.
Email Sarah my PA to put in a date.
Amanda

To my surprise, the reply came in quickly and was promising. To no surprise it was short and to the point.

My instinct had been right. Thank God. Because I really had put everything on the line for this one. Amanda's curiosity had got the better of her, and if I could get Melissa on the coveted front cover of *Avalon*, then I could begin to reposition and rebrand her against all the odds. This is what I'd pitched to Georgina and Nicky. They'd both made it clear they had serious doubts. Messing up wasn't an option – or this would turn into the biggest 'I told you so' humiliation of my brief career. It was sink or swim.

* * *

'What am I going to fucking wear?' I went through all the options with Zoe in the showroom, landing on a black Dixie crewneck cashmere jumper with a white faux-silk Darcy Girl shirt underneath – the collar and cuffs were fine, I just couldn't remove my jumper to reveal the bad stud buttons – and a really good pair of Dante black cord high-waist trousers. This meeting was definitely a fashion fuck-up no-go zone. As I sat in the back of the black cab on route to Mayfair, I went through everything one more time. I had meticulously mapped out the lunch. The location, Cinquecento, the busiest, trendiest place of the moment (for maximum impact); the table, furthest in the corner so Melissa had the longest walk possible through the restaurant (for maximum impact); the timing – late lunch so the room was buzzing (for maximum impact). And, saving the most important for last, the briefing. I had spent hours bringing Melissa up to speed on Amanda's husband, her children, where she lived, what she liked, what she didn't like, and a host of miscellaneous titbits she could use to initiate conversation if it lagged. It was bad form for the PR to be forced to interject a painful silence. I mean, I would do it if absolutely necessary, but Melissa had been enthusiastic – she knew Amanda's influence spread far and wide, and that she could make or break a designer. Now I could only hope she had taken it all on board. I was quietly confident. Melissa knew how to learn lines.

'Don't worry, Frankie. I won't forget a thing,' she had assured me as she chewed on some dried papaya the day before.

In the restaurant, I felt sick with nerves. I thought I might throw up. I'd arrived early, so by the time Amanda got there I had already crumbled a whole basket of bread, strewing crumbs everywhere as my eyes darted nervously to the door and my stomach churned. Amanda had arrived on the dot of two p.m. and graciously ignored the table destruction as she sat down. She was unexpectedly amiable. Perhaps I'd really been right about the pull-power of Melissa? As we chatted about how great Georgina was looking after her latest spa break in the Swiss Alps, I had to stop myself from constantly checking the door as I waited for Melissa to make her entrance. When she did, it was exactly as I had told her. Ten minutes late. So that Amanda could see the reaction of the other diners as she walked into the restaurant. What I really needed was for Amanda to think she'd had the idea, that was actually my idea, that had always been the idea I hoped Amanda would have.

The glass door swung open, and there she was. Melissa's red hair was immaculately blow-dried. She wore a green sequinned one-shoulder cocktail dress, topped off with a brown fur cape, vertiginous black stilettos and giant aviator sunglasses. And as she walked in, every table fell silent and every meal paused. I watched Amanda as she too paused and watched. I knew I had done it before Melissa even sat down. The relief – and a touch of smugness – was real. My utter astonishment that she had chosen evening wear for a lunch appointment was temporarily parked. Now I could enjoy my food. As per usual, I was starving.

In truth, had there not been so much at stake, it would have been one of those instantly forgettable chit-chatty PR lunches. Melissa remembered everything I had told her and effortlessly asked questions about Amanda's children as she picked at some prawns and Amanda nibbled on a rocket salad. I demolished a creamy ham tagliatelle as I sat silently as an observer only. I could have been on another table and they wouldn't have registered. Amanda asked polite, probing questions about how the Satsumi collaboration had come about; did Melissa ever see her *Carlyle Bay* cast members anymore and what film was Gabriel working on next? How had she come up with the delightful names of Dandelion and

Delilah, and did she miss LA now she was based in London? Did she ever want to go back to acting? How was the collection preparation going, what direction was she going in? Melissa answered cheerfully, pretending to be oblivious to the fact that she was being carefully sized up.

I discreetly summoned the waiter over to ask for the bill as they carried on talking. They didn't even notice. I was just the facilitating third wheel. Wallpaper. Neither had addressed me since we had ordered. I would use the GGC credit card and recharge it to Melissa at the end of the month. But what I had to avoid at all costs was any awkwardness at the end of the meal.

'Shall we get the bill?' Amanda looked up from her Americano as the waiter took my card. It was purely rhetorical, as this was just her signal that lunch was now over.

'It's all taken care of.' I smiled beatifically.

'That's very kind. And Melissa, it was a pleasure to meet you.'

'Of course, this was my invitation,' I replied to no one in particular, as the two women were already walking out to their respective waiting cars.

Remember me? I suggested this. I organised it. My idea? Oh, and by the way, it's annoying I didn't get to have the tiramisu.

'How was that? She seemed nice. Did I say the right things? What star sign do you think she is?' Melissa called me from her car a nanosecond after we said goodbye.

'You were brilliant. I'll call you later.' I was being genuine. When she put her mind to it, my God she showed how astute she was. She had handled that encounter with admirable aplomb. I was feeling tentatively triumphant; I knew this was a defining moment for my career. For Melissa. For affirmation from Georgina that she had been right to let me take this account.

It's done. I messaged Zoe as I stood in the biting wind trying to hail a cab. *On my way back.*

She wore an evening dress. To lunch. Charlotte needed to know this important detail.

I would tell James about my lack of pudding later and hope he'd find it in the realms of amusing.

Three hours later I was sitting at my desk, eating a Snickers in lieu of the tiramisu I never got to order. I'd described the lunch in rapturous detail to the team, but it was back to business as usual and I was beginning to feel a bit flat now my bravado had dissipated. I was more than slightly hysterically worried that maybe I'd got it wrong. Jemima and Zoe were debating who would take the show-room appointment waiting downstairs. Andrew was having an argument with *Lancashire Living* about why they couldn't have a Dante top for a shoot, and Nicky had chosen not to come back from her sushi lunch with the Executive Editor of *Madame*.

Suddenly my direct line starting ringing and I saw the *Avalon* number appear on its screen. My heart lurched as I reached for the receiver.

'Frankie, Amanda.'

'Hi, Amanda.' My heart was now pounding.

'Look, I have an idea,' she drawled. 'I want to shoot Melissa for the cover of *Avalon* in a way no one has seen her before. For the February issue. That will come on stand in January, but it will still be there for her first show.'

As I started to gush down the line, she cut me dead. 'Thanks. Speak soon.' She hung up.

No matter and no shame, because BINGO. I was up and running. I screamed and did a celebratory circuit of the office, throwing my Snickers wrapper in the air.

'OhmyGodOhmyGodOhmyGod. What have I done? What have I just gone and done?!!'

'What have you done, Frankie?' Georgina appeared in the doorway, still in the office surprisingly late.

'Oh God, Georgina. I'm sorry. But I've only gone and got the cover of *Avalon* for Melissa!' I picked up the wrapper from the floor sheepishly.

'I'm impressed.' Georgina smiled. I had never seen her smile quite so overtly and as I considered my triumph, she tightened her mouth again. 'Right, Debbie, I'm going home. Can you call my car? I won't be in tomorrow. Anyone got anything else I need to know before I leave?'

Georgina's playbook was well rehearsed. Bark orders. Tell some jokes. Be kind. Be a bitch. Always demand one hundred per cent. Always keep the team on tenterhooks in case she spontaneously appeared, requesting full updates and briefing on current status quo, upon which she seemed to hold a miraculously detailed handle. Oh, and never give out too much praise.

'Your car's here,' Debbie called out.

Georgina waved a vague goodbye to the office and was gone. I felt deflated. Was that all she could say? Couldn't she make an exception just this once, and single me out for a most brilliant job well done?

'If she says she's impressed, I'd take it and live off it for the next month. That's Georgina-speak for "an amazing job", Frankie. Well done. You've done something brilliant.' Andrew had noticed the dismay I'd not been able to hide from my crestfallen face, and stepped into Georgina's vacuum.

I shot him a grateful glance and pulled myself together with a shrug. *Big girl pants, Frankie.* Georgina had taken a risk on me and it was starting to pay off.

'What's going on with you anyway? You've been strangely quiet recently,' I asked Andrew, as it dawned on me this was the first time I had seen him all week. His disappearing acts hadn't abated. No one liked doing external press appointments *that* much. No journalists liked seeing PRs that much, come to think of it.

'Me, no? I've just got a lot on my mind. Stuff. You know.'

I didn't know. Because Andrew was telling stories that were either just too far-fetched to be believed or he wasn't telling any at all. Which was even stranger.

I looked over at Zoe. She raised an eyebrow quizzically. I looked at Jemima. She looked down at her notebook too quickly. With a small flick of my head I gestured Zoe to look at Jemima. She had belied herself unwittingly.

So, what was going on?

PRESS NOTE

Frankie Marks is delighted to announce Melissa Bailey has shot her first cover for Avalon *magazine after a series of mutually beneficial discussions about tutus. The way she lay on duvets was unsurpassed.*

'Our February cover is iconic. It unveils Melissa Bailey in a way that no one has ever seen her before, once more cementing Avalon*'s visionary creativity,' commented the very pleased-with-herself-Amanda Starling, Editor-in-Chief of* Avalon.

ENDS

James had gone on a boys trip to see some European football match and tagged on a couple of days in Amsterdam, leaving me with the flat to myself. I was hoping he'd come back in such a stoned haze he'd have forgotten the night he came in to find me pacing the floor in a panic about the spot Melissa had on her cheek that was threatening to erupt pre shoot day.

The spot had thankfully gone down after an emergency visit to the dermatologist and I wanted to be on set early. Amanda Starling never came on shoots. She always left her team to it. But not today. The transformation of Melissa Bailey was an event she wasn't going to miss. She had cleared her diary and I was ready for her. I had spent weeks working on every detail with the *Avalon* team. We'd had to get this shoot together in record time and put everything on fast forward in order to be ready for the print deadline for the February issue.

'Amanda would like Charlie Simcox to photograph Melissa. Kathy Newell, our Senior Fashion Director, will style. Sergio Knight has agreed to do hair, and Mei Zhang is flying in to do make-up. We're going to build a set in a studio. Amanda and Charlie want a creative direction that will surprise everyone. Our Art Director will be on set all day too.'

I was on the phone to the Photo Editor.

'Can I possibly talk to Kathy before she starts working on the styling boards?'

I emailed the publisher. I needed contracts drawn up. I couldn't have the images or interview sold to anyone without being asked. I couldn't have them doing any PR on the story without being involved. I had discussed the intricacies and possible pitfalls at length with Georgina and she had pointed out what I needed to look out for. Now I was staring at a PDF of looks Kathy was calling in for Melissa to be shot in: Victoriana nightdresses; couture creations of powder-pink silk. Some Dante looks from the last show. Some Celia Johns. Platform lace-up boots, net leggings. I could see where this was going.

Can we please avoid Celia Johns? It's going to cause problems.

Kathy replied.

Well, not really. But let's see on the day.

I needed to explain it all to Melissa.

'I need you to be REALLY open-minded,' I said as I started showing her the proposed looks. 'Remember, they want people to gasp when they see it. And because it's *Avalon*, you're not going to have the control over the images or the styling that you're probably used to.'

'Are they serious? Couture tutus with DMs?'

'You're just going to have to go with it. Charlie Simcox is whimsical. The pictures will be so soft. You have an incredible hair and make-up team. You won't recognise yourself.'

Melissa took a purposeful sip of her alkaline water.

'You'd better be right, Frankie. This is going to be the most important shoot I've ever done.'

You're welcome, I thought. Instead I nodded in vehement agreement that I mustn't get anything wrong. Although, quite frankly, a tutu with DMs was probably preferable to the skin-tight jersey body-con dress with slash shoulder details she was currently wearing with five-inch-heeled black lizard-print ankle boots.

At the shoot, set designers stood on ladders putting the finishing touches to a woodland-themed backdrop. Trellises and roses and chaises longues and beds were artfully positioned all over the room. Charlie Simcox was looking at the monitor with *Avalon*'s Art Director.

'We can start with this, I think,' he was saying as Charlie nodded while looking from monitor to set and back again.

'Sergio, when she gets here, can you tell her Amanda wants to dye that nuclear-red hair back to a dirty blond? I don't care how long it takes, we can shoot into the night if we have to. Kathy, I think we should start with the long pink dress. Set against this corner with the bed. Guys, I'm going to need an extra duvet. For depth.'

I took a deep breath and sauntered over.

'Hi, Frankie from GGC. I'm with Melissa,' I introduced myself.

'Oh, you're *that* Frankie,' Charlie said, giving me the once-over. 'Greg seems to rate you,' he said under his breath, shaking his head and smiling. *Greg had mentioned me? SUCK IN YOUR CHEEKS, FRANKIE*. I flicked my hair in my best girlish who-me-oh-I'm-just-an-unexpectedly-attractive-shoe-model-despite-my-swollen-ankles kind of way.

Kathy, the Fashion Director who was styling the shoot, came running up holding a pink neon leotard. As you do.

'Guys, I really think we should start with this. With the boots. She's got an amazing body, and this will be easier for her to get in the mood. Less fabric to worry about framing around her.' She turned to me. 'Hi, Frankie, how are you? Can't believe we've actually made it. Today's the day!' Kathy was warm. Kathy smoked. Kathy would be my friend in real life.

'Cannot believe it. It's so exciting. Oh, here's Martha. She's Melissa's PA.' I waved at Martha who had entered the studio.

'Hi, everyone. Melissa's here. She's just in the car on a call. Where's her area?' Martha asked.

A girl from production with a headset ran over. 'This is her space.' She showed her a small seating area with a coffee machine, a lit candle and a bunch of white roses.

'Perfect,' said Martha. 'I've brought some extra food that wasn't on her rider. Can you show me the fridge? I've also got some of her clothes that she needs for later; can someone put them on a rail for me? And her iPod with her playlist. Is there a docking station?'

'Can we talk about hair?' I asked. 'If she agrees to dyeing it, what are you thinking?'

Sergio got out a series of reference images. 'Soft. A slight wave. Almost a young Marilyn Monroe. Dreamy. A total contrast to what it looks like now.'

Amanda Starling walked up behind us unannounced. 'And then I need her to wear a hat out in public for three months until we're on stand, so the new hair is a surprise when the cover comes out,' she added, as if it were the most normal request in the world.

I looked at Martha quizzically. I continued to hold it together as Amanda continued.

'Love the set. Love the rails, Kathy. Let's get her in the bloody studio so we can start on the hair . . .'

'MORNING!!'

Melissa had arrived. Dusty-pink velour tracksuit, sunglasses, luminous yellow trainers and a giant logo Louis Vuitton tote bag.

'I am SO excited. I can't believe it. Hi, everyone.' She went around the studio shaking everyone's hand.

'So, what we want, Melissa, is to dye your hair to a dirty blond. Would you be okay with that?' Amanda was telling, not asking.

Melissa looked at me. I nodded.

'Do whatever you want with me, Amanda.'

I would break the news about the hat situation later.

I had been floating around between the dressing area and out front as tints had gone on her hair and manicures, pedicures, tonging and eyebrow brushing had been applied. When Melissa emerged on set four hours later, I gasped. The scarlet hair was gone. In its place was a featherlight blond wave masterfully created by Sergio. Mei had created a soft dewy face, blush-pink lips, smoky eyes. Melissa was unrecognisable. She looked sensational. Kathy's assistant took her robe off her to reveal the pink leotard matched with platform boots and a white fishnet tight. Who was I to argue with Kathy Newell?

Melissa was positioned on the double bed. Kathy fiddled with the leotard neckline. Mei dabbed some highlighter on the bridge of her nose, Sergio placed a curl of hair just so over her forehead, and the Art Director issued instructions to his assistants from the monitor as Charlie started taking his preliminary shots of the set-up and scrutinised the images.

'Push those two pillows further up. Maybe let's lose the trellis over the right-hand side of the headboard. Plump that duvet. Actually, let's get a third duvet on there. Really cocoon her.'

'Melissa, if you could just move up to the right a bit, let's have your left leg slightly straighter. And if you can put your left hand just across your stomach. Yes, exactly, perfect,' yelled Charlie over the eighties R&B playlist.

'Hold on,' Kathy said, 'we're missing something. I need more jewellery. Get me the jewellery table.'

Kathy's two assistants ran to the dressing area and emerged scurrying sideways, holding the small trestle table displaying jewellery options. Kathy spent a few minutes placing rings on and off. On again. Finally, she settled on a giant diamond skull on Melissa's middle finger. That ring was worth a fortune. We knew this because it had been sent accompanied by its own security, who would have to sit and wait in a room with the other jewellery-brand security guys until the end of the shoot to carry their respective wares back with them. Even if they were never shot. The enormous power of an *Avalon* front cover was evident simply by the sheer number of these security guys sitting there in their suits staring at their phones or the ceiling for the entire duration of the day. Each jewellery house was prepared to have them sit it out.

'Okay. We're ready. Just move around a bit, Melissa. I'll keep snapping. Let's see where we get to. Oh beautiful. Amazing. That's incredible. Wow,' Charlie enthused.

Amanda was watching the monitor with a small smile. She knew what she was creating. We could all see the transformation of Melissa Bailey happening before our eyes. I felt exalted. And it was only shot one.

'You look unbelievable,' I said to Melissa quietly as we walked off set for her next change of clothes.

'Really?'

'Really. This is going to blow everyone's mind.'

I also recognised that I was feeling a sense of pride. In Melissa. I was so proud of her, I could burst. And in myself. I had seen an opportunity that others couldn't or wouldn't. I had concocted a strategy for her, I had implemented it and I was now seeing it come to life. *This was what it was all about,* I thought to myself as I watched Melissa step into a tutu while a pair of giant DMs were laced by two assistants at her feet. It was a form of artistry. It occurred to me that perhaps all those years learning how to look beyond the surface in the history of art had paid off after all, as I witnessed these very different types of artists work their craft.

We went from tutus to pink organza, diamonds, pearls, a veil, roses, more duvets, circumnavigating a Celia Johns full-length white spaghetti-strap dress – which I had to concede was incredible, but alas, just too big for Melissa's tiny frame. No seamstress was going to be able to fix it and no amount of bull clips could make it workable. *Such a shame,* I nodded sympathetically to Kathy as I relished in Dominic Carter losing such a great piece of editorial.

I pushed an extreme Dante padded-shoulder sequinned jacket as far as I could without looking subjective, until even I had to relent and accept it didn't work. I would have to explain that to Nicky and Andrew later. But I was so swept up in the magic of the shoot, the way Charlie Simcox was capturing Melissa, the sets she was being shot in, the skill of the hair and make-up, that I spent the rest of the day smiling inanely and almost hopping from side to side.

'That's incredible!'

'Oh, just look at how phenomenal her legs look!'

'Look up, Melissa!'

We all took turns with our expressions of joy. I had my

hand on Kathy's shoulder at one point, squeezing it with excitement each time a new shot came up on the monitor. Every time we went back for an outfit change, we were smiling even more.

Martha stayed in the green room on her laptop working. She fed and watered Melissa whenever she could. She knew when she was getting hungry, dehydrated, or needed to check her phone. The way Martha managed her was impressive. Melissa's mood never wavered. I had never been so grateful for the support. Martha was a true professional. And perhaps a mind reader.

'That's a wrap!' Charlie shouted out, some eight hours later. 'Go and get changed Melissa, and let's look at some of the images together. I'll bring them up on the screen. Won't take me long.'

Once Melissa had got back into her tracksuit, we all crowded around the monitor. The Art Director had done a quick select throughout the day of the best of each shot. He had mocked up a cover option while we had all eaten a hurried lunch earlier.

'What do you think?' he asked as he brought up a portrait shot: eyes to camera, head slightly tilted to the side, roses in soft focus in the background, diamond drop earrings just visible through the soft blond curls. He dragged down the *Avalon* masthead and positioned it at the top of the image. I felt my nose go red – and was that an actual tear in my eye? But it was extraordinary. I grabbed Melissa's hand. She was shaking. Amanda nodded silently.

We all knew. She knew it. I knew it. Amanda knew it. We had done it.

PRESS NOTE

GGC are happy to confirm that the Fashion Week schedule comes together with a click of the finger. Slots are always easy to get, money is never in short supply, humiliating conversations never have to happen.

'I was delighted to investigate chocolate sponsors and beg the organisers of Fashion Week to give us the Tuesday morning slot for Dixie Triton. These key negotiations are what make us grow as a team,' commented Andrew Davies, Account Director, GGC.

ENDS

Georgina banged down her Mont Blanc fountain pen. It was late November. The cover shoot was now in post-production. With hindsight, I realised that had been the easy bit. Now we had to plan the show.

'London Fashion Week is in three months. Make that technically only two, taking into account Christmas and New Year when nothing will happen. We absolutely *have* to have the following show slots: Sunday morning for Melissa. Doesn't matter when. But after nine a.m. Sunday, eight p.m. for Dante as usual; Tuesday ten a.m. for Dixie. I actually don't care what time, as long as it's early enough that the press and buyers won't all have pissed off to Milan already. Just to reiterate, Dixie can't go on Monday. She'll never get the models. Too many big shows and they'll be paying too much for her to compete to get anyone good. Yes? Understood?'

Georgina leant back in her chair and closed her eyes. The schedule negotiations were delicate and required military precision. We needed to take into account when the fashion crowd would get back in from New York and when they would leave again for the first shows in Milan, which was their next stop. We had to know which shows were happening on each day. Who would potentially buy out the top models and keep them on exclusives, precluding other designers from using them. We had to establish where the shows immediately before ours would be taking place, consider the journey time, and work out how late a show would run if the show before was late and on the other side of London. And most importantly, we had to try not to go on the same day as a show that would potentially get more press than ours and steal the next day's front pages. That wasn't just based on their collections. That had just as much to do with how many celebrities they had persuaded to sit front row. It was a cutthroat business. It had never ceased to amaze me over the past couple of years how, during Fashion Week, fashion PRs stopped pretending to be pleasant and became ruthless mercenaries, hell-bent on taking down their opponents – other PRs and their designers. And for us, it was GGC versus Five Star. Ding ding. Let the battle commence.

I scanned the team, who were all frantically scribbling notes and tapping their phones. I stopped doodling and wrote down some *important notes* with asterisks.

'You all know the score. Make it happen. Reconvene this time next week when the relevant conversations have been had. We need to option everyone and everything fast. Before Dominic bloody Carter gets a hint of any of our plans and teams. Understood? And who's been eating eggs in the office again? We've got press coming in today. Someone, please – light more candles.' Georgina was in hurricane mode, and we were all feeling the pressure.

Every designer needed a sponsor. Everyone needed a unique venue. Every client believed they took precedence. It was an almighty headache. And this time we also had Melissa's first show, and all eyes would be on us. Or, more specifically, on me. I was half excited, half terrified but itching to get started and get it done. Then, once I had planned a show, I could help James with his plans for a long-standing weekend away with friends, that helpfully coincided with our sixth anniversary.

'You know, I heard that new chocolate-free chocolate company were looking to get involved in a show,' Andrew piped up. 'They could be good for Dixie. I'll call up their marketing team. I'll probably go and meet with them.'

'Another meeting outside the office? Fine. Just remember, no one wants to have a model eating a non-chocolate chocolate down the runway or anything like that. Any sponsor can have a credit on the invitation, two front-row seats, four standing, backstage access, and promise them an invite to any party,' Georgina barked as she swept out of the room.

'*My Style* is here.' The intern appeared at the side of my desk. 'I've put them in the showroom.'

The showroom was now full of summer samples. November shoots meant February and March issues, so the beginning of the Spring/Summer editorial season. Dixie shawl-collared, belted, lightweight trench coats; Giovanni Castani gladiator sandals; Samira's signature raffia beach bags and a Darcy Girl rail full of . . . well, just a lot of fine pure merino that wasn't quite pure or fine, and a significant number of conversational prints – absurd objects on repeat throughout a garment. I found the watermelons on a pair of cargo trousers particularly disturbing – and quite frankly a conversation stopper. The entire Dante rail had gone to Italy for an Italian *Avalon* special. We wouldn't see it again for a week, but the shoot was worth the gamble that we might lose other potential stories.

'Hey, Susannah, so good to see you.' I leant in for a kiss to greet the Fashion Director of *My Style*, one of the new genre of independent magazines created for millennials that gave them a 'new and unbiased point of view with a fashion-forward twist'. This could be translated as 'producing shoots and content in dark alleys using interesting props and models we found in the local laundrette'.

Susannah was true to form in a red spandex top, eye-wateringly tight drainpipe stonewashed jeans, high-top train-ers and a Sainsbury's shopping bag in place of a handbag.

'You look great,' I said brightly.

'Thanks. I'm trying to be sustainable,' she replied, holding up the shopping bag with no hint of irony.

'So what stories are you working on?' I started moving across the showroom. 'No Dante, I'm afraid. But look over here at Dixie Triton. She's completely underrated, in my opinion, and she's inspired so many of the new designers working now. I think it's time for someone to take the collec-tion and run with it.' I lifted out a pair of green houndstooth check silk trousers with an enormous turn-up. 'I mean, I would style these with a vintage tee and trainers. Whereas someone else would wear the matching jacket' – I pulled that out of the rail too – 'a shirt, and heels.'

Susannah nodded as she felt the fabric. 'They feel good. And I do have a load of great vintage I pulled in from that new place on Portobello. The story is a girl doing her laundry late at night.'

Surprise, surprise.

'Great concept. Okay, well, have a look through the rail and pull out anything you think can work, and then I wanted to show you the new Samira K raffia bags – they're incredible. And check out the Darcy Girl collection of balloon prints. They're fun. And you know what, how about some of the Jessy swimwear? You could use them as bodysuits.'

I took a step back and started checking my phone as I left her to peruse. This was the way it worked best. Put some ideas in their head and pretend it's total coincidence when they walk out with a few Dixie suits, some raffia clutches and a backless black swimsuit.

As Susannah placed the items in my hands, I hung them on the empty rail for call-outs so they could be taken up to Eloise.

'It's interesting – I called in a whole load of Darcy Girl for that story we shot on those four sisters from Warrington in their grandparents' front room. You know, the one that hadn't been touched since the seventies?' I did remember. It was actually a great shoot and I had been frustrated when I saw that they hadn't used any of our clients. 'But I never got a single thing. Literally nothing. We called to chase, but the girl in your sample room kept saying they were on their way. We gave up in the end.'

'Shit. They must have all been held up somewhere else,' I lied. 'I'm so sorry. I'll personally make sure all of this gets put on a courier to you today.'

I ushered her out and marched up to the sample room to find Eloise.

'Why didn't *My Style* get the Darcy pieces they called in?' I almost shouted. 'It was so embarrassing. And we missed a great piece of editorial. What's going on?'

Eloise turned to me, tight-lipped, and I could see a flush coming up on her cheeks, but whether in anger or embarrassment I couldn't tell.

'There's a lot going on in here, Frankie, as you can see.' She waved around at all the samples: hangers held together with pieces of paper pierced through the top of them indicating where they were due to be sent. 'It must have got delayed being collated.'

'Not okay, Eloise. Really not cool. If we lost Darcy Girl, we'd all be fucked. If you're feeling swamped, then ask one of us to help?' Now I was going red in the face. I hated to be confrontational at work, but this was just one miss too many and I was furious.

'Help? You want to do this job?'

'I've always told you I'd help you out. You never reach out. Frankly, for the life of me, I can't understand what the hell you're still doing here.' Now I really was shouting. Jemima came down the stairs.

'What's the shouting for?' she asked.

'She's fucked up again! What is her problem?'

'Frankie, calm down.' Jemima put her hand on my back. 'Georgina will hear you.'

'Let her!' I didn't calm down; now the floodgates were opened, there was no holding me back. I had learned how to curb my tongue and my temper, but when I blew, I blew. 'The whole situation is a joke. She keeps making really damaging mistakes. No one does anything about it. I'm sick of it.' I yelled up the stairs for the intern, who came running down. 'There's a call-in for *My Style*. I've left it on the rail downstairs. Please can you pack it up and send it this afternoon for me?'

I made a mental note to bypass Eloise from now on. I would let the intern deal with all of my client send-outs. I wasn't taking any more risks.

'And this isn't finished, Eloise. It's not rocket science.'

With that, I turned and stomped up the stairs into the office, leaving Jemima to manage whatever I had left behind.

'She wasn't upset, really. Like she didn't care.' Jemima was back at her desk relaying her conversation with Eloise once I had been removed from the situation. 'She just shrugged. She always just shrugs. I think maybe she really is just useless.'

'I don't get it,' I said.

'We've let it go on for too long,' Nicky said.

Is that a new tattoo on her wrist? Concentrate, Frankie. Concentrate.

'Look, it's a shitty job. The conundrum is why Eloise doesn't up and leave and why Georgina keeps her here. Surely her goodwill has been stretched too far by now? I mean, the mistakes are occasional but costly. Hmmmm, I'm suspicious,' Zoe said as she looked up.

'That's what we've been saying for too long. It's all well and good that Georgina's been so magnanimous with her, friend's daughter or not . . . but I agree, Eloise is up to something. It can't be as simple as being shit at her shitty job. I'm done playing nice,' I added. 'Andrew? What do you think? You've not said a word.'

Andrew was still behaving out of sorts. He couldn't even partake in office gossip. It was so unlike him. This kind of conversation was his forte. It was disappointing, to say the least.

'Sorry. Yes, I agree. Whatever you all think,' he said, running his fingers through his meticulously coiffed quiff. 'Do you think my hair still looks good? Or shall I go for a buzz cut? Something new?'

New hair. There it was. This was our universal office alert that there was a relationship happening, ending, about to happen, going wrong, going right – but very definitely going. Andrew's predicament took my mind off Eloise immediately. I would get to the bottom of it eventually.

PRESS NOTE

A glittering event took place at exclusive private members' club The Highline in London's Notting Hill Gate last night. The exclusive soirée was in celebration of the limited-edition collection of Giovanni Castani shoes in collaboration with his dear friend and rising star Mary Foster.

'It was just such a pleasure to work on this collection with someone so dear to my heart. These things always happen organically, and for me, working with Mary was simply wonderful. Together we have created something really special,' commented a delighted and magnificently spray-tanned Giovanni after his first and last meeting with Mary.

ENDS

The designer Giovanni Castani, who had been responsible for my shoe modelling debut, had recently entered into a one-off partnership with the hot new actress Mary Foster, in order to bolster his business by way of association. Mary Foster had agreed to the partnership for a significant six-figure sum and the promise of limitless free shoes – in return for three social media posts, two print interviews and one launch event.

It had been six months in the works. After a protracted series of meetings and negotiations with her agent.

'No, Mary won't do three interviews. Two only. One glossy and one newspaper supplement. And she wants royalties on sales too. And she'll only wear Castani shoes exclusively for one season. And she can do one in-person design meeting. The rest will have to be over email. And she wants full approval over any images. Oh, and no heel height above three inches if you want her to wear them.'

Her agent had been a hard-nosed bitch. But the contract was eventually signed. The design meeting had happened. Giovanni and Mary hugged and congratulated each other as if they were lifelong friends. Zoe had arranged to have some images of them taken together. The two of them sitting over a table artfully strewn with shoes, a misty shot of them perusing a heel held aloft by Giovanni, a pensive Mary, hand on chin, holding a pen pretending to draw something. A loving double portrait in black and white. The de rigueur shot of 'close friends sharing a rare moment of relaxation in Giovanni's well-appointed kitchen'. The shoot of the shoes had also taken place. Six pairs. Two flat, one kitten, three heels. The launch date was set.

Nicky was giving us the lowdown at the end of the Monday meeting, including details of a deal with an organic Wagyu beef supplier and a mixologist sponsored by a gin brand who was happy to work for a small fee and two pairs of shoes for his girlfriend. We would do the event at The Highline, everyone's favoured party venue of the season.

'Now we just need to work out the guest list. I'm thinking two long tables of twenty-five each. Frankie, can you get Melissa to come?'

'She's become a PETA ambassador so won't eat beef, she's got a vodka deal so can't be photographed with gin, and she only wears Manolo's. Plus, she's still wearing a hat in public. So I'm going to say it's a no.'

'For fuck's sake. Okay. We need Mary to bring some guests.

We can work up the press attendees. Then we just need a few more "names", I guess.' Nicky sighed.

Georgina, who had been sitting there listening, stood up abruptly.

'Okay. Unless there's anything else, I'm going. Email me later if you think of anything we haven't discussed. And don't forget to gather all the candles at the end of the dinner for home and the office.'

And with that, Georgina was done for the day, possibly the week. We couldn't be sure until we asked Debbie later.

'I think it should be okay. But guest list, guest list, guest list,' she said as she exited the meeting room.

'Change of plan,' Nicky called out across the room the following morning, throwing her arms in the air in despair. 'Turns out Mary Foster is now out of town until mid-November. Nice of them to let us know now. She can only do first week of December. I'm calling it. December the third. Nightmare.'

A nightmare on so many levels. Nicky sighed. Zoe slammed her head on the table. My heart sank. Third of December was Charlotte's birthday, and I had already promised her I would be at the celebratory dinner. I would ABSOLUTELY NOT FORGET to send her a huge bunch of her favourite flowers with a suitably grovelling message of apology in advance, and a present she would love on the actual day. *I'll have to seriously PR myself out of this one.*

'Double fuck,' screamed Nicky as she banged her phone down. A big-name shoo-in with the papers had just cancelled her attendance at the launch party, and another's assistant had just emailed to say he had a 'slight cold' and didn't think he was going to make it. We all knew a 'slight cold' was a metaphor for 'couldn't be bothered'.

This was all par for the event course, but beyond stressful and irritating each time it happened. And quite frankly, we all felt like developing 'slight colds' at this stage.

'Pull up the seating plan,' Nicky said, 'and let's look at the gaps.'

The problem with the guest list was perennial. It didn't matter who you were, or how popular your brand was. Unless you had major money, or a best-friend group of A-listers, or a celebrity client who wasn't tied to numerous competitive deals, you were only guaranteed to get a couple of great guests and pictures. The rest of the list was superfluous. Although the client was never told that. No, as far as they were concerned, it was a list made up of London's good and great. A smattering of niche 'breakout' stars, key editors, a few influencers, one A-lister, and you were good to go.

'Right, we're still short,' Nicky announced, an hour after shifting seats and names.

'What about Greg White? He should be there. He shot the last few lookbooks,' Jemima said.

My heart stopped. I hadn't even considered that possibility. I still hadn't heard from him since my heart emoji disaster and that was a lifetime ago. A year of social media stalking had got me nowhere but humiliated.

'Shooting in Paris,' Zoe said.

My heart started beating again.

'No, back from Paris,' said Andrew, waving Greg's Instagram feed indicating his location as East London.

'And Josh Brigson. He needs to be on the list.' Jemima was scrolling a celebrity directory for inspiration. 'Big news right now. Modelling for everyone, just started acting. Great friends with Greg. Will help to invite them both.'

'What's wrong with you, Frankie? You've gone all flushed,' Zoe said.

'No, no . . . just that Stacey Powers' PR keeps emailing

me saying she's available and would love to come,' I ventured once I'd checked my pulse. Stacey Powers, the breakfast TV presenter of my inaugural Monday morning newspaper meeting faux pas. Her PR was always emailing me.

'It's a picture for the weeklies,' I went on, 'in case we have any more no-shows.'

'Fuck, I think we may just have to say yes.' Nicky's shoulders drooped. 'Yes, say yes. Then at least the seating's done, pending any last-minute crisis.'

When we arrived at the venue, the poor intern was given the thankless task of doing the door – consulting the guest list on a clipboard. I knew for her this was an internal fist pump moment. Music started playing through the sound system and Nicky looked around at the room, acknowledging a job well done.

Chris, the house photographer, arrived, his signature goatee pointing at almost a right angle.

'Chris!' Zoe embraced him. 'We need pictures of everyone: singles, doubles, full-length and portrait. Umm. Think that's pretty much it. Just the obvious – Stacey Powers on her own only. Mary and Giovanni. Mary alone. Mary and the co-stars. The co-stars on their own. Co-stars together. Josh Brigson on his own. Giovanni with Amanda Starling . . . Oh, and of course pictures of shoes, flowers, gin and beef. Don't forget the beef!'

At precisely 7.01 p.m., Stacey Powers was the first to arrive. In lemon-yellow Celia Johns, I was delighted to note. That was a picture that would be all over the internet before Dominic Carter had time to get it taken down. Let him feel the same pain we had when she had worn Dante in *Brilliant!* magazine. These were small but significant victories. Henny beamed as she stood to have her photo taken before heading over to the tables to furtively look at where she was seated (bottom left corner-of-shame, next to a German journalist who barely spoke English and was only in London for the night).

Slowly a dribble of guests started to arrive. Giovanni rocked up at 7.15, nut-brown and in a shockingly bright pink velvet suit with a purposefully clashing orange silk cravat. Mary Foster walked in at 7.30. Zoe ushered Giovanni away from the bar to have photos taken with her and her gold leather double-ankle-strap pumps. They made a great show of togetherness for three minutes, beaming and giggling for the camera, before heading to separate corners of the room and ignoring each other for the rest of the night.

Gradually the space filled up. Editors, VIPs, celebrities. They all trickled in, including Josh Brigson, the 'model slash actor' Jemima had invited, looking impossibly and casually handsome and brandishing his Castani chocolate suede driving shoes below cropped chinos. Lucy Collins, Dante's stylist, was there. Zoe and I spent a good five minutes analysing every single part of her perfect, 'just thrown together' outfit, the fact she had a zigzag parting in her hair, and appeared to be wearing no make-up but still looked unbelievable.

'She's all I aspire to be,' Zoe said reverently.

'It's not fair,' I whispered.

The volume went up as the drinks were handed around. I flitted from person to person, ensuring everyone was having a simply wonderful time and that all egos were intact. I smiled. I cooed. I congratulated. I talked about great shoots, new haircuts and the latest news, while touching arms and ushering drinks over. Then I stopped talking and apparently forgot how to breathe – Greg had walked in and immediately caught my eye, then strolled directly over.

'So good to see you,' he said holding my hand and giving me a kiss on the cheek.

'Yes,' I squealed, resisting the temptation to clasp my free hand to my heart.

'Catch you later?' I thought I saw him wink at my ankles. I let out a laugh like a nervous hyena and backed away as he smiled and went to grab Josh Brigson in a bear hug.

Georgina was one of the last to arrive. She was wearing a long black satin skirt, an oversized white cotton shirt tucked in at the front and loosely billowing at the back, a great tarnished gold pendant necklace, and a tan cashmere blazer lightly balanced on her shoulders. Even better, she was rocking a pair of Castani trainers. The second I clapped eyes on her I died of outfit envy. She was the best-dressed person in the room and emanated a halo effect of fabulous instantly.

'Sorry I'm late, sorry, sorry.' She flashed a smile as she started to circulate. 'So good to see you,' 'Oh, those shoes look GREAT on you,' 'Love your earrings. Love them.'

From the corner of my eye, I spotted the intern trying not to run but running and whispering in Nicky's ear. That could only mean someone hadn't turned up at the last minute.

'Zoe.' Nicky ushered her over. 'You're going to have to sit for dinner. Sorry.'

This was the worst thing that could happen. What we all dreaded. Being seat fillers when we just didn't have the energy to make any more conversation and had planned on milling around.

'Fuck, why me? Why not Frankie?' Zoe wailed.

'Because Frankie isn't to be trusted not to eat two bread rolls and ask for seconds. Tell you what, just move that girl from *Madame* one over and you'll be next to Josh Brigson. How's that? But don't take him completely away from Amanda. Share him.'

I wasn't offended in the slightest. It was true. I was

delighted. Now I could eat *three* bread rolls at the bar in private and stare at Greg from a good vantage point.

Zoe, in the meantime, was already walk-running to the loos, ostensibly to reapply her lipstick but muttering darkly about wearing the synthetic Darcy Girl knickers she had borrowed from the office when she had realised she needed a change of underwear to avoid VPL under her outfit for the evening. They gave her an electric shock every time she touched them. And they were the wrong side of purple. No matter. She had wriggled out of worse, she reassured us all – but that was before they started crackling with static every time a guest brushed past her.

'So really, what I just want to say to all of you is *grazie a tutti*, thank you all for being here to share this wonderful evening with me.'

Giovanni beamed and raised a glass to Mary, who remembered just in time to look up from her phone and raise hers back with a wide smile. Everyone clapped politely. Chris took his last round of photos – the golden rule always applied. No snapping while anyone was eating. No industry stalwart worth their salt wanted to have a picture circulating of themselves with a mouthful of Wagyu.

The sounds of chatter and glasses and cutlery clinking began to fill the room again. At one end of the first table, I could see Zoe throw her head back laughing and then lean into Josh Brigson, fluttering her very long lashes. On the parallel table, Georgina was in deep conversation with someone wearing chandelier earrings while Amanda had given up on Josh, who was lost to Zoe's charms, and was instead one hundred per cent making her moves on Mary Foster for an *Avalon* cover. We would see that on the newsstands within six months for sure. I was sitting at the bar with Nicky and Chris and my bread rolls, going through images to approve for the news wire. We needed to get them out on the internet as quickly as possible for the newspapers to buy, in order to have those pictures up for the morning so everyone could scroll through them with their breakfast.

'Yes, no, oh awful, nice, that one. Nope. Yes. Got another of Giovanni and Mary together? Make sure you credit that Stacey Powers pic to Celia Johns, will you?' *Our morning gift to Dominic Carter.*

We scrolled, we marked our favourites, we picked at some beef and, most importantly, we kept our eyes and ears open, scanning both tables surreptitiously at all times.

'What time do we think they'll all leave?' I asked Nicky with a hint of desperation as the adrenaline of the evening wore off, and exhaustion began to set in.

'I reckon we've got another half hour. No one will stay for coffee. Watch. Look, Amanda's already pushing her chair back.'

And that was all we needed. The guest who was brave enough to call it a night first, much to the delight of everyone else. Once one chair scraped and one person stooped down to whisper in their host's ear – 'Thank you so much. It was just magical. Really. But I've got such an early start in the morning' – you could literally hear the collective sigh of relief as everyone else knew they could legitimately escape.

It was a strange conundrum. The whole industry pivoted around these moments. Dinners, drinks, parties. And the whole industry spent each event wondering when it would be okay to leave. Me especially.

As predicted, once Amanda and a couple of others made their exit, clutching their shoes in their gift bags, there was a domino effect. Both tables started to empty. The waiters were still offering coffee as coats were shrugged on and goodbye hugs and air kisses and proclamations of 'So sad we didn't get to chat. Lunch next week?' amplified around the room.

Within half an hour of that first chair scrape, the place was almost empty.

'Well done, ladies. Went well. Keep an eye on the coverage,' said Georgina as she laid her tan cashmere blazer back over her shoulders and strolled out to her waiting car. As I watched her leave, I wondered what old maxi skirt and trainers I had languishing at the back of my cupboard that I too could pair with a piece of tailoring.

Giovanni clasped all our hands in succession.

'Beautiful. Beautiful. Now we see what we get from it, no?' he called over his shoulder as he followed Georgina.

Mary Foster had left already with her agent. She didn't bother to say goodbye to us. Her work was now done. Zoe ambled over.

'Success?' I asked.

'With Josh Brigson, or the evening as a whole?'

'Both.'

'Very. On both counts. He asked for my number. And he's already texted me on his way home. I'm considering going to meet him now,' she said with what was definitely a slight sway.

'If you do meet him, do some digging about Greg,' I said quickly in her ear. Zoe scrunched her huge eyes.

'Greg White. Really? Why?' she said, scrunching them even more.

'No, I mean, just . . . see if he enjoyed the shoot . . . if he's around to possibly shoot again . . .' I faltered.

'He's done all the shoots since your one. There's no new shoot coming up. Ohhh . . . Frankie . . . famously frosty Frankie fancies the photographer. Well, this is too good.' She threw her head back.

'Go, go,' said Nicky, ignoring our chatter. 'You're of no use to us now, Zoe. Let's gather the candles up. And who wants to take some flowers home with them?'

I nodded. I was too busy working out how to do a nonchalant wave goodbye to Greg, while smiling seductively and holding in my stomach. As I practised my irresistible farewell, I watched him walk out without so much as a glance back. That would teach me. I had James waiting for me at home. *Karma really was a bitch.*

We blew out all the candles, emptying the hot wax on to the tablecloths, and piled them into two branded Giovanni bags. We grabbed roses from the vases, now sitting wanly on each table, and got our coats. And that was when it hit me. Charlotte's birthday flowers. *Fuckity fuck. How had I forgotten?* I swallowed my dismay.

I had even forgotten to message her to wish her a lovely evening. Somehow my work absorption had once again dropped off the Richter scale. I needed to make amends – and fast. It was before midnight and technically still her birthday. I dashed off a text, full of sad face emojis that I couldn't be with her and a line of birthday poppers to signify I hoped she had had a fabulous evening. But my stomach was in knots. I was utterly in the wrong. There were no excuses. I wondered if there was an unopened candle still in its box that I could send to her in the morning. I'd buy her a family-size bag of Maltesers to accompany it. They were her favourite. Maybe that would make her laugh. Surely she would forgive me. Meanwhile, I scrolled through the pictures on my phone I had taken during the evening and deliberated over the best to post to my Instagram – slide show of the tables, before and after, a close-up of the flowers, a picture of Giovanni and Mary.

I hesitated before tapping 'share'. I knew Charlotte would roll her eyes the minute she saw it, but I needed my industry cohorts to see what we had done. And if I was honest, it had been an amazing night and I wanted to show off. Just a little.

@FrankieMarks WHAT A NIGHT FOR @GIOVANNICASTANI AND @MARY-FOSTER. SO EXCITING TO SEE THESE TWO ICONS COME TOGETHER. WOW. EXHAUSTED! DIDN'T WANT IT TO END!!

Did I seriously just post the word 'wow'? God, I sound like an asshole. I asked my Uber to stop outside the all-night shop around the corner from the flat. They had Maltesers. Small mercies.

And oh my God. Had my phone just pinged? Had Greg just sent me a message? Yes, he had. A gif of a slender ankle.

Charlotte was livid. She framed it as 'disappointed'. A dagger in my heart. She hadn't replied to my message until the next morning. I salvaged a candle that hadn't been lit and a box that hadn't been ripped open to send along with the Maltesers.

'But what did you expect?' James said, when I whimpered about being in trouble. 'You let her down. She's your best friend. You couldn't make it to her birthday dinner, then you forgot to message her to wish her happy birthday or even to ask how the dinner was. You put so much effort into these people you work with, and you need to be careful. What about the rest of us? It's all well and good loving your job – but you know you work to live. You don't live to work. And if you do ... well, you shouldn't. I love you, but it's not as if you're working these hours because you're saving lives. You need to get some perspective. You know we barely communicate anymore. It's kind of depressing.'

That stung. I took the bus to work that morning reflecting on how dramatically I'd changed. But I just wanted to do well. No, not just well – I wanted to excel. James was right about letting Charlotte down. But I wasn't so sure about working to live. What was I supposed to do? It was easy when your office shut up shop by seven p.m. latest, but the thought of telling anyone at work that I couldn't make a launch because it was my best friend's birthday was inconceivable. Those sacrifices were part of the job. And what's more, I loved it. Surely James should understand that by now? Greg would understand, he was in this business. But why did I always feel like I was on the back foot with everyone? If I was waving a paddle at Sotheby's, I'd be lauded for the time I put into my career. But I *had* stopped fully communicating with James. That was true. It was a defence mechanism – he didn't seem interested so I had backed off.

I would focus on our anniversary weekend away in Somerset. Yes, that was when I would be fully present and correct. We would be with friends and the unspoken safety of numbers. We always had guaranteed fun with our friends, didn't we? I couldn't wait to get out of London for a couple of days and have a change of scene. Fun Frankie was due a resurgence. Fun Frankie had a new rendition of Beyoncé's 'Love on Top' with a hairdryer as a wind machine and a pepper pot as a microphone to perform. Fun Frankie was sick of missing out on normal life sometimes. Fashion Frankie also needed to stop thinking about Greg White . . . Somerset would alleviate the tension, and hopefully sort us out.

I was still musing as I bought my breakfast. *Did I have an appointment with* The Forward *magazine today?* I wondered what I could do to right my wrongs against James and Charlotte. I would be a better person. *Had Eloise sent that Samira K bag to* Vita *last night for their last-minute call in?* I would prioritise life outside of the office. *Why did Andrew not turn up to the Dante meeting yesterday?* I would do some food shopping for me and James tonight. *Did I need to finalise the press release for the Darcy Girl balloon-print story this morning?* Shit. SHIT. I'd have to sweet-talk the intern into sending an emergency courier with the candle and Maltesers to Charlotte's office. If I asked Eloise, Charlotte would probably end up with a dark chocolate Bounty bar and a tea light – and right now, I needed to finish off a glowing press release about faux-satin balloons.

PRESS NOTE

Getting a show team together is one of the fundamental steps in making the magic happen. We are delighted to confirm that this season the pre-production necessities of the Melissa Bailey show resulted in Frankie Marks' biggest argument to date with her boyfriend James.

'It's fascinating to watch Frankie become so consumed by her job that she forgets how to treat the people closest to her. She has truly mastered the art of putting her work first. She is to be congratulated,' fumed James, on his own in a double hotel room in Somerset.

ENDS

We needed Jacob McDowell to style Melissa's show. He was one of maybe six or seven hallowed super stylists in the world, famous for his stripped-back aesthetic – and for making designers cry. But if Melissa was serious about the launch of this collection, and indeed launching herself into the fashion arena, then she needed a seriously good stylist. Actually, not just seriously good: great. The best. Georgina had to call Jacob McDowell for me. He was still way above my station. But he and Georgina went way back (Georgina went 'way back' with just about everyone of any importance or influence in the industry). After the first call, Zoe then had to call his agent. Melissa and I had followed up by taking him for a discreet lunch at an exclusive members' club that offered a private entrance to avoid the need for the not-so-subtle leather baseball cap Melissa had taken to wearing to hide her new hair. We had to persuade Jacob she was embarking on a serious endeavour, and hopefully pique his interest enough to want in. Aside from which, a bad leather cap wouldn't have got us off to a good start with one of the greatest stylists in the world.

'I want to show something that surprises everyone,' Melissa had said. 'I'm working on a collection that they really won't be expecting. I poached Carlotta Cadenzi from Celia Johns to create it with me. It's super minimalist. It's really from a female designer's point of view. I want a show that's small. Chic. The best models. The best hair and make-up. Stripped back. But expensive. Do you get what I mean?'

Jacob nodded thoughtfully. 'I'd need to come in six times over the season to look at the progress of the collection,' he had said, wolfing down a huge hamburger and gulping Coca-Cola with an appetite which belied his svelte physique. Nicky had briefed me on what he would be wearing, and she was right about every detail: navy cashmere round-neck jumper (whatever the weather), over a pale blue shirt (no label), black jeans and grey suede Puma trainers (no variation on brand).

'I'll only work with Maureen Gold on production.'

I was furiously scribbling notes as my own burger went cold and untouched.

'I'll only work with Pietro Santiago on casting.'

Noted.

'Music will have to be Marcel.'

Yes.

'I'll need to be kept in the loop on venue choice.'

Of course.

'I only want Gavin for hair and Penny for make-up.'

Absolutely.

It dawned on me that I now had not one but two equally large egos to handle. Great. I was seriously going to have to brush up on my patience and negotiating skills.

'Wonderful!' Melissa said as she popped a steamed broccoli floret into her mouth. 'The team at GGC will get on to your agent this afternoon, won't you, Frankie?'

'HOW MUCH?' Zoe tried not to sound startled as she talked to Jacob's agent that afternoon. 'Jesus. Yes, Okay. Let me take that figure to Melissa and her management. But can I put you in touch with Martha, her PA, to pencil in some preliminary dates in the meantime?'

She hung up. 'We are so in the wrong part of this industry, Frankie. Do you know what his day rate is?!'

'I can guess. But Cole says the money's there. He wants Melissa to have the best team' – I looked out of the window and noted it was absolutely pelting with rain – 'and he's the best in the business, with an ego to match – but we know he's a genius, so I suppose it goes with the territory.'

The costs were racking up. I hoped Cole Fisher really did have the budget he said he did.

A month flashed by. A month of rates being reviewed, costs being assessed, show time being bartered. Endless emails, calls, call-backs, checking dates, checking diaries, checking my never-ending To Do list. I was in the office early, home late, and things were getting more strained with James, who was beginning to refer to himself as the home-help, such was the lack of input I had into even so much as buying toilet roll. The food shop I was going to do with carefully selected organic feta? Course I hadn't. Choosing our hotel room in Somerset? Absolutely no time. But what could I do? I'd worked on many shows before now, but this was the first that I could really call my own and I couldn't fuck it up. I chose to ignore his snarky comments and didn't rise to the bait. Worrying about me and James would have to wait. I only had so much energy and I was conserving it for where I really needed it.

I opened up my emails and started to type.

Martha, can we have a couple of hours this week for a preliminary location meeting – and then a day next week to go and look at venues?

She replied:

Yes. Let me know when. And I can give you next Wednesday for reccies. But after eleven and needs to be done by three.

I emailed Maureen, Jacob's preferred producer.

Maureen, can we have a meeting later this week to look at show venue options before we take Melissa on-site?

Maureen replied.

Yes. End of day Friday, please. I need time to get the team to put some things together and I'm in Paris until then.

I messaged Martha next.

Martha, can Melissa do the preliminary meeting with Maureen on Friday afternoon? Please say she can't. It's such a bad time for me.

I was slightly beside myself. Martha responded straight away.

It's actually the only day she has a few free consecu-tive hours. I'll stick it in the diary.

I slammed my hand against my forehead. Friday after-noon. I had been planning an early exit for our long weekend.

James would be beyond furious. He had booked the time off work already. I emailed Maureen.

> Perfect. Friday it is. Could you come to Melissa's studio?

I sank my head on to the desk.

'Yet again, your job comes first.' James clenched his jaw. 'I'm not waiting for you. You'll have to make your own way there. It's our fucking anniversary.'

I poured myself a glass of wine without offering him one. Not quite cold enough. No ice in the freezer. I drank it anyway. Correction: I inhaled it.

'What can I do? I'm so sorry, but I have to get a venue sorted. Friday afternoon's the only time this woman can do. I just couldn't be the only person who said they couldn't be there.'

I poured myself another glass. There was nothing to eat in the fridge. This wasn't going to end well. I could feel the familiar argument brewing.

'It's a fucking *fashion show*, Frankie. You've turned into a caricature of yourself. It's all so boring. It's just work, work, work with you! You're a fucking fun sponge.'

'Well, thanks a bunch, James,' I then yelled. 'Just because you have a nine-to-five. You know what this job entails. You know how important Fashion Week is. You know it's Melissa's first show. Why do you always have to make me feel so guilty for wanting to do a good job? You know, it wouldn't kill you to be a bit more supportive sometimes. Don't you think I'd rather be on the train to Somerset on Friday afternoon than sitting in an office nibbling fucking dried fruit, going through different fucking options of fucking locations that Melissa is going to fucking reject anyway?'

'Honestly, Frankie, you should hear yourself. I've been as patient as I possibly can, but it's beyond a joke now. You're too fucking intelligent to be running around after Melissa fucking Bailey. I don't even know who you *are* sometimes.'

I took a deep breath, spun on my heel, stomped to the bedroom and flung the door closed. I tried to muster a tear. Tears normally worked to release the pressure valve of my fury while simultaneously garnering his sympathy. But I couldn't. I was still too angry. I messaged Charlotte as I heard the front door slam shut and James storm out.

Frankie
James has just screamed at me about work. Again.

Charlotte
You sure it was him doing the screaming?

Frankie
Well, I may have instigated the screaming.

Charlotte
You do need to stop putting work first

Frankie Not you as well.

Charlotte
Yes me as well. It's taken over your life.

Frankie
But I don't have a fucking choice. I have a fucking job.

Charlotte
You always have a choice, Frankie.

As I sat at the Formica meeting table in Notting Hill at five p.m. on Friday, I considered Charlotte's message. Did I have a choice? Or had I now become so immersed that I just couldn't get myself out? Or, more worryingly, *was* work more important than my relationship? Than seeing my friends and family? Maybe I *was* the 'fun sponge' James had taken to calling me. I was just trying to be the best I could be at my job, but perhaps I really was a self-absorbed pain in the ass? My head spun. But for the time being, I had to focus.

The door opened and in swept a larger-than-life middle-aged lady in a full black sweeping trench coat over a black trapeze dress and giant platform trainers that made her feet look like boats. She looked like she was about to set sail. Multiple colourful bead necklaces and a mobile phone hanging on a cord jangled on her chest.

'Maureen,' she boomed, extending her hand bedecked with multiple rings. Maureen didn't do things by halves.

'Melissa,' said Melissa, standing up and extending her petite one rock-diamond-fingered hand.

Zoe and I also stood up. We were trying our very hardest not to look her up and down.

'So nice to meet you, Maureen. Frankie. And this is Zoe.'

'Lovely. Lovely. And this is my assistant,' she said, gesturing to a small blonde standing behind her heaving under a stack of folders in her arms.

'Let's get down to it. We've scoured all locations open to us on a Sunday morning. We've looked at galleries, hotels, abandoned warehouses, restaurants, covered outdoor spaces, garden squares, theatres, private homes, government buildings. We've whittled it down to five potential options, knowing what Jacob likes, what hasn't been used before, and bearing in mind we only need to seat three hundred. And here they are.'

I glanced at the clock on the wall behind them. James would be on his way to the station now. He had left that morning without saying goodbye. I wondered when we would make up. *If* we would make up. I couldn't imagine my life without James, even when he wore leggings under his football shorts and got excited about interest rates. The room became white noise as I wondered if I had any wine at home, what I could have for supper, whether Greg would ever message me again and then back to thinking fondly (and then guiltily) of the familiarity of James' terrible football attire.

'Yes, could be good.' Zoe was ramming her foot against my ankle to bring me back into the room and holding a photo of some palatial mansion house.

'Oh yes. Looks amazing. Can we go and look at it next week?' I re-entered the zone in the nick of time. 'Wednesday? We have time allocated in Melissa's diary already if we can gain access that afternoon?'

By the time I got home, it was past seven p.m. The flat was depressingly quiet. I wasn't supposed to be in London so had no plans. James still hadn't called, and I knew Charlotte was only going to tell me off if I called her. I opened the fridge. Half a bottle of white, two eggs, some suspiciously dried-out cheese and the remains of the Indian takeaway we had had three nights before. I took the wine and a glass and threw myself on to the sofa, took off my shoes and stretched my legs out on the frayed ottoman. I texted James hopefully.

> **Frankie**
> I'm home. How was the journey? I'll take the train down tomorrow morning?

I saw the bubbles as he messaged back. I suddenly felt nervous.

> **James**
> No point. By the time you get here we'll have left for early pub lunch. Am coming back early Sunday. Going to play football in morning.

> **Frankie**
> Oh. Okay. Say hi and sorry to everyone for me. I'm so depressed I'm not there. Breakfast before footie?

> **James**
> Not sure what time train I'm getting.

He was clearly furious. I decided not to reply. It was only going to turn into a whopping argument. He knew exactly how to push my buttons. I was going to take the adult high road for once.

But I couldn't help myself.

> **Frankie**
> Whatever. Fine. Sorry for being committed to my job. Sorry for always being the bad guy. I'll see you when I see you and btw this is so unfair.

James
There you go. Always making it about you.

Oh God, now I'd started something. I wouldn't text back. I was determined to keep a dignified silence. I held out for thirty seconds.

Frankie
You're such an asshole. Kick me when I'm down. You just have fun.

James
Yup. Will do.

Jesus. Was I really going to let him have the last word?

Frankie
You total and utter dick.

James
Nice one, Frankie. Thought you were a PR. Haven't you learned how to curb your tongue yet? Or do you just save being nice for your clients or the other fuckwits in fashion?

And therein lay my fundamental problem.

Frankie
Hey, Greg. Long time, no text. Just checking in to say hey.

PRESS NOTE

Preparation for London Fashion Week is always highly pressurised yet incredibly inspiring. The entire Melissa Bailey team revelled in the atmosphere and creative process ahead of her highly anticipated debut show.

'It has been thrilling to watch the collection come to life this week. I particularly thrive on the lack of sleep. It's always a joy to discuss ponytails and buttons in exacting detail while snacking on sunflower seeds,' commented Frankie Marks, eating a Jaffa Cake in secret in the toilets.

ENDS

I woke with a start and turned to my side, and there he was. The salt-and-pepper hair ruffled on the pillow. *Oh my God.* Had I really? I grasped the duvet around me and felt around for my clothes. There was no way I was letting him see me naked in the cold light of day. I needed out of this sensational, minimalist, white and steel apartment. Immediately. Before he woke up and noticed I had no access to a toothbrush. My mouth was like sandpaper.

I was in a state of shock. I had never been unfaithful, and I had definitely never done anything like that before. I couldn't even think about how filthy I had been. There had been something about the way he demanded I take off my clothes – and how, in my inebriated state, I had dropped my jeans so fast I forgot to hold my stomach in. Jesus fucking Christ, I'd re-enacted every scene and position from every sex scene in every film I had ever watched with such wild abandon I went red wincing at the memory.

A drink about the latest Giovanni images he had recently shot that we really didn't need to discuss had led to more drinks and a discussion about how I *really* wasn't his normal type but there was just something rather charming about me. I had a hazy recollection of telling him I wanted to lick his hair.

I called Charlotte the minute I got in an Uber.

'I've done something terrible,' I started. 'It was after another argument with James. And you know, I was just feeling so low. And then I texted him.'

'Texted who?'

'Greg. You know, that photographer from ages ago. And oh fuck, I didn't think he'd reply. Then he did. And I went over. And got drunk. And he's got a *really* great loft in Shoreditch. And anyway, I fucking slept with him. Jesus. It's a nightmare. Well, technically it wasn't a nightmare, because of the snaggle teeth, but you know what I mean . . .'

The Uber driver gave me a look in the rear-view mirror. I studiously ignored him.

'*Jesus*, Frankie. That's fucking awful. Okay, let's just try to work out how you move forward. Now's not the time to talk about it. Get yourself home and calm down, make it nice for James when he gets back.' She was clearly appalled with me but wasn't being judgemental, which I was beyond grateful for.

'You know, if you had seen his salt-and-pepper hair and his granite kitchen, you'd understand . . .' I whispered.

When James got back from Somerset, he went straight off to play football and I went to the deli and, in a state of contrition, spent a week's salary on taramasalata, Brie and seeded crackers. I changed Greg's name on my phone to Grace (not that I needed to worry – I didn't hear from him) and did quiet guilty cries in the bathroom approximately every twenty-two minutes. James didn't eat the Brie and he didn't question my new weak bladder.

'Good weekend?' he eventually asked, picking out a sesame seed from his tooth.

'Depressingly quiet,' I mumbled through a mouthful of cheese before I went to the bathroom again. I had a stomach ache from the deception and self-loathing. Or from the excess Brie. But I resolved to soldier on. I didn't really know if I could be a functioning adult without him. Adult life with James was really all I knew.

'Happy anniversary,' I said, raising a tragic toast with my taramasalata.

I decided I had to park the car crash that was my personal life for a minute. James and I went through the normal motions: Christmas at his parents, back down to London for that bit inbetween with mine, and then New Year at a truly terrible party thrown by one of James' work colleagues that had a Club Tropicana theme – and really, that should have been the warning sign before we even walked out the flat door begrudgingly wearing pineapple sunglasses. I buried my infidelity in the recesses of my mind. If I didn't think about it, then it hadn't happened, had it?

It was Melissa's first catwalk show that was really happening. Jacob had been in his preordained six meetings with her and Carlotta – the designer we had poached from Celia Johns – shaping the collection, insisting on more coats, shouting about the lack of green, which was predicted to be 'the' colour of the season. Melissa had called me up after each one of these meetings, exasperated, crying one time, yelling another. Jacob was a hard taskmaster. But that was what she was paying him for.

We had settled on the mansion house as the venue for the show. Now we were here. The week before the show. Well, four days to be precise. But who was counting? Apart from James, who had eventually calmed down after I'd done a lot of apologising and promising that things would change once Fashion Week was over. It was as if he'd put a metaphorical chart on the fridge door and was crossing off the days as he counted down to Ground Zero. He'd threatened to put a physical chart up there but had just stopped short when he'd seen my sense of humour level about it plummeting.

'Morning. Morning, Maureen. Hi, Jacob. Hey, hi, morning.'

As everyone started to set up for the day, I did my rounds clutching my coffee, then headed over to the boards to look at the schedule. Castings all morning. I'd seen the models starting to line up outside the room in their identical black slips handed out by Pietro and his team.

'Girls, try to keep the noise down, please,' Pietro announced with a hint of an Italian accent despite his thirty years as a New Yorker. But as soon as Melissa came through the doors, a reverent hush fell anyway, just as it always seemed to when she entered a room. It was like a magnetic force compelling all eyes on her. Sometimes I genuinely forgot she was so famous until I saw people's reactions.

'Morning, everyone! Sorry to keep you waiting, girls. Thanks so much for coming. Won't be long,' she chirped. I did a hasty U-turn away from the croissants.

'All good?'

'All good. Jacob is at the board.'

'Good morning, Jacob!'

'Hey, Melissa, sleep well?' He turned to give her a kiss.

'Not bad at all. Excited about today. Oh, Frankie, would you mind getting Martha to come down?'

I walked up to the office area.

'Ha – you look how I feel,' Martha said, taking one glance at me.

'I'm fine. Just tired. And hungry. Again. She wants you.'

'Think it'll be a late one?'

'Schedule says finish time approximately midnight. There are castings all morning. First fittings this afternoon. Music meeting at six. Dinner seven. Back to fittings for rest of the night.'

'Okay, then we'll definitely need to get a Chinese for our supper.'

'We will.'

Now that I had a meal plan, I felt better, energised, even. I sat on the sofa next to Melissa as she gave Martha her papaya breakfast order – sliced today – and Pietro stood with a pile of papers for each of the poor girls we were about to see.

'Melissa, this is Helga,' he introduced a lanky blonde model with a hook nose, full lips and hip bones jutting out of her slip. 'Helga, you flew in from New York, yes? But you're originally from Sweden? Helga is seventeen, Melissa. She just opened the Marc Jacobs show. Helga, can you walk for us, please? Do the shoes fit you? Can someone get her the right shoes? Helga, my love, can you tie your hair back for me, please? So just up and down a couple of times.'

Helga with her antelope legs walked up and down a temporary catwalk that had been constructed in the room. Melissa and Jacob watched her. Jacob made notes on her model card. This happened with over a hundred girls over the course of the morning. I wondered if they could see his cross, or tick, or question mark as they came close.

If they looked right, then Jacob would ask to see them in one or two looks. The girls who weren't asked knew they were just moving on to repeat the same process at another designer. I felt for them as I scrolled through my phone and nibbled my way through the sunflower seeds Martha had placed on the table.

'Oh my God, look at this.' Melissa nudged me to look at a picture she had up on her phone from a news story on one of her old down-on-their-luck co-stars from *Carlyle Bay* who had just been announced as one of the competitors on some dancing show.

We giggled conspiratorially. Jacob hushed us.

'Concentrate, please.'

We had been berated like naughty schoolchildren and sat bolt upright to stare at Magdalena from Croatia. And Jasmine from a small town outside Wisconsin. And Zaya from Ethiopia, who was astounding. And sixteen-year-old Sophia from the East Midlands who was accompanied by her mother, Janice, doing her first show season.

Up and down they went.

'Go have a photo taken, darling,' Pietro would say to each and every one of them. More boards went up, photos meticulously placed in symmetrical lines. Girls who would be confirmed. Girls who were a maybe. Girls they knew they wanted before they even walked through the door. In total there would be thirty-five of them. One per look. This was getting expensive.

'I'm going upstairs to work on the press release,' I told the room. I was finding it hard to focus. Everything was becoming overwhelming. I needed some respite, so I went to find Martha. Working with someone who had become a true friend just made everything better.

She was busy in the kitchen, simultaneously booking Melissa and Gabriel's May half-term break somewhere fabulous while tossing prawns in a five-spice dry marinade in a bowl by her laptop, for Melissa's lunch.

'How's it all going?' she asked, adding a pinch of cayenne and scrolling through suite options.

'It's going. I'm not going back down there till this afternoon. I've got to work out how to write a "no-concept concept" press release in more than ten words.'

In terms of a press release, this was almost revolutionary. Normally the PR would be asking the designer to go into the deepest recesses of their brains to find the piece of art they had seen in 1984 with their parents, which had triggered an emotional response they had now applied to a zigzag hemline. My idea was to turn this on its head. These were just clothes women would want to wear. Pure and simple.

I ate two Quality Streets in quick succession from the box hidden in the secret cupboard behind Martha's desk and sat down in front of my laptop with an exaggerated sigh, the blank screen burning my eyes.

For her debut collection, Melissa Bailey presents the notion of the no-concept concept. Here are the clothes that every woman wants to wear. A touch of refinement juxtaposed with a modern fluidity perfectly captures the sense of the perfect woman's wardrobe . . .

Oh God, I was boring myself. I popped a third Quality Street into my mouth and hoped it would inspire me.

After four more Quality Streets and forty-five minutes of wrestling with ways to describe a check shirt and skirt, all I'd managed to come up with was *'an updated version of the iconic eighties skirt suit'*. I gave up and set out to find Martha who was back in the kitchen, in the hope of finding motivation there. But Martha was now dry-frying the prawns, and timing was critical or Melissa's lunch would be spoiled. I went downstairs and poked my head into the catering room, lifting the lids of the silver serving trays to investigate what was on offer. Nothing that inspired me there, thankfully. At least that was a win – one meal skipped would mean extra sweet-and-sour chicken later. I nodded at the production, atelier and casting teams sitting around earnestly eating cauliflower in turmeric and limp salmon fillets and tried to look purposeful as I exited through the swing doors. Admitting defeat, I headed reluctantly back to the other room to see what progress Jacob and Melissa had made.

'Oh, she's fabulous.' Melissa was looking at a young girl fresh in from New York who was being pinned into an A-line purple skirt with drop pockets and wobbling on a pair of lemon wedge boots.

I texted James. *She's doing so well! You'd never know it was her first season! She's so in tune with the stylist!*

You sound like a press release, he replied.

'Oh, that changes everything,' I declared enthusiastically, pointing at a new pocket on a shirt while wondering if I'd have time to exfoliate my face at some point before the show.

Marcel, the show music maestro, arrived for the first music meeting that evening. I occasionally nodded my head with purpose, tapping my fingers to the beat and trying my hardest to look like I knew what I was listening to as he played some options.

'It's morning,' he said, pressing pause. 'You don't want something too hard. But you don't want something everyone has heard before. But you *do* want something they recognise at times.'

'Yes, it's a Sunday. I've seen too many shows where the audience is grimacing at some screeching soundtrack. Let's give the people what they want. Upbeat.' I thought my input was valid without betraying I had no idea what I had just listened to. I was pleased.

'What do you think, Carlotta?' Melissa asked. Carlotta, Melissa's head designer, had done a lot of shows. Not just at

Celia Johns before we poached her, but at the various houses she had worked at previously. I had learned that the industry was populated with these incredibly talented design directors who remained anonymous while working side by side, if not above, the eponymous designers whose name was on the label.

'For me, I like the hip-hop. With something melodic. You know, like a melody? I heard this recently.' She scrolled through her phone and pressed play on some new female artist I of course hadn't heard of, but I showed immense appreciation.

'Yes, she's great,' said Marcel, nodding.

'I love it,' added Melissa reverentially.

'Amazing voice,' I pitched in, then stood up. 'Great, so see you tomorrow, Marcel. I think it's time for dinner. Melissa, you should take a break.'

I was ravenous and I had seen Martha out the corner of my eye take delivery of our Chinese and disappear back upstairs. My sweet and sour was calling me.

'I'd like to work straight through,' Jacob declared. 'We have four girls waiting for their first fittings. Let's just eat in here.'

Fuckity fuck and double damnation. I was not going to be able to bring a deliciously stinking, steaming Chinese downstairs. I could have cried. Instead, I said I needed the loo, jumped the stairs three at a time, body slammed into Martha and threw my face into the container of luminous sunset-orange sweet-and-sour chicken, guzzling mouthful after mouthful before turning to go back down.

'Maybe I can microwave the Singapore noodles for lunch tomorrow,' I said dolefully as I grabbed some plain rice cakes to take down for Melissa and tried to ignore the onset of chronic indigestion.

The next day was essentially a repeat of the last. Except we had the hair and make-up test. Hurrah for some variety. The monotony was killing me. Gavin and Penny the superstar hair and make-up artists came in with three assistants each. We selected four girls from the casting of varying looks, skin tones and hair colour.

Gavin stood in front of the first girl and patted her hair, flicking it from one side to the other. He took out his brush. He pulled back a ponytail.

'Something like this could be super cool. Super natural?' He stood back, showing us a loose pony with some wispy strands of hair falling around her face. To me it looked suspiciously like my ponytail on bad hair days when I gave it a quick spray of dry shampoo and shoved it off my face with an elastic band.

Has Greg been online today? I should just check.

'Oh yes, that could be amazing,' I enthused, wondering why I wasn't being paid to brush people's hair.

Is it James' birthday next week?

'And so for make-up, we'll keep it super light. We'll do a moisturiser, followed by a translucent base. Let's play with the eyes.' Penny was looking at the girls intently.

'Okay, so let's take the girls over to the hair and make-up stations and see you soon,' they said, ushering the girls away to try out the looks.

Two hours later I was sitting back on the studio sofa, nibbling seeds of some description and wishing they were crisps – looking at the girls in their towelling robes with identical ponytails I was still convinced I could have done myself, and a translucent make-up that I was sure was how Nicky normally applied hers. I may also have been thinking, *Kill me now, please.*

Actually, I tell a lie. The hairstyles weren't identical. Each girl had a different parting. Left, right, middle and none at all. We discussed hair partings in earnest seriousness for the best part of an hour. At one point Gavin pulled a strand of hair down over one girl's forehead.

'Oh, amazing,' said Jacob.

Seriously? He just yanked a piece of hair out of an elastic.

'Yeah, that really softens it.' I nodded.

'Yes, I like it. Carlotta, do you like it?' Melissa was scrutinising the strand of hair.

'Me, I like,' Carlotta confirmed.

'So, for make-up, here we've got a nude shadow base on the eye. Then here I've added a gold shimmer to the corner. Here I've left the eye completely bare. And then lastly, we have the option of a brown flick in the corner,' said Penny, pointing at each girl in succession.

How much is she being paid to have an assistant dab some gold shadow on an eyelid? I tried to recall. Or indeed to just put nothing on an eye.

'I think the gold is too much,' Jacob said.

'Lola, wipe,' Penny barked. Lola, one of her assistants who wore a bumbag holding so many brushes and wipes and pencils I wondered how she stayed upright, pulled a wipe out and handed it to Penny.

Penny wiped off the gold.

'Hmmm, nice. Clean,' Jacob said.

'I think you're right. With these clothes, less is more. So, are we saying middle parting, one strand over the right ear, dewy skin and some nude shadow just here?' Gavin cocked his head to the side, waving his hairbrush.

'I think so,' Melissa agreed.

'And the girls with short hair or curls, we can straighten, and if no hair, we can just add a spritz to give texture,' he went on.

'Brilliant,' Penny concurred.

Jesus, I thought. *Really?* They had all been here for four hours and we had all just agreed to do basically nothing.

'I think it looks really strong. Minimal. Understated. But with a powerful fashion message,' I nevertheless asserted in my best PR voice. Charlotte's warning all those years ago started ringing in my ears.

God, maybe I *was* mildly idiotic.

PRESS NOTE

The joy in solving the jigsaw puzzle of a show seating plan is one of the great privileges of a fashion PR. It takes great patience, acumen and a detailed knowledge of the industry hierarchy.

'Sometimes I marvel at the politics of the front row. How something so irrelevant can become a matter of monumental importance. It's moments like these that really propel me on to cater to the inflated egos of people who will never thank me,' said Frankie Marks, sticking her middle finger in the air.

ENDS

'Why don't you just do boy/girl/boy/girl?' James was exasperated and trying to be funny. I wasn't amused. I was reaching the finish line of the show prep, but the floor of our flat was now a sea of Post-it notes with hundreds of names scribbled on them as I attempted to compile the seating plan.

'Sshhh . . . I'm concentrating. It's a nightmare. Melissa's show only has a front row capacity of ninety. Do you know what that means? I'll tell you what that means – utter carnage, tantrums, arguments and cajoling. If I come out of it alive, it'll be a miracle.'

It was still impossible to explain to him the politics and negotiations that went with show seating plans without sounding absurd. My worst arguments had been about front of house. If Amanda wasn't next to Gabriel, Melissa's husband, who wasn't in the eyeline of that reviewer from France, who wasn't directly behind *Avalon's* Fashion Director Kathy Newell, who needed to have a direct line of vision to that actress from the new miniseries who was coming . . . well, it was all unthinkable. But how could anyone of sound mind explain the nuclear explosion that was the seating plan at an eight-minute fashion show?

I was also acutely aware that my knowledge of the average bottom width wasn't a key skill set to shout about.

'I'm going to meet the guys for a drink. Come join us if you can. Text me when you're done.' James stood up and put his jacket on. We were still tiptoeing around each other trying to find our middle ground. Unbeknownst to James, I was also struggling to deal with my guilt. Every time we had a moment when I remembered how much I loved my boyfriend, I had to take myself off to the loo to take a deep breath and hold back tears about what an awful girlfriend I was. The privacy of our bathroom had become my special place.

'Okay. Give me an hour.'

I knew I needed to try to make it, but I was now sitting cross-legged on the floor scratching my head and wondering how I would ever be done. I lit another cigarette and wondered if a drink would be a help or a hindrance at this stage. *This is fucking ridiculous,* I muttered to myself as I headed to the fridge, ten minutes and zero progress later. I needed wine. For my sanity.

My mobile rang. It was Martha.

'Hi. Yes, yes. All great. She okay when I left? I'm still doing the seating. How's it going there? D'you think her mother will definitely be coming? I forgot to ask her earlier. Because I'll need to find her a front-row seat, and at the moment I just don't know where that'll be. Uh huh, yup, sure, no problem. Perfect. Speak later.'

Melissa's mother was indeed coming, Martha confirmed, and was bringing her friend Lesley, who had also never been to a show before. Lesley was so excited. Melissa insisted she also had a front-row seat. I took a large gulp of wine.

Fuckshitbugger. So, Lesley would need to take the seat of the French journalist, who then wouldn't have the direct line of vision, and so Kathy would need to move. I was back to square one.

I finished the glass of wine and lay star-shaped on the floor, staring at the ceiling as I fumbled for my cigarettes and lighter and placed one in my mouth, lighter held aloft. I inhaled deeply and closed my eyes. What an absolute and total waste of my time. These were precious hours of my life I would never get back. I picked up my phone again and called Zoe.

'Can you meet me at the office in the morning? I'm having a total nightmare with the seating for Melissa and I just feel like I can't go back into that studio without it done.'

Zoe sighed back down the phone at me.

'What time? Not too early. Shit, got to go – that's the doorbell. I've got a date.' Zoe put the phone down.

I texted her.

> **Frankie**
> 8 a.m.?

> **Frankie**
> Who's the date?

> **Frankie**
> Where are you going?

> **Frankie**
> Message me when you're home.

> **Frankie**
> I'm jealous.

I texted Martha immediately.

> **Frankie**
> Who's Zoe's date with? How did we not know she had a date? I want a date with someone new and exciting. James hates me tonight.

> **Martha**
> Josh Brigson. Go away. I'm making Melissa a prawn salad for her supper. Her and Jacob have had a row about some dress. She's taken refuge in her office. See you tomorrow.

I messaged Nicky.

> **Frankie**
> Zoe's going on a date with Josh Brigson?

> **Nicky**
> Not a clue. Land back in the morning. Heading straight to Dixie studio.

I scrolled down to Andrew's number and called him.

'You having a seating nightmare tonight as well?' I asked hopefully.

'No! Me and Jemima have almost completed it.'

'Seriously? You lucky bitches.'

So, Zoe was on a hot date. Andrew and Jemima were together, and Nicky was on her way back from her pre-Fashion Week break in the Bahamas (dubiously strange timing, and Zoe had found Nicky's passport in her desk drawer earlier that week while searching for some staples).

'She must have two?' I had said.

'Who has two passports?' Zoe had replied.

And I was on my own, perhaps unprofessionally a little bit drunk, on the floor, surrounded by seating plans, an over-flowing ashtray and with an absent boyfriend who seemed to be downright sick of me.

My phone rang. Maybe James was desperate for me to come down to the bar to join them. I looked at the number ringing. ID withheld.

'Hello, Frankie speaking.'

'Heyyyy. Frankie. Cole. Cole Fisher. Melissa's manager. How ARE you? Sorry to call late. I'm in LA. But I was just on the phone to Melissa and she thought it easiest I call you directly. I'm coming into London for the show, of course. And I'm bringing the team from The American Bedding Company. They need to be front row. Next to me. I left a message for you last week, with a girl in your office. Eloise?'

I HATE MY LIFE, I screamed inside, but I swallowed instead.

'Hey, Cole. That's so great you're bringing them. I've got a slight issue with the front row. Because it's such a small show, the row capacity is tiny. I mean, really small. And we have to seat certain press and buyers. As you know, the sales team is working really hard to get all the major retailers there and we've had huge interest from the press. All the big names are coming . . .' I could detect a quaver in my voice.

'Let me interrupt you there. I need two more front-row seats. Make it happen. The office will send the names in a minute and I'll see you Sunday. You're doing a *magnificent* job, Frankie!'

And then he clicked off. Just like that. *What an asshole. And double asshole Eloise for not letting me know.*

Make it 7 a.m. I messaged Zoe as I pushed all the Post-it notes into one big fat pile of chaos.

PRESS NOTE

We are delighted to confirm that the backstage area for the Melissa Bailey Show at London Fashion Week was a calm and serene environment focussed solely on the show preparation.

'I was just thrilled that my first show was such a well-oiled machine. Every detail had been taken care of so I was free to talk about my commercial endorsements while worrying about a model shoe change. I thrive on multi-tasking,' Melissa Bailey sort-of enthused afterwards.

'The unexpected, early arrival of Cole and his guests was a wonderful addition to the atmosphere backstage. I was delighted to meet them,' said Frankie Marks without a hint of irony.

Martha Chan commented, 'To find there wasn't any sugar-free gum for Melissa in her green room was a delightful moment of added tension.'

ENDS

The alarm was set for five a.m., but there had been no need for it. I'd been awake intermittently all night worrying about missing the alarm, and checking the alarm was still set, and then panicking I had turned off the alarm while checking it. It was show day. I was riddled with nerves. This show *had* to go well, and the enormity of it made my heart constrict. I sent my father a panicky email while still horizontal telling him today was the day. He was an early riser.

I staggered out of bed and switched on the most forgiving of the bathroom lights. Laid out on the floor was my outfit for the day. It was slightly crumpled, but to be fair I had chosen it at two a.m. in the dark while James was sleeping when I got in from the last night at the studio. And anyway, no one would be looking at me. One of the fundamental rules of PR – be invisible unless needed to step in.

I showered as quickly as I could, threw items into my make-up bag, brushed my teeth and scrambled my things together. Trainers for running around all morning. For the show, something resembling a heel. Big necklace for added outfit value. Small bag to carry my phone, phone charger, and chewing gum. Big bag for laptop, wallet, shoes, extra jumper for air conditioning, cigarettes, lighters (I had learned to take many, someone will steal at least two before 10 a.m.). My father had replied. *Focus.* It was short, but to be fair it was only 5.30 a.m., and I felt slightly reassured and just plain grateful that he had acknowledged that I had a job I actually needed to focus on. I started to message our new WhatsApp chat which I had entitled SHOW HELL.

Frankie

I'm in my cab. You in your cab? What time is she arriving? What time's Jacob arriving? Martha did they make sure the green room has a candle? Jemima did you bring the credit sheets? Are you sure Amanda has already flown in?

The journey was marked by a constant pinging. My driver turned up his radio.

> **Frankie**
>
> I'm here. You here? Where are our passes? Which door shall I use? Why has no one put up the stanchions?

There was a knock on the car window. Martha was peering in, hands on hips.

'Morning, and yes, I have the candles. Zoe is getting production to put up the rope and stanchions. Maybe breathe and have a coffee.'

I grabbed my access-all-areas pass from the front desk and entered the fray, game face on.

'Morning. Hi! Soooo great to see you! Oh Gavin – you look amazing, you've clearly had more sleep than me! Hey, Jemima, how did they do with the credit sheets? Did they remember the nail sponsors wanted an apostrophe after their name? Did you tell them the face cream sponsor couldn't be at the top of the sheet? No, not much sleep, but it's fine, thanks. Where's Marcel with the music? What do you mean, Helga isn't here yet? She's opening the show! Send that film crew OUT. Who let them in? I heard Anastasia doesn't land till midday. Nice of her to let us know – let's fill that seat. Yes! Coffee! No! No croissant. We need to make sure there's enough breakfast for the models. *Although I AM starving.* Urggh, what is that? MOVE AWAY FROM THE RAILS WITH THAT JUICE IN YOUR HAND. Yes, you can film the bottom of the rail. But not the top. Don't take a picture of the boards – they're embargoed. Who are you with? Is there someone accompanying you? I think your time slot was five past six to six fifteen. It's six eighteen, you need to leave.'

I had gone into turbo overdrive. Nought to one thousand

in about thirty seconds. I said it all with a smile, but I most definitely wasn't smiling on the inside. *Four hours to go.*

I found Martha on all fours on the floor of the green room trying to work out why the extension lead had fused, an anxious runner from production hovering.

'You need to sort this out.' Martha turned to the runner who was hiding behind her clipboard. 'We need the make-up mirror lights on. Like now. We need the coffee machine on. Like now. *And* the fridge. And these flowers are pink. I said white. And is the gum all sugar-free? Because I really don't think this one is.' She brandished the offending item in her hand, waving it furiously. Every detail mattered when it came to keeping Melissa calm. Everything had to run like clockwork. This was not the time to have sugar in the room.

My phone pinged. Melissa was on her way.

'She's twenty out. Someone go stand at the door to let her in. Kevin – can you go and tell the photographers cameras down. You, runner – sorry, I didn't catch your name – make sure Jacob and Gavin and Penny know she's due soon.'

I was awful. Horrid. The worst version of myself, but it didn't matter. I had no choice but to bulldoze my way through the next few hours to ensure everything ran smoothly. This was all resting on my shoulders.

I navigated my way through the now packed backstage. I was hit with a wave of hairspray, bad deodorant, and unfortunate morning coffee breath as everyone chattered and gushed. There were hundreds of people: models; hair and make-up teams; beauty journalists observing them all so they could write up the 'beauty look'; Jacob's team; and the professional dressers allocated to each girl, in order to get them into their outfits correctly according to the instructions laid out next to photos of each look. There were scores of cameras (still and film), from TV, glossy magazines, online sites, trade magazines, the daily newspapers – not to mention literally dozens of nameless people in black blazers running around with headsets on. Zoe steamed past me waving press releases, looking slightly hysterical and wide-eyed. Hairdryers were whirring, hairspray created a film in the atmosphere, make-up artists were patting down models' faces – 'Beautiful, just like this, dewy, natural, just a touch of light down the nose and across the brow bone. A touch of nude on the eyes.'

Oh, for fuck's sake. Can't this just be over? But actually, maybe there's an assistant who could quickly straighten my hair when no one's looking?

'She's here, she's here!' someone at the entrance was calling to me and generally to anyone who was listening.

I looked at Martha. She looked at me. It was a look that said okay-this-is-a-nightmare-but-I've-got-your-back. We marched up to greet Melissa at the internal entrance to the backstage area. She was in a full-show look, made up for her by the studio team, the two-pocket shirt with a pair of billowing check trousers and a lemon heel boot.

'Morning. Yes, all is great. Going really smoothly. Only a couple of girls we're waiting on. Yes, the boards are here. Jacob wants to change over looks thirteen and twenty-two and there's a bit of an issue with the shoe change between looks three and twenty-five. He's waiting to go through it with you over there,' I said serenely. Jemima had taught me a thing or two about how to project calmness with clients.

'Thanks. I need a coffee. I haven't slept. At all. Can you tell Gavin I need his assistant to blow out my hair? And can you ask Penny if she can send someone with some powder? And can you ask Kevin where I left my bag with my notes? Oh, and so sorry to ask, but can you find Carlotta and get her to meet me at Helga's rail? I was thinking about that shirt and I'm just not sure it needs a brooch.'

I walked and talked. 'Yes, will do. Did you read the notes

for the interviews? Did you remember what I said about the concept being that there is no concept?'

I left Melissa there, examining the high stakes shirt, and saw Nicky wandering through the front of house perusing the seating.

She smiled at me. 'Looks great. But you're definitely going to run out of room on the front row. You'd better hope no one comes in a big coat. Show me the backstage interview list? Need me to do any of them for you?'

I loved Nicky, but this was my show. My client. In the world of Melissa Bailey, we were equals. I had learned fast how to deal with her. Nicky was, however, going to be extremely useful with Cole Fisher, Gabriel and The American Bedding Company. She could talk to anyone.

'Can you look after her management and family for me? I've got the rest of it covered between me, Zoe and Jemima. Andrew's with Dixie today. For the best, really. Melissa hasn't come to terms with his fascination with Gabriel . . . Georgina said she won't be here till just before ten. She's at Dante this morning.'

Melissa's first show was the talk of London Fashion Week. Her critics tasted disaster and had their poison pens at the ready. Her fans were in overdrive, tweeting and posting and already hanging around the venue doors for a glimpse. I was now running on adrenaline overdrive. This show was different from all the others – full of different nuances, potential pitfalls and, if it went well, the opportunity to blast the naysayers and opposition out of the water. And of course, prove myself to everyone – once and for all.

Carlotta and her design team had done a great job. Jacob had stripped the show back to the bare bones of classic minimalism. The room was impressive. The 'no concept' concept was new. There would be no referencing of a pebble found on a beach after a storm in Ireland that had inspired a reflection on the wilderness of the working woman's wardrobe. No. Everyone had agreed with me that no one wants to wear a concept. Just beautiful, wearable clothes. *Maybe this fashion outsider had the right idea after all?*

I went back out to the front of house. The benches were out and Jemima was directing the team on exactly how to place the press release and notes on the seats. The catwalk cover was on. The riser for the photographers was in place at the front of the catwalk for them to get the best shots of the girls. There was such a crackle of anticipation in the air, you could almost reach out and touch it.

Melissa was with Jacob and Carlotta, looking at each girl's outfit and making changes. The running order was up on the boards. Monitors were being turned on. It was really all happening. It had taken months and months, but here we finally were.

'Sorry we're early.' Cole Fisher was walking towards me through the crowd backstage, followed by two rather chic but most definitely New York power women with swinging blow-dries and ridiculously high shoes. My heart sank.

'Let me introduce you to Frankie. Frankie, meet The American Bedding Company team.' I smiled and shook hands.

'So great to have you here today.' *But not now. Not right now.*

'It's amazing back here. Wow. What a scene. Do you think we'll have any time to say hi to Melissa after the show?' asked one in a distinct New York accent, extending a perfectly manicured hand. 'You know, when we saw Melissa in that incredible *Avalon* shoot surrounded by those duvets, well, I said to everyone – they should be OUR duvets! We can't wait to start working with her.'

'That shoot was all Frankie. Wasn't it incredible?' Cole interjected. 'And Melissa and American Bedding will be such an unexpected collaboration . . . so exciting. Frankie, let's all sit down with the team before they head back to LA this week, to talk about moving everything forward.'

FOR FUCK'S SAKE! Didn't he know how busy I was? Couldn't these people see what was going on around them? Seriously?

'So great to meet you. Oh look, here's my colleague Nicky. Nicky, this is Cole. And some bedding people. They do duvets. Nicky will look after you all and see you to your seats later.'

I whispered urgently into Nicky's ear away from the group. 'Get them a corner back here to wait. I don't trust them to not take any photographs or post anything. Don't let them out for the rehearsal. Shove a pain au chocolat up those women's bony asses. Anything. But please can you keep them out of the way of everything?'

'*So* lovely to meet you all,' Nicky gushed to the group. 'It's just going to get a bit more frantic here over the next hour – why don't I take you out for coffee while we wait? There's a wonderful cafe just around the corner. Do the best almond lattes in London.' She already had her hand firmly planted on the women's backs, pushing them gently towards the backstage exit. *God, I love Nicky and her shiny hair.*

I waved them all off with a huge sigh of relief.

PRESS NOTE

GGC are thrilled to confirm that the Melissa Bailey Show was oversubscribed and caused a seating frenzy in the front row.

Laura Cole, Fashion Director of Madame, *commented, 'Perhaps in future, certain fashion PRs will allocate enough room on the front row to important people such as myself and unfortunate incidents such as these will be avoided.' She added, 'Fortunately, when I fell off my seat I didn't sustain any serious injuries.'*

ENDS

> **Jemma**
> Can we open doors front of house? How late are we starting? What's going on back there? Had people waiting outside now for twenty minutes. Really think we need to start letting them in.

Jemima was on the extended WhatsApp SHOW DAY group – it included the production team so I couldn't name this one in my customary fashion. I had to maintain my professional demeanour with external participants.

I typed. I didn't have my headset on yet.

> **Frankie**
> We need to be opening doors.

> **Jemma**
> Doors opening

> **Frankie**
> Okay. It's going to be a scrum. Nicky you'll have to take Gabriel when he arrives. Melissa's mum is fine on her own she said. Is the seating team in order?

Zoe sent a thumbs-up emoji.

> **Frankie**
> Okay. Let's do this. Good luck everyone.

I put my phone down. I was backstage with Amanda and Melissa. Standing at the boards, looking at the looks. We were doing a preview – key, I now knew, to any catwalk show – taking selected editors and reviewers through the collection boards, the colours, the design process, the fabrics. The concept – if there was one. A show went by in a flash and they needed to know details to incorporate into their reviews. We hadn't done many, I was too nervous. But Amanda Starling always came backstage at the shows she was interested in for a private walk-through before taking her seat, and she had to be accommodated. She had a vested interest in her cover girl.

'Talk me through it,' Amanda drawled.

'Well, really, for me, this first show is all about dressing a woman from a woman's point of view. I mean, when people ask me what the concept is, I just say there is no concept.

Because who wants to wear a concept?' Melissa touched Amanda's arm gently.

'So you know, we're showing thirty-five looks. And my real favourite is this windowpane check skirt with Argyle jumper. It's super chic. And looks really simple. But actually, the pattern on the skirt is really complicated. And for me, that's the essence of the whole collection. Deceptively simple.'

Melissa was doing well. I released the breath I'd been holding and acknowledged that the collection really was amazing. I believed in it. I wanted to wear it. I would be bedecked in check skirting and high-waisted turquoise trousers next season.

'What about the evening wear? That's really strong.' I directed Melissa to other key stories as she stalled.

'Oh yes, the evening wear. Well, it's really about a new modern take on evening wear. Because no one wants to wear full-length anymore. You need to be able to be comfortable. But chic. And not complicated.'

Okay. Jesus. She's overusing 'chic' and 'complicated'. Move her on.

'But the colour's really key, isn't it?' I interjected again.

'Yes, yes. Frankie's right. For me it's really important that colour is used in an interesting way. So it's chic, but not too complicated.'

Oh God. 'You know what, Melissa, I'm so sorry, but I'm going to need to pull you away. I can see Jacob wants you over there.' I pointed aimlessly. 'Amanda, shall I show you some of the rails as I take you out and I can seat you?' Amanda didn't bat an eyelid. She gave Melissa a kiss on each cheek, wished her luck and said that the collection looked 'strong'.

I began the ceremonial procession to lead Amanda Starling to her seat. No eye contact. No speaking unless spoken to. I gestured with one hand to the space with her seat and we silently nodded at each other as she sat down. One down, 299 to go – I looked over at Zoe and raised a *for fuck's sake* eyebrow.

I saw Zoe was having her own issues with Laura, the Fashion Director from *Madame*. She had made an almighty fuss when her invitation arrived last week and she didn't have a front-row seat. She didn't merit a front row – but the arguments and emails and phone calls had just been so incessant, and such a waste of time, that Zoe had relented at the last minute and I had squashed Laura into a seat that didn't physically exist.

Zoe spied her walking into the venue and caught her before one of the poor unsuspecting interns was accosted.

'Morning, Laura. Here you go.' She ushered her to a postage-stamp-sized space on the corner of the last bench on the front row, next to an enormous Italian journalist with a hefty bosom and pink-framed glasses.

'Or there's an actual seat for you just behind in the second row, if you prefer?'

Laura nodded indiscernibly. She didn't take off her sunglasses.

'This'll be fine,' she muttered as she manoeuvred her bottom to the perilous edge while officiously extracting a notebook and pen from her shiny black structured handbag. Typical. Anything to look relevant. Zoe gritted her teeth and smiled before spinning on her heel to see what actual notables needed assistance.

Over on the other side of the room, Nicky was leading the duvet contingent and Cole, laughing loudly as she smoothly placed them in their allotted seats before turning her attention to a man in a bad brocade suit who was waving his invitation in the air, gesticulating wildly at his fourth-row seat, and shouting at the bewildered intern. She marched over and a furious argument ensued. He was from a Danish independent style magazine. The fourth row was where he belonged.

Snippets of his wrath could be heard as he protested his right to be moved forward, along with Nicky's clipped 'it's just not possible' and 'take it or leave it' replies. She won. Brocade man sat down, defeated, shamed and slightly red in the face.

Gabriel's arrived, Martha texted.

I moved backstage, where preparations were in full and final flow. The girls were lined up in their looks. Jacob was tweaking a waistband. Carlotta had a lint roller out, giving them all a final brush down. Melissa was holding hands with her six-foot-four, lightly tanned, dark-haired husband sporting a handlebar moustache required for his current role, looking at the board.

This was the first time I had met Gabriel, on a rare break from his busy filming schedule.

'Babe, this is Frankie who I've been telling you about. She eats carbs!' said Melissa.

'Hey, Frankie. Looks great,' Gabriel said, in the instantly recognisable, husky tone that had won him an adoring fan base across the world. I would store that carb comment away ready to regale Charlotte with it over a glass of wine and a bowl of triple-cooked chips.

'Can't believe what's going on back here. I had no idea. This is crazy! It's best the girls didn't come. Too overwhelming.' He turned to Melissa to reassure her that the decision to not expose Dandelion and Delilah had been the right one.

I interjected. 'Nearly there. Nice to meet you. Are you guys going to be okay if Nicky takes you to your seat, Gabriel? You're next to Amanda from *Avalon*. Take one for the team, Gabriel, as we say. Cameras will be on you!'

'Hey, I got this. Good luck, darling. So proud.' And he gave Melissa a peck on the forehead as he left.

'Martha! I need someone to bring me powder! For my forehead,' she screamed.

Nicky ushered Gabriel through the back and out to the

front row. I couldn't resist following, just to see what the atmosphere was like out there. There was a ripple of excitement as all eyes turned on Gabriel. Then a sudden surge of photographers raced to capture their shot as he sat down. He smiled. No, he dazzled. He kissed Amanda as if they were long-lost friends, then picked up the press release and credit sheet and began reading them intently – ever the adoring, supportive husband who really *was* interested to know who had done the models' nails for the show (at the bottom of credit sheet, in the tiniest print we could give this gripping piece of information). There was a barrage of clicks and flashes, and I already knew I had the front pages in the morning, whatever the actual show reviews were going to be.

'Thank you. Enough. The show's about to start. Please go back to your positions,' Nicky said politely to the photographers. Then, when they didn't move, a little less politely, 'Don't make me have to get security over here. Please. To your positions. NOW.'

They dispersed like ants. I ran back one last time to check all was okay backstage. The frenzied mayhem had somehow metamorphosised into a semblance of calm. I felt like I was having an outer-body experience. I had put everything into this. And I could do no more. The models were lined up in order, standing on their names, which were taped to the floor. Jacob, Melissa and Carlotta were doing their final smoothing, tucking and pulling at the clothes. The hair and make-up teams were doing last-minute spot checks on skin and pony-tails. Photographers were taking their final backstage images. Now they needed to vacate the area. Production removed them, and I knew we were minutes away from lift-off.

'Right, I'm going back out front. Turnout is brilliant. You okay? It'll be great! Good luck! See you after.' I gave a slightly ashen-faced Melissa a little hug, smiled at Jacob and put on my headset.

'Guys, I'm out front. Looks like we're fully seated.'
'All ready back here.'
'Catwalk cover can come off.'
'Marcel, wait for your cue.'
'Zoe! I can see an empty seat third row, block C. Fill it!!'
'Move those standers out of the aisle.'
'Get those bags in block A under the benches. They'll be in shot.'

Four men, jeans perilously low over their backsides, started to unroll the catwalk cover revealing the chequerboard floor. It was a painstaking job. I was willing them to speed up. My stomach was in knots. The chatter and buzz of earlier had descended into a hush of anticipation.

'Lights, ready?'

We raced to our positions to watch. Our job now was to assess reactions from press and buyers alike. How many notes were taken? Which outfit got the most camera flashes? We had to notice when pens went down. When phones went up. We switched off our headsets; there was nothing more to be done.

Boom. Lights down. Blackness. Boom. Lights up. Glaring. Pause. The first girl was about to emerge at the top of the chequerboard catwalk. The Italian journalist in the front row stifled a cough and shuffled her bottom backwards. But in her precarious outer bench position, this was enough to topple Laura from *Madame* off the corner of the seat. The muffled thud resonated around the room. Everyone turned to stare. Scrambling back up as quickly as she could, Laura repositioned herself – but with no dignity left intact. We stifled our giggles, not entirely successfully. *Bloody well serves her right!*

Heads and eyes back to the catwalk. I could feel my heart pounding in my chest. This was it. The music filled the room with a crescendo. Marcel's nineties hip-hop beat was mixed with that soulful female voice we had all loved. I nodded knowingly. The first look (on Helga) was making its way down towards the photographers. Her lemon wedge boots stomped. The clicking and flashing of the photographers was frenetic. The resounding bass of the hip-hop track reverberated through the floor. Every phone was held aloft. Every reviewing journalist was scribbling notes.

From our vantage point, Nicky, Jemima, Zoe, Martha and I all looked at each other. Had we really pulled this off?

'Shit. I forgot to change my shoes,' I whispered as I looked down at my feet bedecked in my wretched old Converse trainers.

'Tsk, no one's looking at you,' Nicky chided, as I looked up to see Georgina standing in between the benches on the other side of the catwalk glancing at my feet with a slightly raised eyebrow.

PRESS NOTE

The conceptual non-concept of the Melissa Bailey Show was a standout moment of London Fashion Week. Frankie Marks is to be applauded for her remarkable risk taking in the realms of the press release.

'I was just delighted to finally be able to eat chips in public while being lauded for my foresight,' Frankie commented as she triumphantly read the first show reviews while asking for more ketchup.

ENDS

'Oh my God. YOU DID IT!'

Everyone was high-fiving each other, clapping each other on the back while I restrained a swarm of well-wishers who had crowded into the backstage area.

Melissa looked shell-shocked. Teary, almost. Nicky pushed her way through the crowds with Gabriel, Cole and the rest of Melissa's entourage.

Everyone took a respectful step back as Gabriel came in to wrap Melissa in a hug.

'Well done, baby. It was awesome!'

The not-so-private moment was captured by another horde of photographers who had spotted their second Monday morning front-cover image. The newsrooms would have a field day with their headlines, which would likely be along the lines of '*Mel and Gabe Stop the Show at London Fashion Week*' once the picture hit their inboxes. Gabriel graciously moved to the side as Nicky edged in with Cole. Ever the loving husband – and consummate professional. The photographers raced out to send their images to the photo desks.

'I knew you could do it.' Cole squeezed both Melissa's shoulders. 'Just for one moment say hello to the American Bedding team,' he whispered in her ear, 'it's important.'

I watched Melissa grimace, and then force herself to smile widely.

'Thank you so much for coming. I hope you enjoyed it.'

'It was spectacular,' the women gushed, 'we can't wait to work with you!'

'I'm so sorry, but there's a line of press who need to talk to Melissa,' Nicky said. 'Would you mind dreadfully if we pulled her away?' She pressed her hand into Melissa's back and pushed her firmly away from the duvet contingent.

Once again, I thanked God for Nicky and her heaven-sent intervention; I had a baying crowd to contend with, phones on record mode at the ready.

'How does it feel to have presented your first collection here in London?'

'What was your overriding inspiration?'

'We all just loved the windowpane check. Can you tell us the significance?'

'What was your starting point? You said in your notes that the concept was simply about dressing modern women. Are you the woman you want to dress?'

'Will Gabriel move to the UK full-time? Now you've based your business here?'

Oh, bugger off. 'Melissa is only talking about the collection today,' I intervened. 'So back to the question about the concept.'

'The concept was that there really was no concept. No one

wants to dress in a concept – but you know, I just wanted something chic but not complicated,' said Melissa, on autopilot.

Repetition is recognition. I had taught her that early on.
She just didn't need to repeat 'chic' and 'complicated' *quite*
so often. Finally, the crowd dispersed and the teams started
to pack up. What had been the epicentre of excitement and
frenetic activity was now just an empty set of conference
rooms being packed into boxes.

'We still have to do some TV front of stage,' I reminded
Melissa. She looked like she really had had enough. The show
itself may have been over, but we had only just begun on the
post-show requirements. She needed to get with the programme.

'Oh God, okay. Where's someone to powder me down? Has
Gavin left anyone to fix my hair? Who do I have to talk to?'

'Two American online shows. *Breakfast Banters*. All the
European publications and a film crew from Dubai. Just
repeat what you said just now so brilliantly. And add some
gratitude for the UK fashion industry and London Fashion
Week. The fact there are so many of them is amazing. It
means everyone wants a piece of you. The buzz is phenomenal.' I needed to pep her up before she waned.

We were swift. We were professional. Melissa excelled in
every interview until we got to Dubai and she repeated the word
'chic' ten times. At that point, I called it a wrap and thanked
everyone profusely as Jemima and Zoe saw them out for me.

Back in the green room, Martha was hanging Melissa's
change of clothes. Gabriel was sitting on his phone, and Cole
was gushing to the Americans. As we entered the room,
Melissa turned to me anxiously. Her impeccable game face
had momentarily dropped.

'What do you think? Did it go well? Do you think they all
liked it? Honestly?'

'I *really* feel like you're going to get good reviews. They
were all taking notes like crazy.'

'Really? Shall we look now? I don't know if I can wait. I just need to know!'

'You need to give them a chance to write them! They'll start in their cars to the next show. But you're going to have to be patient. I won't have anything in for a couple of hours.'

Patience was not Melissa's virtue. I looked at Martha. A look that I hoped said get-them-out-of-here-fast-so-we-can-lie-down-for-ten-minutes-and-then-go-and-have-some-lunch-in-peace.

'Oh God, waiting is going to be agony. You have to be sitting right next to me when they come through. We'll all go to lunch together,' Melissa announced. 'Martha, can you make the table bigger?'

My heart sank. I had really needed a few moments alone to regroup and drop the gushing PR veneer. On the other hand, my ego was only human – and Melissa wanting me with her made me feel important, and my role validated. In this job, I sometimes found myself completely conflicted.

'How lovely,' I beamed.

Cinquecento was full of Sunday lunchers who were beyond thrilled at their surprise celebrity co-diners, but busy pretending not to notice. My phone sat next to my wine glass, staring at me.

'Anything yet?' It was the tenth time Melissa had asked.

'I'll get an alert as soon as something comes in.'

I tried to eat my Milanese with a side of frites, but I was too nervous. I said a little prayer and took a large sip of wine.

'The bedding company thought you were fabulous, Melissa.' Cole flashed his wide too white smile as he leaned across the table for the salt.

'Course they did.' Gabriel flashed an even wider smile as he looked at her adoringly.

PING. I snatched my phone up and swiped.

BAILEY BLOWS HER CRITICS OUT OF THE WATER

I have to admit I was more than reticent about another celebrity turned designer. But today those tables were turned. Melissa Bailey showed us all how it can be done with a singularly classic collection, full of to-die-for pieces that perfectly sum up what a woman's wardrobe needs . . .

I didn't need to read any more. I grabbed her arm.

'Oh my God! First one is in. And it's AMAZING.'

My eyes started watering. Which was hugely embarrassing. But the relief was so immense and the joy so real that I just wanted to cry. I proceeded to read the full review that was up on *Avalon*'s website and tried to stop my voice from cracking.

'"And if this is the beginning, who only knows what we have to look forward to."'

I put down my phone in triumph, smiling inanely. Melissa clasped my hand in disbelief and blinked back her own tears. Gabriel raised a toast. Cole even stopped talking about duvets. Martha winked at me across the table and I heartily shoved a handful of chips into my mouth, my hunger revived. We carried on squeezing each other's hands under the table – in friendship, solidarity and enormous relief.

'Well, if they've given you a good review, it's a great sign that the next ones that come in will likely be positive. We can relax a bit. This is great. Better than great. Amazing. God, I'm so happy.' I could sense the tip of my nose going red as I started to get emotional again.

The rest of lunch passed in an exuberant haze, punctuated with a few selfie requests with Melissa and Gabriel, made by eager diners who couldn't resist. No one minded the interruptions, and I forgot my exhaustion and tucked into my tiramisu. Alert after alert vibrated, with not a negative review among them, and we toasted each and every one. I excused myself to the bathroom.

D-DAY

Zoe
Have you seen?!!

Frankie
Yes!

Jemima
OMG, well done you.

Nicky
Is she happy?

Frankie
Beyond.

Jemima
See you at Dante!

Zoe
Heard from Georgina?

Frankie
She said she's 'pleased'.

Nicky
Georgina-speak for thrilled.

The whole GGC team – bar Eloise – shared in my excellent good fortune. Even she was included on the chat out of work etiquette, but not once did she interact. The rest of the team, on the other hand, were my support network, and I loved them for it. I knew I had a few hours left of unadulterated self-congratulation before I'd have to come down from cloud nine and get back to business – and the Dante show. And James. I absolutely *had* to try to see him, or at least speak to him, before I entered the fray again. I was fully dedicated to persuading myself that everything between the two of us was normal, and I knew it was the right thing to share my news with him. I called him on the way back from the loo.

'It's done! Reviews are coming in and are all great. We're just at lunch, then I'm coming home to change, then I've got to leave again,' I said into his voicemail when he didn't pick up. I hadn't stopped to consider it was his Sunday too and he was probably out with friends and too busy to hear about chequerboard catwalks. I was too joyously wrapped up in my own world to care.

I practically skipped back to the table.

'Nice shoes,' whispered Melissa mischievously.

PRESS NOTE

Melissa Bailey and her remarkable team arrived for their flight well prepared and raring to go for their next whirlwind trip to Los Angeles. How do they do it? It's testament to their dedication.

'It's always a thrill to be packing again. I am constantly amazed at the array of travel-size deodorants I am able to amass,' commented Frankie Marks, trying to sort out her washbag.

ENDS

The show was universally well received. The sales team took the collection to Europe and the States, and sales were strong. The *Avalon* cover had also been a resounding success when it came out a few weeks before the show. After much delicately aggressive back and forth with the *Avalon* press office, we had settled on releasing the cover, the bed shot, and one black and white image of Melissa in the tutu on a chair surrounded by roses. The press release contained gushing quotes from Amanda (written by the magazine's press office) and Melissa (written by me). Amanda was so 'thrilled', Melissa was so 'humbled'. Together they had created something truly 'special'. Amanda had conducted and written the interview herself – unheard of, and the biggest industry affirmation we could get. We gave the images and excerpts from the interview text to the *Daily Post* as an exclusive. Eloise had thrown that day's issue in the bin, so it was slightly crumpled, but still it read:

SCARLET SIREN TO BEGUILING BOMBSHELL!
Melissa Bailey sizzles in a dramatically different look as she features on the cover of style bible British Avalon for the first time.

So ran the headlines, followed by editorial *'Ms Bailey is launching her first foray into high fashion'* – along with our carefully chosen quotes – *'I always knew my heart belonged to fashion'*, *'I never expected to be accepted'*, *'My family life with Gabriel is sacrosanct but he's behind me every step of the way'*. Every tabloid clamoured for it. Everyone wrote about it, posted about it, talked about it. The cover had been a hot topic all through fashion week. It was discussed on breakfast TV; it even made the evening news. The transformation of Melissa Bailey was a big story. It was *Avalon*'s fastest selling issue ever. Oh, and it had secured us the duvet deal. My mother bought every copy of every magazine and newspaper Melissa's cover was in. My father even emailed me to say he'd seen it in the *Reporter*, and managed to say 'well done', causing my heart to swell. Charlotte and I discussed the coverage endlessly every evening for a week, and James had the cover printed and framed in what I thought was the most romantic peacemaking gesture ever – until he said it could only go above the loo. Now I had done the show, he was so relieved he had resumed showing flashes of his brilliant humour and I felt like I could just move on from my monumental mistake with Greg and appreciate the relationship I had. But most deliciously, I knew that the Melissa Bailey success story would have Sockless Dominic Carter spinning with fury till his too white teeth spontaneously smashed.

But as was the norm in this strange world of ours, once that cover and round of shows were done and the excitement over, life went back to the usual day-to-day grind over the next six months or so. We did another show season, press days, press lunches, call-ins, appointments, social media strategies, celebrity dressing, bitching about other designers, moaning about Eloise, obsessing over Georgina, haggling, negotiating, creating documents, building press books, eating tuna sandwiches on white when we really needed to be eating salads.

Andrew nurtured and loved Dante, his biggest client. He cooed and shouted. He spent time in their studio fervently discussing why the velour hadn't worked, why the seersucker *would,* and how Celia Johns had most definitely copied their three-pocket lamé shirt last season. Come to think of it, he seemed to spend an inordinate amount of time at their studio.

Jemima caressed and cared for Dixie as if she were her own mother. She took a briefcase of Carraway diamond necklaces on a series of appointments to editors' desks to make them feel special, rather than asking them to come to the showroom. She went to every men's publication as well, pointing out how well they would work on Christmas gift specials and that husbands and boyfriends always appreciated the help.

Nicky massaged Giovanni's ego and wore his new patent ballet flat to all her breakfasts, lunches and dinners for a full two weeks in order to sell them to all who saw how versatile and chic they were. She did the same for Samira K. She carried a black raffia woven tote around with her for the best part of a month.

Zoe and I carried on extolling the virtues of the high street and threw on as much Darcy Girl as we could on a daily basis. 'This jacket? I know! Right? Can you believe? Looks like it's from the catwalk! Yes, I can send you one in navy this afternoon. Do you want to shoot it with the matching trouser?'

Eloise remained sulky. She had chosen not to come to any of our shows but curiously had been spotted by one of our press contacts standing at the back of the Celia Johns show, Five Star's biggest event of the week, which caused frenzied speculation over our desks. Was there a bigger story behind her appalling tights? I wanted to interrogate her, but it was impossible. Since our showdown, she was even less willing to communicate with me, save for telling me about things that she hadn't been able to send to shoots two days after they should have been sent.

For Melissa, we did day trips to Europe for shopping events with department stores in Madrid, Paris and Dublin. There was a magazine conference in Berlin where Melissa did an onstage interview with an editor; a lunch in Bruges for the top high-net-worth customers at their chicest boutique; a signing event at a multi-brand store in Lisbon; a dinner to celebrate an Italian magazine cover shoot in Milan. The six months following Melissa's Fashion Week debut were an arduous marathon of flights, early mornings, late nights, hair, make-up, press releases, step and repeats, photo approvals, selfies with fans and Instagram posts. We went on three-day turnaround trips to New York, LA and Toronto, booking our flights with precision, taking into account timings, tailwinds, plane seating formations. My suitcases were on a constant conveyor belt of packing and unpacking. I had enough adapter plugs from Amazon to service an international convention, and so many travel-size deodorants it was ridiculous – I couldn't risk one running out, so I just kept buying them. But still I always forgot to pack the right knickers.

It was relentless and I was permanently jet-lagged, but the truth was that we also laughed so much. In between screaming, holding our hands to the heavens, sanitising Melissa's hands at meet-and-greets and, occasionally, crying with exhaustion and arguing like alley cats, Martha, me, Melissa – and, as often as I could bring her (budget and her other clients' needs dependent), Zoe – travelled and worked as a close-knit pack. No one would ever understand what we did, how we did it, how tired we were, or how funny it was when the interpreter on stage in Korea sobbed while meeting Melissa, and how we had frantically corralled innocent grocery shoppers in malls in Dubai to join the queue for signings when the lines weren't long enough. They would also never understand how Martha's urgent search for perfectly textured papayas for Melissa was a constant mission of international importance. We had nights of hotel room revelry together where we got inordinately drunk and Melissa got us to re-enact her cheesiest *Carlyle Bay* lines while she gave us stage directions. We analysed our horoscopes and learned when Venus was rising. We became so close through all of it. And as a result, we retreated more and more into our own private world.

James settled into the new routine too. Seeing each other less somehow decreased the tension in our relationship, and we maintained a peace plateau that gave me hope we would be able to make it work. I bought him a hideous snow globe every time I travelled to a new country and spent a considerable amount of time asking him about different currencies (which made him positively blush with delight). The frenetic pace allowed me to continue to pretend my indiscretion with Greg had never happened. It also alleviated my secret misery that Greg had eventually only ever sent me one message after our one-nightstand – *Well that was fun* – before he went offline and out of my life.

Georgina may not have always outwardly shown her

appreciation for my professional success, but it was signified by a generous pay rise. My father's misgivings were at least partially mitigated by my increased income, and my mother started sending me overexcited texts every time she saw a flash of my hair behind Melissa in paparazzi shots. Things were also pacified due to their delight that once she graduated with a First, Tilda had been accepted at law school, so they eased up on me a bit. And for that I was immensely grateful to my sister.

Next up on our schedule was another intensive trip to LA. It was a big one. To promote the bedding, do some TV appearances, attend a shoot and fit in some dinners. I was packing. Again.

I stood in front of the wardrobe. James looked at me from the bed, one eyebrow raised. He had seen this all before. He gave nothing away – whether he was happy or sad to see me go again – and I followed his lead.

'Shall I take a leather jacket? Or just denim?' I asked him, holding them up. I knew it was a rhetorical question he wouldn't bother answering, and that I would take both anyway.

I packed strategically. A row of tightly packed tees. Two fine-gauge knits in neutral colours carefully folded on top. Shorts, one pair. Jeans, the cropped flared ones. Skirt. Culottes. Shoes: Gucci slides, Prada velvets, the very heavy suede clogs I took everywhere just in case, but never actually wore. These were small testaments to my increased salary. Trainers: one pair to travel in; a different colour packed for colour-coding and wet weather emergencies.

Workout clothes: one pair of leggings, Lycra bra, vest top, sports socks. They wouldn't leave the case. But to have had the good intent was enough. That reminded me – more socks. For the trainers.

I took my customary deep dive into my underwear drawer. Where were my nude seamless knickers?

Make-up. Toiletries. Would I need sunscreen? That suggested I would have time to sunbathe. I'd take it just in case. I wouldn't use it. Or a swimsuit. I shoved one inside a suede clog anyway.

'Do you think I can wear this crossbody bag with a larger handbag, plus a carry-on, and get away with it?'

'We have the same conversation every time. And every time you do. Just don't forget your knickers again . . .'

Wallet. Passport.

'I'll wear the leather. Pack the denim.'

'You will, Frankie,' he said without taking his eyes off the telly.

'I will, James,' I said as I put my full body weight on the case and started to zip it shut. *I will also remember my parents' wedding anniversary this week,* I reminded myself. I made a mental note to call them from LA.

The flight had been carefully managed as usual. We boarded the plane last to maximise Melissa's privacy and minimise her wait time. As we stepped onboard, an overeager Cabin Services Director was all over us.

Martha had seated Melissa in first class, and then came to meet me and Zoe in the business class section. The three of us were next to each other in the middle bank of seats, and thankfully the fourth seat was empty.

'Welcome on board, ladies. *So* pleased to have you with us,' said Geoffrey (according to his name badge). 'I'm Geoffrey. I'll be your Cabin Services Director, do let me know if you need anything. You're with Melissa Bailey, aren't you? I must say I'm *so* excited to have her on board. I absolutely adore her. And again, if there's anything I can do for you, please let me know and I'll see to it immediately. In case you didn't catch it, my name's Geoffrey.'

We all smiled mutely.

'Yes, Geoffrey, we are, and we did,' Martha concurred as she heaved her hand luggage into the hold above her head. 'Can you please do us a massive favour? If Ms Bailey asks for any of us to go and see her during the flight, could you please tell her we're asleep.'

Geoffrey gave her a conspiratorial wink. 'Oh, I understand. I've got you. Water, champagne or orange juice?'

Was that a rhetorical question?

'Champagne please, Geoffrey.' Martha flashed him her best smile as we all started to unpack our hand luggage. Tracksuits to change into. Make-up remover. Lavender mist for general aroma. Hand sanitiser. Disinfectant wipes for the seat area. Kindles. Laptops. AirPods. Moisturisers. Phone chargers.

'What will we watch?' I asked, scrolling the channels.

'I've got to finish the schedule first,' said Martha.

'And I've got to finish the briefing notes for the bedding collection interview,' said Zoe.

'Urghh. Travel bores. Fine. I'll type up the production notes for the *John Isaacs Show*. Then I'm watching a movie.' Of course, I messaged Charlotte before I got out my laptop. She was now fully ensconced with Filipe 31D and had recently taken on a new case involving human trafficking, and made my heart swell with pride at having such an honourable best friend who didn't mind me sending her banal messages. I didn't disappoint with this one.

> **Frankie**
> On runway waiting to take off. La La land here I come.

And then James.

Frankie

About to take off. If I crash, don't tell anyone I went to discuss duvets. Tell them I was on my way to a UN conference.

I made myself comfortable and considered my surroundings. When I had time to stop and think, I realised my trajectory in the world of fashion had been fast by anyone's standards. God, I was lucky.

I must have fallen asleep mid-thought, because I woke several hours later with a start, sensing someone was there. Someone was: Melissa. Perched on my footrest.

'What are you doing, you weren't sleeping, were you?' She grinned as she put her grey slippered feet beneath her like a small Buddha. It really was remarkable how she had toned everything down. The blond hair was a revelation. There was no bad velour tracksuit. In its place she wore a pair of grey cashmere leggings with oversized matching hoodie. She was naturally very pretty. I admired her for a second.

'No, no. Must have dozed for a minute,' I mumbled, shuffling myself back into an upright position. 'Everything okay?'

'Yes. Just got bored. Nothing to watch and there's a man across the aisle who's trying to make conversation with me about season five of *Carlyle Bay*, so I wanted to escape. Anything we need to go through for when we get there?'

'Well, Zoe's finishing up her briefing notes for the *C'MON!* show interview. I'm typing up the *John Isaacs* pre-production notes from our call, and Martha's doing the schedule now.' I patted my unopened laptop.

'Don't forget we're going to Spinning Souls in the morning. Martha, are the bikes booked?'

'Yup.'

'Great,' I whimpered. 'You sure you want me there? I'll be useless.'

'You'll be great! It'll be fun!'

'Can I get you something to drink, Ms Bailey?' Geoffrey was leaning over my seat.

'A peppermint tea would be lovely, thank you,' she replied.

So, she was staying for a while.

'Are Brian and Penny meeting us at the hotel?' she asked Martha.

'Do we have approvals over the lighting at the interview, Zoe?'

'Is Gabriel definitely not going to make it back from set to see me while we're there?' she questioned Martha again. Sometimes I wondered why she couldn't just do an old-fashioned text to her husband and ask him herself.

'No. Night shoots in Vancouver,' Martha replied, looking at her laptop.

'How is it with your boyfriend, Frankie?' Melissa suddenly changed the subject from her relationship to mine. I had realised over time that she had an uncanny knack for noticing unsaid things.

'Yeah, you know, it's hard. I love him, we've been together forever. But he's not interested in fashion, he doesn't understand PR, and the pressure we're all under, and why I'm hardly at home with him like I used to be . . . I'm not really sure where it's all going to go.' I surprised myself by answering so candidly and finally admitting to myself how problematic it all really was.

She took my hand. 'My therapist always says you may think the grass is greener somewhere else, but you should just concentrate on watering your own grass.' *Crikey.*

Martha and Zoe looked up at the air-conditioning units and then down at their seat belts.

'Well yes, that's a really valid way of looking at it,' I said, slowly taking my hand back.

'And my meditation guru gave me this mantra: "Out of the darkness and into the light, to all that is good and all that is bright." You know, for when you feel stressed or anything. I use it when I'm cross about things like my fruit being too ripe ... or an outfit not working,' she added earnestly.

Right. This conversation has to end. And it has to end now.

'Your tea, Ms Bailey.' Geoffrey handed over Melissa's tea while he gazed at her with unadulterated adulation. I couldn't have loved Geoffrey more for his timing as she smiled at him as if it were the greatest serving of tea she'd ever experienced and started to peruse my in-flight dinner menu.

'Oh look, Frankie. They've got a cheesy pasta bake. You'll like that. Last time I had cream was in 2011,' she quipped.

And that, really, was what I loved about Melissa. Because she knew I would cheerfully eat airplane food. Because she liked to make fun of herself. Because she treated uber fans like Geoffrey humanely. Because she was aware of what was going on around her – when she wanted to be. But mainly because, underneath it all, when she wasn't in diva mode, she was a laugh – and, almost in spite of herself, she was actually rather sweet.

PRESS NOTE

The marriage of fashion and exercise is an almost holistic coming together of two key categories. We are proud to announce that Frankie Marks experienced her first Spinning Souls class in Los Angeles this morning.

'It was inspiring to see someone so hopeless yet so keen try so very hard in one of my classes. She may be a beginner, but she's a warrior. While keeping to the rhythm may be a challenge for some, Frankie took it to the next level. She will find the beat. Eventually,' commented Angelica Ferrera, fanatical Spinning Souls instructor.

ENDS

I had forgotten to pack my workout leggings accidentally-on-purpose. I'd been wide awake in my hotel room, praying for sleep since 3.30 a.m. Jet lag was not my friend, and although it was now past 5 a.m., my dead-weight limbs showed no inclination to move. I clutched the duvet around me and stared hollow-eyed at the ceiling. I reached for my phone to scroll through Instagram and see what had happened in London when I was asleep. Inevitably, it was someone's birthday, a picture of Charlotte and Felipe howling with laughter on a tandem bike in the park, and a reel telling me what had happened in the Netflix show I was saving to watch. I felt a flicker of angst at what I kept missing out on, then pulled myself together from my ludicrously luxurious soft satin sheets, surrounded by a vista of Los Angeles. As I was wondering what I would have for breakfast and whether a bath or shower would work best to trick myself into work mode, the silence of my room was shattered by the phone ringing in my hand, jolting me upright.

'Morning, Melissa.' I tried not to sigh.

'Spinning Souls at seven a.m.!'

'Oh God, you know what, I just realised I left my workout leggings in London! I think I should probably take the time to go through the emails that have come in and prep for the day.'

'Oh, don't worry,' Melissa trilled down the phone, 'I've got some freebies they sent me; I'll bring them for you when I come and get you. I'll be with you at six thirty.'

'Great. See you soon.' I collapsed back down on the pillows for personal dramatic effect. *Fuck.*

At 6.28 I was standing in the minimalist lobby of the hotel, looking out for the car. I was always punctual to a fault. Melissa was always late. Ten minutes later, the black SUV glided into the hotel drive. I plastered my face with a smile and jumped in the back.

'Hi. Hello,' I acknowledged Paul, our security guy, who was driving us.

'Here you go.' Melissa passed over a pair of leggings from the passenger seat. 'Sorry, they really are hideous. Which is why I haven't worn them, but I've been waiting to get someone else into them for a laugh. I'm sure they'll fit you. They stretch.'

I allowed the comment to go over my head as I wriggled and twisted my way into them on the back seat while trying unsuccessfully to hide my modesty from poor Paul, who was strictly eyes-to-the-front. The leggings were truly terrible. Emblazoned with logos that wrapped around my thighs, they created that dreaded sausage-leg effect that screamed 'she eats carbs' like a neon sign flashing above my head. As we pulled up at the studio, I got out of the car and immediately started stuttering apologies to anyone unlucky enough to catch sight of me and the offending items. 'Sorry, borrowed,' 'Yup, I know,' I muttered, employing – I hoped – my best British irony.

'You have bikes three and four. Here are your shoes!' The girl at reception was abnormally springy – and possibly over-excited to see Melissa – as she took us through to the lockers and waited to see us into the studio. I was fully aware that we were being given the top VIP service, and I was not looking the part. Melissa, on the other hand – well, she didn't disappoint. The peak of her cap was pulled down low over opaque black sunglasses. Her perfectly coordinated crop top and leggings revealed a delicate six-pack and thigh gap. I was sure I saw some pitying side-stares coming at me and at my leggings as we were ushered to our bikes. *Fuck you all*, I thought to myself as I smiled serenely.

Thank God the room was dark and candlelit. But candle-light? Seriously?! Weren't candles for long baths and power cuts? I decided to ignore the ridiculousness of my surround-ings and channel gratitude for small mercies as I watched beautiful people in bra tops and men in no tops pedalling furiously, stretching and taking sips out of their personalised water bottles. I clambered on to the bike, clipped my shoes in, tied my hair up and tried to stretch one side to the other with-out losing my balance, while surreptitiously scanning the room for anyone I recognised or, God forbid, anyone I actu-ally knew. *Please God, just don't let anyone see me here looking like this.*

'We're here together to give us all some SOUL, to reaf-firm what we know is great about ourselves. We made it. We're here. This is YOUR forty-five minutes. Let NO ONE take them away from you.' The instructor Angelica, who resembled some sort of ninja, had begun her invocation. Everyone was whooping and cheering. I wasn't. I was thinking that this was going to be the longest forty-five minutes of my life and wondering whether Martha would wait for me for breakfast, and if I would have time for a blow-dry before work began.

Angelica was evangelical. She was beautiful. She was adored by the room. She didn't break a sweat. I, on the other hand, felt sick. I was drenched, gasping for air as my throat burned with the effort. I spotted a Kardashian at the end of row one. I could do this. I would not give up. Next to me, Melissa looked like she was having some sort of divine intervention. *Make it stop*, I prayed. It's highly possible I said this out loud. I couldn't be entirely sure.

'Let's take this home people, let's TAKE. THIS. HOME.'

After what felt like an eternity, Angelica raised her arms in the air and I was finally embarking on the last Sexy Corners manoeuvre (swing to the left, to the right, take it back, swing to the left, then to the right again, try not to fall off your bike). And it was done. Riders fist-pumped their neighbours, cheering. With soul, apparently. I took the moment to apologise to those around me for being so out of time. The lights went up. GOOD GOD. I came face to face with my reflection in the vast mirror that lined the wall in front of us. I was nuclear red. Hair wet with sweat and plastered to my forehead. There was nothing for it but to make as quick an exit as possible, get my sunglasses on, drape a towel over my head and slink back to the car without being seen. I was queuing to leave the room and high-five Angelica – 'Great job, great class' – when I felt a tap on my shoulder.

'Hey, Frankie, I thought it was you.' I froze and turned slowly around. Oh, Christ – it was Dante's stylist Lucy Collins, looking like she had just come out of a juice bar. I hadn't seen her since Zoe and I had worshipped her from afar at the Castani dinner. There wasn't an ounce of sweat. Not a chafed thigh to be had. I needed the ground to swallow me up with immediate effect. It didn't.

'The leggings aren't mine, I just borrowed them,' I squealed. 'But great to see you, oh, and here's Melissa! Hey, Melissa, look who I just bumped into.'

'Don't look at Frankie's leggings, they're hideous!' Melissa said, pointing directly at my legs.

'Jeez, thanks,' I sighed under my breath, and sloped off to die quietly and get my stuff from my locker. At least I'd thought it was my locker, but of course I was so spent and lacking oxygen, I couldn't now remember which one was mine and had to spend ten minutes assuring the other cyclers that I wasn't a thief as I tried every locker's combination. Finally I felt the Holy Grail of the opening click.

'Okay, okay, I'm ready.' I walked up to where Lucy and Melissa were still chatting. Melissa turned to face me.

'Frankie, let's meet with Lucy when we're all in London. I want to talk about vintage inspirations with her. Can you arrange with Martha to talk to Lucy's agent about putting a time in?'

I hadn't even had my first coffee of the day. I was broken, I was a tomato, I was in the worst leggings ever created by mankind.

'Great idea – of course! Can't wait to see you in London. So much to discuss. We've got so many vintage ideas.' I went into autopilot PR-speak, nodding effusively and effusing enthusiasm.

'Didn't you love that?' Melissa enthused from the front seat of the car, reapplying lip gloss and adjusting the peak of her baseball cap to just the right angle of don't-look-at-me-but-look-at-me-I'm-in-disguise-but-yes-it's-me.

'Umm yeah. I mean, it was hard. And I don't think I'll be fit for purpose for a few hours till my face returns to some kind of normal colour,' I mumbled from the back seat. 'But it was good to see Lucy.'

Melissa's spur-of-the-moment whim to discuss vintage was nonsense. I knew she basically had a girl crush on Lucy, as did the whole industry, and she had made that up on the spot. Shit. Was this – tirelessly accommodating Melissa's every whim – always going to be my life? The car drew up at the hotel.

'Okay, so I'll shower and go through all the scripts for today, and Martha and I will be at your hotel at lunchtime. You need to go into hair and make-up at one.' I heaved my logo-covered legs out of the car and jumped down. 'See you later,' I called out as I headed into the hotel lobby. 'Thanks, Paul.'

Back in the room I peeled off the sausage leggings and put them directly in the bin. It was only right and proper that they never saw the light of day again. As I struggled to manoeuvre myself, Houdini-like, out of my sports bra, my mobile rang.

'Hang on a sec, Martha, I'm putting you on speaker. My hands and half my head are stuck inside this fucking bra top,' I yelled at the phone as I desperately attempted to extricate myself from the sodden Lycra.

'Done. Thank God. Hold on again,' I shouted, 'I'm just getting my cigarettes and going on the balcony.'

Finally, I was standing in my bathrobe on the hotel room's minuscule balcony overlooking Sunset Boulevard – cigarette in one hand, phone in the other.

'Jesus, you're so lucky you didn't come this morning. It was a nightmare. I told her I was going through the scripts and we'd be there at lunchtime to set up glam. Fancy going for some egg whites and a quick blow-dry?'

'Already booked,' Martha replied quickly. 'What do you think I am? An amateur? Meet me downstairs in twenty.

Zoe's getting room service. She doesn't have enough hair for a blow-dry.'

It was still only eight a.m. I showered thankfully and put all the upmarket hotel toiletries in my washbag, knowing they would be replenished later. What was the point of all the travelling without taking some of the benefits? I lived off hotel shower and bath gels.

'Our appointment is at eight thirty, just across the street. I've turned my phone off. I need an hour's respite – she's not stopped messaging me since five a.m. Mainly about the papayas in her fridge not being ripe enough.' Martha gesticulated as we crossed the boulevard and entered the Blow Bar.

'Two appointments for beach blow-outs in the name of Martha at eight thirty a.m.,' she told the girl at the front desk.

'I mean, if this is what they think is "beach", then what the fuck is "bouncy"?' I whispered as we paid at the cash desk half an hour later, looking dismally at our reflections in the mirror. 'I clearly said no root lift. This had better drop before this afternoon.'

LA was not being kind to us. Our skin was dry. Our hair was big.

'I'm starving. Can we have pancakes instead of a bloody egg-white omelette?' I said as we waited for the lights to change. It was already getting warm, and I could feel the LA humidity adding frizz to my big hair.

'We can. Let's go back to the hotel. Breakfast is fine there. And it's been paid for already.'

We walked back into a blast of delicious air conditioning and headed to the restaurant.

'Goooood morning,' said the unfeasibly chirpy host at the entrance.

'Table for two, please,' Martha said.

'Are you staying with us, madam?'

'Yes, room two-three-four. We'd like to be by the window, please.' Martha headed directly to the table she wanted without waiting for his reply.

As we crossed the room, I surveyed our surroundings. Men in expensive, well-cut suits wielding iPads and drinking coffee. Impossibly thin women in their best athleisure outfits meeting for a post-school-run fruit salad. A group of possibly Scandinavian film-makers talking too loudly. And then something familiar about the group in the far corner caught my eye, and I did a double take. I grabbed Martha's arm.

'Ouch,' she said. 'Frankie, that hurt.'

Seated in a white leather corner banquette were the Dante boys – Lloyd and Jonathan. With them was Dominic Carter. Laughing and joking. Dominic was making notes in a smart leather folder.

'Oh-my-fucking-God.'

I whipped out my phone and scrabbled for Nicky's number to fire off a message.

> **Frankie**
> Call me the minute you wake up. Emergency.

PRESS NOTE

Melissa Bailey shone on the John Isaacs Show, *which aired at 11 p.m. EST last night.*

'I couldn't be more delighted than to stick my hand in the box of mashed fruit. I'm always game for a laugh. And oh how we laughed. I am eternally grateful to my PR, Frankie Marks, for always pushing me to go the extra mile,' commented Melissa Bailey through gritted teeth.

ENDS

We'll deal with it, was the unanimous response back from Georgina and Nicky about Dominic and Dante. I forwarded the email on to Zoe who was staying back at the hotel working so we could discuss it in detail when I saw her.

Meanwhile, driving into the studio parking lot was complicated. Approaching the barrier and the first security hut, I held out my ID.

'I'm here with Melissa Bailey. She just went through in the car in front?' I offered my driving licence through the passenger window for inspection.

'Hold on, madam,' said Bernie, whose name tag was firmly fixed below his lapel. He disappeared into his hut and came back holding a clipboard with names. He was not in a rush.

Martha called. 'She wouldn't wait for you. We've gone in. Once you get to the artists' entrance, ask for Conrad. He's the runner. He knows you're coming. He'll bring you in. But hurry. Got to go, getting in lift.'

Bernie ambled over to the window and handed back my licence.

'Thank you, madam, you can go through now. Turn right over there, then left and then straight ahead. The car can't wait for you. Have a great day.' He activated the barrier.

I could see who I presumed to be Conrad in the distance, headset on, smiling broadly as I approached.

'Conrad?'

'Hey there! Here, let me help you,' he said, holding out a hand to help me jump down from the extraordinarily high car.

'Thanks so much,' I said as I unpicked my skirt, which was rather unseemingly stuck to my backside from sitting against the sticky leather seat and was feeling worryingly damp. 'I'm a bit late, I got stuck at security; can you take me directly to her room please?'

I followed him down a maze of corridors emblazoned with bright glossy photos of white-toothed presenters in cobalt clothes. We passed a series of very busy-looking people with remarkably straight hair holding jumbo-sized drinks with jumbo-sized straws. It was like some kind of cult where everyone ends up weirdly identical. I spotted Paul from security loitering, and knew we were close to her room.

TALENT: Melissa Bailey said the sign on the door. I nodded at Paul. Professional PR mode today. Bad cycle leggings a distant memory.

Conrad knocked and then opened the door. 'Let me know if you need anything. I'll be right out here. John will come to see Melissa half an hour before the show starts. Production will come to mic her up shortly after.'

I walked into the room. Four people, one sofa, two armchairs, a make-up station, TV on the wall, a vast platter of fruit, and a gift box of branded T-shirts and enormous mugs. Melissa was looking thunderous, sitting in the make-up chair going through the briefing notes.

'I told you I didn't want to do that stupid game with the mashed fruit,' she snapped as soon as she caught sight of me.

'And I told you, it was that or putting you on the Wheel of Death, so this was the best option. Everyone does it. It'll be good for you to be seen to loosen up. In return, you're allowed to mention the duvet collection twice PLUS credit your own website,' I snapped back. I took a deep breath and reminded myself to rein it in and channel some of my inner Jemima.

We needed this show appearance to promote Melissa's new bedding collection, launching with The American Bedding Company, the biggest home retailer across the States. Crucially, she was also wearing the red dress from her own collection that wasn't shifting in store anywhere, and I'd made them promise she could talk about the new season's collection.

I gave Martha a sideways glance. She raised her eyebrows, then went back to her laptop where she was busy ordering Melissa some furry slipper slides she had seen on Instagram and had to have NOW.

'Shall we do a messy updo?' Brian, Melissa's friend and hair stylist, was jumping around her chair, dancing to the Britney Spears track playing out of the wall-mounted TV.

'You should,' I agreed. 'Then we can see the neckline on the dress more clearly, and when you walk in and wave, if you turn around, the buttoned back detail will be visible.'

'Good point,' said Melissa, still frowning as she read her notes.

'And let's do a strong eye.' I turned to Sally the make-up artist who was brushing up Melissa's eyebrows.

'So, John will come and see you in about half an hour,' I continued. 'The team will come in to talk you through everything first – but it's pretty much going over everything we did in the pre-production call yesterday. You'll be miked up after that – hopefully they can run the wire down the back, so it doesn't interfere with the dress. I'm just going down now to look at the lighting. I'll be back soon.'

I opened the door to find Keen Conrad patiently waiting on the other side.

'Conrad, could you take me down to the show floor so I can have a look, and then can we go into the gallery so I can see the screens and camera angles?' I remembered to apply some common courtesy just in the nick of time. 'Please?'

'No problemo! Follow me!'

I marched behind him as he moved quickly through the maze of corridors.

'You'll take me back to the dressing room afterwards, won't you? I'll never find my way back,' I panted.

'Sure, sure. No problemo! So, this is where she'll be brought.' We were standing side of stage behind a wooden screen. 'And if she doesn't mind, we'll just do a few shots of her over here with the signage in the background.' He pointed at a jazzy pink neon sign: THE JOHN ISAACS SHOW. 'Then she'll be taken by me up to this point' – he stood at a red cross painted on to the floor – 'and I'll just push her in the right direction. John will get up to greet her and she'll sit in the chair nearest to him over there.' He was pointing to the stage set. 'Then afterwards the social team will do a few Instagram videos over here.' He gestured to a lit box with a stool.

These stage sets were always so much smaller in real life. A table for the host, a couple of chairs, about a hundred and fifty metres of floor space, an enormous array of cameras on wheels and then a small seating area for the audience. I scanned the floor space. I had done this so many times now – from Dublin to Dubrovnik – and it always gave me a bit of a thrill.

'Then – and we're sooo happy she's agreed to do it – John will lead her over here to play Mashed in Space.' He pointed to the left of stage where a Perspex box would be filled, apparently hilariously, with over-ripe fruit. 'She just needs to put her hand in the box and find the banana. Which will be placed top left. That's it! Then she's done!'

'Okay, sounds great. So when she comes off – she'll exit where?'

'Over there on the left, and you can wait for her there. She'll do the videos and then we'll bring you back to the dressing room, and you can either leave directly or wait for the show to end. There'll be lots of drinks in the green room.' Conrad led me round the back, up to the gallery room.

'Hey, guys, this is Frankie, she's with Melissa Bailey; she just wanted to see the set-up and the lighting from in here.' Conrad was speaking to a dimly lit room of seated production crew with headsets on, in front of a frightening number of knobs and buttons and a bank of screens. They turned to look at me with undisguised contempt. No one wanted a busybody PR in their space – but it was at times like these that I had to put on my thickest skin and assume an air of entitlement in order to get what I needed. And I *always* needed to check camera angles.

'Sorry to intrude, everyone.' I gave a limp wave in half greeting, half apology. 'It'd be great if you could run me through the camera angles. It'll just help with her make-up. And it would also be great if you could avoid zooming in on her nose. Bad lighting does nothing for her nostrils.'

There was a deafening silence. I added a muted 'please', as they continued to stare me down. I knew I had about thirty seconds before I was not so politely asked to leave, so I quickly clocked each screen, checking where they hit the guest chair, and then turned to Conrad to indicate I was done.

As we came out of the room my phone pinged.

Where did you put the birthday present for my dad? Can't find it anywhere, James had texted.

God, I had totally forgotten to pick it up from the post office before I left London. I'd promised to collect it after I'd been in the shower and failed to hear the doorbell I had specifically promised to stay in to hear last weekend.

> **Frankie**
> At the post office. Shit. Sorry. Can you collect? I typed as I walked.

> **James**
> FFS.

> **Frankie**
> Don't be moody. It's round the corner. I'm in talk-show hell. Wish all I had to worry about was walking to a post office.

> **James**
> Whatever, Frankie.

I bit my lip. Great. But I'd have to deal with that later. These types of exchanges with James always seemed to happen when I was in my most heightened work mode, and the ensuing days of frosty silence just gave me added anxiety in the pit of my stomach. They were also a potent reminder that I had been unfaithful, and that as persistently guilty as I felt, no one happy had a night swinging from a chandelier with someone like Greg. I made a mental note to spend some time dissecting the current state of my relationship once I got back from LA.

But right now, I had to check Melissa could roll her sleeves up enough to avoid staining her dress with mashed fruit. Add that to the list of career highs and state of relationship lows . . . I went back into the dressing room.

'You look INCREDIBLE,' gushed Brian, tweaking Melissa's ponytail and practically twerking. I held back my giant eye-roll.

'I've been on set and I managed to get into the gallery room. Two camera angles, keep your head slightly to the left and don't cross your legs too high. Paul, entry and exit on-and offstage is easy.' I had just started before the door knocked again.

'Hey there, it's Jerry, I'm with the crew, I just wanna run through the notes quickly. Check John has everything he needs.' Jerry was sporting an impressive beard and long-sleeved Metallica tour T-shirt as he scanned the notes on his iPad. 'So, he's going to start by asking you about the family, how you're enjoying living back in the UK. We're going to show this Instagram picture of you all sitting around the piano so he can ask about the family and music.' He held aloft an image of Melissa and Gabriel with the children in a soft haze filter. 'He'll probably make a joke about *The Sound of Music*. Then he'll move on to soft questions about press intrusion. That'll be quick. Then he'll say he loves your dress. That's when you'll talk about your collections and we'll show some images from the last show that your team provided. After that, he'll move on to the bedding and this image of you will come up.' He showed her another picture on his iPad, the one of her lying on the bed with many duvets from our *Avalon* shoot.

'Oh, she can mention the website at this point, Jerry, can't she?' I interrupted. There were broadcast rules we were supposed to adhere to regarding self-promotion, but at the end of the day, that's what this was all about. I flashed him my best megawatt smile.

'Yeah, sure. Just once though, please. Then John'll wrap it up nice and quick and take you over to Mashed in Space. That segment will last one minute. And then you're done. Easy. Can I send someone in to mic you up now?' Jerry and his beard had other guests to get to.

'Don't forget the banana will be in the top left of the box,' I told her quickly but firmly. Melissa needed the information and I didn't need to dwell on the banana. Fortunately, I was saved from further discussion.

'HELLOOOOO!!' The door swung open and the host John Isaacs came bounding in. He was like Tigger on steroids. Melissa swung around in her chair. He was much shorter than I had imagined, and wearing a lot of foundation for a man in his thirties – even by TV lighting standards. 'How're Gabriel and the kids? Soooo great to have you on tonight! I'll make it all super light and easy. Don't worry about a thing,' he boomed, nodding in everyone's direction but not making eye contact with anyone but Melissa.

'John! Haven't seen you for ages! We're all great. Thanks so much for having me on, I'm really looking forward to it.' I had to hand it to Melissa – she could really turn on the charm. They exchanged a few more gushes and disingenuous pleasantries as we all hovered, smiling politely and being ignored. I knew Melissa and John barely knew each other. But to watch them now, you'd think they'd shared baths as toddlers. I guess that was part of John's appeal. He made his audience feel like his guests were his best friends. The energy in our tiny room had amplified in thirty seconds. It was why the show was such a massive hit, and why I knew we needed it to go perfectly for Melissa.

'See you out there!' He bounded out as quickly as he had come in.

The second the door clicked shut behind him, Melissa swivelled to face me. 'I'm still furious about the stupid mashed fruit thing.'

Where's your bloody mantra now? Thankfully, before I could say anything, there was another knock at the door, and an efficient-looking blonde came in.

'Just here to mic you up now, if that's okay; do you mind if I put my hand up your skirt?' she asked, lifting Melissa's dress and edging the wires up her back. 'I'll clip the box just here and if you wouldn't mind clipping the mic to the front for me.'

'Yeah, yeah, I've been at this rodeo before. I can do it.' Melissa was getting impatient, which was bad news when I needed her on sparkling form. Martha stood up to make a timely intervention.

'I've made reservations for dinner at Sky Kitchen for straight after the show. We can leave as soon as you're done,' she said in an effort to divert Melissa's attention.

'Oh. Okay, great. We'll all go. Brian, you too?' She relaxed for a minute.

Brian looked like all his Christmases had come at once. 'I'm soooooo free,' he said, twerking in her direction.

'She started life as the darling of Britain's favourite soap,' boomed John Isaacs from behind his table on stage, above the noise of the audience clapping and cheering as images of a young Melissa in her *Carlyle Bay* days flashed up on the monitors in front of them. 'Then she went on to be the darling of Gabriel Bannon, and our very own darling of LA.' More clapping, more cheering, some pictures of her and Gabriel flashing on the screen. 'She's also a doting mother of two' – cue perfectly filtered Instagram images of the family – 'and then she left us to go back to the UK' – John mimed a sad face, before continuing – 'to launch her very own fashion label.' Now cutaways from the last fashion show were on the screens. 'Is there nothing my next guest can't do? Well, she's back, and she's here with us

tonight, and we couldn't be happier. Ladies and gentlemen, please show your appreciation for ... MELISSA
BAILEY!'

The house band turned it up a notch and the warm-up
guy turned around and waved his hands up to the audience
to keep cheering as Melissa appeared in the doorway, hands
clasped together as if in prayer before nodding and waving to
the raptures of the audience.

The dress looked good. I watched the monitors to see
what the TV audiences would be seeing, and then looked
at her live. My eyes darted up and back down, up and back
down again.

Melissa took John's hands in hers and they kissed each
other effusively on both cheeks before she sat down and
smoothed her dress.

'Oh my goodness! It's so good to be back, John.'

The audience cheered. 'Love you, Melissa,' shouted out an
enthusiastic male voice in row four.

'Love you too.' She beamed and blew a kiss. The audience
cheered again.

'So, Melissa, here you are at last. Can you tell how much
we've missed you? Welcome back – we thought we'd lost you
forever!' John started. 'How's life in the UK, and most importantly – are you missing us?'

'Well, I can't tell a lie, John, you're all we talk about at
home.' She turned to the audience and winked. They bellowed
their approval. John held his hand to his heart dramatically.

And so it went on. As production had promised, up flashed
an Instagram image of the whole family around a piano, with
a light reference to Julie Andrews, followed by one gentle
question about press intrusion.

'You know, we can't complain. It is what it is. Sometimes
it's just a bit much. But we're not the kind of people to moan.
We just try to get on with our lives in as normal a way as

possible and keep our girls out of the spotlight. You'd be amazed how boring we really are! I mean, my idea of a wild Saturday night is takeaway pizza in front of the telly and an early bed.' She had the audience in the palm of her hand. God, she was good. She was even convincingly pretending she ate pizza.

'Noooo. Never boring, Melissa. And let me just say, your dress. You look amazing, doesn't she, guys?' More applause. One wolf whistle. Or maybe two. I was now on tenterhooks. She mustn't forget to plug the dress and the collection.

'Well, thank you! This dress is from my newest collection. It's in store now. Or online at MelissaBailey.com.' *WELL DONE.* John Isaacs went on to show more catwalk images and another clip from the last show.

'But because you're not busy enough already, you're also launching a bedding line?'

'I am, John. You know, when The American Bedding Company came to me and asked if I wanted to collaborate with them, I jumped at the chance. I love my bed!'

'OOOOOOH,' exclaimed the audience.

'Noooo!' She laughed. 'Not like that, you lot are terrible, honestly! But I guess when you're married to Gabriel, you would, wouldn't you?' She winked. Again. They all laughed. 'No, what with being a working mum, my sleep is just so important, and I've been obsessed with The American Bedding Company for so long.'

'Well, we know you like a comfy bed. You even take it on shoots with you!' John exclaimed as the *Avalon* image of her cocooned in duvets came up on the screen. More audience laughter. 'Is that on your rider? One full bed with two duvets?' The warm-up guy whooped the audience to howl with laughter once more. I looked at them all with some combination of contempt, pity and immense gratitude that they believed everything they were seeing with such exceptional enthusiasm.

'I wish! No, but seriously, they came to me with this wonderful concept of a bedding range in organic cottons and I just couldn't say no. And it launches nationwide next month!'

WELL DONE AGAIN. I was bursting with pride. She had remembered everything.

'I can't let you go, Melissa, without us playing our favourite game: Mashed in Space! But tonight we've renamed it just for you: Melissa's Mash. Let's goooo.'

John bounded from his chair as the house band played its signature funky accompanying music. Melissa followed. She kept up a brave smile, but I could tell she was hating every second. I, on the other hand, was rather beginning to enjoy myself. There was a certain sense of karma to it all. The music played to a crescendo as John whipped back a black-sequinned cloth to reveal a clear, rectangular box filled to the brim with, well, with mushy fruit. This was literally Melissa's worst nightmare – as we all knew too well, she was fussy to a fault over the ripeness of her fruit.

'Okay, Melissa, I'm just going to ask you three questions. When, or IF, you get them wrong, you'll need to stick your hand in the box and find the banana.' John bent double with laughter, the audience following his lead. 'But of course, we can't make it TOO easy – so you'll be blindfolded. Can I do the honours?'

Melissa managed a brittle smile as he tied a black silk scarf over her eyes and led her to the box.

'Ready?'

'Always ready for you, John,' she replied.

'What year did *Carlyle Bay* start?'

'Oh, that's an easy one – 2001.'

'CORRECT.' Clapping.

'What year did you and Gabriel tie the knot?'

'Well, how could I forget THAT. 2010!'

'CORRECT. You've got this! And last, but certainly not least: what is the optimal thread count for an Egyptian cotton pillowcase?'

'Really?'

'Yes, Melissa, really.' Now it was John's turn to wink conspiratorially at the audience, who were beside themselves.

'I mean, well, I haven't got a clue, John!'

'Neither have I! But you know what that means. MASH IT UP, MELISSA.'

'MASH IT! MASH IT!' chanted the audience.

I could see Melissa gritting her teeth and laughing along gamely as she felt for her dress sleeve and pushed it up above her elbow. She hovered her hand above the box and then shoved it in. Swirling and searching.

'Ewww! This is so GROSS,' she squealed.

'Gross is the name of the game,' he shouted back.

'MASH IT! MASH IT!' The audience was in a frenzy.

She squelched around in the box for a few seconds looking for the strategically placed banana in the left-hand corner, where I had told her to find it. Except she didn't find it. It wasn't there. She squelched some more. I felt my stomach tighten with hysteria. Where was the fucking banana, Conrad? It was agonising. Time stood still as she swirled and I watched her smile tighten. *Please God, don't let your game face falter. You need to be a woman of the people for one more minute.* After what felt like an eternity, she located it. Fucking top right. She made a grab for it and pulled the banana out triumphantly, removing the blindfold with her other hand.

Holding it as far away from her as she possibly could, she turned to her host.

'Want a bite, John?'

'Oh-my-God-isn't-she-incredible. Melissa Bailey, you really are game for a laugh. Thank you so much. Here you go.' He handed her a linen towel to wipe her arm and hand down with.

'Ladies and gentlemen, Melissa Bailey! Don't forget to look out for her stunning duvets!'

And with that, he ushered her offstage with a handshake. I ran back to meet her.

'Happy now?' Melissa barked at me, pulling her sleeve down. 'Why the *hell* wasn't that banana where you said it would be? I looked like an asshole. That's a major fuck-up, Frankie.'

'They said it would be on the left. I wouldn't classify it as a major fuck-up. I would rank it as slightly irritating.' My blood was boiling. Conrad mouthed a sorry. *Big fucking problem, Mr 'No Problemo'.*

'And as it happens, yes, I'm very happy. Because for one dumb banana game, you got the website credited, plugged the bedding and earned yourself a million new fans. So it's a win-win. You showed everyone you've got a great sense of humour,' I pondered for a second how to turn the mood around and fast, 'the audience adored you, and your hair and make-up looked sensational.' Sometimes I was astounded at how shallow I could be to get what I needed, particularly when I was now so infuriated with her I wanted to pull that fucking bun off her head, and hopefully yank some extensions out with it.

'Oh really? Did they? Thanks.' Melissa patted her messy updo. 'We'll discuss the banana and how you could have got that so wrong later.'

I didn't register a response. I wasn't arguing about fruit.

'Now, just some social to do over here,' I led her to the neon sign, 'and one message to record over here. And then we're done.'

As I ushered her over and watched her do the last record, I remembered I needed to check in with Georgina and Nicky back in London. They were going to call Lloyd and Jonathan and find out what the hell they were doing with Dominic. I was dying to know what had happened.

'I'm Melissa Bailey and I love mashing fruit,' she was saying in front of the neon signage. 'Am I done now?' She looked at me with a grimace.

'You are.' I gritted my teeth as I scrolled through my new emails and saw the message from Nicky with the subject heading – *Fucking Dominic Carter.*

PRESS NOTE

The shoot for The American Bedding Company was a triumph. Melissa Bailey sank into every duvet with conviction. This is a collaboration of true passion. She has truly understood the value of 1,000-thread-count Egyptian cotton.

'Melissa is an inspiration. Her commitment to the King-size cover with embroidery detail took us all by surprise. It's not often you come across a celebrity so willing to pretend to embrace a collaboration with such integrity,' gushed Dana Goldberg, CMO, Head of Marketing and all things concerning duvets for American Bedding Co.

'It's always thrilling to be a part of a significant moment in bedding history. Sadly, in the excitement Frankie forgot to call her parents on their fortieth wedding anniversary. Her father said he will forgive her when she finally stops trailing around after a nonsensical celebrity,' commented Zoe Shepperton as she admired a pillowcase.

ENDS

Melissa and I had a frosty hour when we wouldn't look at each other. I hated her. She in turn sat at the opposite end of the table and pointedly ignored me, until our alcohol intake led us to abandon our mutual loathing, and the dinner at Sky Kitchen turned into a raucous affair. The following morning, I was feeling the after-effects and had a hazy memory of downing the last vodka shot and joining Brian in some twerking while Martha was organising the bill. Now I felt a little bit dreadful. James had gone stony-cold silent over post office-gate and my anxiety was swirling around in the fog of my brain. Would I dare have a coffee or would a hot water and lemon be safer? Should I just go all in for French toast with bacon and maple syrup, or keep it clean with some fresh fruit and oatmeal? The former, obviously. And I would one hundred per cent be taking my breakfast in my bed with easy access to the en suite, in case of emergency.

I drank a gallon of water, popped two paracetamol and slowly propped myself up. My head was thumping, but surprisingly I didn't feel nauseous. It was the straight vodka. 'No mixers, no sugar, no hangover,' I vaguely recollected Melissa reassuring me as I had knocked another one back. Well, I suppose she was half right.

I called room service. This was an emergency order: full-fat cappuccino, fresh orange juice, French toast, extra crispy bacon. Oh, and a bowl of berries. And perhaps I should also have the energy-booster green juice with added alkaline and chia seeds? Yes, that would do it. Today, jet lag was my friend. It was still only 7 a.m. and our call time on the duvet set was 10 a.m. I was having a lie-in.

I checked my emails. Nicky had written to me and Georgina.

Lloyd said they were ambushed. Dominic 'bumped into them' at Catch on Melrose. The boys had been out to dinner with Lucy Collins. They had also had a quick conversation with Usher, who was at the next table and a big fan of their work. But that was by the by.

Invited them for breakfast and did a whole pitch on them. They said they thought he was a creep. But I think we need to keep an eye. God knows what he's promised them.

What's bizarre though is that Dominic knew about that collection leak a few seasons ago and about your trip to that Spanish spa, Georgina? Hope LA is going well, we'll be checking on pick-up from the *John Isaacs Show*. But so far the mashed fruit segment has had more views online than anything else he's done this year. Also, Andrew not himself – can we discuss when you're back, Georgina?

Hope you're having a great break.

Nicky.

I felt a glow of satisfaction about the success of the banana – and the fact that Melissa would have to acknowledge she had had a wholly disproportionate temper tantrum – as I sat happily surveying my breakfast laid out around me. Honestly, I didn't know what to eat first. But it was all going down very well. I felt almost normal by my third French toast. Dominic knew about that time the Dante collection images were released a day early? How on earth would Sockless Carter know about that? I pondered over the weirdness as I crunched on my crispy bacon and considered Andrew's mood swings and disappearing acts. Could they be connected? No, it couldn't be. No way would Andrew be talking to Dominic Carter and Five Star. *Surely not?* My phone pinged.

Meet downstairs at 9.40. Car will take us to collect Melissa then straight on to studio.

It was Martha. Martha wasn't eating breakfast for three, lying in her bathrobe and slippers. She was clear-headed and organising our day. Clever Martha. I sighed at the thought of the day ahead, my happy reveries over.

Frankie

Zoe, I'm wearing the Darcy culotte. Don't wear if you brought them.

> **Zoe**
> Got it

She had spent last night tidying up the notes for the pre-record interview Melissa was doing this afternoon for the *C'MON!* show, before going on a date with some music guy she had originally met in London who had moved to LA but hadn't quite got her and her pageboy cut out of his head.

> **Frankie**
> Successful night?

> **Zoe**
> Extremely!

That was most excellent. She would be firing on all cylinders while I took my time to get my momentum and my mojo up.

> **Frankie**
> Getting in shower. See you later

I audio-texted as I drank my energy smoothie, holding my nose with my free hand.

'Heyyyy, so great to meet you! I'm Dana!' A woman with an immaculate bob, an enormous pink sapphire ring and silk paisley pyjama outfit with absurdly high heels approached us. 'I head up the American Bedding marketing division. I'm so happy you're here and we are DOING THIS!'

'Hi, Dana, I'm Frankie. This is Melissa, Zoe, Martha.' Everyone shook hands and then we followed Dana into the cavernous studio where I could see a set made up of a double, a super king, a single, and . . . oh God, bunk beds.

'We want to show Melissa as a mother,' she said to me, when she saw my frown.

I spotted the pair of women from backstage at Melissa's show last February, sitting at a long table behind super-sized laptops. They jumped up as soon as they saw us walking through the set.

'Well, here we are. Can you believe it? We are actually DOING THIS,' they both cried out pretty much in unison. Yup. I got it. We were DOING THIS. We were doing it for the money and a bigger profile in middle America. They were proclaiming it as if we were all about to sit down and nail the cure for cancer.

'We're so excited. Aren't we excited, Melissa?' I turned to her and poked her arm as she stared in horror at the bunk beds.

'Thrilled. Honestly, thrilled,' she managed to bleat.

'You were incredible on *John Isaacs* last night! How did you find the banana so fast?' they raved.

The shoot itself should have been simple. But it was hell. The photographer did his best to incorporate the props while keeping me and Melissa happy; Dana grinned furiously behind her whitened teeth while talking very loudly about *keeping it commercial*, and how we must bear in mind we needed an image that would work on a swing tag for the pillowcases. Melissa managed to remember the money and keep smiling while looking aghast at the shots on the monitor. She dropped in a comment that she perhaps looked a tiny bit ridiculous hanging off the edge of the top bunk. I did my best to soothe and placate and mediate between them all, while screaming inside. Behind their laptops, the two New York power women were so starstruck and delighted with their decision to use Melissa they didn't know which side of the fence they should be sitting.

I wasn't enjoying myself. I wondered if James had finally

forgiven me for the forgotten birthday present and if he would message me when he woke up. I enjoyed the time difference in the mornings when I knew he was at work and the pressure was off. As it got later and I sensed he was on his way home, I always got a tiny pang – a confusing combination of missing him, yet dreading hearing from him.

Zoe was working on her laptop, ensuring she got the messaging right for the *C'MON!* interview taking place that afternoon and intently discussing Egyptian cotton and competitive pricing. She needed to let Melissa know how many stores the collaboration would be available in, the price points of every single versus king duvet, the delicate embroidery on what we had decided to name the Dandelion collection, the more playful prints on the Delilah single sets. Like me, Zoe was starting to wonder if any of this fell under the umbrella term of fashion PR.

After an interminable morning, it seemed we had enough shots to argue over and approve. Melissa, however, was furious.

'You said the photographer was great!' she fumed as she changed.

'He is great. At least it's done now. I'll find the best images. And we need to turn this around fast. This collection is going in store in a month.' I was cross. I was tired. I wasn't getting anything for working on this collaboration. The only winners were her, Cole and The American Bedding Company. Yet here I was coordinating, managing, arguing. And I hadn't even got to the lengthy approvals process yet. Another argument was brewing.

'Right, here are your briefing notes.' I was saved by the Zoe bell as she approached. 'I've given you the price list, the distribution, images of the prints, and a few key bits of wording. See here,' – she pointed at the highlighted sentences on the pieces of paper – 'machine washable, perfect for any age, Dandelion and Delilah personally chose the two collections in their names, they loved them, Gabriel found the four-hundred thread count to be his personal favourite. Aspirational yet affordable, really has the Melissa Bailey stamp on all of it, the embroidery really mirrors everything you try to do in your collections, it's a piece of Melissa Bailey but on your bed. Etcetera.'

'The *C'MON* team is setting up over there.' Martha pointed to a corner of the studio currently busy with a camera crew, the anchor and other people fussing around. 'What's she wearing?'

'She's going to wear the yellow skirt and shirt with these orange pumps.' I pulled out the look from the rail. 'It's in store now.'

We talked about Melissa like she was a commodity and mollycoddled her like she was a child. But the whole point of doing anything painful like a *C'MON!* show interview to talk about duvets was to get maximum use out of it. We would sell a lot of that yellow look if she wore it on prime-time TV.

'Was that okay?' Melissa asked me as she walked off set. I was in a fog of delayed fury. Now I had done what I needed to do, I looked at her through squinted eyes. I refused to be shouted at about bananas. I wasn't going to take being berated for a duvet shoot. I was sick of her.

'It was perfect,' interjected Zoe. Thank God we had each other. She had seen me zoning out – succumbing to exhaustion, frustration and yes, homesickness. She put a hand on my back. These were the moments where I was grateful for the fact that we weren't just colleagues. Our travel bubble – me, Zoe, Martha, and even Melissa – were really good friends. As we left the studio, I got a brief but irate email from my father.

Would you like to call your mother? It was our wedding anniversary yesterday.

Fuck. I urgently and desperately wanted to get home. Just one more shopping event, and I would soon be on that plane.

Will I have Branston pickle or mustard on my cheese on toast when I eventually get there?

'She's decided she hates her room.' Martha banged her head against an imaginary brick wall. 'Apparently there's not enough closet space, the minibar is whirring and the extra fridge I had put in for her papayas and supplements is an eyesore. The view isn't right, the curtains are dirty, and the sofa is uncomfortable. Shoot. Me. Now.'

'She'll get over it.' I shrugged. 'Zoe, where do we have to go with these clothes?'

We had a shopping event to get through. We had suitcases full to the brim of salmon-coloured samples – it was the colour of the new season.

'Penthouse suite. We should go and start hanging them up.'

'I'm not going anywhere, because I'm going to look for an attractive fridge and argue with the concierge about getting a different room,' Martha said.

We were there for a shopping event with overly keen and hysterical women who, once they caught glimpse of Melissa, would lose all social propriety and jostle, push and shove their phones in the air. The worst. But what was more pressing was the current LA humidity and its effect on our hair.

'How do we fight the fucking frizz? That's really the most urgent situation, if you don't mind me saying,' I said, gently patting my ever-increasing volume. 'It's not our best look and it's only going to get worse. Even for you, Zoe.'

'Your hair isn't the only problem. I'm sorry, Frankie, but the dress you wanted to wear tonight has now gone to the billionaire from Palm Springs' daughter. Yes, she is only twelve but she's trialling it for her batmitzvah. Melissa wants her to wear it.'

'Well, what the hell am I going to wear? I forgot my seamless knickers again.'

'Remember, Frankie, no one will be looking at you,' Martha and Zoe said in unison and then fell over themselves laughing.

'That may be true, but it's not funny,' I retorted and shoved two chips into the corners of my mouth to create some fangs. 'Are Brian and Sally setting up in her room?'

'Oh yes. They're all sharing her papaya as we speak.' Martha rolled her eyes. Melissa's hair and make-up teams always declared their passion for prawns and papaya when they were with Melissa. We knew they were probably secretly craving spaghetti bolognese. Actually, we definitively knew they were – because our favourite game was to look at their room service bills at the end of each trip when Martha was signing off their expenses, and see what they had ordered in private.

'I like the salmon pink because I just like it,' Melissa said belligerently to the poor, overexcited journalist from the *LA Bugle* as we did our last round of print interviews. She scrolled through her phone and took a long, passive-aggressive slurp of her drink through her straw.

I was furious. Livid. I shot her a look, and then turned to the flustered journalist.

'What Melissa means is she *adores* salmon pink, so it really was just a given that it would feature so heavily in this next collection. Isn't that right, Melissa?'

'Yes. Yes, that's right.' She crossed her legs and leaned back against the sofa she had now been sitting on for three hours.

'You cannot tell a journalist you've chosen a colour *just because you like it*.' I turned to Melissa as soon as I'd shut the door for the final time. 'I know you're tired. I know you haven't slept. But these people are excited to meet you. *They're* not sick of talking about salmon pink, because it's the first time they've ever talked about salmon pink with Melissa Bailey. That just wasn't okay.'

She shrugged. There was an uneasy silence.

'You know we're all tired. We're all away from home. We all have jet lag, and we're *all* bored of shaking people's hands and telling them we love their handbags. But we just need to get through today, and then we will be flying home.'

The balance of mine and Melissa's relationship was impossible to explain to anyone. I may have been on the payroll but I was her friend, her security blanket, her gatekeeper and sometimes her moral compass, all rolled into one. It was a lot of pressure. And I just wasn't having it. I was sick of her. Sick of James. Sick of life.

'In better news than salmon pink and crying journalists, Josh Brigson messaged me last night. I haven't heard from him for a while.' Zoe was lying on my bed with me later that day.

'And?'

'He wants to meet up when I'm back. Seems he can't stop thinking about me since that dinner. Well, he definitely wasn't thinking about me when he was out with the blonde from that girl band. And he absolutely *had* forgotten about me when he was on the red carpet with that ex-Disney star. When he was telling me what he's been up to, I had to pretend I hadn't been stalking him and act surprised. Seems he had never minded about my purple Darcy Girl knickers.'

'It's almost a love story.' I laughed.

'Well, you know, he's hot. I'll give it another whirl.'

'You will.'

'I will.'

'Did he mention Greg at all?'

'Anything you want to tell me about Greg?' Zoe looked at me.

'Nothing of any consequence. No, nothing. It was nothing,' I said.

When Zoe went back to her own room to continue sexting Josh Brigson, I was suddenly overcome with loneliness. Desperate loneliness. I called Charlotte. No answer. I took my chances and called James.

'Only me.' I was talking in my woeful small voice when he picked up.

'Oh hi, how's it going?'

'It's going. Pretty relentless. Done the TV. Done the duvet shoot. Been polite to a lot of ladies who didn't care about me but just wanted to get to Melissa. I'm exhausted.'

'I'm about to get on the tube to work. That's how we roll in the normal world.'

'I'm so tired, James. I just want to come home.'

'So tired in your five-star hotel, in your chauffeur-driven car, with security and a first-class flight? Come on, Frankie. Stop feeling sorry for yourself. No one forced you into this. It's me who's left behind back here, picking up birthday presents and fixing the dishwasher. Anyway, look, I've got to go, going into a tunnel.'

And with a muted farewell, the phone went dead.

Actually, I flew business. But it didn't seem the right time to correct him. Or to tell him I had forgotten the correct knickers. Again. The state of our relationship wasn't currently up to in-jokes.

I got back from LA in a blur of suitcases, jet lag and an empty fridge. James clearly had no desire to be in the flat waiting for me with a cup of coffee and a hot bath. I messaged him to say I'd landed. He messaged back a thumbs-up emoji. I had brought him back an absurd super-sized John Isaacs mug from the green room. I hoped he'd think it was funny. But truth be told, I was getting cross. These trips were exhausting – mentally and physically. And he kept talking about them as if I'd been on a spa break. 'Yeah, Frankie's trips are gruelling – I mean, what with flying first, dinners out, blow-dries and carrying Melissa's handbag – I don't know how she does it,' he would laughingly tell our friends. But I felt patronised, and not for the first time. He had never been on board with how fashion PR could become a worthwhile career. And now I had reached a modicum of success, he still couldn't come to terms with it. I also knew it was a pretty accurate precis of what he thought I did. It was decidedly unfair, as he knew how hard I worked – and that sometimes my blow-dries were a *disaster*. I stuck the kettle on and ran my own bath as I started unpacking again.

Once I was back at my desk, it was like I had never been away. After each trip I was always so happy to be back with everyone at GGC. It still took me by surprise. Eloise was still the most unpopular girl in the gang. Nicky the most groomed. Zoe the bombshell. Jemima was everyone's friend, and Andrew was sporting a new red tint in his hair and had taken a mysterious long weekend break without documenting it on Instagram, which led us to believe it hadn't really happened. Georgina popped in and asked for a quick debrief on LA, we bitched about Dominic and worried about Dante; Zoe relayed the bunk-bed story. Everyone screeched with laughter about the banana. We went on a massive charm offensive with Jonathan and Lloyd, who had started to question decisions and press coverage in a way that clients only did when they were getting itchy feet or other offers.

The office was my happy place more often than not. I was increasingly perplexed as to why my commitment to my work still seemed to cause James and my father such affront, and why Charlotte didn't stick up for me unconditionally, but I started to compartmentalise. I needed to focus my energy on all the other clients I had neglected when I was away. I did a large lunch for a bunch of stylists for Darcy Girl where I gushed over the upcoming winter drop of mohair mix knits; I pushed Jessy swimwear on every winter holiday newspaper supplement story I found out about. I created a gifting list for the Samira K sparkle evening clutch and got the intern to package twenty of them up and send them to the most relevant celebrities and editors. I told Holly Lars at *The Forward* about the limited-edition Giovanni Castani neon sandal that she could have on an exclusive for her February issue introducing the new summer collections. I was on a whirlwind of breakfasts, lunches and dinners. I attended every party I had to. I took so many appointments in the showroom even Georgina noticed and suggested I might like to let the intern take the less important ones for me. I was a typhoon. I talked about the trouser of the season. The shoe of the year. The most impressive culotte of the high street. I was fully entrenched. Yet I knew I was floundering.

I had secured Melissa the cover of *Vita* magazine. Second only to *Avalon* in terms of kudos.

'I want Mendel to shoot me.' Melissa shrugged defiantly.

Don't fucking start with me, lady. Not again.

'But you know he doesn't want to shoot you. Plus, he only shoots in New York and we're shooting in London. Look, here are the other options. There are some great photographers. Look at this guy, Robert Cook – he's doing so well. He's the next big thing. He could really do something new and innovative with you.'

I pulled up some images of his work on my phone. I was in Melissa's office, ensconced on the deep purple sofa, leaning my elbows on my knees and picking out the cashews from a bowl of nuts and seeds on the coffee table. I popped a few in my mouth as she zoomed in and out of the images.

'I'm not convinced. Who are our hair and make-up options? Who's styling? What's the location? You know I really don't want to shoot in a studio again. I'd like something dramatic, outdoors. Like a quarry, something big – but it can't be too far from home. I don't want too early a call time, and make sure Martha knows I want to make it home for supper. That's my new rule. Home for supper.'

I smiled passively. Inside, my stomach was already churning. A quarry near London. Location shoots were expensive. This was supposed to be fun. Why was this not fun? Melissa should have thanked me for the coverage with a tear in her eye. We should be triple-somersaulting around the office. I had a new moonwalk I could perform at any given opportunity.

'Absolutely. Sure, no problem. Leave it with me. I'll talk to Martha now. But I just think you need to be open-minded about shooting in a studio. I'm not sure they'll have the budget for a location shoot. And as it's for March, you're going to be in Spring/Summer and we really don't want you in a swimsuit in a thunderstorm in a quarry. But you know, this is great. Couldn't be better.' I couldn't quite hide my irritation as I got up and started to walk towards the door.

'I do trust you, Frankie,' Melissa said.

'I know you do,' I replied gratefully.

'Let's drink vodka next week. I'll get Martha to look at the diary.'

'Let's absolutely drink vodka. We've earned it.' Despite all Melissa's foibles and demands, I just couldn't help but like her. She knew when she had pushed me too far and how to bring me back from the edge.

I ambled over to Martha's desk. She pretended to ignore me. 'Want a cup of tea before I go?' I said, moonwalking.

'Oh no, here we go. What do you want? You only offer to make me a cup of tea when you're going to annoy me, mess up my diary and cause me problems.'

I smiled as sweetly as I could, bringing my moonwalk to a halt while peering over her shoulder at the colour-coded diary up on the screen that was jam-packed to the last hundredth of a second.

'No, it's not a problem. I just need her for a full day. In London. Before the end of November.'

Martha fixed me with her most steely look, tucked her hair behind her ears and emitted an enormous sigh.

'Oh yes, Frankie. That's easy. Because there really are thirty-five days in November . . . You'd better see if there are any Hobnobs in the kitchen too.'

I ran to stick the kettle on. It was going to take more than a cup of tea and a biscuit to get me back firing on all cylinders. I had started to feel like this was all finishing me off.

PRESS NOTE

Shooting a cover is a joyous and wonderfully collaborative, creative process. We are thrilled to confirm Melissa Bailey will be the March cover star of Vita *magazine.*

'I was delighted to be told what I could and couldn't style the subject matter in by the bloody PR. It was definitely a new experience for me,' raged super stylist Lucy Collins.

ENDS

'Morning! Morning! Hey, so great to see you. Oh my goodness, look at you, you look amazing. Have you been on holiday? Oh hi, Robert! Thanks so much for flying in to do this. We are SO grateful.'

'Where's Lucy?' I asked one of the assistants as I scanned the room. We were lucky to have convinced Lucy Collins to style this shoot, thanks to our run-in at Spinning Souls. She was so ensconced with Dante – and the vintage discussions Melissa had suggested on a whim had, of course, never materialised – that I was surprised she had agreed to do this. But the way Lucy mixed vintage with new season was unsurpassed, Melissa had insisted. And she wanted her. Despite of – or probably because of – Lucy's affiliation with Dante. There was no love lost between Melissa and Dante. She knew how Jonathan and Lloyd derided her, so doing a shoot with Lucy would cause them immense irritation. It was also another impressive show of her dogged determination to be immersed among the fashion elite. Melissa never took her eyes off the prize.

I skimmed the hanging clothes with my fingers and spied some ruffles that weren't going to work. I made a mental note to have them removed before Melissa got there.

'Is Martha here yet?' I asked no one in particular, assuming someone who knew the answer would hear me. 'Robert, can I look at the set-up, please?' I called out. 'Did anyone bring that balconette Eres bra I asked for?' 'Gavin, you know you can't use anything oil-based on the extensions, yes?' 'Carol, did you bring that foundation shade two I emailed about? Her skin is quite tanned at the moment.' My brain whirred. 'Terry, I really hope you have that nude shade for her toes this time, the other one was just too pink last week.'

I was on high alert. Everything needed to be set up and perfect. Clothes needed to be steamed and ready. The mirror needed to be full-length and the robe needed to be cotton, not silk.

'WHERE ARE THE SLIPPERS?' I cried out.

A hand brandishing them appeared.

The door opened and Martha walked in, NDAs in hand. Rider to be checked off:

1. White flowers (no greenery). Check
2. Sunflower seeds. Wholefoods. Check
3. Sugar-free peppermint (not spearmint) gum. Check
4. Alkaline water (glass bottles, not plastic). Check
5. Sriracha sauce. Organic. Check
6. Fig candles. Diptyque. Check
7. Papaya. Peeled. Check
8. Prawns. Small. M&S only. Check
9. Sea salt. From Cornwall. Check

'So, guys, can I just gather you round quickly before she gets here?' I called out, trying at once to be a team player but also to reaffirm who was in charge. The *Vita* magazine Art Director's plane was stuck in a snowstorm on the runway coming back from a shoot in Finland. She had sent through copious notes and instructions, but her absence was a blessing. One less expectation to manage, more room for me to take control.

'She's on her way. Has everyone signed their NDAs? You really don't need to read them. They're completely standard.' I needed to protect Melissa in case she talked about Delilah not doing her homework or Gabriel hating his co-star in earshot of someone with loose lips and a tabloid on speed dial. It was an occupational hazard. 'Robert – what are you thinking?' I made sure I kept my voice light as I barked out instructions. I couldn't afford to get them offside.

The photographer Robert really was the new hot ticket, and Melissa had finally agreed to use him once she had seen his shoots with JLo for Italian *Bella*. He had flown in directly from Milan and was known for being both charming and an arrogant asshole.

He was wearing a very nice white T-shirt, I noticed. Just the right side of worn in. Faded black jeans. Old-school Adidas trainers. Glasses on top of his head. I twirled my hair. *I wonder if James would like some old-school Adidas trainers? Stop looking at other men and their trainers, Frankie. You have a boyfriend. James has some lovely Nikes.*

Robert looked up from checking his cameras.

'So, *you're* Frankie. Wow, Greg was right, not his usual type at all.'

For crying out loud. Did these photographers overshare everything? I raised an eyebrow in what I hoped was an expression of crushing dissent with an element of yes-I-hear-that-a-lot-but-actually-I'm-devastatingly-sexy. It seemed to go right over Robert's head. I needed to practise my I'm-vulnerable-and-unexpected-and-will-take-you-by-surprise look. I also needed to stop being reminded what a terrible person I had been.

Robert went on. 'Yeah, right. What I'm thinking is to use this corner. Slightly seventies. Some black and white. Let's just really feel it. I'll use daylight. Really make it feel natural. How's her hair at the moment?'

I nodded thoughtfully, collaboratively, even. Then I stared into the middle distance for thirty seconds as if to contemplate.

'No,' I said, 'sorry, daylight won't work. Too hard. Never works for her. I want soft lights. She's exhausted. She's been travelling. We did a lot of black and white for the cover of Spanish *Elite* so let's avoid that.'

He must hate me. I hate Greg more.

'Sorry, sorry, my car was late.' Lucy, the stylist, skipped into the room like a gazelle. Slightly wet, dishevelled, shoulder-length black hair, denim shirt nonchalantly stuffed into a pair of what must have been black wide-leg Celine trousers, indeterminable trainers that I now needed to own immediately. Rings on every finger, a couple of gold chains thrown over her neck, fine gold earrings in five holes in her ears. She was everything, as usual. I prayed she had forgotten my Spinning Souls leggings.

'Robert!' She grabbed him into a bear hug. 'How the fuck are you? I haven't seen you since we shot Miley in LA. God, that shoot was great. But this is going to be great too.'

I sidled over.

'Hey, Lucy, great to see you. Don't worry, I'm not going to interfere too much, just here to, you know, sit on the sidelines . . . can we just go through the mood boards together before Melissa arrives?'

The three of us took out tear sheets and reference images. We ushered Gavin over and discussed tousled hair down versus loose ponytail up with intensity. We talked looks, positions, double-page, portrait. The cover absolutely had to feature Dior, because they had taken major advertising for the March issue. The editor insisted.

Oh. The Dior. The offending yellow ruffles.

'Lucy, can I have a quick word?' I ushered her over to the rails. 'The problem is, Melissa will hate this look. I know before she's even tried it on. It's going to swamp her. The colour's dreadful for her. Can we rethink cover options? Does it have to be Dior?'

'She's here,' Martha said, 'and she's brought the dog.'

'Back in a minute, Lucy, can we discuss when she's settled in the chair?' I asked quietly.

Melissa arrived in a pair of baggy jeans, big polo neck and trainers. Boy, had she come a long way since her ghastly get-up at that first *Avalon* shoot.

'Hi, everyone! I'm so excited. Oh, Robert, so great to finally work with you. Lucy! I love your trousers. Terry, can you start by taking off these old gels, and do you have that nice nude shade? Gavin, don't use oil on my hair. Carol, I can only use foundation two. Frankie, are there any slippers? Martha, can I have some papaya, thinly sliced? Sorry to ask, I'm starving.'

Melissa was all smiles. She engaged with everyone. 'She's so down to earth,' all the assistants she'd never met before muttered to themselves. Not how they imagined at all. My phone beeped. Melissa. A text: *Can you come over here please?*

I speed-walked over to where she was placing her handbag on the floor in the corner of the dressing area.

'I hate everything I can see on that rail. I can't stand the photographer's aftershave, and last time we worked with Carol, I looked like a drag queen. Can I leave it with you?'

My heart sank as I nodded and tried to appease her. 'Sure, don't worry.' I smiled, turned and exited. Straight to my bag to grab my phone and fags, and out of the studio. Standing outside the doors on the street, I lit up.

'Fuck you. Fuck fuck this shit,' I spat under my breath in between drags. I dialled Zoe.

'It's a fucking joke. I don't need to be dealing with this shit. She ASKED for Carol. She WANTED Lucy. She AGREED to Robert. Can you please come down and be my buffer? Nicky won't mind. Just for a couple of hours? I'm about to go into battle at the rail over ruffles. RUFFLES! This is NOT a career high.' I didn't stop for breath.

'Okay, I'll come down. What studio are you in? Do you want anything?' Zoe sounded like she wouldn't mind an outing away from the office for a few hours.

Just hearing her voice helped. I looked up at the sky, which was unusually blue, and had a fleeting moment of calm.

'Yes – another packet of Marlboro Lights; one of those lemon waters out of Georgina's fridge if she's not there; a packet of prawn cocktail crisps. And some arsenic. Thanks. See you soon. Hurry.'

'On my way. The arsenic may delay me, though. Just warning you.'

I stubbed my cigarette out on the pavement, pulled out a gum from the deep recesses of my jeans pockets and ventured back into the studio.

'Oh my God, Gavin, it was HYSTERICAL.' Melissa was holding court. In between charming everyone around her, I could see she had spotted me coming back in. My phone pinged. *You spoken to Lucy and Carol yet?* No 'please' this time. I pinged back *Just about to* as I walked straight past the hair station to where Carol's assistants were fiddling with make-up brushes.

'And then it was just SO funny. We drank SO much. It was the BEST PARTY EVER.' I could hear Melissa carry on regaling Gavin with stories as I moved past them. I hated her when she was like this. Part diva, part actress, part fashionista. And everyone's best friend – unless, of course, you worked for her and things weren't exactly how she wanted them.

'Hey, Carol, you know, I was just thinking – let's keep the make-up really light today. Like natural. Almost not there. And then, you know, build it up once we've seen how it looks on the monitor?' I ventured gently to the make-up artist as she was straightening her eyeshadow compacts in rows.

'Darling, course. Not a problem. I just need to be careful around her lips. They're bigger than I remember from last time. But I hear you. Light. Natural. A little sun-kissed. We'll just accentuate the tan.' Carol pointed to a bronzer.

My mind had wandered already but I remembered to nod. 'Perfect, yes! I knew you'd understand.'

At that moment I literally couldn't care less. But I forged ahead.

'Lucy.' I walked up to the rail where she was handing clothes to be steamed. 'Look, don't shoot the messenger, but I really feel we need to simplify the looks today. Melissa wants to look, you know, un-styled? Does that make sense? Like she just threw the clothes on? She just loves how you use vintage. So, you know, I'm just not sure that Dior ruffle is going to work. How about we shoot her in something like this for the cover.' I picked up a green ruffle dress from Melissa's own collection. If it was ruffles they wanted, I could give them ruffles. 'And use those Dior stud earrings for the credit?'

Lucy stiffened. *Also hates me.*

'The earrings won't be enough of a credit for them, and I don't know if I can have her in her own collection on the cover. Besides, I really don't really think green will work. Look, I got this in specially from Dante and these cowboy boots are vintage. Let's just try her in a few things when she's had her hair done?'

Lucy had grabbed a purple Dante seersucker trouser suit from the rail. Melissa would look great in it. Lucy really was a genius stylist. And I knew Andrew would be furious if I missed this editorial opportunity for them – *on pain of death* may have been his actual words.

'Okay, sure, let's try a few things on,' I said in a low voice, 'but let's not tell her exactly when we're shooting the cover look. It'll be easier that way – I'll deal with her afterwards. Thanks, Lucy.' She looked slightly mollified so I thought I could try my luck. 'By the way, where are your trainers from?'

'Oh God, it was just AMAZING. We laughed SO much.' Melissa was still entertaining the team as Terry worked on her toes while her hair was simultaneously being sprayed and tonged.

'Carol, you can start on her in two minutes,' Gavin called out. 'I'll just grip her hair back, hold on.'

'How's this colour?' Terry asked from the floor at Melissa's feet.

I moved swiftly by, until their conversations were just a low hum, and went back outside to wait for Zoe and have another ciggy. Martha joined me. She was so tiny in pink cashmere she looked like a little blancmange. I liked to call her the baby-faced assassin. Appearances were so misleading. She lit up and took a huge drag.

'If I have to slice papaya ONE MORE FUCKING TIME, I'll kill myself,' she said, exhaling. 'And any minute now, I'll have to take the fucking dog for a walk. Not to mention I'm also breaking in her new fucking shoes for her so she can wear them for some lunch tomorrow and not get blisters.'

I looked down to examine the wholly inappropriate mint-green stiletto pumps she was wearing.

'Oh God, you poor thing. But I'm also relieved – I'd been wondering about your choice of shoes all morning.'

'Well, thanks a bunch,' she replied, but we were both smiling now.

'I've told Zoe to come down,' I said. 'We need an extra man on the ground. We need all the help we can get today.'

We sighed.

'At least she wants to be home for dinner tonight. So it won't be a late one. We really need them to start shooting soon.' Martha wriggled her feet. 'How many shots? When is the interview happening? Did you remind them she's tired?'

We stared into space, contemplating what still lay ahead.

'How long have you been with her now?' I asked. It was a rhetorical question. I knew the answer. Five years.

'Five years this April.' Martha sighed again.

'How much longer do you think you can keep it up?' I asked. I realised I was wondering more for myself than for her.

'I dunno. Not forever. I'll burn out soon,' she replied.

'I think I'm nearly burned out already,' I said. 'I don't know how much longer I can put someone else first. It's hard, isn't it? I mean, we have a laugh, we like her even when we hate her. And what would we do if we didn't speak to each other every day?'

'Have a life?' Martha said.

'Look at you both! Here's your lemon water.' Zoe appeared, thrusting the bottle in front of my face. 'And I got you Skips 'cos there were no other prawn cocktail crisps. And here are your fags. I couldn't get arsenic.'

'Thanks. I already want to go home, and we haven't even started shooting,' I wailed.

'My feet are killing me. She'd better not expect me to walk the dog in these motherfuckers,' Martha muttered.

'And polite reminder, I've come down as a favour to you both, so cheer up,' Zoe said. 'Let's all go back in and check what's going on. And FYI, Frankie, we all know you secretly love these shoots. You thrive on them. This moaning of yours is just all part of the ritual.'

I chose to ignore this rather perceptive analysis of hers.

'Martha! Martha!' Melissa called out as soon as she saw her across the studio. Martha started running as fast as she could in her heels.

'This papaya is too ripe,' Melissa hissed in her ear.

PRESS NOTE

The Vita *magazine interview that accompanied the Melissa Bailey cover shoot was a breath of fresh air. She answered every question with a sense of honesty and openness that is rare to find these days.*

'Of course, as a public figure, I am mindful of the interest in my personal life. I'm always happy to share personal insights with my fans. However, if one more interfering journalist asks me where my husband is, I'll kill them,' Melissa Bailey commented while nibbling on a slice of papaya.

ENDS

Hours passed as I checked the lighting on Melissa's nose and the position of her feet. By now I had looked at images of Melissa through so many monitors on so many shoots that I was on autopilot – mechanically going through the motions and issuing a steady stream of instructions.

I messaged Martha and Zoe on our newest group chat entitled 'Fuck this 4 a laugh'.

> **Frankie**
> How's the food looking? I'm starving.

Zoe
Yeah, quite nice. I see something that looks like a curry. When do you think you'll break for lunch?

Martha
When Melissa's hungry I guess.

Frankie
Urghhhh.

Studio shoots always made me starving, and if there wasn't a Dorito in my mouth it was a Haribo. I tried not to drink too much on set. I hated sharing bathrooms with strangers. It was unhygienic and I didn't like people I was trying to maintain an air of professional authority with hearing me wee.

'That's done,' said Robert, putting down his camera. 'Lucy, shall we try the purple Dante seersucker now?'

Melissa was walking towards the changing area.

Lucy held up the purple seersucker suit. 'I really want to see how you look in this, if that's okay.'

Zoe was on tenterhooks. 'Oh wow, that'd look sensational on you, Melissa,' she said.

I wasn't the only one willing to stoop to new levels of shallow to get a good outcome for one of our clients. Especially one who was actively being courted by Dominic Carter.

But Melissa didn't like having to compete with Dante for attention at GGC, and she wasn't ever overly generous in lending her selling power to anyone she conceived as a competitive designer.

'It would be really nice to show your support by being shot in one of their looks,' I ventured quietly.

'Right. I'll try it. Can you get me out of this top first, please,' she said to Lucy's assistant who was waiting behind the modesty screens.

'Wow. You look amazing in that!' said Zoe.

'Totally – such a strong look,' I added.

'Let's just try these boots on with it,' said Lucy, holding up the cowboy boots.

'I need to get that piece of hair out of the collar.' Gavin appeared as if from nowhere with his comb.

'Just a little bit of powder on your nose, hold on,' Carol said, waving a compact.

'The dog just shat on the floor,' Martha announced.

Ignoring her, Melissa looked at herself in the mirror. It did look good. I could tell she was admiring the cut – albeit reluctantly.

'Okay. Let's do this. And then I really want to break for lunch,' she called out as she walked on set. I did a surreptitious fist pump as we passed Martha, who was on her knees with a pooper scooper and a packet of disinfectant wipes.

Melissa was eating at the make-up station while FaceTiming Gabriel on set in Vancouver.

Martha, Zoe and I sat at the long communal wooden table on a mezzanine level eating a sweet potato curry, the dog at Martha's feet.

'How many more shots?'

'I think three. But I'm going to suggest a double-page spread for one to make it two,' I said between mouthfuls. Fuck, I was hungry.

'When's the interview happening?'

'End of day. It had better be snappy.'

One of the production runners appeared.

'Are you Frankie?'

'Uh huh.'

'Someone called Dominique's here and asking for you. She says she's here for the interview.'

Well, that was just downright irritating. I did not want the journalist in the room watching the shoot before the interview happened – that was an open invitation for some 'colour' when Melissa got tetchy. Which was why I had scheduled the interview for the end of the day.

'Save me a piece of that chocolate brownie,' I said as I left the table and thumped down the stairs.

'Hey, Dominique. Great to see you, but I'm afraid I don't think the interview is scheduled till five p.m.? I'm not sure if you want to hang around till then or if you'd rather just come back later?'

Dominique would clearly rather hang around, as she was already taking off her jacket and making herself comfortable on the sofa to the side of the set.

'Oh, I'm good to wait. It's going to be helpful to watch her in action. Give me some colour for the story.'

'Oh wonderful. But listen, I'm operating a closed set. So I'm going to need to ask you to wait upstairs. There's food if you haven't eaten?'

'I won't get in the way. I've got lots to be getting on with. Here is fine.' She edged her bottom further into the leather sofa.

This was now a delicate balancing act. I didn't want this Dominique watching. But equally I didn't want to piss her off before she'd even started the interview.

I smiled sympathetically and put my hands in my pockets.

'Of course. Well, I'll see you in a couple of hours then.' I wanted to slap her.

'You know what, Gavin, I'm not sure I like this piece of hair falling like this on this side.' Melissa was back in the hair and make-up chair.

I leaned down and whispered in her ear, 'The journalist

doing the interview has decided to turn up early. I need you to be on your BEST behaviour for the last few shots. Okay?'

She looked at me as if butter wouldn't melt. 'Sure.'

I wasn't sure. But there was nothing I could do. I kept one eye on Melissa, one on the monitor and the eye in the back of my head on the journalist who was pretending to work on her laptop but was absolutely taking notes.

Vita may have finally given us this cover, but I didn't believe for one second that they wouldn't try to garner some headlines with the interview copy. They would want to make everyone forget that *Avalon* had broken the Melissa Bailey revamp – there was no room to play sloppy seconds. This shoot needed to be seen as part of the *Vita* strategy, and within that strategy I was absolutely certain there would be the search for a headline-grabbing story. This was the PR tightrope I walked whenever I agreed to any kind of shoot or interview. It was always nerve-wracking, and I loved it.

Melissa behaved impeccably until one of the stylists' pins, which had been holding a trouser waist, came loose and stabbed her. She screeched a litany of profanities. The journalist's pen flew across the page. The next two shots thankfully went seamlessly. I ate a packet of Jelly Babies and stared at the monitor. I had seen what the cover could look like, I had options and I was ready to wrap it up and get this interview done.

'That's a wrap,' Robert called out. We all clapped. 'You were wonderful,' he said, pushing his glasses back up on his head as he and Melissa faux hugged.

'Thank you so much, it was great. Do you think we got a cover?' Melissa asked, as she walked up to the monitor and glanced at the images that were on the screen.

'So many options for the cover,' Lucy said as she placed her hand on Melissa's shoulder assuredly.

I was acutely aware I was on a deadline – it was five p.m. already and Dominique would be expecting an hour with her. Melissa would want to give her half. I would settle on forty-five minutes.

I introduced Melissa to Dominique and messaged Martha to bring over her slippers. I wasn't leaving the pair alone for one second with Melissa in this mood. Dominique placed her Dictaphone recorder on the table and activated Voice Memos on her phone. 'Just in case one doesn't work,' she said. 'How was the shoot? Looked so great. I love this look.' She pointed at the shirt and knickers Melissa was sporting.

'Oh, it was wonderful; I've wanted to work with Robert for so long. I'd seen some of his work and I said to Frankie, "I want to work with him the next time I have a shoot." He's the one to watch. Didn't I, Frankie?'

'Oh, absolutely, yes. You're always so great at spotting new talent.' I didn't take offence. I knew I was never publicly going to get the credit for anything. *Excuse me as I just disappear into the woodwork.*

'So, tell me a little bit about living in London. Your studio is now here full-time, isn't it?'

'That's right. You know, once the business started really taking shape, it just didn't make sense to have the offices anywhere else. And the talent here is so wonderful. I feel so lucky to be able to work in such an inspirational environment.'

Dominique nodded and smiled genially while looking through her notes. She asked a few more questions about Melissa's collections, Cole, London Fashion Week, the children. Being a working mother. Being back home. I knew where this was headed.

'It must be hard to live apart from Gabriel?'

Here we go.

'Well, you know, technically we don't live apart. I mean, he's always worked away, been on location for long periods of time. It's just that now, in between projects, we have the option to be together here or LA. Honestly, it's the dream scenario.' She touched Dominique's knee gently and conspiratorially. 'And who doesn't love a bit of "me" time?' She winked. 'But really, I'm not here to answer questions about my husband. It's just so obvious.' Her mood and tone turned. This was not okay, and it required intervention.

'I mean, it's great to be here and have the time to work on the February collection, isn't it?' I said jovially as Dominique eyeballed me.

'Frankie's right. It's actually worked out brilliantly. I can work on the collection. Me and the kids will head back to LA for Christmas and New Year, where we'll love a bit of quality family time. Then I'll head back here in good time for the girls to get back to school and for me to prepare for the show in February. And Gabriel will be here for that. He wouldn't miss it for the world. Which is what I'm sure you *really* want to know.' She raised an eyebrow and picked up her phone.

Holy hell. This was not fun. I had given her clear instructions. Why couldn't she just stick to the script for once? I needed this to be over.

'I'm going to need to wrap this up in a minute, Dominique. Melissa needs to be home for dinner with the children. Did you have any more questions?'

'Yes, okay.' She crossed her legs and frowned. 'You've been nominated for Designer of the Year in the Fashion Awards in December, I saw. That must feel like a massive achievement. From soap star to serious fashion player.'

'God, I was so shocked. Humbled. I mean, what an honour.' Melissa put her hand to her heart. 'But of course, I don't expect to win. There's such incredible talent out there. I'm just so grateful to be in such inspiring company after such a short time in the industry.'

She fully expected to win. I needed to tell her she hadn't. That was my next hurdle.

PRESS NOTE

Choosing outfits to wear for the Fashion Awards is always an exciting chance for the GGC team to showcase their clients. Just because the team aren't all model-sized and don't quite fit into the samples doesn't stop them giving it their very best shot.

'I was thrilled to be asked to wear a Dante suit two sizes too small in support of one of our clients. This is what the industry is all about. Inclusiveness,' commented Frankie Marks, holding in her stomach and sighing.

ENDS

All I had really wanted was to wear the long crêpe de Chine low-back dress from Melissa's Spring/Summer collection to the Fashion Awards. Problem was, I just couldn't get into the damn showroom press sample. No full-body Spanx was going to cut it. That zip was not getting anywhere *near* closed.

I was standing in the middle of the showroom with Nicky, Zoe and Jemima amidst a pile of options while Andrew stood empathetically on the sidelines, eating a packet of cheese and onion crisps while doling out guidance and passing judgement with a nod or shake of his head. He had turned down his seat at the Dante table for what seemed to be a variety of reasons – stretching from not being able to get the shoes he wanted from Tom Ford, to having dinner with his stepbrother, who had just flown in from Stockholm, depending on who had asked.

'He's lying,' Zoe had said.

'Course he is,' I had affirmed.

'I'm worried.' Jemima had frowned.

'We haven't got time to worry about it,' Nicky had concluded. 'Plus, I've just heard that Georgina has agreed a new contract with the boys. Dominic Carter went one step too far, apparently. Told them he didn't think they should use velour anymore, which sent Lloyd into a spiral, and then quoted them some astronomical fee. So what Andrew does or doesn't do is small fry at this point, quite frankly.'

Now Nicky pulled the crêpe de Chine from my grasp and threw it on over her jeans and jumper. 'Maybe I should wear it,' she said. I couldn't deal with how much room she had to spare. 'Just means you have to wear Dante, Frankie.' Nicky pointed at a new iteration of the purple velour suit which hung like a sort of phantom menace.

Zoe screeched with laughter.

'Don't know what you're laughing about, Zoe, this Dixie double-breasted tuxedo-dress thing has your name all over it.' I held up the offending item and threw it in her direction.

'What about shoes, ladies? Who's sample size for these Castanis?' Andrew held aloft a pair of gold faux-python-print six-inch sandals. 'Someone has to also fly his flag, plus we really didn't get him good editorial this month, so it'd be doing us all a favour.'

'That'll be Nicky.' I shrugged. 'I'm going flat. I'm going to have to dig out some shoes from home. Do you think if I'm in a suit I can just wear trainers? Because, you know, they are the *Fashion* Awards? Oh shit, I can barely do the button up.' I was heaving the trousers on. Either their sizing was extremely small, or I had eaten a few Haribo too many.

'I think you can,' said Nicky. She was now resplendent in her gown with one python shoe on, her jumper sleeves protruding out of the crêpe de Chine. Honestly, if she'd gone out just like that, she'd have been able to carry it off as a look. Sometimes life was so unfair.

Zoe was stuffing herself into the double-breasted tuxedo dress. It was hideous. But if anyone could pull it off, it was Zoe and her Jessica Rabbit body.

'You can do it, Zoe.' Andrew was doubled up howling with laughter, clutching his stomach and empty crisp packet.

'Oh, I don't think it looks so bad,' Jemima said encouragingly. 'Think I'll just borrow some shoes and a jacket. I'm not staying for dinner. I'm just going to help you out with the red carpet then I'm out of there. I'm on annual leave next week but I won't abandon you all.'

God, Jemima is literally the nicest person I've ever met.

Georgina was going to be missing the Fashion Awards too. A holiday to Puerto Rico for her best friend's fiftieth. According to Nicky, it wasn't the first time. 'I'll never forget the year she called me to say she was stuck with lawyers and I distinctly heard a bath running in the background,' she recalled. Georgina did exactly as Georgina wanted. She had earned the right to cherry-pick her appearances.

It was going to be a big night. Melissa and Dante were both nominated for Designer of the Year. Dante had won twice already. We all knew they'd clinched it again, and not only had Melissa not won, she had also only made the shortlist due to my relentless campaign to get her on it. *Think of the press she'll get you on the red carpet*, I had implored the powers that be. *If you don't put her on the list, we can't guarantee she'll come.* These days my bartering skills would put a Turkish rug seller to shame. We all knew Melissa still had a way to go to prove herself to the industry, but as part of my role as her advocate and therapist, I knew it was essential for her ego and well-being that she was on that list, so I'd pushed hard. Giovanni Castani was nominated in the accessories category. And Dixie was . . . well, she was Dixie Triton, stalwart of the industry and a fixture at every major event; revered by all, but no longer relevant enough to be awarded.

'Who are you sitting with, Frankie?' Andrew turned to me.

'Well, obviously no room for the PR on Amanda Starling's table. Melissa's on it with the actress Judy Chaloner, who's coming into London 'cos she has her film premiere the next night. Although she's wearing Celia Johns – bloody Dominic Carter lucked out again – and refused to even look at anything of Melissa's that we sent to her stylist. I'm sitting on the BFC table across the way. With the good-looking short one from that new boy band, some magazine editor from India, and the CFO of Hunter & Fitch.

'Not so bad . . . and we know Hunter & Fitch are coming to the end of their contract with Five Star, so do some subtle pitching over a breadstick and then shove it up Dominic Carter's ass,' said Nicky.

Nicky would be with Dante and a smattering of hot new talent. Given her place in the industry, she was basically going to a fun drunken supper with friends – not to mention she was sitting with the designers who we all already knew were going to be the big winners of the night. While Nicky was negotiating her client's win and who they would like to present them with their award 'by surprise', I had had to break the news to Melissa that she hadn't won.

'But it's still really important that you're there, Melissa, to show you own your place in the industry and to support your peers,' I had told her.

'I don't want to go if I haven't won. It's humiliating.'

'It's not humiliating. It's only your first year of shows. Being nominated is an honour in itself. And please don't forget, you're not supposed to know you haven't won.' I was losing patience.

'Why should I give them all the press from me attending when they aren't giving me an award?' Melissa's face had flushed.

'You will go,' I had said calmly, 'and it will work in your favour in the long run. Not going *really* isn't an option. Let's discuss what you're going to wear.'

'Well, think of me,' interjected Zoe, still standing in the middle of the showroom stuffed into her outfit. 'I'll be in this dress, on the sponsors' table next to the toilets.'

'Best place to be,' said Andrew, 'closest to the exit for surreptitious fag breaks.' He'd made an excellent point. Zoe was appeased.

The Fashion Awards were a bore at the best of times. Each year was a variation on a theme of the last – the red carpet had to be handled before everyone could sit down in an over-crowded, lilac-lit room, full of tables too close to each other and terrible salmon mousse starters already congealing in situ. The name of the game was to avoid drinking too much warm white wine and peaking too early, while ensuring you took home as many of the sponsors' crystals that bedecked the table as possible, for your daughter, goddaughter or niece. It was a long night.

Tables were marketed as Premier or Standard. Just a few tens of thousands of pounds delineated between rows one to five. Table positions in their respective rows were negotiated delicately. Seating plans changed up until the last second. (Thank God those plans weren't our problem.) Presenters were promised. Presenters cancelled. We endured dubious live performances, listened to worthy speeches with clenched jaws, and we air-kissed and exchanged platitudes. All. Night. Long. I hated it with a passion. Crowds, strangers, pleasantries. My idea of hell.

'I'm really looking forward to it this year. It's going to be so much better than all the shit years I've had to suffer,' Nicky said.

'Well, I'm dreading it. DREAD. ING. IT,' said Zoe.

'I would literally rather be home watching *EastEnders* eating a pizza and arguing with James,' I moaned. 'It's going to be hideous.'

'How's it going with James? Does he still hate us all?' Zoe asked.

'It's going. You know . . . well, I don't know. It's fine. I still would rather be home with him. I think,' I replied.

'Oh dear, well, sorry to rub it in, but while you're all on duty, I'll be having a fat Chinese to celebrate not having to go this year,' Andrew said.

'Thought you were seeing your stepbrother,' I said.

'Yes, a takeaway with my stepbrother,' he said, shuffling his feet and not quite making eye contact. I knew he would usually be devastated to miss witnessing Dante's win – he was their Account Director, after all. I was increasingly suspicious.

Jemima looked at us all, wide-eyed.

'I don't know why you're all complaining. Isn't this the biggest night of the year? Isn't this why we do our jobs? Isn't this why we all love fashion so much?'

We all just turned and stared at her.

PRESS NOTE

It was at the awards where Frankie's PR skills really came to the fore. The way she navigated the red carpet and Melissa's salmon mousse crisis were exemplary.

'I was thrilled to be screamed at by the press pen as I got in their shot. It wasn't humiliating at all. It was a wonderful learning curve, and I embrace constructive criticism,' muttered Frankie while holding Melissa Bailey's handbag for her so she could look her best as she entered the event.

ENDS

Early December and the Royal Albert Hall was lit neon pink. I could see it in the distance as I marched up the Kensington side street where I had been dropped off – road closures stopped the 'normal' guests from driving any further. No glamorous kerbside drop-off for us . . . I thanked God for my trainers. I didn't thank God for the muffin top being squeezed over the edges of my too tight Dante trouser suit. I also noted with some despair that because of this, I wouldn't be able to take the jacket off all night.

As I got closer, the noise became a low hum and I joined more groups of people walking up to the entrance. Lasers were spinning up and across the sky. The outfits on display were astonishing. Astonishingly bad, that was. Deep Vs with breasts miraculously pushed to the sides, showing only an expanse of sternum. Shoulder details involving butterflies sticking out a metre either side of a ridiculously skinny blonde. Clutch bags in the shape of serpents. Headpieces that could take someone's eye out. I stopped to observe for a minute and heard my phone buzzing in my bag.

'I'm by the ropes at the top.' It was Jemima. 'I see you, look, I'm waving.'

I strained my eyes into the distance and spotted an arm frantically gesticulating.

'Yup, I see you,' I said, walking towards an ever-growing throng of people.

'Crikey, it's chaos,' said Jemima as she was elbowed out of the way by another over-zealous PR, ushering someone in who I vaguely recognised from one of the better reality shows.

'Okay, I'm just going to check out the lie of the land and find security to talk about Melissa's entrance. Will you wait here for Nicky and Zoe? D'you know what time the Dante boys and Dixie are getting here?'

'Nicky's in the car with Dante now. Zoe's going to wait for Dixie. In her tuxedo-dress thing. I'll wait for you here,' Jemima replied, but I had already started to move away. I had spotted Melissa's security for the night.

'Evening.' He nodded.

'Evening.' I nodded back.

'So, the car will come up to this point. She'll be on the driver's side. When she gets out, she'll walk this way' – he pointed round the back of the stanchions – 'and go straight on to the carpet. When you've done the carpet, I'll be waiting at the other end.'

'Okay. Seems painless. Let me just get a view of the press pen.' I walked on to the edge of the red carpet to take a look, just behind the reality-show star. I heard a cacophony of boos.

'OI, YOU! GET OFF,' screamed the photographers. I was ruining their wide shot. Oh, the humiliation, particularly as I turned to see Dominic Carter smirking from the sidelines.

I walked backwards, waving in apology and praying I wasn't going too red.

I spotted Nicky and went over to the car that had pulled up carrying her, Lloyd and Jonathan. Nicky was in an excellent mood. As she bloody well should be. No booing for her.

'Evening. I'll take the boys on to the carpet,' she said and walked briskly past as she ushered them through. She went to speak to the organisers. 'I have the Dante boys, but they're not sharing the carpet with *her*.' Nicky pointed in the direction of the reality star who was milking her moment in the spotlight. Within seconds, said 'star' had been ushered off, and Nicky pushed the boys on to the carpet. Flashbulbs popped.

'Over here,' the photographers screamed. 'To the right.' 'To the left.' The boys turned and posed and turned again.

I spotted security waving me over as Melissa's car drew up. I raced over to stand next to him, and once it came to a slow halt, I positioned myself in front of the car door as he opened it, shielding her from view as she stepped out.

'How's my skirt, can you pull it down at the bottom?'

Behind the open car door, I found myself on my knees pulling the hem down, bottom in the air, jacket creeping above my waistline, trousers pulling down perilously low. *Please God, let no one see me.*

'Hi, Frankie.'

God wasn't listening. I glanced to my right. Greg fucking White, with an Amazonian blonde. After all this time. *Why now?* I gave my best ironic smile as he walked right over, just to get the perfect view of my muffin top pouring over my waistband. I was pretty sure my bum crack was also on full display.

'Hi.' *Good God, you're still divine.*

'Yeah, hi.' I strained my neck and looked up, fighting to keep my rising blush down.

'Nice to see you. Been forever. This is Celeste.'

Of course she was called Celeste. She was fucking celestial.

'Bit tied up here.' I tugged a bit of hem to demonstrate.

'Well, great to see you. Maybe see you inside.'

'Sure. See you in there.' *Surely not. I will try to avoid you all night.*

'My skirt, Frankie!' came a banshee wail above my head.

I stood and pulled my waistband up as I watched him and the goddess glide away. I felt like the wind had been taken out of my sails and slapped my cheek to bring myself back to the task at hand.

'A fly,' I said, catching my breath as Melissa looked at me like I was mad. 'Okay, all good, just a bit more powder on your forehead. It's shiny. Then let's get the carpet done.'

'I have Melissa Bailey,' I announced to the bossy stick insect in charge of the red carpet, who was clutching a walkie-talkie and talking officiously into her headset.

'This way,' said Bossy Stick Insect.

I watched in admiration as Melissa completely ignored Stick Insect, smoothing down the front of her long navy satin skirt and stepping graciously on to the carpet to field the barrage of blinding flashes and frenzied orders from the waiting photographers.

'Looking great, Melissa,' shouted one.

'This way.'

'Over here.'

'Where's Gabriel?' someone from the back yelled.

'Melissa, Melissa. Look over here.'

Melissa twirled and whirled as she worked the first bank of photographers and then moved on to the second – until she noticed the Dante boys were still there. There was an uncomfortable pause as she waited.

'Clear the carpet,' I screamed at Stick Insect, and then ducked behind the screens to run to the other side so I could be ready to lead her off.

I raced as fast as I could, but too late – my heart sank as I watched while Melissa was cajoled into posing with Lloyd and Jonathan. Nicky and I stood stock-still, bottoms clenching. We had lost control for three minutes. Unacceptable.

'On your own now, Melissa,' screamed the photographers.

The Dante boys came off.

'We did NOT want to be photographed with her,' Lloyd stage-whispered to Nicky.

'Oops, sorry, Frankie' – Jonathan nodded at me, clearly delighted that I had heard – 'but that velour looks SENSATIONAL on you.'

'Just one more looking this way, Melissa,' the photographers shouted.

'That's enough now.' I leaned in and waved my hand to usher her off.

'I did NOT want to be photographed with those boys. Their last collection was shit,' she hissed under her breath as she remained all smiles while we climbed the stairs. 'Here, can you take my bag, I need to lift up my skirt.'

'But you liked the seersucker suit at the shoot? Anyway, it's fine. It's good for you to look like you have friends in the industry.' I was now gently sweating, holding my bag, Melissa's bag and her phone – plus, the dreaded velour was beginning to take effect as it started chafing between my thighs. 'Let's just go in and find Amanda and the table,' I said, as we reached the maze of corridors and walkways.

'So great to see you!'
'Oh, I love your outfit.'
'Wow, I didn't know you'd be here tonight.'
'Congratulations on the nomination!'
'You're so much prettier in real life!'

We were engulfed in waves of social niceties, air-kissing, smiles and chit-chat. Everyone wanted to see and be seen in close proximity to Melissa, who was one of the most highly anticipated guests of the night – and I acknowledged my inner delight at being the person glued to her side. *Yes, yes. I am with her. I know. And no, this suit isn't too tight at all.* It took twenty minutes just to work the labyrinth of corridors and avoid all the camera crews with giant microphones being thrust in Melissa's face for sound bites, before security managed to get us to the entrance to the show floor, where the tables were. Amanda Starling's table was, of course, in pole position – front row and centre. Celia Johns was on a table to the right – where, much to my chagrin, I saw that Dominic Carter was also going to be sitting, with his client, as he preened himself like the cat that had got the cream. Nicky and the Dante boys were to the left. GGC's other clients Dixie and Giovanni were seated with the event organisers, two tables behind. Zoe was indeed by the exit marked for the loos, and I glanced at my table across the gangway, which was already occupied by a bunch of strangers I would have to make painful small talk with for the duration. Oh well, at least James would have a field day at my expense when I told him. He had just got back from a work conference in Scotland. I had listened to stories of whisky and bagpipes and the state of the Scottish economy in light of Brexit. He would listen to my Fashion Awards recap even if it killed him.

Amanda was standing by her table greeting her guests.

'Melissa, I'm so glad you're here. I put you in between me and Judy.' Amanda was in her element. I, on the other hand, was greeted with a perfunctory 'Oh hi' as if we'd once bumped trolleys at the supermarket and she couldn't quite place me. I nodded a quick 'Hello, Amanda' as I did a circuit of the table to check all the placement cards. Yup, all present and correct. No ringers. No no-shows. Thank God for that.

'I'll be at that table over there,' I whispered in Melissa's ear. 'If you need anything, text me. Or wave.' I was never off duty. Not for one second. Melissa touched my hand briefly, signalling it was okay to leave her, and I saw Jemima walking towards me.

'I'm leaving in a minute. Zoe and Dixie are on their way in. Heads-up – Dixie's upset because her red carpet was a bit of a damp squib. Giovanni's going to be here soon. He had a siesta and woke up late, so he overran once he'd had his spray tan. But I'll just go and tell them he's on his way. Have fun! I'll check the wire for images. Text me if you need anything.'

How was Jemima always in a good mood? I quickly looked at my phone: 7.53 p.m. *Only three and a half hours to go,* I thought, crossing my fingers behind my bag as I wandered over to my table.

There was my name card – in between the boy band guy and, quite fortuitously, the Hunter & Fitch CFO I was supposed to be pitching to.

'Excuse me, sorry, hi.' I smiled apologetically as I squeezed my way around to get to my chair and looked down at the sickly pink salmon mousse in front of me.

I texted Martha.

> **Frankie**
> Salmon mousse. Do they have her dietary??

> **Martha**
> Yes. Don't panic. It's sorted.

For a split second it hit me – how had I reached a point in my life when I cared about someone else's food as though it was a matter of life and death? Here I was, looking like Tinky Winky, sweating in purple velour and stressing about Melissa Bailey's salmon fucking mousse.

Our WhatsApp chat was up and running. I'd called this one IT'S JUST ONE NIGHT as a message of solidarity.

> **Zoe**
> There's a really cute guy on my table. And I can see he smokes. Maybe this isn't going to be as bad as I thought.

> **Nicky**
> What about Josh, Zoe?! All great here! Lucy's on her best form. Lloyd's already drinking which is good. I'm not eating this mousse thing.

> **Frankie**
> The trousers have cut off all circulation. I may never be able to have children. Oh God, Melissa already typing . . .

A new message appeared.

> **Melissa**
> Where's my papaya? There's a mousse in front of me.

I texted Martha off group:

> **Frankie**
> Melissa has mousse. Not papaya.

I texted Melissa:

> **Frankie**
> Martha calling them now. She organised your food.

Martha replied:

> **Melissa**
> I bloody called them to triple-check this morning.
> I'm on it. Can't she just move it around the plate?

I typed quickly:

> **Frankie**
> Apparently not. Music starting. Text soon.

'WELCOME TO THE BRITISH FASHION AWARDS! HERE'S YOUR HOST FOR THE EVENING – JACK LANGLEY!'

Jack Langley bounded on to the stage and launched into his opening patter. He was a comic in his twenties with a podcast, a Netflix show and a lot of influential fans and friends. I reached for the warm wine.

'Let me get that for you,' said young boy band guy.

'Oh, thanks so much – Frankie, by the way.'

'Gary.' He nodded in that I'm-famous-but-extremely-down-to-earth-and-would-never-assume-you-know-my-name kind of way.

'Been to many of these?' he asked, topping up my glass.

'Too many.' I took a large gulp. Good grief, it was disgusting. They really must have struggled with sponsorship money this year. Oh well. I took a second gulp and started amassing the crystals strewn across the table into a pile to put in my bag.

'I'm just here to present the men's accessories award. Soon as I'm done, I'm going to do a ghosty.'

'Absolutely don't blame you. So would I if I could.'

'Who you here with?'

'Melissa Bailey. She's over there.' I gestured to Melissa's table where I could see her pushing food around her plate as she talked animatedly to Amanda Starling.

'She nice? I've never met her,' Gary asked.

'She's interesting.' I shrugged, taking another gulp, and turned to my right. I really couldn't be bothered to engage any further.

'Hi. Frankie.' I introduced myself to the Hunter & Fitch guy – at least he had finished puberty and was wearing a beautifully cut dark grey suit.

'Matthew Bradbury.' He held out his hand.

'Ah. Hunter & Fitch. I love what you do. We were talking about you earlier. I'm with GGC.'

'And you know we're looking at putting the contract out to pitch next month?'

I smiled with what I believed to be my most winning smile.

'Of course – we were just chatting about it in the office. We'd love the opportunity to show you what we could do for you.' I fished around in my bag and found a business card. 'This is me. Now that we've put a face to a name, perhaps we could come in and see you in the new year?'

I slid the card across to him and then forcibly concentrated on the stage, feigning nonchalance. We weren't desperate for a hunting/fishing client. We just wanted to get one over on Dominic Carter.

'PLEASE WELCOME JUDY CHALONER TO THE STAGE, EVERYONE!' yelled Jack Langley, desperately trying to keep the audience's attention as the bottles of booze mounted and interest waned.

IT'S JUST ONE NIGHT

Zoe
I'm going for a fag with this bloke.

Nicky
I'm peaking too early on the warm wine.

Frankie
I'm going to the loos to undo trousers to prevent amputation of torso.

As I weaved around the tables to the loos, I nodded imperceptibly at Melissa. She didn't nod back – which meant she was completely fine. For now, at least.

When I reached the corridor, I bumped into Dominic Carter loitering and looking smug in dark green velvet *and no fucking socks again.*

'Oh hi,' I muttered, trying to get past him as quickly as possible.

'Shame you're not sitting with Melissa?' he said, raising an aggressively quizzical eyebrow.

'Oh no, I needed to be on a separate table. I've got a LOT to do here tonight.' I raised an enigmatic eyebrow back at the asshole.

'Celia's dress looks great on Judy, doesn't it? And you look nice in purple. Although I really could never represent designers who work with velour,' Dominic added. He was like a bloody terrier. I needed to shut him up and make my getaway.

'Yes, she looks stunning. I find velour just so versatile. Listen, I'm in a rush – got to change my tampon. Really heavy flow tonight.' *That should do it.*

'Sure. Right,' he said, reddening, but still managed to regain enough composure to add, 'See you at the *Vita* event tomorrow.'

'Yeah, yup. See you there.' WTF – I tapped out a message to the group as fast as I could.

> **Frankie**
> WTF IS THE *VITA* EVENT TOMORROW?

Melissa was about to appear on the cover. How could we not be invited to any event?

'God, that was agony,' Melissa muttered, as we weaved our way out of the room, stopping for a few selfies. She turned to our security guy. 'Get us out of here fast as you can.'

He led us purposefully out into the corridor, warning us, 'There's a lot of paps outside.'

'Frankie, let's just go to the bathroom so I can check my make-up.'

I felt my heart sink. So near, yet so far to an exit.

As Melissa applied her powder and lip gloss, I checked my phone: 11.42 p.m. I could feasibly be in bed by 12.30. Maybe James would be awake and could make me a cup of tea?

'Let's go, best to get out before the throngs,' I bleated.

'Not before we have a quick swig of this.' She brought out a tiny hip flask, and we both gulped a burning shot of vodka. *My kind of girl. Sometimes.*

The camera flashes were blinding as we walked down the steps outside. Melissa walked closely behind security. I kept my head down. I wasn't being caught out like a rabbit in the headlights with a double chin in yet another paparazzi picture. Not this time. (I had once been a thumbnail story in a weekly magazine asking why Melissa Bailey's 'friend' hadn't brushed her hair, accompanied by a picture of the two of us – featuring me looking particularly frazzled while she was shiny and groomed with a tight jawline. James had announced I had finally 'arrived'. My mother had sent me a link to a new Tangle Teezer.) I texted the group.

> **Frankie**
> Leaving now.

> **Martha**
> How was it?

> **Frankie**
> Like pulling teeth.

> **Zoe**
> I've just snogged that bloke. Think I'll go to the after-party.

Melissa's car pulled up.

'Can you send me all the photos when you get them in? Before you go to sleep.'

'Sure.' I nodded and kept smiling for as long as I waved her off.

I texted Jemima from the cab.

> **Frankie**
> Hey. Any photos up yet?

> **Jemima**
> Sending now.

A bank of images came in over the phone. Melissa on her own. Melissa with the Dante boys. Melissa with Judy Chaloner in her Celia Johns dress. Melissa hugging Amanda. Melissa smiling into the middle distance. Melissa caught mid-laugh with a hint of a double chin. Shit.

> **Frankie**
> Can we get that laughing picture off the wire asap?

I frantically texted Jemima.

> **Jemima**
> Too late. *Daily Post* picked it up already.

Melissa had been online.

> **Melissa**
> Can you get that laughing picture down off the *Post*??

> **Frankie**
> Trying.

Melissa
I hate it.

> **Frankie**
> I know.

Melissa
Is it down yet?

> **Frankie**
> It's only been three minutes. We're trying.

Melissa
We need photo approvals.

> **Frankie**
> We can't get approvals at an event we don't run
> with over 1,000 guests.

Melissa
It's awful. I hate everything about it.

Frankie

It's really not that bad. You look friendly. People will like it.

Melissa

I knew I shouldn't have gone tonight. And Mercury is in retrograde.

Jesus.

I went straight into the kitchen, undoing my trouser button as I walked. The blessed relief of releasing my waist was overwhelming. I reached for a cigarette. I allowed myself to succumb to my moment of deep humiliation over Greg as I listened to James snoring. The familiar sound made me feel guilty for even thinking about Greg as James slept peacefully. But Jesus, couldn't he just sleep a little bit more quietly if he wasn't going to be up and greeting me with a hot drink and a sympathetic ear?

I scrolled through some more online images. There I was, on the edge of the red carpet with my hands up, apologising in the background of the reality star's image. There was Judy Chaloner with Celia Johns. Melissa with her hand on her hip, one leg forward. *Quite a good shot*, I mused. The double-chin image was there, but I was beyond caring. Then there was my new friend Gary from the boy band looking fashionably scruffy in his bright yellow suit with Converse. And in the background, I could just make out Dominic Carter on the edge of the carpet – in what appeared to be mid-conversation with Dixie Triton. He may have lost the battle for Dante so far, but he was still up to something. I just knew it.

I also knew I just hadn't enjoyed the evening at all. I

couldn't get away from the feeling that my life was starting to slip by me in a merry-go-round of niceties, battles, press releases, air kisses and apologies. I was constantly swinging from elation to despair, self-pity to self-importance, resolve to confusion on a daily basis. I needed to save myself, my job and/or my relationship.

Time to stop procrastinating and make a bloody decision, Frankie.

PRESS NOTE

Press day is the most important seasonal moment for all fashion PR agencies. The GGC team revel in promoting their clients and entertaining journalists at their beautifully appointed showrooms.

'I talked about faux-python shoes for nine hours today. I was thrilled,' said Nicky Harris. 'I used the repetitive motion of picking them up and putting them back down as part of my daily workout routine. I love how I can work on my core strength while admiring a kitten heel.'

ENDS

As it turned out, there was no *Vita* party. It was a baby shower for one of their feature writers. Dominic Carter was just vile. Anyway, if there had been a party I would have been ill-inclined to attend since I got a call from their copy team the morning after the Fashion Awards checking on information for the interview from a 'source' who had told them Melissa was devastated and furious not to have won an award. Only the GGC team knew about her fury. Surely they wouldn't have said anything to anyone? After my emphatic denial and a few threats including the word 'legal', they decided not to print it and the immediate panic was over, but I really didn't want to think about who that source was. Andrew's off-kilter behaviour flashed in my mind momentarily, but I dismissed the thought as fast as it crept in. Eloise and her apples also came to mind. I didn't dismiss that thought quite so quickly.

Christmas was incoming again – but this year I was truly dreading it. I had a sense of foreboding over what increasingly felt like the slow demise of my relationship, the rounds and rounds of work parties, seeing my parents, and my annual sobbing on New Year's Eve – which always happened for no particular reason apart from too much alcohol, too high expectations and a massive comedown. I had it all to come.

GGC received copious season's greetings – mainly digital, with flashing gifs and magazine teams doing dances as gnomes on what we had to tell them were 'hilarious' cards. We received more boxes of champagne and mulled wine sets than we knew what to do with. We sent out hundreds of cards and gifts of our own. I got a round-robin 'Merry Xmas' message from Greg, which I deleted. There was nothing merry about it.

Georgina was just back from Puerto Rico. Nicky was departing for the Maldives imminently. Yet another holiday. She'd only just got back. I wondered how much money Mark, her husband, must earn. I also wanted to remember to ask her if she had two passports. Jemima was going on a girls' holiday to Egypt. Zoe had too many plans to keep up with, but Josh Brigson seemed to be a part of some of them. Andrew was keen to insist he was going on an extended round of debauchery but was suspiciously vague on the details. Georgina didn't tell us where she would be or who she would be with, and as for Eloise, well, no one asked her what she was doing.

James and I had agreed to be with our respective families for the festive period. He was spending time with his old friends up in Durham, and my New Year's Eve would be spent at

Charlotte's. She and Felipe were having an extremely grown-up dinner party where I would absolutely get inappropriately drunk and spend the night crying in her spare room. She assured me there were going to be some great guests from the world of human rights and I would be fine.

'It'll be good for us to be with old friends and family, I guess?' I said to James the week before.

'It's only ten days. It'll be fine.'

'Will you miss me?' I asked, wondering if I would miss him.

'Course. But let's be honest, you're away a lot, so I'm used to it. But you know, absence makes the heart grow fonder and all that. We both need time to think. It'll be fine, Frankie.' He gave me one of his best bear hugs and I felt my New Year tears brewing early.

I ploughed on. For Christmas, I bought Melissa a year's subscription to an astrology app. She bought me a silver bracelet I had chosen for myself – with Martha, so she could tell Melissa to buy it for me. Darcy Girl sent me a bomber jacket with a daisy-embroidered sleeve that I immediately wrapped to give to Tilda, and Giovanni sent me a bottle of dessert wine with a panettone, which I would give to my parents. I gave James a beautiful tortoiseshell frame with a photo of the two of us laughing together on holiday in Italy in our uni days, and a new pair of football boots. I snivelled as I wrapped the photograph, feeling all at once nostalgic, cross that we were no longer love's moon in June, and just down-right weary. The reality of what spending Christmas apart *really* meant hit me.

Christmas Day itself was uneventful. It was just the four of us: Mum, Dad, Tilda and I. We ate and drank too much and argued over the inevitable game of Trivial Pursuit where I only excelled at Entertainment and failed miserably at Arts and Literature, much to my embarrassment and my father's disdain. The feeling of being at home alone with my parents over the festive season was deeply depressing, and I wallowed in self-pity. I had tossed and turned in my teenage single bed the night before as I stared at an old Beyoncé poster and asked her how it had all come to this (Charlotte and I had debated WWBD – What Would Beyoncé Do? – throughout our teens). *God, I'm miserable,* I told Beyoncé. I found myself broaching my misery with my family at some point in the evening of Christmas Day, after a few glasses of Baileys had cemented my Yuletide gloom.

'So, I don't know if it's time to think about moving on from GGC. It's been years. Also, I feel like James and I could be on the brink of breaking up. He's really been trying, but he can't take it anymore. I'm miserable or tired or both, so much of the time. I'm not sure if it's the job, James or me. But I've been thinking about looking at other options,' I announced from the folds of the beige leather sofa, taking myself by surprise by offloading to my family. My voice cracked slightly.

'You know how much we like James. But you've been together a long time and you're still young. You need to do what's best for you. And as for GGC, you've created a real career for yourself. You're earning a serious salary. And you're good at it. Whatever "it" actually is, you've applied yourself – and from what I can see, even that Melissa person has become relevant,' my father replied. What? This was not what I had been expecting.

I was so taken aback I stared at him for a minute before getting my words out. Well, one word to be precise.

'Oh.'

'Yeah, you know, even my friends at law school talk about Melissa now. And anyway, if James thinks you're busy, he should try dating a lawyer,' Tilda chipped in.

'Honestly, sweetie, you just need to look after yourself a

little better. Your relationship has suffered, and we've barely seen you. The receptionist at the hairdresser said she saw a picture of you looking a little bit too thin at some event with Melissa in *Hiya!* magazine,' my mother added, handing over a plate of mince pies.

Well, that was one silver lining.

James threw his holdall on to the kitchen counter and I literally body-surfed him, lunging for a hug.

'You had your usual New Year slump then.' He laughed.

'Course. And I'm just really, really pleased to see you,' I said, nestling my head into his chest.

'I missed you too. Everyone did. It wasn't the same without arguing over the merits of cranberry sauce with you,' he said.

'Bread sauce all the way,' I replied.

But the post-Christmas honeymoon period only lasted a couple of days before we backed resentfully into our respective corners and resumed sniping. Once we were settled in our daily routine, the sound of him swallowing was beginning to be enough to make me want to murder him. I fell back into a malaise.

'It's worth fighting for. One last shot,' Charlotte had counselled. I decided to give my relationship the time she suggested. I resolved to have sex with James at least once a week, and not with my flannel pyjama top still on. As for Melissa and GGC, I went back into the offices on 4 January still feeling like the job was all just getting to be too much. I was struggling, and the exhaustion was causing me to resent it more often than I was loving it. Although my father's unexpected support had given me the validation I had long yearned for, I still spent a significant amount of time daydreaming about what would happen if I actually did call it quits. *Oh yes, I was a fashion PR for years, but I'm just so happy to now be helping small children and giving back to the community. My hair? Yes, I know. I haven't brushed it for months. So liberating.*

But by 6 January, I was already so steeped in approvals for Melissa's *Vita* shoot and arguing about the budget for the benches for the February show, I put everything to one side. Just one more season. That was what I would do. One more season and then I would sit myself down and properly consider my options.

Another season came and went. We had our press day: the day to show off all our clients' collections to a stream of stylists, influencers, and anyone with a pink blazer paired with silk tracksuit bottoms, an excellent crossbody bag and a TikTok account.

'It may be polyester, but the fabrication is so incredible it could be silk.' Jemima repeated this line by the Darcy Girl rail continuously.

'You may not want to wear seersucker yourself, but my God, it photographs well, and the retailers are just lapping it up,' enthused Andrew by the Dante rail.

'No, not real python obviously. Giovanni is very sensitive when it comes to exotic skins,' Nicky could be heard to say at intervals.

'I know. Isn't it just incredible what she's done in such a short time?' I would say, enthusiastically holding up a Melissa Bailey windowpane check, time after time, and forcing myself to smile.

'Dixie just *knows* what women want to wear,' Zoe would gush, as she yanked out a newly reimagined tuxedo dress a hundred times.

'They just weren't happy at Five Star!' I explained as I stroked Hunter & Fitch belts, my well-earned prize from the Fashion Awards.

We went on. And on. As the door shut on the last press attendee, we all gathered round the visitors' book for affirmation we had done a good job before Georgina came to inspect it.

'I sold seersucker like I've never sold anything before,' Andrew said.

'What about that new guy from *Madame*? He was cute, Andrew. And I think he was flirting with you.' Zoe nudged him.

'Oh, I didn't notice. Really? I don't feel it,' he replied distractedly. This was not the same Andrew I met all those years ago. He would never, in a million years, not have picked up and run with that one. The rest of us all exchanged glances. We were always second-guessing everything Andrew said these days.

'I don't know why we do this,' Nicky said, sitting up against the wall, having pushed the clothes to one side and thrown some shoes into a pile to give herself some space. She rubbed her ankle tattoo distractedly.

'Oh, come on, it's not so bad,' piped up the perennially glass-half-full Jemima. 'We do actually like some of the press. We do have some amazing clients. And luckily, we all love each other. I enjoyed today.'

'I nominate you to take all the requests into Eloise tomorrow, in that case. I mean, the way she was lurking and staring throughout those appointments but not actually speaking to anyone.' Nicky knocked back her drink. 'She has got to go. She actually gives me the creeps. Right, I'm going to gather my things. I'm out for dinner.'

'Jesus, how can you be bothered?' Zoe exclaimed. 'I can't wait to go home and put a face mask on.'

'I'm one hundred per cent with you. I'm going to go home, try to not have an argument with James, and wash my hair.'

'Poor James,' Jemima said. She really was Switzerland.

I was lying on the showroom floor when my phone pinged.

> **Melissa**
> How did it go today? Good reaction? Gabriel just flew back to LA. You free for supper?

FUCK. That wasn't a polite request. That was an order to accept.

'No, no, no.' I banged my hand against my forehead.

'What's happened?'

'I have to go for dinner with Melissa, that's what. Shoot. Me. Now.'

'Well, I did warn you.' Georgina was standing in the doorway observing us all prostrate on the ground in various guises. 'These kinds of clients live off you like you're their oxygen. Anyway, good job, everyone. I've looked at the visitors' book. Great turnout. I'm going. See you next week. We have our anniversary party to start organising, so get some rest and be ready.'

And with that, she did what Georgina did. Turned in her immaculate outfit, shouted to Debbie to ask if her car was outside and left. Like a puff of smoke. Now you see her, now you don't.

'Who has deodorant and a mascara I can borrow?' I pulled myself upright and typed out my now perfunctory message to James saying I wouldn't be home till late. To which he replied with his now perfunctory message *So what's new?*

I woke up the following morning to incoming messages from Andrew. I had forgotten to silence my phone when I got back late after dinner with Melissa. It was only seven a.m. I didn't have to be up for another hour. How incredibly irritating.

> **Andrew**
> Awake?

> **Andrew**
> I can't come in today.

> **Andrew**
> Can you take my meetings please.

> **Andrew**
> And get some Dante leggings back from *The Forward* to go to *Avalon*.

> **Andrew**
> And *My Style* need shoes. I forgot to send.

I replied but it didn't deliver. I called and Andrew's phone was already off. I poked James awake. We had been having a better week so far.

'Huh?'

'Look at this.' I showed him Andrew's messages.

James rubbed his eyes and squinted at my phone.

'So? Leggings? And? Put the kettle on.'

I pulled on my pyjama bottoms left crumpled on the floor and went upstairs. James and I had had sex last night. I hadn't exactly channelled my inner *Fifty Shades*, but at least I'd managed not to think about Greg or what I was going to have for dinner the next night in the middle of it. As the kettle filled, I stared into space.

'Blimey, thank you.' James smiled and sat up against the headboard as I made a ceremonial walk with coffee and toast. I even remembered butter and jam.

'I can do breakfast. I'm not entirely useless,' I said

unconvincingly. 'And I wanted to talk to you. I'm knackered. I think LA really finished me off. Melissa was the worst version of herself – over a fucking banana. Plus I hated those awards with a passion. Press day was agony. I think it might be time to really reconsider everything.'

James smiled sleepily and stretched out his hand to pull me down into a hug. He smelt warm. Like mornings, like normal life. Like it used to be.

'Halle-fucking-lujah,' he exclaimed as I sighed and appreciated the little bit of hair sticking out from the crown of his head.

'We should talk everything through,' I said. 'I'll go first.'

Just then my phone rang.

'Hold on. Hello? Melissa? I can't hear you properly. What? Yes. Okay. See you in thirty.'

I looked at James. He put his coffee down on the bedside table and got up in furious silence. Yet again, he had been dismissed by someone at work taking precedence. We were in the throes of a life-affirming conversation. Possibly a relationship-saving heart-to-heart. But what could I do? Melissa was hysterical. I couldn't admit to him it was because she couldn't zip up the back of her dress and her housekeeper was out buying oat milk and chia seeds, and Martha had booked a day off.

James and I took turns in the bathroom, edging past each other, careful not to touch. We didn't speak again. He thundered out of the flat. I picked up my cigarettes, phone, charger, wallet and threw them into the handbag I still hadn't emptied from my last flight. I saw a boarding pass stub and my passport floating around the bottom along with my hand sanitiser, Kindle and lavender spray. I shut the front door with a sinking heart. What was it they said? There was nothing lonelier than being with someone and still feeling alone.

PRESS NOTE

Leading agency GGC celebrated their 10th anniversary with an intimate party at the Golden Goose last night. The great and the good of the London fashion scene came together in honour of Georgina Galvin and her team for an evening to remember.

'It was like being at a wet T-shirt wrestling match with cocktails in the middle of a soap opera. I was thrilled to have witnessed such a dramatic turn of events,' commented Malcolm Fulwell, CEO of Darcy Girl, beaming with his feet up on his desk.

ENDS

We were having a party for our anniversary. The agency. Not me and James – that ship was continuing to sail further and further away.

I agreed to go to the venue to check on everything the day before the party. Nicky was too busy, Andrew was AWOL. Jemima wouldn't shout enough to get what she wanted, and Zoe was going out with her new sort-of boyfriend, Josh Brigson. I *knew* I'd smelt celebrity sex on her.

I hotfooted it down to the Golden Goose just off Portobello Road. It belonged to the godson of a friend of Georgina's, had just seen a much-talked-about relaunch, and was perfect capacity. Enough space for us to have our clients, press, a few retailers, and any VIPs if we wanted to. Not enough space for any of us to bring our partners. Apart from Zoe, but Josh was off on assignment in Greece in the morning. Which we all agreed was a little bit annoying – he would have been a great photo.

When I arrived at the venue, I was greeted by a vision.

'Hi. Kieran,' said Kieran. The godson. I felt my heart fall to my stomach, trip down my legs, do a mini somersault and revert back up to standing position. Kieran, as it turned out, was divine. My kind of divine. Tall, straggly brown hair, white shirt, jeans, some battered-up retro trainers. Plus, he had a packet of Marlboro Lights sticking out of his back pocket and was eating a Mars bar.

'Sorry, not had time to eat today,' he said, wiping the chocolate from his lips.

'No problem.' I smiled in the most bashful manner I could muster while resisting the urge to lick the chocolate off him myself. I put my tongue back in. 'Frankie.' I gave Kieran a firm handshake. One that told of confidence, made it clear that I had a boyfriend, and that I hadn't noticed his mouth. 'So, all set for tomorrow? How many staff will be passing drinks and food? How many barmen? Bar's open, but let's try to encourage the passionfruit Martini and white wine so costs don't go through the roof. DJ? He has Georgina's preferred playlist? Food? Proper food? Mini chicken skewers, risottos . . .'

By this stage I couldn't have cared if he'd suggested a Burger King delivery. But I went through my well-oiled motions as I marched around the space.

'We'll have candles in the booths, yes? You'll have a security guy on the door? Invite says from eight p.m. We'll all be down by seven. What time is your licence till? How many people are manning the cloakroom? We won't be doing any formal photos. Just our house photographer roaming – Chris. With the goatee. You'll recognise him.'

On and on I went. Like a bull in a china shop, pushing

down my urge to body-slam him there and then, and ask him where he'd been all my life.

'Wow. Okay. Yup. You seem to have everything covered. That's some impressive checklist,' Kieran said, popping the last of the Mars bar in his mouth and sticking the wrapper in his front pocket. 'Katya will be dealing with everything. She's done loads of these kinds of events.'

And then in stepped Katya. Vintage T-shirt with a Grateful Dead logo. Fingers full of heavy silver rings. Hair scraped up into a high bun. Beautiful Katya. Who wrapped her left arm around Kieran's waist in a sign of easy intimacy that was currently so lacking with me and James.

Well, that was that, then.

'We'll have some VIPs. Let's reserve this banquette area for them. Lighting will be lower than this, won't it?' I went on. And on. I thought I saw them exchange a glance.

I left the venue and walked home. The joy of not being in East London for a change was overwhelming. Imagine how quickly I would get home tomorrow night. But the flippity flip of my stomach when I met Kieran was another mammoth warning bell I just couldn't get to stop ringing. My one-night acrobatic show with Greg, I had mostly managed to put down to being flattered a demi-god had got past my muffin top – and an impulsive desire to escape the need to try to fix me and James for one night. My head hadn't been turned since. Being without James was unimaginable. Couples had come out the other side of worse, hadn't they? I still clung on. But how had it gone so wrong? Was it the job? Was it me? Was I potentially throwing away the best thing I had, for the sake of clients who wouldn't remember me in five years' time? In particular for Melissa, who I sometimes couldn't work out if I loved or loathed?

'I'm sorry we're not allowed to bring partners,' I said to James as I applied mascara. I wasn't sorry, but I now knew how to practise acceptable social interactions – even if we were allowed, I would have told him we weren't. Truth was, I didn't have room for James in my work bubble. It would have been like fitting a square peg into a round hole and the two did not belong together. I didn't have the headspace to worry about whether James had a drink or someone to talk to when I was in full PR turbo mode.

'Honestly, Frankie, there's nowhere I'd less want to go. It's my idea of hell,' he replied indifferently, pulling up his football socks.

I looked at him out the corner of my eye. And I felt nothing. I wasn't upset he wasn't upset. I was worryingly neutral. For years, I had been painfully desperate for his approval. I had wanted him to secretly long to be a part of my exclusive club that wouldn't allow him membership. Now, I was more concerned with finding my lip liner from the depths of my make-up bag and getting to the venue quickly.

'Right, see you, then,' I said as I shrugged on my leather jacket and threw a bag across me. I was going casual tonight. I wanted to be able to dance if I could. Old vintage jeans, an oversized, collared, green and white striped Melissa shirt, large gold pendant, hair up, trainers. With hindsight, I would probably have worn a top that wouldn't have gone see-through when Lloyd threw that drink that misdirected and hit me.

I didn't give James a second thought as I took the eight-minute cab ride to the Golden Goose. I was only thinking about how the intern would cope on the door and if I had enough vape charge to last the evening.

When I pulled up at the unassuming red entrance, Jemima was already there. Zoe was running late, par for the course. Nicky was in the loo applying lip gloss, and Andrew was by the bar, solemnly downing a bright green cocktail.

It looked good. Low lights, flickering candles, playlist on, two barmen prepping the Martinis and four more waitstaff ready to pass drinks and food. There was no branding anywhere. Georgina felt that kind of self-promotion would be tacky. This was a private party for us to celebrate with our nearest and dearest. Translate to: clients, press, people we needed to thank, people we needed stories from, a few prospective clients who weren't ours yet but perhaps should be, and so on. Chris, our erstwhile event photographer, was there with his goatee. That facial hair brought me great comfort in its familiarity.

Debbie came in.

'Georgina is five out. Mood is great. She's looking forward to it,' she assured us all.

Katya emerged from the door behind the bar in another great vintage tee, some oversized red and white striped trousers and flip-flops. I wanted to wear big striped trousers with flip-flops. I wished I could wear them. God, she was cool.

'Hey, Frankie. All looks good, no?' She kissed me on both cheeks, emitting a waft of fresh linen. She deserved Kieran. She was practically perfect.

'Kieran isn't coming tonight. There's a crisis in the kitchen in Shoreditch, so he's had to be there.'

I was secretly relieved. My ten-minute crush had been humiliating. And the life crisis it had reignited had been parked temporarily.

'No problem. Oh look, Georgina's here. Excuse me.'

Georgina was standing in the doorway giving everything the once-over, Debbie by her side. It was a familiar sight. Her razor-sharp antennae were up. She scanned everything. I held my breath. She nodded. And then she smiled.

I exhaled and grinned. She was in a Dante trouser suit. Black gaberdine. Precision tailoring at the shoulder. Straight-legged trousers that just hung over her navy round-toed Giovanni pumps. White silk Dixie T-shirt. A long, spiders'-web-thin, diamond Carraway necklace. Navy Samira K clutch. She was a walking advertisement for her favourite clients. They would all be thrilled. She would likely tell Darcy Girl she was wearing one of their bras. Jessy would forgive her for not being in a swimsuit and I would tell Melissa she was saving the striped suit from her last collection for the *Avalon* Christmas party.

Zoe came careering in, all boobs and bottom poured into a green Dixie jumpsuit.

'Glad you could join us,' Georgina said in a rare moment of levity. 'Let's all get a drink.'

We stood at the bar, Georgina in the centre, and raised our Martinis.

'To GGC. I love you all and thank you. Really. Thank you. Here's to a great night.'

The guests arrived thick and fast. Malcolm from Darcy Girl was just beyond delighted to be there. For him this was a big night, mixing with the most influential press, high-end designers and a couple of key retailers he had known when he was the Buying Director at a multi-brand store in the nineties. He flashed a smile and threw back a couple of Martinis immediately. Zoe gushed, standing close. At one point I absolutely saw her peel down the zip of her jumpsuit to show him the Darcy Girl bra she was sporting. He nearly spat out his last mouthful as he went a shade of crimson but carried on smiling even more widely.

All our clients were in attendance. Every important editor and VIP we had ever worked with. Even Mary Foster turned up. Her star had risen even further since we'd done that collaboration with Giovanni and his shoes, and we knew she wouldn't stay long. But that was fine, we'd still get her photo. The room started filling. The music was cranked up a notch. The atmosphere was light. Fun. The GGC team escaped everyone and had a shot at the bar together as Georgina carried on circulating.

Quite frankly, it just couldn't get any better, we all agreed. People would talk about this party for all the right reasons. Dixie had earlier decreed Dominic the biggest creep in the industry, and gleefully announced to us all that she had taken great pleasure in allowing him to take her to dinner last year at her favourite, eye-wateringly expensive caviar restaurant, before telling him over a blini that she wouldn't join Five Star even if their services were being offered for free. We regaled the story to each other, clinking our glasses. We howled, reminiscing Eloise's scowl when she said she was busy tonight, but acknowledged it must be sad to be her.

Martha
Melissa is ten out.

It was Martha. Shit. I had momentarily forgotten Melissa was coming. How could I have forgotten? She was who everyone was waiting to see. Forget about the Mary Fosters of this world. Even now, after all this time, I sometimes failed to completely comprehend the fascination Melissa commanded. But it was very real.

Frankie
Will wait outside for her.

'Andrew? Where's Andrew?' Jemima nodded towards a door at the back of the bar. He had barricaded himself in the gents. I opened the door an inch and called in: 'I have to go and meet Melissa. Are you even going to come out? This is just weird now.'

I had no better comment to offer and moved through the now crowded room towards the door. I air-kissed everyone I passed. I complimented outfits. I gushed over new cover shoots. I told Jessy her newest collection inspired by palm trees was all I wanted to wear on my next beach holiday.

The black 4x4 pulled up directly outside the door where I was waiting alongside the intern, who was still smiling and clutching a clipboard of names. The Golden Goose security guy had never showed. But we weren't bothered. It was an easy, invite-only event.

Out Melissa came, black sunglasses although the light was already dimming outside, a full look from the last show, head-to-toe – high-neck turquoise silk jumpsuit, with an orange shoe peeping out of the hem. A fine gold chain belt and a purple clutch bag. She looked great, if completely overdressed for the venue. But this was the Melissa I had nurtured and created. She had taken every style lesson and applied it diligently – if on occasion a little too literally.

'You look amazing.' I greeted her with two kisses.

CLICK.

I looked to my right to see a paparazzi jump out from the car behind. Shit. They'd been followed. We had told all the guests this was a private party. Now I knew when we emerged at the end of the night there would be a crowd of photographers. That was how it worked. One became two, two became four and so on. I ushered her in through the door, fast, while quickly telling the girl on the door to keep an eye out for any more lenses.

'This is cosy,' Melissa muttered as we went into the throng.

'It's crowded, but follow me. I've reserved a booth for you.' I led her directly to the table I had asked Katya to hold back. I ushered Zoe over. Giovanni made it to where we were at breakneck speed.

'*Ciao*, so wonderful to meet you.' He leaned down over the table. 'Giovanni Castani.' He was practically bowing as he held out his hand rather formally.

'Hello. Melissa,' she said in her customary perfunctory manner while holding out her hand, rather taken aback as he proceeded to sit down opposite her.

Once she warmed up, I left them to have a mutually

beneficial conversation congratulating each other on how brilliant they both were and how they should definitely work together one day. I got Melissa a drink from the bar. I had made sure we had a bottle of her vodka sponsor in case she was photographed.

By the time I was headed back with the branded glass, I could see Georgina was busy talking to Melissa, Giovanni was smiling like the Cheshire cat who got the cream, and Zoe was hovering.

Andrew, in the meantime, was now cowering on the other side of the room, eyes fixed on the door. Every client was ensconced with someone they needed to be with. Everyone was eating a bit, drinking heavily and being merry. I knocked back a Martini, feeling like I could sort of relax, and doing a little dance on the spot when Nicky whacked me on my back.

'Ouch. What?' I exclaimed and turned to look at her. She was staring at the door. Where Dominic Carter had just walked in with *Eloise* of all people, followed by a flustered – no, frantic – intern. No fucking way.

What the hell was he doing here? With Eloise? How come Eloise had make-up on? And had most definitely had a blow-dry? And was smiling?! I hadn't seen her smile once in all the time she'd been in that sample cupboard. Dominic smiled slimily. He perused the room, caught our eyes and nonchalantly strolled in, seemingly without a care in the world. The intern was literally chasing him. If it hadn't been so dreadful, it would have been hilarious.

Debbie spotted them too and proceeded to speed-walk over to Georgina, who was still charming Melissa. She whispered in her ear. In the meantime, Nicky had marched over to Dominic and Eloise.

'What are you doing here?' she half shouted, 'and what the fuck are YOU doing here with him?' She moved closer into Eloise's smirking face.

'Oh, we're having a late dinner with Kathy tonight, and she suggested we meet her here first. I was sure you wouldn't mind. I told her we were all professional friends, just another face in the crowd,' Dominic murmured, as he took in the room.

'But we do mind,' Nicky retorted. 'Don't worry, it's not your fault.' She turned to the intern, who was close to tears. 'We all know when someone bulldozes their way in where they're not wanted.'

I felt my hackles rising and a furiously strong sense of solidarity and stepped forward to Nicky's side. I threw myself in.

'And as for you, Eloise. Want to explain yourself? You hate GGC so much you turn up to your own work party with this? I mean, him!' I added, my pitch rising. 'And wearing really good bronzer,' I muttered as a begrudging aside.

'Dominic invited me to dinner. I've handed in my notice. I left a letter on Georgina's desk this evening. I'm now a Junior Account Manager at Five Star. Dominic always does the right thing,' she replied in that irritatingly monotone voice of hers while looking up at Dominic adoringly. I checked out her much-improved outfit, hair and make-up. No technicolour tights. God, that she could scrub up okay was just one more thing to scream about.

'The right thing? What do you fucking *mean*?' Zoe yelled.

'Oh, Eloise and I are very close. For years now, actually.' Dominic smiled. 'She's been so helpful to me.'

Helpful? What was he talking about?

Slowly the rest of the team walked up, until we were all surrounding them in collective disbelief. All the other guests pretended not to notice but their eyes were glued. Andrew hung around the back. Georgina pushed herself to the front, just in time to hear Dominic finish speaking.

'I appreciated Eloise's eye for detail. Her overview on

exactly what you lot were doing. Her forgetfulness to send things out on time or make diary entries was just an added bonus,' he smirked.

Holy fucking mother of holy shit. All this time? *Eloise* had taken a side hustle spying for *Dominic*?

The realisation hit all of us simultaneously. We had speculated, we had discussed, and we had complained about her, but we had waited too long to do anything about it. We were now like a volcano waiting to erupt. Georgina took control.

'Get out.'

'Come on, Georgina. Let's not be dramatic. It's just a party. We've been at plenty of parties together.'

'This is *my* party. You've tried to destroy my business. You used a naive, misguided girl,' she looked at Eloise, 'and now you dare to turn up here, uninvited, with your pawn in tow.'

'That *naive, misguided girl* who you overlooked, treated like shit, left to rot in a sample cupboard while you surrounded yourself with this bunch of sycophants who are so self-absorbed they even blur their professional boundaries with clients?' With this, he looked directly at Andrew, and then eyed each one of us up and down, his finger flailing in the air. 'Everyone knows you're a washed-up old has-been, Georgina. Your glory days are over. It's a new era.'

'Yes, she is a *naive, misguided girl*,' Georgina said, her voice never rising, but white rage emanating as she looked at Eloise, 'who's now tied to you, whose reputation is ruined, and who'll never be able to get another job. No one else in the industry will ever employ her. You're stuck there with him, Eloise. You understand that? What he's done to you is the death knell for your career.'

I thought I saw a flicker of anguish cross Eloise's face. I nearly felt sorry for her.

'Talking of destroying careers, perhaps he can explain what he's done with *him*,' he said, first pointing at Andrew and then somewhere that looked to me to be in the direction of the Dante boys. 'Everybody's talking about it. Seems like Lloyd and *you lot* are the last to know.'

That was when Dominic laughed. The final straw.

Georgina slapped him.

Right then and there. In the middle of the party. It was a neat slap. But hard. Stinging, even. And as one, all our mouths fell open, like the frog chorus. Georgina then turned her back, told Debbie to get them out, and took a sip of her drink with a slightly shaking hand and went to chat to Amanda Starling. What we had failed to notice was the paparazzi from the street who had slunk in the unattended front door. I saw the flashes. *Oh fuck.*

At that moment, I realised Andrew had come forward. He had come into the fray and into direct contact with Lloyd and Jonathan. He looked at Jonathan in despair. Lloyd stepped forward.

'So it *is* true. You disgusting piece of shit.' He spat the words out, leaning into Andrew, and then, as if in slow motion, went to throw his drink at him. Jonathan put out his hand to push it down. It sprayed to the other side. All over me. I looked down as my shirt absorbed the pink liquid and clung, transparent, to my left breast. Even in the chaos, I spotted Malcolm from Darcy Girl's neck swivel as he had a good old look.

Having missed his target, Lloyd didn't quite know what to do. He was on his tippy toes.

'I'm sorry,' Andrew managed to whisper.

'What?' Lloyd spat out.

'I said I'm—'

THWACK.

Lloyd punched him. Right on the cheek. I didn't know who was more surprised: Andrew, Jonathan, everyone else watching, or Lloyd himself. Who I was pretty sure had never hit anyone before in his life.

'You. Out!' Jemima was shoving the paparazzi out the door.

'You. With me.' Nicky yanked Lloyd and Jonathan to one of the booths.

'I think I'd like to go now.' Melissa was standing next to me.

PRESS NOTE

As a team, GGC support each other through thick and thin. They always remain calm and collected. Emotions are placed to one side as each problem is strategically thought through.

'I could slap Andrew for what he's done,' commented Frankie Marks.

'If I get my hands on Eloise, I'll kill her,' added Nicky Harris.

ENDS

It had been an unmitigated disaster. There was very little PR spin we could put on it to suggest otherwise. The only saving grace from my point of view had been the surprise arrival of Kieran, somewhere between the slap and the spill. When he handed me over a tea towel to try to retain some of my dignity, I felt a tiny charge of electricity. Whether it was mutual or if I had just elevated him to divine superhero status in my mind was undetermined.

I stepped through the dimly lit room with him and surveyed the remnants of the night once the last stragglers had left. It wasn't a pretty sight.

'Did I miss something?' he joked as I patted myself dry.

In a red leather booth, Andrew was nursing his black eye and swollen cheek with a tumbler of ice. On the banquette in the far corner, I could see Nicky talking into her mobile in slow rhythmic sentences as she stared into space. Presumably to the Dante boys, who she had ordered a car for and seen out swiftly.

The affair with Jonathan had been going on, on and off, for years. That was what we now knew. All those hair tints we had noted were markers of moments in the relationship. All those disappearing acts. The wild stories. The non-stories. Andrew protested that he just didn't know how to get out of it. Not that he even *wanted* to. But he knew he had created the most almighty mess, and the aftermath was going to be nuclear if they were ever caught out. He had reached his pinnacle of panic over the past month. Lloyd had found suggestive text messages. Jonathan had tried to make light of it. Lloyd had destroyed an entire roll of very expensive satin with very large fabric scissors. Jonathan had broken down and confessed he'd *thought* about it, but of course he couldn't live without Lloyd – or Dante. Lloyd conceded he would never find anyone to share his frustrations about velour with in quite the same way and chose to believe him. Dominic's public outing of the betrayal was testament not only to his willingness to stoop to any level, but also confirmation that he truly had his eyes, ears and spies *everywhere* in the industry – not just in our sample cupboard.

So, when Andrew had regaled us all with tales of illicit one-night stands, filthy nights out, and alcohol-and-drug-fuelled debauchery, what he failed to mention was that almost every single one of those encounters were with Jonathan. When he had disappeared from the office, it was to catch snatched moments together.

It had started by mistake, he admitted. He had gone to their studio with a stylist to discuss bespoke looks for some starlet. Lloyd wasn't there. He'd taken to his bed in a fit of malaise over seersucker or velour. *Fucking velour. Always going to haunt us one way or another.* Jonathan had always liked

Andrew. His lack of melancholy was a breath of fresh air. Well, that was Andrew's story.

The meeting had gone well. The stylist had left and Jonathan had taken out a bottle of extremely expensive tequila gifted by Amanda Starling. Just one shot each, they had said. It had been a long week. Two shots later – 'Will we have tiny bump?' Jonathan had suggested, taking out a wrap from his desk drawer. 'Oh, I shouldn't,' Andrew had smiled, 'but okay, then.'

At some point early that morning, things changed. Neither of them could pinpoint it. But they did. And afterwards they were both full of remorse and did their respective walks of shame home.

Andrew was telling us all this between heaving sobs and a lot of snot.

'Georgina will fucking fire you,' I said despairingly.

'I'll have to do the right thing and just hand in my resignation. Save her from having to sack me.' He ran his fingers through his hair and threw his head into his hands.

I patted his back. I wasn't really very good at moments like this. I continued patting firmly but gently as we then moved on to drama number two. Or was it drama number one? What *was* the worst drama tonight?

'I can't believe it. I literally can't. Eloise. How could we not have realised?' Zoe said.

'We all knew she couldn't have just been that shit at her job. But we were too busy to really dig down to what was going on. But to be moonlighting for the competitor, for all those years? Who does that? While only eating apples?' My pitch was rising.

'Like a double agent,' Andrew said.

'Oh, he's back in the room,' Nicky said, smiling, having ended her call and come to join us.

'Well, we're all great at our jobs. We should have known things couldn't have been going wrong just because I wasn't around enough,' he said, laughing nervously.

'That's how he knew Dante were in LA that time,' I said. 'And why Stacey Powers was sent their clothes. And oh my God, all the missed calls, wrong diary entries, stories not sent for.'

'Poor Eloise,' Jemima said. 'Our jobs are hard enough as it is. Imagine having to deal with Dominic and sneak around behind our backs, all at the same time as packing up some bikinis to go to *Avalon*.'

Nicky gave her a light slap to the shoulder.

'Never use the words "poor" and "Eloise" together again. She's a snake – and she isn't poor. She's been getting a double fucking salary!'

The smell of stale alcohol was heavy in the air as Jemima carefully stepped over the spilt drinks to pick her way through the now unattended cloakroom, gathering all of our coats. Lovely, calm Jemima. Always practical and dependable.

Back at the bar, Zoe was shaking her head in despair as she perched on a stool scrolling through the online news sites.

I could see the banner headline from where I was standing: WHEN FASHION GOT UGLY, it screamed above a series of images which showed Georgina slapping Dominic and Melissa exiting the building, holding her hands up to shield her face from a flurry of flashbulbs. It had all only happened a couple of hours ago. Christ, those tabloids worked fast.

'At least we still all look sensational. Well, most of us.' Zoe shrugged, looking at one of the images of us all with our mouths hitting the floor – me in my soaked shirt looking like a drowned rat and showing too much of the old nude M&S bra I'd unwittingly chosen to wear. 'Come on. Let's get out of here. There's nothing more to be done tonight. We can deal with it in the morning.'

I gave Kieran a little morose wave as the door opened on to the – now late – London night, and we all trooped out one by one to a line of waiting minicabs Debbie had arranged. Georgina had left quietly half an hour before. As we each stepped into our respective cars, I looked over at them all. They were my work family. But this evening had been a fiasco. I didn't know if I could do this anymore. I was mortified, embarrassed and wet. I buckled my seat belt and threw my head back, closing my eyes.

PRESS NOTE

Appearances are everything. As a PR, you learn to set problems aside and work out how to solve them while maintaining an air of total normalcy. It's a wonderful skill set.

'Just because one of the team has been having a catastrophic love affair with a client and another member has been trying to sabotage our business for years, that doesn't mean we don't continue to love and support each other and our clients and pretend everything is fine,' Jemima Sahar commented while smiling and calmly stroking Andrew's hair as he wept.

ENDS

The next morning, back at the office, we all sat at our desks sipping coffees and picking at food we couldn't face eating. We all looked rough. Apart from Zoe, of course. But today, even Nicky hadn't been able to bring herself to blow-dry her hair. We were raking over the shocking turn of events in the cold light of day.

'How could none of us have realised about Andrew?' Nicky asked.

Jemima smiled gamely while shaking her head. 'I warned him when I got a sniff of it, but he refused to confess so I dropped it. This was a disaster waiting to happen.'

We were right when we suspected she knew something was up, all that time ago.

'Jesus. The shit has really hit the fan.' Zoe rubbed her eyes. 'Andrew. And Jonathan? Jonathan, one half of Dante? Dante, our prize possession? Lloyd's partner and boyfriend? Lloyd, the most overwrought, hysterical person any of us has ever met? You know what, the shit hasn't just hit the fan. Andrew's face is going to be pushed into the fan and sliced up into a million bloody pieces by Georgina when she sits down with him.'

'What's the plan then?' I asked. 'How will we PR this catastrophe – and our other situation?'

'We take cover under our desks and duvets until someone's dead, and pray it isn't one of us?' Zoe offered.

'Apart from that,' Nicky replied.

'Where's Andrew now?'

'In hiding. Waiting to be sacked.'

Nicky shook her head. 'How could you not have said anything, Jemima? Jesus.'

'He wouldn't admit it to me. What was I going to do?'

'I'm calling Andrew right fucking now.' Zoe picked up her phone and bashed through her contacts. I could see her hands were shaking as she pressed his number. She placed it on the table in front of us all as it rang out. 'Jesus.'

Later on, Nicky called Dominic in a fit of rage from her desk.

'How fucking *dare* you? Where do you get off? Don't you have any remorse? Any sense of right and wrong? This is unbelievable, Dominic. Unbe-fucking-lievable.' She banged down the receiver, before admitting he hadn't picked up and she'd been screaming into his voicemail. Then she promptly started crying. Our loyalty to Georgina was impregnable. Try to take GGC down and we all come up fighting. It was this pack spirit that I loved. That was what had kept me there, above all else.

We busied ourselves with the daily work that needed to be done. The intern took over the samples. That wheel kept on turning. From the outside looking in, it was business as usual. We were consummate PRs and we would spin this to our advantage.

'*Absolutely* we can get that suit to you.'

'I'm afraid I'll have to decline a guest appearance at the hosiery awards. She's very busy finalising her new queen-size bedding range while working on the new season collection. We'll be showing it in that new revolving restaurant space on Aldwych. Yes, I know, really exciting.'

'Of course, we can get a quote for you for your tailoring story. What's the deadline?'

I considered how I was able to switch it off and on like this. It wasn't normal, I knew that. I also knew that the skill set required to gush and smile and talk about cashmere in the middle of two catastrophes was an acquired one. For a split second, I tried to remember what my thesis had been about. Something to do with the art market? 'Aesthetics versus Values'. Well, there was a synergy in the subject matter at least, if not the intellect. Where was the person who researched and read and wrote, without the excessive use of exclamation marks? Was I still her? Buried under press releases and bias-cut hemlines?

Andrew appeared in the office mid-morning. Like a ghost. Debbie marched up to his desk.

'Georgina wants to see you. Today. Before lunch. At her flat. I'm just warning you. She's apoplectic with rage.'

Andrew went even whiter. Our poor, beloved Andrew. I couldn't cope. He was a shell of himself. I missed old Andrew. Fun Andrew. Soup-fanatic Andrew. I wanted it dealt with, harmony restored, and for life to resume as normal, whatever that meant.

He left the office like a dead man walking. Nicky was on the phone to *Avalon* about a potential interview with Dixie for a Designer of the Decades story. Zoe was emailing *The Forward* about a swimwear shoot. They couldn't have the high-waist navy and yellow check bikini they wanted, because it wasn't due back in time from another shoot in the Maldives. Jemima was taking an appointment downstairs with the *Herald*. I started emailing the *Scottish Post* to decline their monthly interview request with Melissa, and the intern was busy packing up some send-outs in the sample cupboard.

The PR cycle didn't stop for a personal crisis. Print deadlines weren't delayed because Andrew was in the throes of a tragic love affair; appointments weren't cancelled because someone within our ranks had tried to sabotage us. No. Tartan versus tweed still took precedence.

I stopped to think about it for a minute. What was wrong with us? Were we so institutionalised that we just kept on going, no matter what?

I pondered. Then I carried on typing:

. . . thank you so much for your kind interest in Melissa. Sadly at this time she is unavailable for interview. As you can imagine, we get a huge amount of requests globally and are only able to fulfil a certain amount of them. Please do get in touch in the future . . .

PRESS NOTE

To spin good from bad is what keeps this industry turning, and GGC are proud of their ability to turn all press to good press.

'When the PR needs some PR, perhaps it's time to quit,' Frankie Marks lamented as she looked at pictures of herself in the tabloids that she had been unable to get removed.

ENDS

I had gone to bed the night before in turmoil. I'd had a drink thrown over me, witnessed a client punch a PR, watched Dominic Carter and Eloise walk in like they owned the joint, had a CEO leer at me, had spent hours of my life panicking about Melissa and her vodka and who she was talking to and how to get her out of there, and had realised that Georgina was only human. There was a picture of me in the papers with my mouth open and my bra exposed, which my mother would one hundred per cent see and show my father. James' notion of the absurdity of my career would finally be confirmed, and I couldn't deal with his implicit I-told-you-so. I went out on to the pavement outside the GGC office and called Charlotte.

'I think I've hit my wall.'

'What does that mean?'

'I don't think I can do this for much longer.'

'Praise the Lord.'

'No, seriously. I'm depressed. It's all gone horribly wrong and I don't know what to do. You free tonight?'

'Yes. Come over here. I'll cook you some supper.'

I felt a vestige of relief. The prospect of a normal evening outside of this insular bubble got me through the rest of the day.

Georgina came into the office that afternoon in a cream trouser suit, perfectly starched white shirt and box-fresh trainers – a picture of poised calm. We all gathered in the meeting room for the debrief from hell. Eloise was just a sample manager who had been hoodwinked, she told us. Dominic was desperate – and if he needed to stoop so low, then shame for him, quite honestly, and poor stupid Eloise was now always going to be branded a liar in the industry. Andrew was a fool. Georgina was furious with him. (He said later that he hadn't received a dressing-down like it since he was caught in the showers with Barry at school by his sports teacher.) What Andrew and Jonathan decided to do was up to them. But he should bear in mind the consequences for the agency and Dante, who would most certainly have to leave if the relationship continued in any shape or form. And that was *if* Lloyd and Jonathan could even continue to work as a design duo after this. It was foolish, selfish and reckless of him. But, Georgina said, when push came to shove, her loyalties were with Andrew. She wouldn't accept his resignation and she didn't sack him. And now he needed to get out of her sight as she waited for Lloyd to simmer down.

She went on. 'Malcolm messaged to say he had the night of his life. Mary Foster asked Dixie to make her a dress for her next round of interviews to promote season two of her show. Holly Lars talked to Jessy for a good half hour and wants to do a story on her for *The Forward*. Melissa was on good form. There are loads of messages about how great she looked. And Giovanni and Samira K will both be in *Vita*'s hot accessories shoot after their editor saw my shoes and bag. And as we all know: all press is good press. So, let's make use of our unexpected splash in all the tabloids. Turn it to our advantage. Suddenly the brand-name GGC is in the general domain. So, some upsides.'

She was so matter-of-fact. So cool. Just so, well – PR and Georgina, about it all. I, on the other hand, was fidgety. Worried about calling Melissa, who'd be furious about her picture being used in the same context as a story entitled 'When Fashion Got Ugly'. The familiar gnawing in the pit of my stomach was at full pelt. And not just because of Melissa. Because, well, because I was embarrassed. There, I had admitted to myself. Was I also ashamed? That what I had sometimes thought to be the greatest job in the world now amounted to terrible tabloid headlines? This wasn't chic. This wasn't fashion. This most *certainly* wasn't strategic.

'*Ghastly people*,' my father had said repeatedly. Maybe he had been right all along?

None of us were staying late at the office that night. Andrew went home alone, bruised and red-eyed. Nicky announced her husband was taking her to dinner at Cinquecento to cheer her up. Zoe was waiting for Josh to land later that evening. I left at the same time as Jemima.

'It's going to be fine, Frankie,' she said gently. 'Tomorrow's fish and chip paper, and all that.' She gave me a kiss on the cheek and headed the other way down the road.

As I arrived at the red-brick mansion block where Charlotte now newly resided with her boyfriend, Felipe 31D, I pulled shut the old-fashioned lift doors and burst into tears. By the time I was knocking on the flat door, I was bawling my eyes out.

Charlotte hugged me for a very long time. I wasn't a hugger. But I needed serious consolation. And a glass of wine, which she provided the minute she let go of me. I sat on a stool at the kitchen island as she stirred something in a saucepan and I blew my nose.

'From the top,' she said, as she ground in some pepper.

'Last night was a disaster. James is a disaster. I hated everything about the clients, the situation, myself. I really don't think I can do this anymore. It's highly possible I might really be done this time.' I took a gulp of wine, had an enormous drag of my vape and blew my nose again, scrunching the tissue in my hand. 'It was ugly. It was demeaning. And through it all, I still had to worry about everyone else. After Dante, Melissa and Dominic left, I still had to spend an hour circulating, placating, pretending everything was fine. Talking about fabrics, lingerie stories, how much I fucking loved Mary Foster's patchwork miniskirt. Which I didn't, incidentally. It was disgusting.'

I took another drag. Another swig of wine. Charlotte refilled my glass.

'Then today I had to grovel to Melissa. Melissa Bailey. To tell her she looked great in the pictures, and not to worry. Looked great? She had fucking sunglasses on at ten p.m. at night! She looked ridiculous. I had to promise that no one would associate her name with the headline. Well, that was a lie. That's going to stick. And who's going to have to unstick it? Me.'

I looked up at the ceiling and noticed Charlotte had a lovely fifties' pendant light hanging over the kitchen.

'I love that light, by the way,' I commented before ploughing on. 'And then look. Just look at you. You're happy. Settled. Even Zoe has a sort-of boyfriend. Martha's still with Aiden. At least Andrew had some romance. Some drama. I had a disastrous one-night stand and me and James are . . . well, in a rut. I even fancied the restaurant owner, for Christ's sake. Something has got to give.'

Charlotte put down her wooden spoon and stopped stirring. She leaned across the island.

'First things first: James. Frankie, maybe it's really over? You've been so absent for so long – physically and emotionally. He wants your old life and your old relationship. It doesn't exist anymore. Not to mention that photographer incident . . . sometimes these things come to a natural end. It's life. And as for that job of yours – you've done incredible things. You've achieved so much. You're respected. You have great friends at work. You've travelled the world. You've experienced things you never would have otherwise. But it has taken over.' She took a breath as she put down the pepper grinder. 'I'm glad you're seeing what it is you've got yourself into. And now you can think about getting out. If that's what you want.'

I nodded pathetically.

'And stop looking at everyone else. Georgina's probably lonely. Andrew's most likely in bed, weeping. Martha's dealing with Melissa. And Melissa, well. She's too reliant on you. You've done too good a job. Maybe it's time to cut those apron strings?' She threw a cucumber at me. 'Chop this, will you?'

'Dangerous to give someone so vulnerable a knife, don't you think?'

'Just chop, for God's sake.'

PRESS NOTE

Once a PR, always a PR. It's part of the DNA of this business that no one ever leaves.

'It has been a mortifying experience to realise I am so entrenched in the industry I don't know how to get out,' Frankie Marks whispered in horror, as she lay on her bed eating a family pack of prawn cocktail crisps and contemplating her life choices.

ENDS

> **Frankie**
> I need to talk to you later.

I texted James the next morning, after he'd left for work. I spent the day with a knot in my stomach but feeling brave. I had finally made the big decision.

When he walked into the flat that night, I could feel my heart pounding. James took off his jacket, sauntered over to the kitchen and re-emerged from the fridge with a Corona in his hand as he plonked himself on the sofa.

'How was your day?' I asked.

'Fine, thanks.'

My stomach pitched and I grabbed my glass of white to steady my shaking hands. I sat down next to James and curled my feet under me as I steadied myself to speak.

'You know . . . it's just . . . I can't do it anymore. I really think it's time for a change . . . I really think it's over.' I touched his hand lightly.

'Oh my God, Frankie, I'm so pleased.' He took a gulp from the bottle and squeezed my fingers. 'Have you told Georgina? Melissa?'

Oh fuck fuck fuck. I felt the blood drain from my face.

'Oh God, shit, no, James, I . . . I'm so sorry. I mean us. It's over with us. And I really am deeply sorry and sad about it.'

'I did it.' Later, I was blubbing down the phone to Charlotte.

'Aww, Frankie, that's huge. You did it – you finally quit.'

'No,' I snivelled, 'I broke up with James. I mean, let's face it, it was mutual – it's just me who finally called time. I think he was relieved. So that's it. I'm officially single in a job that makes meaningful relationships practically impossible.'

'Fuck, that's even huger. But let's be honest, you both tried. We all knew it had run its course. You two were just the last to admit it. At least it sounds like you've ended amicably, but I'm sorry. I'll miss him. What did he say?'

'I know, I know. We hugged it out. He told me he loved me but couldn't cope with PR-me. One final dig. Then he said there was no rush to pack up my stuff – it was all so sad. I just need to process this particular bombshell, see Melissa through the next show, and then I think I'm well and truly done. Ready to drop the next one.'

'You've been saying that for a while.'

'I have?'

'You have.'

'It's just so hard to let go. There are so many things I've done that won't come out for months, and I just can't bear to not be around to see the results of my hard work. Or worse, see someone else take the credit for it because I'm long gone ... Not to mention, so many pairs of Giovanni shoes for next season that I want to get my hands on. So many plans for Melissa. And I'd miss everyone so much. And there I go – I don't even know who I am anymore outside of this fucking job.'

'You're Frankie Marks. Late twenties. A London girl. Funny. Popular. Intelligent. Been missing in action for years. Time to come back, Frankie, one way or another. Time to come back.'

'Can I come stay with you for a while – just till I find myself somewhere to live and have officially found my way back?'

I tortured myself for the next few weeks. I worked as hard as ever, but it felt surreal to be back to business as usual when my life had changed so seismically. I cried off all but the absolutely unavoidable evening work invitations and came home to the spare room at Charlotte and Felipe's every night. But it was also good. I needed the quiet to spend time with myself. I went and picked up the remainder of my things from James' flat, where he patiently helped me pull out drawers to find bras and pants lost for years which were wedged behind them. We laughed and hugged as I triumphantly held up an Elsa sock from my GGC interview day retrieved from the back of the bottom drawer. Truly a full-circle moment. I invested in a vast array of scented candles and diffusers, which I dotted around my room. I bought a new Le Creuset casserole pot which never actually made it to the oven. Instead, I worked my way through every takeaway delivery service within a two-kilometre radius. I bought flowers from the stall at the end of the road almost every day, but there were never enough vases. I looked up the latest exhibitions every weekend, but never quite made it. I was too restless, my thoughts unruly, and I just couldn't find the resolve to, well, *resolve*.

I confided in Zoe. She understood, to an extent. But on

the other hand, she just couldn't comprehend why I wasn't delighted to be a PR girl about town. To enjoy my success. Be free to flirt, go out when and where I wanted, to have none of the shackles of a relationship and all the freedom to concentrate on the best job in the world.

'There are plenty more Gregs in the fashion sea, you know,' she said. It was kind of her to not have mentioned she had known about it all this time. I should have known she would sniff it out.

It was ironic, really. Zoe was now in a fully fledged relationship with Josh Brigson and becoming a red-carpet fixture. The name on other PR agencies' party guest lists.

Martha was totally with me. If she didn't have a mortgage to worry about, she'd be out of there like a shot. I was lucky, she told me. I could survive for a few months without a job if need be. I had, over seven years with James, learned a thing or two about savings, and had set aside more than enough to keep myself going for a while. If only I could extricate myself from the industry.

Still, I avoided talking to Georgina. She had the power to mesmerise me to such an extent that she would have persuaded me my job was comparable to brokering world peace and I couldn't leave. I looked at Nicky, Andrew and Jemima and wondered why they were so content.

I also couldn't imagine Melissa doing any of it without me. And despite everything, I liked her. I *really* liked her. Plus, I had to admit, I loved having an endless wardrobe of free or discounted clothes. I knew that secretly I loved all the travel, thrived on the adrenaline of shoots, and still got a thrill from a great piece of editorial and the satisfaction of developing a great strategy for the new season. But the nagging doubt at the back of my mind refused to disappear in the usual flurry of anticipation of the challenges ahead, as it had done so many times before.

The anxiety didn't dissipate. I made a list of the pros and cons of my working life, stuck it on poor Felipe's fridge and added to it over the weeks.

'"Discounts on dresses" doesn't really count as a stand-alone pro,' Charlotte suggested as she watched both lists grow.

'Does the planned trip with Melissa to Beijing go in pros or cons?' I waved my pen in the air.

'It spreads across both. Pros: being in China. Cons: jet lag and potential conjunctivitis from the smog,' she replied.

'New one for cons – having to decide on the name of the Darcy Girl polyester pizza-print collection.' I sighed.

And so it went on, until my list of cons made it all the way to the freezer door and, for one final time, Charlotte gave me a look that said enough was enough.

It was a normal morning. I had my usual coffee. My morning cigarette. I scowled at everyone on the bus into work. I was wearing an excellent pair of jeans with my new Giovanni loafers and was examining the ribbed hem of my navy Melissa Bailey jumper as I approached the office. I was going to hand in my notice. A now-or-never moment that I resolved to act upon the minute Georgina came in – before I changed my mind again.

'It's really hard for me to say this after everything you've done for me,' I started, facing Georgina from the other side of her desk.

'Go on,' Georgina said.

'I just think it's time for me to move on. I'm worried I've lost sight of myself. I love it here. Truly I do. But I've put my personal life on the back-burner, it's a miracle I haven't murdered Melissa yet, and I just need time out to think about my next steps.' And then I started to cry. Of course I did. I *did* love it at GGC. That wasn't a lie.

'I just don't know if I have it in me to constantly put other people first anymore. I don't want to regret never using my degree,' I went on.

'I want you to think about it, Frankie. Don't make a decision now. Don't write a formal letter yet. You've come so far. I see so much of myself in you. I had a great degree too – Italian, as it happens.' That explained Georgina's life in Milan. 'And I understand the sacrifices we make in our personal lives sometimes.' There was my hint at her undisclosed relationship status.

I nodded and wondered if my jumper also came in beige. I would be the best-dressed art historian in London.

'Give it a few weeks. You're a really great PR – perhaps not the most conventional PR, but you're smart, Frankie. You can go far. Honestly, I don't know what the team would do without you.'

'Thank you, Georgina. I'll think about it. But I think my mind is made up.'

'And I think that you would miss it too much. I think the thought of Melissa doing so much as a wee without you knowing will be too hard for you. But I'll leave that with you. Go, I've got a lunch and I can hear your line ringing.'

And with that I was dismissed. Now I just needed to get over the Melissa hurdle. I booked in a meeting for that afternoon. As I walked in, I could barely look at Martha, but clocked her discreet thumbs-up out of the corner of my eye.

Melissa was immaculate, as always. Her hair was glossy and blow-dry perfect, her make-up expertly applied, and she was wearing a full double-denim trouser-suit look from the last show. But as the words came out, there was no pout, no stiffening of her features; instead, they fell, a fleeting slump before she recomposed them. Let no one forget she had been the star of *Carlyle Bay*.

'Oh. I really wasn't expecting this. Think about it for a while, will you? We can make it work. Perhaps you could come in-house? Or consult for me? We can find a way. You're the best, Frankie . . . I couldn't have done it without you. And I don't want to do it with anyone else. Mercury is rising. Did you know? Shall we have a vodka?'

Well, that threw me. I was expecting a cool *thanks* and *okay* and *great to have known you.* I wasn't anticipating she'd be sad to see me go, or that she'd try to make me stay on in some capacity. Obviously, she didn't understand that it was the pressures of looking after her that had finally worn me down. But PRs were a dime a dozen. There were many more where I'd come from . . .

Or maybe I really am good at this? And bloody hell, maybe we're actually friends and she's going to miss me? This doesn't help. At all. I have so many friends now.

Melissa's fleeting lapse was just that – fleeting. She pretended the conversation had never taken place and we carried on as normal. There just wasn't time for me to agonise over it as the usual demands kicked in. Georgina didn't push. Zoe was pragmatic, but made it clear she didn't understand why on earth I would leave. Martha was diplomatic, as ever. The rest of the team didn't need to know – they were too busy anyway.

Now that Zoe was officially going out with Josh, it was astonishing – she was glowing. She ceremoniously disabled her Tinder and Hinge apps. We also all noticed that Nicky had stopped drinking coffee. She didn't say anything to any of us – she didn't need to, we were already discussing every detail of her new oversized look and latte deprivation in hushed tones over the kettle in the kitchen on a daily basis until she told us. When the big reveal had finally come, she also confessed that most of the holidays she had been taking were actually time off for gruelling rounds of IVF. 'I told you no one has two passports,' Zoe said. Georgina had told Nicky to take all the time she needed. Her tans were out of a bottle to make her feel halfway human after the battering her hormones and body had taken. Jemima had a new boyfriend, Carlos. He headed up IT at a publishing house on Euston Road, and she was taking him to her niece's christening. Debbie was, well, just Debbie. She got a new laptop and she was happy. We never spoke of Eloise again until Jemima heard on the PR grapevine that she wasn't exactly the most popular or successful hire at Five Star, and we all took immense satisfaction at the news. Andrew had recommended a full-on circuit of London's hot spots, but occasionally his wicked grins didn't quite reach his eyes. He acknowledged that Jonathan and Lloyd were happier than ever. In fact, it seemed that Andrew had done them a massive favour and forced them to look at their relationship. Jonathan even called him to thank him – and just to check that Jemima was now their Account Director, mentioning it was probably best if Andrew didn't go to any of their events or shows for the foreseeable. When Andrew put the phone down, he stuck two fingers at the receiver and then asked what soup was the special today. And Georgina. She didn't change. She was exactly the same. Commanding rooms, looking sensational, popping in and out and being revered by one and all.

But, with Charlotte's encouragement, driven by her utter desperation, and after some crisis casseroles with my parents, I felt I had finally reached a decision. My work friends had been my extended family, but I could live without seeing them every day, and I could live without the stress of wondering if Melissa had blown her nose before yet another camera focused straight up her nostrils. I had learned so many work and life skills that I could now take with me. I'd probably take a month off: I'd read, I'd go to galleries, I'd join a gym. I would even take the time to have tea with my mother – just because it was a Wednesday and I could. I would concentrate on finding my own place to live and I would remember everyone's birthdays. I would refine and perfect my CV and I'd probably look for a job in the marketing department of one of the auction houses. I could write up notes on a Rubens and resist the urge to use exclamation marks. I'd read the weekend papers at leisure with a latte and without a pack of Post-its and a fluorescent marker pen.

As for my love life? Well . . . I had to go back to the Golden Goose to debrief Kieran on the party, and check they hadn't suffered any adverse publicity from all the coverage (they hadn't – in fact, bookings and covers had soared). Turned out Katya was his sister. FFS. I'd felt like such a fool – but my heart did that funny somersault thing again and I found myself sucking in my tummy as we perched on the bar stools and knocked back a few shots while I regaled him with every gory detail of the night. It was a revelation. He laughed with me, he got it. He found my stories funny and, dare I say it – he was genuinely interested in my job, which was a revelation. I slipped down off my bar stool, slightly unsteady from maybe one tequila too many, and my tummy did a triple backflip when he suggested drinks again – another time, when we could make a night of it.

And so it was that with a spring in my step and a new-found belief that I could follow a new path, I marched up to the black front door of the GGC offices with my coffee for what was probably the ten thousandth time. Today was most definitely the day. Butterflies fluttered in my stomach. I sat down at my desk, switched on my laptop and started typing my formal letter of resignation.

My phone rang.

'Frankie Marks speaking.' I tore the corner off my almond croissant. 'Hold on while I just jot down the details. The cover? And a trip to Australia? Recreating Melissa's Autumn/ Winter show on Sydney Harbour Bridge?'

I took a bigger bite. I could feel the familiar thrill as my heart raced and my brain whirred. I didn't stop scribbling notes – dropping flakes of croissant as I scrolled through both mine and Melissa's diaries.

There was no way, not a chance that anyone else was doing that show who wasn't me. Georgina was right. I wasn't going anywhere.

Uh.oh . . .

THE 10 COMMANDMENTS . . . OF FASHION PR
(according to Frankie Marks)

1) You will not treat everyone as equals.
2) You will say the cover isn't everything. But it is.
3) You will not steal samples. Until the end of the season.
4) You will smile at people you dislike.
5) You will learn appearances are everything.
6) You will spend time explaining to normal people what it is you actually do.
7) You will go to parties when you want to watch TV in your slippers.
8) You will gush over tweed and only refer to garments in the singular. Shoe. Culotte. Pant.
9) You will pretend you don't touch red meat or carbs and eat shepherd's pie in secret.
10) You will hate everyone. Especially other fashion PRs.

AND THERE'S JUST ONE MORE

11) You will never leave. You will think you will leave, many times. But you never will.

Acknowledgements

After decades in fashion PR and recounting ridiculous tales to my children – old and new (my career pre-dated their arrival by some time) – my daughter begged me to write a book. Well Sylvie, I did. And Remi – you don't have to read it. There's nothing in it about football.

I have so many people to thank I'm not sure exactly where to start. But I'll go with the beginning. Brower Lewis PR: the agency that I founded with my close friend Tracy Brower back in 1995, with no money, no clients and not much experience – and which went on to become a hub for great stylists, journalists and PRs for many years. We could only do it with the help of Pete Ward, our silent partner, who I can never thank enough. Everyone has a story from the Brower Lewis days. For this book I went back and interviewed as many of our old staff as I could find, harass, and beg. Thank you to Marsha, Atul, Hadley, Filiz, Rod, Sara, Liana, Jess, Miranda, Claudia, Alistair and all the others who I either couldn't track down, who I can't remember or who were fired for numerous misdemeanours and didn't want to talk to me.

During the next phase of my working life as a freelance consultant I also got to work with an amazing group of people including Sarah, Flo, Laura, Fiona, Caroline, Melissa, Leon, Edward, Sophie, Hugo, Ella, Barry, and the one and only Jo Milloy. Not just work colleagues but friends.

And we couldn't all have done this ridiculous yet brilliant

business of fashion without all the clients that shaped our careers and all the stories that ensued. Natalie Massenet and net-a-porter.com, Tamara Mellon and Jimmy Choo, Ruth and Tom Chapman and Matches, Betty Jackson, Anya Hindmarch, Bella Freud, Victoria Beckham, Claudia Schiffer, Marie-Chantal of Greece. To name but a few.

I informally took my kernel of an idea for this book to an agent a friend knew. Great idea, she said. *What's your narrative* arc? she asked. *What's a narrative arc?* I wailed. *Better get yourself on a creative writing course,* she suggested – and directed me to Curtis Brown Creative. My time on their courses shaped how I wrote. Special thanks to Jennifer Kerslake and my tutor Laura Barnett, but mostly thank you to the writer friends I made, in particular Abigail Johnson for being a tireless sounding board, and Lisa Sargeant for keeping our troop together and generally being our mother hen. They, along with Anna, Steve, Steven, James, Emma, Vivienne, Colette and Rick have been an unbelievable support over the past few years. And then, once I signed my deal, I met an amazing group of fellow 2023 debut authors. There's too many to list but they all know who they are . . . Never have I met a more inspiring and original group of people to whom I sent copious messages about deadlines and semi colons and always received enthusiastic replies and positive reinforcement. You will likely all read their wonderful books and will be incredibly lucky to do so.

And then to all my greatest friends who kept me sane. My very first beta readers Catherine Robinson and Ruth Joseph who both tirelessly listened to my anxiety and didn't shout at me when they really ought to have. Those who read excruciatingly bad, very early drafts or sample chapters and didn't tell me they were rubbish – Tom Konig-Oppenheimer, Kate Driver, Harriet Whitehorn, Minnie Driver, Bella Blenkinsopp, Daisy Donovan, Jane Suitor, Ruth Kennedy, my goddaughter

Lillie, Tracy (again, who had to read an early draft with me sitting next to her staring at her for the entire duration), Sarah Hiscox, and very importantly Abigail Hearne. To Fred Berger, Robert Ferrell and Mariel Redlin, I also owe an enormous debt of thanks for loving Frankie and sometimes laughing at my jokes over Zoom. Special mention also to Francesca Amfitheatrof for letting me discuss my proofreading in the middle of my actual day job, and to my decade long book club who helped my love of reading over the years (when we've finished discussing our families, the energy crisis and if we're going to be drinking): Ruth Joseph (again), Susannah Paisner, Annie Woolf, Tammy Ward, Jane Lewis and Kate Southworth; and my WhatsApp group who I talk to about books and things that definitely aren't to do with books – Claire Pizey, Dalya Shear, Maxine Levi and Beth Silver.

There are also those friends, colleagues, and acquaintances who along the way help you more than they could ever have imagined at the time. With just one email, one comment, one introduction, one message of support, one chocolate croissant, one walk in the park when you're flailing, one metaphorical slap across the cheek – Bella, Vassi, Bryony, Pippa V, Pippa H, Annabel, Martha, Olympia, Jemima, Esta, Tamzin, Claudia, Neris, Flavia, Fran, Cathy, Hadley, Izzy, Josie, Gayle, Anthony, David. I noted them and I banked them.

But most importantly, I need to thank Tara Henry. Who has been my rock and my de facto teacher – fully immersing herself in Frankie's world for over a year. Our calls and emails to and from London and Adelaide will always remain my greatest memory of this whole process. I literally couldn't have done it without her.

I also need to mention two wonderful authors. Paula Hawkins, who (after I stopped fangirling) very kindly took the time to Zoom and email with me and answer my questions about pacing, and Clare Pooley who I was introduced to right when I was losing the will to live and was so generous with her time and advice.

Then you get to the big stuff. My amazing agent, Katie Fulford – in whom I am so lucky to have found my advocate and has gifted me with the greatest email line of my life: 'sadly my agent says no.' Finally, I have someone looking after me rather than the other way around. Everyone at Hodder & Stoughton who believed in my book. My incredible editor Amy Batley who got Frankie from the outset and has dedicated herself to understanding that I don't understand how to use tracked changes and has made everything fun, has calmed me down and hasn't told me off once for excessive emailing. And the rest of the wonderful Hodder team – Oliver Martin, Laura Bartholomew, Katy Aries, Natalie Chen, Kay Gale, Sharona Selby.

Deciding you want to do something different at the ripe old age of 50 is daunting, and without the support of my family I'm not sure I'd have dared believe I could do it. So, to my mother Hannah who still asks what exactly I do for a living, and my father David who really did tell me a mule was a donkey, not a backless shoe – thank you for your endless encouragement. The same applies to my sister Jane and my oldest friend Beth who really is family.

Last but by no means least the biggest thank you (and congratulations and commiserations) to my husband Max for putting up with me and holding the family fort as I travelled for work for years – and then, just when he thought it was all over, had to put up with me again when I suddenly never travelled anywhere but from my laptop to the kettle, muttering about plot and telling everyone to be quiet.

But most importantly this book is for my late sister Catherine who I wish more than anything had been here to tell me what a pile of nonsense worrying about a mirrored catwalk really was.